WORLD WAR 3.2

THE AXIS OF TIME

JOHN BIRMINGHAM

GIGANTIC
BOMBS
CORP.

AUTHOR'S NOTE

World War 3.2

This book continues the series that began with *Weapons of Choice*. Including novellas and ebooks, it is the seventh title in that series, but you can safely start with *World War 3.1* if you want. Just take a deep breath, close your eyes, and imagine a multinational battle group from the twenty-first century, falling backasswards through a wormhole and popping out into the Pacific on the eve of the Battle of Midway. That would mess up your high school history texts, wouldn't it?

Or, you could just go read *Weapons of Choice*. There's certain to be a dog-eared copy lying around your local library. Either way, I wrote this book, and the many to follow, because I loved this series, the premise and the characters. It was written at the turn of the century when things were, let's face it, simpler. Returning to this alternate history has been a little like escaping a timeline that went badly wrong. I suspect that's why so many readers have asked me to get back to it for so many years.

I had intended to finish this story with the next book in this trilogy, *World War 3.3*, but halfway through writing this book, I realised there was zero chance I'd be able to do that. To give this world and these characters their due regard, I'm gonna have to write another five or six books. So that's what I'll do. But I promise I won't take twenty years to do it this time.

1

Cairo. Five weeks ago.

DAN BLACK SAT at a small table in a backstreet café, hunkered over a bitter black coffee. It was hidden in the dogleg turn of an alleyway in Cairo's old town that stank of sweat, spices, and diesel fumes. Dan, hidden under a lightweight dishdasha, took a slow sip of the coffee, not looking at the two men seated several tables away, sweating through their masquerade as the afternoon heat pressed down on the city. They were Russians, NKVD for sure. Dark woollen suits that would have been quite comfortable in a cold Lubyanka basement, here grabbed and gripped at dank armpits and ample bellies.

He'd been following them for days, watching them stumble through streets that had been swallowing empires for thousands of years. He recognised their tells now, the way the shorter one habitually tugged at the sweat-stained collar of his shirt, the way his partner's fingers tapped an unlit cigarette against the table, a nervous metronome marking time until their next mistake. The men were used to shadow work, but not here. Cairo's ten thousand alleys were often dark, even as the noonday sun baked the city's rooftops, but darkness, while universal, was also many in its forms, and these fools had blundered for three days through the shadows of a city that was ancient thousands of years before Moscow's tinpot empire was born.

The taller one—bald spot spreading like a stain through what remained of his hair—checked his watch for the fifth time in as many minutes. Beside him, his partner hunched over their table like a sparrow sensing a hawk's shadow, eyes darting to the doorway where dust motes danced in the afternoon light. A car horn cut through the café's drowsy murmur, and both men snapped to attention.

The taller Russian dropped a few coins onto the table, not waiting for change as he stepped toward the doorway. His partner followed closely behind, the same nervous energy rolling off him as they pushed through the narrow door into the street.

The sleek black sedan outside waited among Cairo's rusted river of battered vehicles like a diplomat at a dock workers' pub. The rear door opened, and the first Russian slipped inside without a word. The other hesitated for a moment, casting a final glance around the street before climbing in after him.

The car door slammed shut, and the engine revved.

Dan downed the last of his coffee in one gulp. He threw a few coins on the table, and rose to his feet, slipping into the close heat of the old quarter. He knew where it would deliver them to the main thoroughfare, and he could cut through the backstreets to intercept at their destination. The Cairo Hilton.

Before him, ancient pathways meandered like the creases of a well-worn map. A stone arch loomed ahead, and as he ducked beneath it, the alley narrowed further, the buildings above nodding toward each other as if sharing confidences about the stranger below. He could hear the distinctive blare of the sedan's horn bouncing off the stone walls and tin roofs, the driver eager to leave the narrow confines of the souk behind and break out onto the wider roads.

He emerged from the narrow alleyway onto a wider street, the buildings giving way to open sky. This was the transition point, where old Cairo began to dissolve into the modern city, where the slums brushed up against the gleaming structures that had risen after the war.

Dan crossed the road quickly, slipping between a donkey-drawn cart and an old delivery truck before turning onto Prince Farouk

Avenue. He quickened his pace, reaching the edge of the slum just as the sedan sped past in a dirty blast of hot air and grit. Ahead of him, the Cairo Hilton stood not so much across the road as in another world. The blue glass towers gleamed in the afternoon sun, their angular form suggesting the pyramids of Giza.

Pausing as the sedan motored toward the hotel's entrance, Dan watched it pull up to the valet station. The Russians joined the stream of vehicles that ferried diplomats, foreign dignitaries, and more than a few covert players to the peace conference at the hotel. He kept to the edges, slipping through the gates on foot, avoiding the staff in their crisp uniforms. Instead, he veered left, moving along the path where palm trees bordered the drive. A few turns brought him to a side entrance, where staff shuffled in and out, carrying trays of food, linens, and other supplies.

Dan glanced over his shoulder, confirming that the Russians had left their car and were approaching the garden party. He kept his distance. The scent of jasmine and freshly mowed grass was strong as he passed through a shaded archway leading to the expansive gardens. White tents billowed gently in the warm breeze, and a soft murmur of conversation floated over to him, voices rising and falling like birdsong, the world pretending, briefly, to be at peace.

He took a moment to observe his surroundings.

A peace conference, they called it.

He moved among the guests as though he belonged. Nobody noticed him. Nobody ever did unless he wanted them to.

The Russians, though, were not doing as well. Stiff-backed and wary-eyed, they cut awkward figures among the diplomats, business-people, and well-dressed peacemongers. Dan trailed them at a safe distance, keeping to the fringes of the gathering. Whatever they were up to, it would happen soon enough.

He slowed as the Russians neared the far edge of the garden, where the crowd thinned. Dan watched from beneath the swaying palm trees as they threaded their way deeper into the grounds. Beads of sweat trickled down his brow, but he remained motionless as they moved with purpose, shoulders stiff, eyes scanning the crowd, searching for someone.

And then Dan saw her, walking down from the hotel.

Recognition came not with shock, but with the sick awareness of a man who had just read the last page of a book he meant never to pick up again, let alone finish.

Julia Duffy appeared in the distance through a gap in the crowd, and for a second, the noise of the garden party faded to nothing. Ten years folded in on themselves, time and space physically compressing in a violent collapse. He'd known she was here in Cairo. With Harry, of course. That was part of his briefing packet on Skarov. But the NKVD man, rather than his former lover, was why he'd flown to Egypt, and Dan had resisted the temptation to see her, even from afar.

He shoved down hard on the surge of raw feeling that came at him. His eyes flicked back to the Russians. He couldn't lose sight of them.

The taller of the two NKVD agents paused for a beat, glancing in Julia's direction. It was a subtle movement, but enough for Dan to recognise with accelerating dread what was happening. The Russians had target locked on her. His jaw tightened as he saw the taller of the two nudge his partner, murmuring something.

Without another word, they peeled off from the party, their course shifting toward Julia, and their intent clear. Dan remained still. His eyes tracked every move as the Russians split up to flank her. She seemed unaware of the danger, lost in her own thoughts, her focus entirely on whatever assignment had brought her here. The conference, he presumed.

Dan's pulse quickened, and his fingers brushed the grip of his pistol, concealed beneath his jacket. The Russians were getting closer to her, their pace quickening without any apparent effort. This, at least, was something they knew how to do.

He kept to the garden's edge, blending into the shadows cast by the towering palms. The taller Russian, his hand reaching casually inside his jacket, was already positioning himself on her blindside. The shorter one lagged slightly, blocking any potential retreat.

Julia faltered, and the lead Russian was on her in an instant, slipping in close and muttering something into her ear. His partner closed the gap from behind, seizing her arm in a quick, practised grip.

Dan moved, his heartbeat quickening.

They steered her toward a black sedan coming down the driveway, the one he'd followed from the old town. Julia walked with them, her head turning slightly, as if assessing her captors. As the taller man pushed her toward the open door, she twisted her body and screamed at him before slamming the heel of her boot into his shin. The Russian's grip loosened just long enough for Julia to rip her arm free and drive her elbow back into his face.

Dan kept moving, closing the distance but staying low. He hadn't expected her to fight so well after all these years, but she moved swiftly, with no wasted motion. She drove the first man's head into the corner of the car door with a wet crunch that Dan could hear from thirty meters away. Blood sprayed across the white gravel driveway and her bright, cream tank top.

Christ, she hasn't lost a step.

The second man was already closing in, but Julia was pivoting, hands coming up in defence. The blade caught her across the small of her back. Dan saw her arch, saw the line of red appear on her torn silk blouse. He was running now, no longer caring about cover or mission protocols. The Russian with the knife was bigger than Julia, heavier, and she was bleeding, but as he watched, she deflected the strike, caught his arm, and broke it at the elbow.

She stripped the blade and drove the stiletto into the bigger man's eye. He went down screaming, clawing at his face. But his partner was back, reaching for her. Julia stepped up to him and drove the knife up under his chin. His weight carried him forward, knocking her down beneath his falling bulk.

Dan was ten meters out when the driver climbed from behind the wheel, pistol in hand. The man's face was sickly green as he surveyed the carnage, and he fired wildly, barking orders in Russian, telling Julia to get in the car. Dan dropped to one knee and put three rounds into his centre mass before the Russian could squeeze his trigger.

Hotel staff were already running toward the scene, shouts in Arabic and English peeling through the garden as they rushed to Julia's aid. She had slumped to the ground, and he started to withdraw. She couldn't know it had been him.

He'd been dead for over ten years.

Dan holstered his pistol and slipped away into the chaos behind him. Guests and conference attendees scrambled for cover. Some hotel staff ran toward the commotion, their faces pale with fear, while others simply froze, unsure what to do.

A man barked orders in Arabic, gesturing for other men to secure the area. Dan stayed low, watching as he knelt beside the bodies, checking for signs of life. The security men fanned out to secure a perimeter. Julia, still dazed, wiped at her face with shaking hands. Her gaze seemed to linger on him for a half-second, but then it moved on, her focus shifting to the security chief kneeling beside her. Dan was just another mook in a bedsheet.

His heart rate steadied as he watched a knot of hotel staff gather around her. A woman in a Hilton jacket gently took her by the arm, guiding her toward the main entrance, and she let them, her legs shaky beneath her.

Satisfied but shaken, Dan Black turned and retreated into the afternoon heat, unseen and unknown.

2

Washington.

IT LOOKED VERY MUCH like the Oval Office as Robert Menzies remembered it, and yet it was so very different. The furniture, obviously, changed every couple of years, and he recalled from President Roosevelt's time the inescapable smell of the Camel cigarettes FDR had smoked. Reason enough to change the couch and curtains regularly, he assumed. But sitting next to the British ambassador, waiting for the reporters to leave, Menzies noted other changes, too.

The huge black Bakelite telephone that had sat on Roosevelt's desk had been replaced by a much sleeker unit, one of those touchscreen thingies he had so much trouble using. Something about his fingertips, they said. More likely it was something about the ridiculous touchscreen, Menzies thought, but there was no telling those computer louts anything. His fingers had no trouble turning the dial on a proper phone. But no. The problem was his fingertips. Not the phone that didn't work.

The television, of course, was new, very new, one of those monstrous things as big as a picture window and not much thicker than a couple of volumes of *Britannica*. It was blank at the moment, turned off, for which he was grateful. Some fellows, when you visited them, loved to show off all of their modern doodads and whatnot, and Robert Menzies found it very distracting, not to mention unconscionably rude. There had even been talk of installing one in the bar at the Melbourne Club so that the Members might watch the Cup or the cricket, and the Prime Minister had both lobbied and voted against that invasion, now happily defeated.

Here and there in this odd set-up of President Kolhammer's, there were, of course, so many little intrusions from the future that you could not see.

He still wore the watch his father had given him when he was admitted as a lawyer. And Lord Templesmith, the British ambassador, he knew, still had the watch he'd worn as a destroyer captain in the North Atlantic. But the president liked to flash around one of those sports watch thingies, the ones that spoke to satellites and counted how many steps you took during the day and would probably make you a decent serve of beans on toast if you asked. He wasn't wearing it now, of course. They had all surrendered all of their electronical devices before arriving here. Not that Menzies had many to surrender. The Australian Prime Minister was a traditionalist in that, as in so many things. Wristwatches were meant to be worn on the wrist and checked occasionally to tell the time, not to encourage one to run a marathon or to cook up a full Scottish breakfast.

Menzies nodded to the last of the reporters leaving the room after the live press conference: young Talbot Duckmanton from the Australian Broadcasting Commission. That was another thing which was different, of course. The last time he'd done a press thing with an American leader, there'd been more than a hundred reporters in attendance, most of them American, of course, and so much better behaved than the rabble of the Australian press. This evening, there had been but four in attendance because of the security requirements for a real-time transmission: Duckmanton from Australia, a fellow from the BBC, and two Americans, including one shooting a little movie of the event on his pocket phone.

Menzies wasn't quite sure why the reporters got to keep their pocket phones when everybody else had to give up theirs. But perhaps they were special units that were somehow more secure than everybody else's. He didn't think that likely, but the Americans, and particularly the Americans under Kolhammer since the murder of Mr. Eisenhower, were absolute devils for detail when it came to that sort of thing. Menzies didn't bother questioning any of it. He just did as they asked, or rather, he instructed his staff to do as they asked, and he focused instead on why he was here.

"Thank you, gentlemen," President Kolhammer said as his chief of staff closed the door behind the last reporter. She stayed in the room, which spoke to the level of trust Kolhammer had in her. A quite remarkable woman, Menzies thought, not simply because she was a woman. It was unusual, but not entirely remarkable, to find a few ladies in these roles now.

But even by that standard, Lia Pao was noteworthy. Fierce-looking, Chinese, or maybe American Chinese, he supposed. Well, perhaps not Chinese exactly, but certainly from one of the Asian races, as best Menzies could tell. And yet she spoke with such a strong midwestern drawl. It always surprised him to hear such a voice from an Asian face, even now, a decade after the Transition. You'd think he'd be used to it, and publicly, he had to be. But it still vexed Robert Menzies to speak to someone like, say, Captain Nguyen from the Navy and hear a broad, nasal Australian twang coming from that unmistakably Vietnamese face.

"Mr. Prime Minister?"

Menzies shook his head, snapping out of his reverie. He'd been lost in thought for a minute, which was most unusual. "Mr. President, my apologies," he said, "and my condolences, too. We haven't had a chance to speak in person since..." He trailed off, uncertain how to phrase it.

"Since President Eisenhower was murdered," Kolhammer finished for him.

"Yes, indeed," Menzies said.

"Well, thank you, sir," Kolhammer replied. "The condolences are appreciated, but unfortunately, unless a lot more people are to die at the hands of Mr. Beria... That's why I wanted to talk to both of you tonight. About the submarines."

"Of course," Menzies agreed, "the AUKUS submarines."

Templesmith, the British ambassador, had said nothing yet, and he kept his counsel now.

"I'm not sure what more we can do for you, Mr. President," Robert Menzies said. "Our two operational nuclear submarines have already sortied north and, although they're not beyond communications range, we're not in contact with them for obvious reasons."

"Yeah," Kolhammer said. "I get that. And they're doing a great job bottling up the Russians in Vladivostok, for which we are very grateful."

Menzies waved away the thanks. "Well, we have two submarines there. You have at least thirteen, so I think it's fair to say you're doing most of the work."

"Every little bit helps," Kolhammer said, inclining his head toward Lord Templesmith. "For which I must thank Her Majesty's Government, Mr. Ambassador. The rapid deployment of HMS *Ajax* from Singapore to Vladivostok was crucial to preventing a Russian breakout into the Pacific."

The British Ambassador nodded. "I shall pass on your thanks to Downing Street, Mr. President, but I don't imagine that's why you asked us here. If this were simply a matter of expressing your appreciation, you could have sent a thank-you note."

Kolhammer huffed out a short laugh. "Yeah, could have. Not really my style, though. No, I wanted to talk to you both about moving more boats into the Atlantic. And, Mr. Prime Minister," he said, turning to Menzies, "getting your third AUKUS sub off sea trials and into the Atlantic as soon as possible."

Menzies frowned. "I understand the haste, Mr. President, but that third boat is what the Navy calls an evolved design. It's taken in a lot of the lessons we learned building the first two boats, and my boffins tell me those trials are important. We've hurried the process along, but there are all sorts of things that could go wrong."

"Things can always go wrong," Kolhammer said. "That's the nature of war. Even when things go right, they're going wrong for somebody. They've gone about as bad as they can go for us since the Russian attack. Between us in this room, gentlemen, I can tell you we may lose Europe within the next month. The prospect of Red Army tanks reaching the French coast is real."

Neither Menzies nor Templesmith spoke for a moment. Finally, Templesmith nodded slowly, as if Kolhammer had just confirmed information he'd received independently.

"I see," said Robert Menzies. "And how would pulling our third submarine out of sea trials make any difference? I doubt it could get there in time, and the Russians are not advancing across the Atlantic. Yet. They're moving across Germany."

"They are," Kolhammer said, "and they're doing it a hell of a lot faster than I'd like. They're moving so fast that there's a chance all effective resistance could collapse. If that happens before Operation Reforger delivers significant US forces to continental Europe, we'll be back in 1941, with a hostile dictatorship controlling the entire continent. And, Mr Ambassador, Beria won't make Hitler's mistake. When he reaches Paris and the French government collapses, he'll order his forces to turn north to the Channel, and the United Kingdom will come under immediate and sustained attack."

He turned from Templesmith back to Menzies, before continuing, "So, Mr. Prime Minister, any contribution that you can make to the defence of Europe, and specifically to the success of Operation Reforger, would not simply be appreciated, it'd be vital to our success in this war. The alternative is the use of tactical nuclear weapons to stall the Soviet advance."

He let that hang in the air, the threat of it. The horror.

"Her Majesty's government," Templesmith said quietly, "is, of course, fully committed to this fight."

"I don't doubt it," Kolhammer said. "I had breakfast with Sir Winston not long ago. He'd strap on a parachute and jump into the Fulda Gap himself, if he thought it'd help. But you have an AUKUS sub in the Mediterranean. As important as that theatre is, it doesn't come near the importance of getting American forces into Europe as quickly as possible. The Sovs know we're coming. They know that most of our materiel is coming by sea, and many of our personnel, too. They had a dozen of their nukes in the North Atlantic, before the orbital bombardment which took out the Fifth Army. Even more of their old diesel boats."

Menzies shifted on the couch, which he found uncomfortably

deep. He very much wanted a cup of tea, but didn't think he could ask for one.

Kolhammer wasn't looking at him or Templesmith now. He seemed to be staring past them, and Menzies wondered if he was thinking about the great naval battle he'd fought near Taiwan.

"Those submarines, by our standards, are not good," the president said. "They're big and they're noisy. But there's a lot of them. And we lost most of our Atlantic fleet in the attack on Norfolk."

"Quantity does have a quality all of its own," Menzies said, quoting old Joe Stalin.

"Reference acknowledged," Kolhammer agreed. "But quality counts too. And the best way to kill a shitty Russian submarine is with a much better American, or British, or," he turned back to Menzies, "Australian submarine, that's smaller, faster, quieter, and armed with much better weapons. We have that advantage over them, thanks to Jane Willet."

Menzies nodded at that. He could accept the president's thanks on behalf of Captain Willet, but the situation was not as simple as Kolhammer made out. Jane Willet had run the program developing what became known as the AUKUS submarines, but her position in that role was not uncontested. Many influential voices within the defence hierarchy back in Australia thought it a waste of money to spend so much on such an exquisite, boutique capability, especially when so many other technologies had come through the Transition. And it irked him to admit that Willet, as a colonial, did not necessarily enjoy the respect in the corridors of Whitehall that a British submariner might have.

Nor did it help that she was a woman. Glancing at Lia Pao, he understood that some fellows might cut up rough answering to a lady, especially from the antipodes. But there was no denying that Captain Willet and *HMAS Havoc* had served with distinction and to great effect in the last war. And there was simply nobody else in the world who knew as much about nuclear submarines.

Of course, Menzies thought, a lot of the resistance came down to most admirals just not liking submarines because most of them spent their careers jaunting about on top of the water, not underneath it.

"What about the situation in Japan and Korea?" Lord Temple-smith asked. "It is the opinion of Her Majesty's government that both of those theatres could turn bad very quickly, and to prevent a breakout into Southeast Asia, it will be necessary to have the most capable forces in the region. Without the AUKUS boats, even with the US Pacific fleet, you might struggle to contain them, don't you think?"

"I don't think," Kolhammer said. "I know. But neither the North Korean nor the Japanese communist regimes have the power projection capabilities to be more than a nuisance throughout Southeast Asia. I'm confident that the forces we have in place will be enough to handle them."

"Even though you propose to divert those forces to the Atlantic?" Templesmith asked.

"Yeah," Kolhammer said. "Gentlemen, I don't know how to make this any simpler for you. The Russians cleaned our fucking clock at Norfolk. The control of the North Atlantic is still being contested, and there's no guarantee that contest will end in our favour. If those Russian subs get hold of the Reforger convoys, we'll lose not just the Atlantic, but everything."

Menzies knew he would face all manner of unpleasant questions from the opposition and the press when he returned home, but he didn't see any way out of this. Kolhammer was right. As barbaric as the regimes in North Korea and the DPRJ might be, they were primitive backwaters compared to the Soviet Union. The fall of South Korea and Free Japan to communist aggression would be a disaster for their people and a long-term threat to Southeast Asia, and eventually to Australia. But if Beria took Paris and then London, it would only be a matter of time before the hammer and sickle was raised over Washington, and certainly over Canberra, unless they all died in a nuclear conflagration beforehand.

"Mr. President," he said, "you can have your submarine. But even if I pulled it out of sea trials tonight, I don't understand how it could help in time."

"Thank you, Mr. Prime Minister," Kolhammer said. "And don't worry about the logistics. I know a shortcut."

Kolhammer looked like he was about to lean on the British ambassador for a similar commitment when a knock at the door drew their attention. His chief of staff, Lia Pao, opened the door and took a message from a young military officer, a Navy man, Menzies thought, from the glimpse he got of the fellow's uniform.

Miss Pao closed the door and walked briskly over to Kolhammer. She leaned down and whispered a few words. He nodded and thanked her.

"Gentlemen, I'm sorry to interrupt, and Mr. Ambassador, you and I will surely return to this conversation, but you'll want to see this." He picked up a long black pointer from his desk and gestured at the television screen Menzies had been admiring. It came to life with surprising speed.

"This is a feed from the Pentagon," he said. "It's coming in via fibre optic cable, so the signal can't be intercepted unless the Soviets have managed to physically tap into the line. And they'd find that very difficult—impossible, really—so you can trust what we're seeing."

Menzies had some trouble understanding what, indeed, he was seeing at first. It looked like a grey field, and then he realised it was the ocean at night. Three stars came into view. No, not stars. He realised they were missiles, rockets of some sort. Their exhaust cones showed as bright white spears against the grey background of the ocean.

Data appeared on screen to frame the image. He couldn't understand much of it, but he did recognise the rapidly changing numbers and figures that signified longitude and latitude.

"What are we looking at here, Mr. President?" Lord Templesmith asked.

"Three cruise missiles, sub-launched, from a Russian boat," Kolhammer explained, "heading towards Washington. The White House, probably."

"Oh dear," Robert Menzies said.

"Yeah, don't worry about it," Kolhammer said. "They're not going to get ashore, and if they did, obviously they wouldn't find us in this room."

"Do you think they're targeting us?" Menzies asked.

"For sure, Bob. That was my plan when I set up this meeting."

Menzies nodded. His mouth was dry, and he rather did wish for that cup of tea now. He wondered if it would be awful of him to ask the chief of staff for one and assumed that it probably would. Firstly, she wasn't a tea lady, and secondly, well, she was a lady. In his experience over the last ten years, the ladies had become rather difficult about simple questions such as who should fetch the tea. Why, there was even talk of the President tapping one of the Congressional ladies on the shoulder for the job of Vice President. He imagined that if you looked closely enough, you might well find Miss Pao's fingerprints all over that decision.

Another screen opened up, or another window, he corrected himself, that's what the computer louts called them, and Kolhammer grunted with satisfaction. He sounded like a man who had ordered a beer at the bar and been served two and a complimentary packet of nuts.

"Outstanding," he growled. "That, gentlemen, is a satellite image from Norfolk Naval Base. You can't see it there, but... Ah, there we go."

The image flared, and three bright streaks of light arced away from the coast.

"They're interceptors, ground-to-air missiles," Kolhammer explained. "They'll take out the Russian cruise missiles, but if they don't, we have other defences, which will knock 'em down before they get anywhere near the city."

Sitting in this rather good facsimile of the Oval Office, which he had entered half an hour earlier, Robert Menzies was relieved. He was a good safe distance from the White House, of course. They all were, but he no more enjoyed the idea of Mr. Beria being able to reach out and stick a missile through the window than he imagined President Kolhammer would be. He didn't bother asking the obvious question of how Kolhammer knew the Russians would try this on. The man had his sources, and he was, Menzies reminded himself, an admiral of long-standing, and thus, quite used to the games that admirals play with each other. In this game with Admiral Kuznetsov, it appeared Philip Kolhammer had just sprung his trap.

"How long will it take?" Lord Templesmith asked.

"Not long," Kolhammer assured him. "Those Russian cruise missiles are pretty primitive, but they're still fast movers. Ours are a lot better, and they're moving at nearly twice the speed of sound. It shouldn't be long before—"

The windows on the television screen flared white. A new window popped open.

The view was still elevated somewhere above the sea, but Menzies could tell it was coming from a much lower elevation and was not directly above the track of the rockets, but some distance away from them. Off to the side, he thought; not being a military man himself, he was sure they had some term of art for it.

"This feed is coming from one of our anti-submarine planes," Kolhammer explained. "They'll have a fix on the launch position of the Soviet attack, and they'll be vectoring in three other anti-submarine aircraft on that position."

"Will you get him?" Templesmith asked.

Kolhammer nodded. "They're not getting out of this trap," he said.

"And do you know, Mr. President, whether this was the boat which launched the sneak attack on Norfolk?"

"We have high confidence in the intelligence," Kolhammer said. "This is the boat. The Russians had two submarines capable of pulling off that mission, and the Royal Air Force is currently tracking one of them in the North Sea, Mr. Ambassador. So yeah, to answer your question, these are the assholes who hit us at Norfolk."

Menzies watched the footage of the counter-attack, fascinated. Burning debris fell from the skies where the three Russian rockets had been intercepted. It fell for under a minute before hitting the ocean's surface and extinguishing the fires.

"How long will it take?" he asked.

"Well, that's harder to say," Kolhammer said. "The Russians will have dived immediately after launching, and they'll probably go dead in the water once they reach what they consider a safe depth. Their drive systems are still garbage compared to ours," he nodded to Menzies, "Thanks to Jane Willet and your HMAS *Havoc*. And of course, we're hunting them with augmented technology."

"Well, it wasn't my submarine," Menzies allowed, somewhat

graciously, he thought. "Perhaps my grandchildren could take credit for that, but I'm glad to see the program put to good use."

Kolhammer flicked off the television. "This could go on for an hour," he said, "I wonder, Ambassador Templesmith, if we could return to the question of that last AUKUS submarine."

EXTRACT

'Studs Terkel Talks About *The Transitions: An Oral History of the Future.*'
By Harold L. Winikoff
The New Yorker | March 13, 1954 | Vol. 29, No. 5 | pp. 51–66

Louis 'Studs' Terkel orders black coffee in a bar on 57th, a corner joint with a stuffed pheasant behind the register and a piano that hasn't been tuned since the last war. It's late afternoon, and the windows are fogged from the inside, thick with the kind of secondhand smoke and first-rate banter that Terkel seems to carry with him like static charge.

He's wearing a scuffed houndstooth jacket, baggy at the shoulders, and he carries a tape recorder heavy enough to bend the table legs. He sets it down but doesn't turn it on. Instead, he produces a notebook with dog-eared pages and flips through it like a gambler working his patented system at the track. Terkel is not, by his own admission, a historian.

"I'm a listener," he says. "That's the whole secret. Shut up long enough, and people will tell you everything."

We're talking about The Transitions, his forthcoming oral history of the last decade and change. He's reluctant to call it a book yet. It's more of an excavation, he says, and some of the bones are still warm.

"The generals have their maps. Scientists have their microscopes. What I've got is a waitress in Akron who dreams about flying in a space shuttle. A pipefitter in Queens who swears the sun's a different colour now. And this kid in St. Louis who talks like he's sixty and writes like he's twenty-one in 2025."

Terkel's eyes crinkle when he smiles, which is often, but it never quite erases the shadows underneath. He's been travelling more or less nonstop since late '52, chasing stories through church basements, union halls, student lounges, jazz clubs, and military depots. What he's teased out is less a straight line than a messy braid of voices: astonished, furious, adrift, hopeful and haunted.

"I'm not trying to explain the Transition," he says. "That's someone else's job. Professor Einstein, maybe. I'm just trying to remember it while it's still happening. Before people start making up stories instead of just telling them."

There's a pause while the bartender delivers a second coffee.

"I'll tell you this," Terkel says. "If we're to get through this—and that's still an open question—we'll need more than physics and math to explain what happened. We're gonna need voices. Real ones."

He takes a sip, grimaces politely, and returns to his notes. "Anyway," he says, "enough about me. Let's listen to someone else. You've heard of this Kerouac kid, right?"

3

Germany.

THE RAIN DRUMMED STEADILY on the slate roof of the half-timbered house, every fucking drop finding its way through the jagged shell holes to puddle on the floors below. Admittedly, the floor was already a bit of a mess. Panzer 59 sat quietly in what had been someone's living room, its main gun jutting through the blown-out front wall, pointing at the intersection where the B251 met the L743. Through his binoculars, Joachim Boosfeld could see the railroad tracks cutting across the approach road, the wet steel rails gleaming dully in the grey afternoon light.

The village of Brilon-Wald stretched along the Hoppecke Valley like a discarded ribbon, three kilometres of empty houses and abandoned shops pressed between the forested slopes of the Sauerland hills. The residents had taken one look at his company's approaching panzers and done the sensible thing, run like hell toward Willingen. They knew what was coming. Anyone who'd lived through the last war understood that when the tanks arrived, the killing and the dying started soon after.

Rain dripped from Boosfeld's peaked cap and ran down his neck as he surveyed his killing ground. Fucking miserable weather for a fucking miserable job. At least the clouds would keep the Red ground-attack aircraft grounded for a few more hours. He would take all the small mercies on offer.

He supposed he should be happy with what they'd accomplished so far, rather than being angry that he had manifestly failed to keep the Reds from pushing deeper into the Fatherland. In a month of fighting, he'd seen half his command turned into smoking scrap metal across a dozen battlefields.

The major action a week earlier at Kassel had started so well, but then things had gone bad for the Allies. Their armoured thrust had plunged into the shoulder of the Red salient ten kilometres along Route Seven, before running into very powerful Soviet blocking forces and belt upon belt of hastily laid anti-tank mines.

Before their penetration was pinched off, Corps had decided to head northwest and hold onto Highway 44. They were partially successful. His presence in this half-shattered house in Brilon-Wald testified to that. It could also be, he thought, that the Reds are behind us and nobody has bothered to tell me. In which case, they were so deep in the shit that even the fucking flies had given up and gone home for want of anything better to—

The shriek started as a whisper in the distance, then built to a freight-train howl that made Boosfeld's teeth ache. Incoming artillery. He didn't bother to button up. He could already tell the rounds would fall short, and they did, throwing up in geysers of black earth and splintered timber two hundred meters south. Ivan was finding his range. The concussion slapped against his face, and he tasted cordite on the wind.

He sat in his tank, which sat in the living room, keeping the binoculars pressed to his eyes, scanning the empty ribbon of asphalt that wound between the pine-covered slopes. Intel had it that their latest customers were elements of the 25th Tank Division, mixed in with a few Czech motor-rifle units. In his experience, Czechs fought harder than Russians, but he couldn't blame them for that. They had legitimate grudges and, unlike the average Russian kulak, they were not culturally broken.

Artillery continued to walk closer, each salvo shaking loose mortar from the damaged walls around him. Dust drifted down onto his map case as he traced the B251 with a gloved finger, the only good way north into Brilon proper. A chunk of plaster bounced off his helmet.

Boosfeld's company held the road, but the math was simple enough. Given the correlation of forces, as the communists like to say, it was a question of how badly the Russians wanted it. They surely had the mass to sweep him aside. Rain drummed harder on the broken slate above, finding new leaks that sent cold streams down his neck. His smile felt like a winter dawn as he folded the map and stuffed it back into its case.

2nd Company was prepared to do a leapfrogging break-contact drill all the way to the next town. They would make the Russians bleed rivers. The radio crackled with reports from his platoon leaders, their voices calm and professional despite the incoming fire. And there was a company of Panzergrenadiere just north of his position, dug into the houses with Panzerfausts, mortars and machine guns. He could see their camouflaged positions through his binoculars, dark shapes waiting among the pine boughs.

Brilon-Wald was not going to be cheap for Comrade Beria.

More artillery began walking toward him, the rounds impacting closer with each salvo. The Russians were probing, feeling for his positions like a blind man with a stick. Boosfeld remained standing in his turret, the cold rain mixing with sweat on his neck despite the autumn chill. The steel deck plates vibrated under his boots with each distant explosion. Both sides wanted the same thing, for someone's nerves to break, for the prey to flee and reveal themselves. That's when the real killing would begin.

Movement. A glint of steel through the trees.

Boosfeld lifted his binoculars with deliberate slowness, cupping his left hand over the objective lens to kill any reflection. His pulse quickened—the old familiar surge. There they were: BTR-152s, three of them, creeping along the road like cautious beetles. Their six wheels kissed the wet asphalt, and their stubby turrets swivelled left and right like the heads of hunting dogs.

They would sense they were being watched. They would also note the empty windows, the abandoned cars, the complete absence of civilian life. Boosfeld wondered if they'd probe a bit more, then fall back to bring up the main force. Four M-60s waited in the forward ambush, including his own. Rangefinders preset, the gunners' hands rested on their controls, but no one fired. Good. He had been very specific that he alone would initiate contact.

The BTRs halted at the railroad crossing. Their turrets rotated slowly, gun barrels probing like insect antennae. Boosfeld controlled his breathing, willing them to turn around, to report back that the village looked abandoned, or lightly held at best. Come on, comrades. Take the bait. Just a nibble

Then some shit-for-brains in the tree line opened up.

The MG3's distinctive buzz-saw rip shattered the afternoon quiet. Boosfeld watched the 7.62mm tracers streak past the lead BTR like angry fireflies, sparking harmlessly off its armoured flanks. The rounds chewed divots from the asphalt and whined away into the forest. He cursed silently. If that infantryman lived through the next hour, Bosfeld would personally introduce him to the business end of his boot.

The BTRs responded instantly, their heavy machine guns hammering the tree line with thumb-sized slugs that splintered pine trees and filled the air with sawdust. Then, mission accomplished, they spun around and disappeared back down the road in a cloud of diesel smoke and rubber.

Boosfeld lowered his binoculars and spat into the rubble at his feet; now the Reds knew Brilon-Wald was defended. His first instinct was to find that trigger-happy machine gunner and introduce his face to the nearest wall. The whole point of an ambush was to let the enemy blunder into it. Now the communists knew exactly where his forward positions lay.

But as Boosfeld shifted his weight in the commander's cupola, clenching his numb buttocks to squeeze a bit of life back into them, he reconsidered. The burst had been too high, too hasty, typically nervous fire from some idiot kid who'd probably shit his pants at the same time. But those tracers had streaked past the BTRs without penetrating. From the Russians' perspective, what had they seen?

A single machine gun position. Infantry weapons only. No tank guns, no anti-tank rockets, nothing that could threaten armour. The

BTRs had withdrawn not because they were outgunned, but because they'd completed their recon. Standard doctrine: probe, identify, report back.

Boosfeld rubbed his stubbled jaw, the leather of his gloves rough against his skin. Maybe that kid had done him a favour after all. With any luck, the Sovs would assume the village was held by nothing more than a few squads of infantry, easy meat for a tank company. They'd come in fast and heavy, hoping to overrun the position before the defenders could call in artillery support.

Which was exactly what he wanted them to think. Boosfeld settled back into his cupola and waited. The rain continued its steady drumming on the broken slate above, and somewhere in the distance an artillery round exploded with a muffled thump. He checked his watch, adjusted his binoculars, and kept his eyes on the road. The Reds would be back; the only question was how soon and in what strength.

Fifteen minutes later, shapes moved through the drizzle along the road, infantry advancing in textbook bounds. These weren't the screaming hordes of the last war, charging forward, screaming "URRAAAH!" until the machine guns cut them down in windrows. These bastards moved in short rushes, one team providing overwatch while the next sprinted forward to cover.

"Fucking Czechs," he muttered.

Boosfeld could see at least a platoon on the road itself, but there would be more, flanking teams pushing through the pine forests on both sides, invisible among the dark trees. His skin crawled with the certainty that sniper scopes were already crawling over his position.

He carefully keyed his radio to the artillery net. "Tannenberg Base, this is Lehr Two-Six. Fire mission. Grid 325587. Infantry in the open, over."

"Lehr Two-Six, Tannenberg Base. Grid 325587, infantry in the open. Shot, over."

"Shot, out."

The first incoming round announced itself with a howl that made his eardrums pop. It detonated beyond the bend with a rolling CRUMP that shook pine needles from the trees. Close, but long. The Czechs were already scattering.

"Two-Six, splash, over. Adjust fire."

"Tannenberg Base, splash, drop two hundred, over."

"Roger, Two-Six. Drop two hundred." A pause. "Shot, over."

"Shot, out."

Twenty seconds later, another 155mm shell landed between the advancing Reds and his position, closer this time. Boosfeld felt the ground tremor through his tank's suspension.

Bracketing fire. The next round would split the difference and land right on top of the poor bastards out there. He smiled and keyed his mic.

"Add one hundred and fire for effect."

They didn't bother to call back. A coal-train roar split the heavens, and the earth erupted in a geyser of black soil, shattered stone, and human remains. The follow-up rounds came in a steady drumbeat that hammered the ground into a moonscape of overlapping craters. Each explosion sent shock waves through Panzer 59's hull that Boosfeld felt in his bones and his teeth. Pine trees snapped like matchsticks. The stench of burning and torn earth filled his nostrils.

When the barrage lifted, the road ahead lay empty except for smoking crater lips and scattered equipment. But Boosfeld knew better than to relax. The Reds would regroup, call in armour, and try again.

The diesel roar reached him before he saw them, T-55s and T-72s pushing forward at speed, their tracks chewing up the asphalt as they accelerated out of the tree line. He nodded. Smart, but ignorant. They'd decided Brilon-Wald was held by nothing more than infantry and were rushing to mix it up close, where artillery couldn't touch them without hitting friendlies.

The lead tank was an old T-55, its steel flanks scarred by a dozen battles. Boosfeld pressed his lips into a thin line. Same old Russian tactics, send the expendable shit forward, men and machines, to soak up the fire. More armour appeared around the bend, another T-55, then a modern T-72 with reactive armour tiles bolted to its hide like metal scales. This was no probe. This was a battalion-sized push.

"Perfect," he muttered.

Boosfeld keyed his radio to the company net and spoke the single word to start the killing: "Initiate." His gunner's response was immediate—the 105 mm gun fired with a sound like the world cracking open. The T-55 erupted in a ball of white-hot flame as its ammunition detonated.

The moment Panzer 59's gun spoke, his other three tanks opened up in sequence, their guns bellowing like dragons. The Panzer grenadiers followed suit, Panzerfausts streaking out from concealed positions to slam into the BTRs bunched up at the intersection.

The WHACK of a Panzerfaust launch was followed instantly by the metallic CLANG of shaped charge meeting steel. The BTR lurched sideways, its right track torn away, and erupted in orange flame that climbed toward the sombre sky. Men tumbled from the burning hull, some of them on fire.

The T-72 commander panicked, traversing his gun wildly and firing high-explosive rounds into the tree line where he thought the infantry were hiding. Each shot was a thunderclap that rattled windows in the abandoned houses. Behind them, the rest of the column hit their brakes hard and bunched up at the intersection. The T-72 sat broadside to Boosfeld's position, its commander's hatch open, the crewman screaming orders Boosfeld couldn't hear over the engine noise.

Now. To his gunner, "Target, tank. Get the T-72 on the other side of the intersection."

"Identified," Sergeant Pickelhaupt replied, his tone as calm as if he were ordering coffee.

The 105 mm gun fired with a sound like the world cracking open. Boosfeld felt the recoil slam through the tank's hull as the round streaked across the intersection faster than thought. The T-72's turret rang like a struck bell, then vanished in a ball of white-hot fire as its ammunition detonated. The turret sailed a hundred meters through the air before crashing into a cottage.

His other three tanks followed up in sequence, their guns bellowing like dragons. Soviet armour died in fuel explosions that rose in filthy mushroom clouds, secondary detonations that threw off track links and steel wheels, crews bailing out only to be cut down by coaxial machine gun fire.

One T-55 tried to escape by driving along the railroad bed, its tracks sparking against the steel rails.

"Gunner, on the railroad tracks there."

"Identified."

Another tungsten dart, another funeral pyre.

This fight was his. Soviet armour burned along a two-hundred-meter stretch of road, and Boosfeld allowed himself a moment of dark satisfaction.

Then it all went to hell.

The screaming came from above, a sound like a circular saw cutting through sheet metal. The explosion that followed blurred Boosfeld's vision, and the clang that followed was like standing inside the world's biggest church bell when someone hit it with a sledgehammer.

Lieutenant Strohmeyer's tank, fifty meters to his right, was hemorrhaging greasy black smoke through holes punched in its turret. Secondary explosions boomed as the ammunition cooked off, each detonation lifting the sixty-ton hull slightly off its suspension.

Boosfeld scanned the burning Soviet vehicles ahead, looking for the shooter. His remaining tanks were still engaging targets, and another BTR died in flames as he watched. Then he heard it again, that buzz-saw roar of a turbofan at low altitude, followed by the distinctive thunk-thunk-thunk of 30 mm cannon fire. Behind him, another explosion shook the ground.

Frogfoot. Sturmovik. Whatever the fuck they were calling them now.

Boosfeld searched the overcast sky but saw nothing. The bastard was up there somewhere, probably coming around for another pass. He keyed his radio.

"All Lehr Two elements. Air attack!"

The words brought back memories he'd tried to bury. Dive-bombers screaming down out of the sun, the helpless feeling of being hunted from above.

As if summoned by his thoughts, more Soviet tanks appeared around the bend. The lead vehicle was another T-72, its gun firing on the move, muzzle flash strobing like lightning. The tanks behind it were firing too, their rounds whistling overhead to explode among the houses where his infantry were dug in.

The artillery was picking up again, heavier stuff this time, 152mm rounds that made the earth jump like a struck drum. Somewhere above the clouds, that attack aircraft circled, waiting for another chance to gut his remaining tanks.

Boosfeld felt the familiar weight pressing down on him. Stay and fight, and 2nd Company would die here in this shattered village. But movement was risky too, breaking contact always was. The Frogfoot would love to catch his tanks in the open.

A sharp thump from the tree line behind him, followed by a thin white contrail streaking up through the grey overcast. The Redeye missile, the Americans' latest gift to the Bundeswehr, climbed steadily toward the circling Sturmovik, its infrared seeker locked onto the aircraft's hot exhaust.

Boosfeld held his breath. The missile was new, barely tested in combat.

The explosion bloomed orange against the clouds, followed by the satisfying shriek of turbofan blades tearing themselves apart. Burning debris rained down into the pine forest, and somewhere a fuel tank detonated with a secondary boom that shook rainwater from the trees.

"First platoon, leapfrog per SOP to the rear," he ordered. "Second platoon, support."

By morning, Brilon-Wald would be in Soviet hands, and another piece of Germany would have fallen to the Red Army. But every hour he bought meant another hour for the Corps to dig in somewhere else, another hour for the refugees who had lived here to reach safety, another hour closer to winter when the Reds would bog down in the mud.

It wasn't victory. But it wasn't surrender either. He prepared to withdraw.

Captain Joachim Boosfeld had been fighting losing battles his entire life, and he'd gotten very good at it.

4

Germany.

DANTE HIMSELF COULD NOT HAVE CONJURED A MORE wretched procession than the endless river of refugees on Road 67. Geert took a long drag from his cigarette and watched an old woman, a grand-mother he would've wagered, pushing a wheelbarrow. Inside lay two small children and a pitifully small bundle of rags that represented everything left of their lives. Behind her, a businessman in a torn suit carried a briefcase in one hand and dragged a sobbing teenage boy with the other. They all dragged themselves west with the desperate, broken shuffle of the damned.

Like the walking dead fleeing Judgment Day, he thought, and then frowned. There was a banned television show called The Walking Dead, he thought. Or an uptime movie called Judgment Day. He couldn't remember, and it bugged him more than it should, because what did it fucking matter anyway?

What did anything matter?

He checked his watch. They'd kept Bernadette in this farmyard outside Dülmen for nearly an hour, the longest they'd stayed in one place since the retreat began. Around him, the survivors of B Battery tried to catch their breath. Eighteen men from the original forty-two.

"Opper," Bauke Aukema called from inside Bernadette's fighting compartment. "We're fucked badly for ammo."

Geert carefully stubbed out his smoke against the steel hull, preserving the butt of the rolled cigarette for later. You never knew when you'd get a fresh supply of tobacco and papers. Or if you'd get one. "How badly fucked, Bauke?"

"Ten rounds. Three HE set for super-quick, the rest are Willie-Pete and illum." Aukema held onto his bookkeeper's precision even as the world burned. "Might as well fart at the orcs, eh?"

Peter Ter Velde leaned over from the gunner's position. "If we could bottle your farts, sure. The HE rounds, though, we can kill something with them, no?"

"If we're close enough," Geert muttered. Super-quick fusing meant the shells would detonate on first contact, which was perfectly fine for soft targets but nearly useless against tank armour. And white phosphorus? Illumination rounds? In broad daylight against Soviet main battle tanks, they were less useful than Aukema's farts.

Heero Bloemsma sat slumped in the driver's seat, staring at nothing. The young carpenter had been getting worse. Geert had seen it enough now, even in regular army guys. Heero was at his breaking point.

Geert looked across the small farmyard over to see Lieutenant Eikelboom talking to Gun One's crew, his CO's expression grim under several days of beard growth. He supposed all their expressions were a bit grim these days, but that young man had aged ten or fifteen years in five weeks.

"Bloemsma," Eikelboom called as he approached Bernadette. "Fuel status?"

No response. Heero continued staring at the refugee stream.

"Driver!" Geert barked. "The LT asked you a question."

Heero startled, rubbing his eyes. "Sorry, what?"

Eikelboom's jaw worked silently for a moment. "How much diesel do you have left?"

"Maybe an hour's drive, if we're lucky."

"Wonderful." Eikelboom's voice was ragged with exhaustion and bitterness, but Geert could not say which was stronger. Maybe the bitterness. The poor fellow had seen his command annihilated. "At this rate, we'll be walking with the reffos, soon enough."

Geert was sorry that he'd stubbed out his smoke. He wasn't even sure why now. There were—

A scream cut through the air. A human scream, not the metal shriek of incoming. He spun toward the road and felt his stomach drop. The refugee column was already scattering, people running and pointing back east. Through the panicked voices, one word rang out clear as a church bell:

"Russen!"

Geert was already moving before conscious thought kicked in. Around him, his crew scrambled for their positions, Aukema diving for the loader's station, Ter Velde sliding behind his sight, Bloemsma already reaching for the ignition. He plugged in his CVC helmet and peered through the gunner's sight toward the eastern approach. There. Low, angular shapes moving fast along the road. BTR-80s, probably a reconnaissance element. Maybe a kilometre and a half out.

"Heero, start her up!" Geert called out. If those scout cars radioed back their position, they'd be dead as soon as the main Russian force arrived.

"Starting now, Opper!" The diesel engine coughed to life with a reassuring rumble. The alarm seemed to snap Heero out of his torpor, too.

The radio crackled. "All elements, move out! Now!" There was a sharp edge to Eikelboom's voice that hadn't been there before.

The much-reduced unit lurched into motion, Gun One smashing straight through the farmyard's wooden fence in a shower of splintered planks. Bernadette followed, her steel hull clipping the corner of a barn, sending heavy chunks of timber flying as they crashed through the debris. Bernadette, Gun Three, brought up the rear, serving as the column's tail-end Charlie. Through his commander's periscope, Geert watched the BTRs growing larger. They'd stopped, probably calling in the contact.

"Heero, why are we crawling?" Geert asked.

"The refugees! There's nowhere to go!"

Ahead of them, desperate families pressed against roadside fences and stumbled into drainage ditches, trying to clear a path for the enormous military vehicles. A woman with a baby clutched to her chest tripped over a fallen suitcase, spilling its contents across the road. Geert watched an old man stumble and fall, helped up by a boy.

They were normal people, like his neighbours in Utrecht, like Aukje's parents—

He forced himself to stop. That way lay madness.

"Listen carefully," Geert told his driver. "If we come under fire, you drive through whatever's in front of us. That's a direct order."

"I'll run over kids, Opper. Families. I'll kill them."

"No, I gave the order, so I will be killing them. Not you. You will do as you're told."

Bloemsma muttered something that Geert ignored as the convoy picked up speed around a bend, temporarily losing visual contact with the Soviet scouts.

For twenty minutes, they rolled west in fits and starts, the refugee stream quickly thinning as word of approaching Russian forces moved ahead of them. Geert swept his periscope back and forth across their six o'clock, scanning the empty road behind them. Nothing yet, but he could see dust clouds rising in the distance, far too much dust for refugee foot traffic. Through the haze of exhaust and settling debris from their hasty escape, dark shapes flickered in and out of view along the horizon.

Movement caught his eye. Low and fast, coming up the road behind them. Not a BTR this time, the unmistakable turtle-shell silhouette of a T-72 main battle tank. Moving at speed, not caring what got in its way.

As Geert watched, a tiny figure, a human being, disappeared under the tank's tracks. No sound at this distance, but he could imagine the screams if he chose to.

He did not.

"Bravo 6, this is Gun Three," he called over the radio. "Enemy tank in sight. Engaging." Then. "Driver, halt!" They couldn't outrun a tank, and Bernadette couldn't hit anything while she was rolling. Geert knew he was probably killing them all, but what choice did he have?

"Target tank, bearing 095, range 1400 meters."

"I see him," Ter Velde called from the gunner's position.

"HE, super-quick," Geert ordered, knowing it was all but useless against armour. Maybe they'd get lucky and hit a track or a vision block.

The T-72's main gun flashed. Geert instinctively ducked as the round screamed past and exploded in a field to their left. The Russian had fired on the move, a difficult shot, but they were walking their fire closer.

"Deflection set," Ter Velde reported.

"Range set," Aukema added.

"Fire!"

Bernadette bucked as the 155 mm gun roared. Through the smoke, Geert saw their round impact directly on the T-72's turret. For a heart-stopping moment, nothing happened. Then the Soviet tank disappeared in a greasy black fireball.

"The fuck!" Ter Velde yelled. "We got him!"

"Reload, move!" Geert ordered. A lucky hit, but where there was one tank, there would be more. "Driver, get us behind those trees!"

As Bernadette lurched forward, Geert popped up in the commander's hatch to navigate. The sight that greeted him would haunt his dreams forever—if he lived long enough to have dreams again. Bodies lay everywhere. Refugees cut down by fire, or simply crushed on the road. As he watched, their tracks rolled over something that might once have been a woman. He was grateful that the dead did not scream.

"Jesus," he whispered.

Behind the tree line, Geert looked back and felt his ass try to fall off as he spied not one tank, nor two, but an entire company of T-72s and support vehicles, deploying into formation. A dozen main battle tanks, supported by BMPs and BTRs.

"Bravo 6, we've got a full tank company back here!" he called over the radio, feeling strangely numb.

No, he supposed while he waited for a response. It wasn't strange. He was already dead, so what was he supposed to feel?

Geert waited. No response.

He tried again. "Bravo 6, this is Gun Three, do you copy?"

Silence. Then, faintly: "All Bravo elements, scat—"

The transmission cut off in a burst of static and distant explosions.

"Reload! HE." Geert yelled, but even as Aukema rammed another shell into the breach, he knew it was hopeless. One gun against a company? They had perhaps two minutes before those tanks zeroed in on their position.

"Driver, I don't care where you go or what you hit. Get us out of here!"

The diesel engine screamed as Bernadette crashed through the tree line, zigzagging desperately as Soviet tank rounds walked closer. The first shot hit fifty meters to their right, showering them with clods of earth and shattered branches. Geert felt the concussion through the steel hull.

"Left! Go left!" he screamed at Bloemsma, but his words were swallowed by the shriek of another incoming round.

This one landed close enough that Bernadette lifted off her tracks for a half-second. The impact threw Geert against the commander's hatch, the steel rim catching him across the ribs with a crack he felt as much as heard. Stars exploded behind his eyes as the taste of copper filled his mouth.

He watched a T-72's main gun swivel toward them. The muzzle flash bloomed, and Geert's bowels let go. He could see the shell coming, a dark streak against the smoke-hazed sky, growing larger, larger—

It passed so close overhead that he felt the displacement, the sucking void it carved through the air. The round detonated behind them in a mushroom of flame and debris that rained down on Bernadette's rear deck with metallic pings.

"Jesus fuck, Jesus fuck, Jesus fuck," Ter Velde chanted from his gunner's position, his voice climbing toward hysteria.

Bloemsma yanked the steering levers hard right, sending them careening toward a drainage ditch. For a moment, Geert thought they'd flip—fifty tons of artillery piece rolling like a child's toy—but somehow Bernadette's tracks found purchase and they lunged forward again.

The next round didn't miss by much. Every loose object in the fighting compartment became a projectile, including a thermos that broke open against the turret wall and showered them with warm coffee.

Geert tasted blood and realised he'd bitten into his tongue. His ears were ringing so badly he could barely hear his own voice as he screamed orders that made no sense. The acrid smell of cordite mixed with diesel fumes and something else—the sweet, cloying stench of fear-sweat and fresh shit.

Another shell screamed past, and the detonation cracked one of the periscope blocks. Fragments of armoured glass peppered Geert's face, tiny cuts that burned like fire. He could feel blood trickling down his cheek as he tried to look through the damaged optics again as soon as they hit a relatively benign stretch of flat ground.

He could see enough. A BTR-80 raced up from their left flank, its 30 mm cannon already traversing toward them. The first burst of automatic fire sparked off Bernadette's armour like angry hornets, each impact sending shock waves through the steel that felt like blows from a giant's hammer.

"They're on us! They're fucking on us!" Aukema was screaming now, his voice cracking with panic.

Bloemsma threw them into another desperate turn, and Geert felt something give way in his shoulder as he was hurled against the turret wall. The pain was immediate and stunning, radiating down his arm like liquid fire. But through the agony, through the chaos and the screaming and the endless mechanical shriek of incoming death, some part of his mind remained cold and composed.

They couldn't keep this up. Bernadette was tough, but she was an artillery piece, not a tank. Her armour was designed to stop fragments and small arms, not main gun rounds from a T-72 or a sustained burst from a chain gun. It was only a matter of time before—

The next shell hit close enough to drive Geert to his knees, his helmet bouncing off the commander's seat with enough force to crack the plastic. His vision greyed at the edges, and for a weirdly comforting moment, he thought he might pass out. How nice it might be to simply lie down and sleep, never to wake into this hell again.

But he forced himself upright, and suddenly, impossibly, the explosions were behind them.

The shooting continued, muzzle flashes still bloomed in his mirrors, and he could hear the angry chatter of automatic weapons fire, but the rounds fell short now, kicking up geysers of dirt and smoke in their wake. They'd broken contact, somehow. They were still alive.

"All Bravo elements, this is Gun Three," he called over the radio. "Report status."

"Supply Two, still rolling."

"Gun One, behind Supply Two. Don't see anybody else."

That was it. Three vehicles and no officers on the net.

Geert realised with dawning horror that he was the ranking NCO. An Opperwachtmeester—a senior sergeant—who not long ago had been worrying about tree roots in the University Chancellor's toilet.

He thought of Aukje, hopefully evacuated west by now with the twins and the new baby. If they were lucky. If the Dutch government had—

If, if, if...

"All Bravo elements," he called over the radio, his voice steadier than he felt. "This is Gun Three. I'm assuming command unless someone who outranks me speaks up."

And just like that, Opperwachtmeester Geert Veenstra—plumber to the professors—commanded what remained of B Battery, 3rd Artillery Battalion, Royal Netherlands Army.

"Supply two, Roger. We've got Eikelboom, but he's... he's messed up."

Geert closed his eyes for a moment.

"Supply Two, roger."

He looked back at the smoke rising from where they'd left more of their dead. Very soon, they'd run out of diesel. The Russians were in front of them and behind them. They had almost no ammunition left and no contact with higher command.

But they were still alive. Still fighting.

They were still Dutch and free.

"Heero," he called to his driver. "What's our fuel situation?"

"We'll be walking soon."

The radio crackled again. "Gun Three, Supply Two! Tanks ahead! Soviet tanks!"

Geert looked west and saw them—more T-72s blocking the road. They were trapped.

He reached for his tobacco pouch and found it empty. Somehow, that seemed perfect. He keyed the radio.

"All elements, prepare for contact front and rear. We've got them right where we want them. Let's kill them all."

5

Washington.

THE WALLS of the Oval Office came down before Kolhammer could get out from behind the Resolute Desk, or as good a facsimile of it as the carpenters at CBS could make. The Potemkin Desk, he called it. From where Menzies and Templesmith sat, it looked exactly like its famous counterpart. But after sitting behind it, Kolhammer knew it was just pine struts and plywood with some nicely finished veneer glued to the front.

The make-believe office came apart as the Secret Service poured in. Behind them, teamsters in black t-shirts were already yanking down the cream-colored canvas flats that served as the Oval Office walls, revealing the warehouse's bare concrete. Stage lights powered down with audible clicks, their cooling fans winding to silence. Two crew members rolled up the rug with the presidential seal, while others coiled thick camera cables and dismantled the professional lighting rigs that had made the set glow much more vividly than the real thing. Kolhammer waved the Secret Service off momentarily, watching his performative presidency efficiently packed away into road cases and wheeled platforms.

"I just want to thank these guys," he said.

"Of course, Mr President," his detail chief replied, "but we're moving in two minutes."

Kolhammer sometimes wondered who worked for whom in this gig, but he took the two-minute warning on board and moved quickly to grab Bob Quinn, the CBS producer who'd organised all of this.

"Bob, great job," Kolhammer said. "Just needed to say thanks. I could do the usual schtick about your grateful country thanking you properly, but honestly, the reward will probably come in the ratings over the next few weeks."

Quinn laughed. "Happy to help, Mr President." His smile faded. "I had a nephew serving at Norfolk. He's okay. He got through, but you know, a lot of his buddies didn't."

Kolhammer nodded. "No, they didn't."

Quinn looked at him inquisitively. "So... will this work? Did you get a result tonight?"

Kolhammer smiled. "Bob, I can't tell you anything right now. But I do want to thank you for your help and understanding about keeping everything quiet. We couldn't have done it without you guys, and I think you'll be happy with the results. Please pass on my regards to everyone involved, from the big boss down to the kids running coffee tonight. I'd appreciate it. I have to go now and get back to my office."

"Your real office," Quinn said.

"Yeah, the real one. Still standing, thanks to you guys."

They shook hands as the teamsters arrived on set to carry away the couch Menzies and Templesmith had been sitting on. The set would probably break down in five or six minutes and return to New York before dawn. The daily shoot on *All The President's Men* started at 0800, Quinn had told him, and he didn't doubt that if he'd leaned on the broadcaster to keep the fit out for another day—or even a week—they would've made it happen. But he was glad the subterfuge had paid off quickly.

It was bizarre that prestige historical TV dramas were now set years into the future. That used to be called sci-fi, where he came from, and there was a whole cable network devoted to it. (Two, if you counted Apple TV). But he came from the future, and he conceded that was a shit-ton weirder.

Lia Pao appeared at his left shoulder, her heels clicking in sync with his stride as they crossed the sound stage. Secret Service agents formed a loose diamond around them, their earpieces and hair cream glinting under the industrial lighting. The warehouse's massive roll-up door groaned open ahead, letting in a blast of warm air carrying the smell of wet asphalt and diesel fumes from the idling convoy.

"Menzies and Templesmith?" he asked.

"Already rolling," she said. "I leaned on Templesmith, and he promised his support, but you could seal the deal by catching up with him later this evening. He'll make time."

"Will we have time?" Kolhammer asked.

"We'll make it," Pao said. "You want that submarine."

"We need it," Kolhammer corrected. He loosened his tie as they passed disassembled lighting rigs being rolled out to waiting trucks.

Pao stepped in a bit closer and lowered her voice.

"I've also got Griffiths and Guggenheim coming around for meet-ups. Not at the same time, of course. Guggenheim's pretty much nocturnal, so you can talk to her after Templesmith. But I think we should have her tested for vampire genes or something. I've never seen the woman during the day."

Kolhammer felt his frustration getting the better of him even as Pao joked. He was taking all sorts of bullshit and heat for not having picked a Vice President yet, but every time his people went to the House or the Senate with a name, they got a polite 'fuck you very much' back in reply. He had his suspicions about who was behind it all, but there wasn't much he could do about that.

"Fine," he grunted. "So, situation room next?"

She nodded. "They're tracking the hunt for Red October."

He smiled at that. In reality, they were tracking the *Alexey Schastny*, a Novgorod-class submarine, which they were 98% certain had launched the cruise missile attack on Norfolk Naval Station at the start of the war.

"Still nothing?" Kolhammer asked.

"I couldn't say, Mr. President. But we can plug you in once you're on the move."

They strode away from the temporary studio—a warehouse in

outer DC off Maryland Route 355—into the car park, where a convoy
of Humvees and LAVs waited under sodium vapour lights that turned
everything a sickly yellow. A hot wind whipped debris across the wet
asphalt, the idling engines adding their heat to the already sweltering
night air. Besides the military personnel standing rigidly at attention
in their digital camo, the only people outside worked for him or CBS.
The TV guys were easy to spot in their T-shirts and cargo pants,
equipment belts sagging with tools and radios. They lined the path to
his vehicle, clapping and cheering as he passed. He waved back,
doing the political bullshit he hated so much, forcing a confident
smile because he had no news to share about the sub hunt yet.

At least the teamsters and caterers thought it would all end well.
Not so well for the fucking Russians obviously, but that was the
whole point of this bait-n-switch. Giving them a big fat target they
couldn't resist, then sucker-punching 'em when they took the shot.

His Secret Service guys ushered him into the back of an
armoured vehicle. Lia climbed in after him. The interior was a
cramped command centre, with banks of screens and communications equipment lining both walls. Four fixed swivel chairs were
bolted to the deck plating, each facing a dedicated workstation. LED
indicators and switches cast a blue-green glow across the metal
surfaces. Bundled cables snaked along the ceiling, connecting the
arrays of monitors, radios, and satellite uplink equipment.
Kolhammer took one chair and Lia the one nearest to it.

An army corporal sitting in one of the remaining spots jumped up
and snapped out a salute so fast Kolhammer worried he'd break his
fingers or his neck on the armour plating overhead.

"Thank you, son," Kolhammer said. "But get back to your work.
I'll call out if I need a hand."

"Yes, Mr. President."

The corporal resumed his seat and set headphones over his ears
as he began working his consoles.

Lia leaned forward and gave Kolhammer a side-eye before asking
in a low voice, "Can that guy hear us?"

He cocked his head. "Lia, you know the clearance procedures as
well as I do. You supervise some of it. He's been positively vetted. He's
cleared. Anything we say stays in here with us." He surveyed the

cramped interior, noting the blinking status lights, rows of toggle switches labelled in military block lettering, and the soft hum of encrypted comms gear. "Unless I leave a hot mic on and broadcast it to the eastern seaboard, but that's also part of his job, making sure we don't do something stupid like that."

She nodded and leaned back, still looking at the technician as though she didn't quite trust him. Lia was a great chief of staff, but she sometimes took her calling to cover his ass more seriously than Kolhammer thought necessary.

The LAV was idling quietly. Augmented technology copied from the eight-wheeled fighting vehicles the Australians had carried through the Transition, the engine growled, and they lurched forward, stopped, and started moving again. Lia relaxed as soon as they were mobile, but her idea of relaxation was to pull a flexipad out of her tote bag, power it up, and fill the screen with documents and windows.

"I've booked a slot for Templesmith to join you for a nightcap in the Oval in three hours," she said. "Menzies was happy to take a limo back to Australia House. I think he's already up past his bedtime, and he's probably worried his warm milk will go off before he gets back."

Kolhammer snorted. He wasn't close to the Australian Prime Minister. To be honest, he found him very old-fashioned and an unreconstructed bore. But he couldn't fault the man as an ally. He'd provided full access to Jane Willets' HMAS *Havoc*, the only nuclear-powered submarine in the world, without hesitation or strings attached. And it'd been a reverse-engineered goldmine; every circuit, every weapons system, and every piece of tech from that sub had been studied down to the molecular level and replicated as far as possible. Just like they'd done with his ship, the Big Hill. The AUKUS subs were the prize; for now, they were the only thing denying Beria control of the Atlantic. Like the carriers of the Pacific War, he thought, except this time the decisive battles would be fought in the cold depths rather than high up in the open skies.

"Mr. President," the corporal said from the other end of the compartment, "I have the live feed from the Situation Room if you want it now."

Kolhammer nodded. "Hook me up, son."

Two screens flickered to life in front of them. The first displayed a grid of six live camera feeds from hundreds of miles out in the Atlantic. The second showed Admiral Paul Tisevich, Chairman of the Joint Chiefs, waiting to brief them.

Tisevich was smiling for the first time in weeks.

"Admiral," Kolhammer said. "Good news for a change?"

"Excellent news, Mr President. We got 'em. A P3 out of Norfolk put a swordfish through them a few minutes ago. Subsea drones confirmed the hit."

"Fuck yeah," said Lia Pao beside him.

Kolhammer closed his eyes and took a deep breath, slowly letting it go but nodding and smiling as he did.

"Thank you, Paul. Outstanding work by everyone involved. If you could get the deets to me, I'd like to thank the flight crew of that Orion."

"Of course, Mr President. I do know that was one of yours on the stick, sir. A Captain Nova Paris. You may have trouble getting through to her, though," Tisevich smiled. "I think there's going to be a long line of folks buying them all drinks when they get home."

Kolhammer tried to pull the name up out of his memory. By 'one of his', he knew Tisevich meant an uptimer, but more than ten thousand people came through the Transition with him, and if Captain Paris was flying P3s now, it meant she was probably pretty junior back then.

"I'm glad it was a crew out of Norfolk," he said. "Now, anything else happen since I went into the studio that I need to know about?"

Tisevich's smile faded. "Nothing got worse, Mr. President. But nailing that sub was the only happy news. We have a link to SACEUR scheduled in one hour. General Jones will bring you up to speed, but the Russians continue to grind forward. We're making them pay for every inch, and the Germans in particular are bleeding them, but there's a lot of them to bleed."

Kolhammer nodded.

"Okay. Lonesome can brief me on that. You be sure and take a moment to enjoy this one, Paul. And get me the names of Captain Paris's crew."

"Will do, Mister President."

The link dropped out.

Kolhammer turned to his Chief of Staff, expecting to find her grinning at last, ready to spin this small tactical win into some great political victory, but instead he found her scowling into her personal screen, mouthing what he was sure were the words, 'ratbastard' and 'motherfucker'.

He could be reasonably sure he was right, because he'd had so much practice seeing her describe his opponents in just those terms.

"What's up, Lia?" he asked,

"Joe McCarthy," she said. "That ratbastard motherfucker is up to something."

EXTRACT

'The Transitions: An Oral History of the Future, by Studs Terkel.'
The New Yorker, March 13, 1954, Vol. 29, No. 5, pp. 51–56.

Nora Benedetti, bookstore clerk, City Lights, San Francisco.
(Interview conducted in late 1952. Benedetti works afternoons at the front desk of City Lights. She holds a thin cigarillo with fingers stained from forty years of stamping receipts.)

Oh, the first Skywire readings. Jesus, that was... what, '50? Maybe early '51? Just after they got the dishes working steady. We had one of the first setups in North Beach. Lawrence talked the satellite company into giving us a receiver. Cost him six months' rent, but he said he wanted poetry in space, not war mongers' rockets. (laughs) He might've been right.

We were listening to Jack Kerouac. Not a recording. Him. Live. Broadcasting from wherever he happened to be that week. That was the beauty of Skywire. You didn't need to know where he was—New York, Nebraska, the goddamn desert somewhere. His voice just came down out of the sky like rain.

He'd taken to the road as soon as he could, trying to make sense of it all. Can you imagine? Every book he was ever gonna write had already been published. Some of them were on our shelves before he'd written a word. On the Road, Big Sur, Visions of Cody. He couldn't bear it. Said he had to go live those pages now. Said he was going to be the Gonzo Scrivener of the New America.

We'd set up folding chairs in the back of the shop, twenty, maybe thirty people. At first it was mostly working guys. Longshoremen, merchant sailors, a few barflies from Vesuvio's who wandered in looking for heat. But then the college kids started showing up. Not just from UCLA either. Sharp kids. Smart. Buzzing with ideas. Some of them already dressed like beatniks or hippies or rappers. A couple of the girls leaning into the uptime style. It was all beautiful chaos.

McCarthy's thugs would drop by. They'd sit in the back, scribbling like they were collecting names for the Book of Revelation. Lawrence didn't care, and Jack surely didn't. Sometimes he was brilliant. Sometimes he just rambled. But always, always, it felt like he was right there in the room with us. Skywire wasn't like radio. Radio was polished. Safe. This was jagged. Alive. You could hear the wind in the background, traffic sometimes, a jukebox, a girl laughing. A whole country passing through his mouth. And you could talk back, of course. That was the real magic. That exchange of ideas.

And when the signal fuzzed out, we'd all lean forward like that would help. People craved the sound of him and the others. It felt like stealing something from the gods.

Sure, the narcs made me nervous. But when Jack's voice filled that little room, people forgot to be afraid. Just for a little while, they remembered how to dream.

There was this one kid—skinny, maybe eighteen—never missed a reading. Always wore a clean shirt, but his hands were caked in engine grease. He'd write everything down, word for word. After the readings, he'd hang back and ask me about the books.

"Miss, you think I could write like that someday?"

What could I tell him? The whole world was coming unglued. These voices from the sky, from the future, because that's what they were, talking about travelling down roads we hadn't built yet, in a country that hadn't decided what it wanted to be.

6

Washington.

JOE MCCARTHY CONSIDERED his dick again. He frowned a little as he inspected the damn thing, noticing a new spot at the end that hadn't been there last week. It was small and white. The spot, that is. Not his member. That was plenty big enough. But worry crept in as he thought of that woman down in Biloxi. Self-proclaimed good Christian lady, she was. Said she followed all the tenets of cleanliness and so on. But that business in the motel room, that'd been anything but pure, hadn't it?

It was all good fun at the time, sure enough. You couldn't blame a fella for having his fun. But now, standing in the water closet of his Senate office, Joe wondered whether she'd truly been as clean and wholesome as she'd promised. His frown deepened. Probably not. They never were.

Bending over in the confined space, he examined himself more careful-like. His goddamn belly kept getting in the way, and he was leaking a little bit, which made things messier than they needed to be. Was the leakage a sign that something was wrong? Or just the natural wear of things? Pipes and faucets do get a bit leaky over time. That's what happened to everything, eventually.

And now he had warm piss all over his fingers. Goddamnit. He shuffled around in the bathroom, which he reckoned was one of the smaller water closets in the Senate building. Pitiful comparison to Bigelow's spacious facility, which he'd visited just the night before. You could swing a live cat all the way around and back in that one. But this one? Hell, you could barely twirl a dead mouse by the tail.

He shuffled around in the barely adequate space, still leaking and dripping. But now dripping from his fingertips as well. He turned on the faucet to clean himself up. "Like that whore in Biloxi should've done last week," he muttered.

The water came out too fast and splashed over the front of his pants, making it look like he'd lost complete control of himself. "God-dammit," he cursed.

A soft knock sounded on the door behind him.

"Everything okay in there, Senator?" a voice asked.

"No!" he roared back. "It's not. Just give me a second, Roy. I just got to clean myself up."

"They're waiting for you, Senator."

"And they can wait another good goddamn minute for me," McCarthy barked back. "Unless you would advise me that I should do this press conference all piss-stained and wet-fingered, Roy. Is that what you're advising, Roy?"

Roy Cohn's voice came back, as measured and strangely soothing as McCarthy always found it. "No, Senator. They are here at your convenience and pleasure. And they can wait all day if necessary. They will. They're Hearst men, for the most part. They'll do as they're told."

That mollified him some. Joe liked it when people did as they were told. Made life a lot simpler. A lot more predictable. Especially compared to the unholy mess everyone was wading through now, thanks to Kolhammer and his bastard friends.

Senator Joe McCarthy pulled up his underpants, tucked himself away, and did up his belt. Then he remembered he was gonna have to change his pants because he'd splashed water all over himself in his rage and dishevelment.

One of the smart things Cohn had suggested when he came on board as McCarthy's main advisor was that they should always keep a couple of spare suits in the office. Joe was partial to a beer and some baby back pork ribs, and it wasn't unusual for him to find he'd left sticky-fingered reminders of his appetites all over his shirt and his coat. But to Cohn's credit, he hadn't made a big deal about it. He'd simply reminded him, "That's why you have free dry cleaning, Senator. So you can look your best for the American people."

McCarthy needed to look his best today. Today was the day he was gonna show the American people they needed new leadership if they were to pass through the valley of their travails. It would not be under the guidance of someone like Kolhammer. If the Republic wasn't to fall backasswards to the hammer and sickle, it would have to return to those first principles which had made America great in the first place.

"Get me a new suit," he said as he stepped out into the main office. "Goddamn faucets splashed water all over me."

Roy Cohn turned to his secretary, "Mary, get the senator's blue suit."

McCarthy patted his pockets looking for his speaking notes while Mary disappeared into the other office to fetch his change of clothes.

"I've got them here, sir," Roy Cohn said, holding up a small piece of paper. An envelope, actually. McCarthy saw he'd jotted notes down on the back of an envelope. Joe was relieved. The guy he'd had before Roy had been forever trying to get him to use one of those newfangled devices, which were diabolical and worse than useless, the way they vexed a fella. But a few notes in good, thick, solid American block letters, written on the back of an envelope? That was how a man organised his thoughts. That was something Joe McCarthy and millions of other Americans could work with.

"So these reporters, they're all from Hearst, you say?" McCarthy asked.

Cohn shook his head. "Not all, sir. That wouldn't look right. But you can be assured that everyone is on board with this. They'll ask the questions that need to be asked. And Walter's here. He'll ask you questions you're going to need. Throw to Walter when you're good and warmed up."

McCarthy stopped patting his pockets, which he'd kept doing even when his aide had offered him the envelope. He wasn't quite sure what he was looking for, but there was something that felt off.

"Walter? Good. That's good. But I think I need a belt, Roy."

Mary called out from the next room, "Your suit is coming, sir, with the right belt."

"No, not that...goddammit, Roy. I just need a shot of something to grease the groove and get the wheels rolling," he insisted.

"No, sir, you do not," Roy Cohn replied coolly. "A shot is the last thing you need right now."

McCarthy felt the heat rise quickly. Who was this Jew to tell him what he couldn't do? But Cohn—who seemed to have an unnatural ability to remain calm amid even the fiercest storm—smiled, shook his head, and reached into his pocket for a small bottle.

"You just need your medicine, Senator," he said, pulling out the small bottle and giving it a quick shake. The rattling sound had a strangely soothing effect on Joe McCarthy. It wasn't quite as good as throwing back a shot of bourbon, of course, but the ungovernable rage that'd been threatening to undo him just moments earlier suddenly abated.

Cohn gave the tiny bottle another shake before he twisted off the cap with a distinctly satisfying crack. A new bottle, then. Even better,

McCarthy held out his hand, and Roy Cohn dropped a single pink pill into his palm. For a moment, Joe simply stared at the pill. Even looking at it was enough to calm him down a ways.

"Here you go, sir," Cohn said, passing him a glass of water.

McCarthy blinked. He hadn't even seen his aide fetch the glass or noticed it in the room earlier. But he wasn't here for magic tricks. He was here for the American people, goddammit.

He swallowed the pill with a quick gulp. Almost instantly, a warm wave began to dissolve, replaced by a languid lightness. The building storm inside him quieted. The jagged edges of his thoughts softened, replaced by a smoothness that made everything wrong in the world feel distant and unreal.

When Mary returned with his new set of clothes, McCarthy was already climbing out of his pants without a thought for her. She made a little squeaky sound and exited the room quickly.

"Give me a hand here, would you, Roy?" he called, struggling to get into his jacket. He was a big fellow through the chest, and he sometimes found it challenging to get his elbows back far enough to get his arms through easily.

"Of course, sir," Roy Cohn said, moving behind him like a good tailor, holding the jacket steady so that McCarthy could easily slip his arms in.

Once the jacket was on, McCarthy shrugged and examined himself in the office mirror. He was transformed. Marvellous, really, what a decent set of duds could do for a man. It was a small thing when he thought about it, but when he did think about it, that was definitely one of those things he found most objectionable about the Kolhammer people. The ones he'd brought with him. And even worse, the people he'd lured from the good and narrow path after his arrival. They seemed to have no sense of decorum whatsoever.

He recalled going out to California, where the contagion was at its strongest and its worst. He'd seen folks wandering the streets in all manner of dress. Even men in dresses. Actual goddamned dresses. He'd seen it for himself once while visiting Old Mr. Hearst before he passed away. Two fellows walking down the street hand in hand. One of them wearing shorts like some sort of boy at summer camp. The other one in a dress. He had, quite frankly, stood and gaped at them on the street. And one of these perverts dared to wink at him as they walked past.

But with Kolhammer in the Oval Office, that sort of incidental perversity was the least of his concerns. Not with Beria's hordes raging through Europe.

"Will this do? I think this will do," he said.

"It will do fine, Senator," Roy Cohn said, brushing a piece of lint from his lapel. "You've got the talking points."

Still holding the envelope scrunched up in his hand, McCarthy unfolded it, scanned the brief passage of text, and nodded.

"I've got it. Let's go."

The press gaggle was waiting for them just a few minutes away. Artfully arranged by Cohn to make it seem as though they were there to grab a comment from any passing senator. But of course they were not. The gaggle erupted as McCarthy rounded the corner. He pushed back his shoulders and nodded to them as though they were his men and he was about to lead them into battle. Which, in a sense, they were.

Old-fashioned camera light bulbs flashed in his face. A barrage burst of harsh, incandescent lights that wanted so to blind him. Each flash a quick, bright shock against his eyeballs. But Joe McCarthy maintained his resolute expression, being careful, as Roy Cohn had taught him, to pick one of the reporters who wasn't holding a flash camera and to look mostly at his chest. Occasionally lifting his eyes to catch his gaze.

The questions were coming now as he stopped in front of the pack, and he let them come. Let them wash over him. Roy had taught him to stand calmly in the face of shouted questions with the mildest of smiles, all to create the impression of control and authority. To put the country in mind of a firm but indulgent father figure. That's what they needed right now. Not the clown show in the White House. But his medicine had taken effect, and he was not at all perturbed by their poor manners and uppity questions. He waited until the moment was right, and then he indicated with a gesture that he would take a question from Charles Haverford.

"The White House says the Navy has confirmed the sinking of the Russian submarine that attacked Norfolk, Senator McCarthy. Do you believe them?"

McCarthy paused, letting the question ripple through the press pack before raising a hand for silence.

"The White House? I don't believe a damn thing they say," he said, pausing to let that land. "But I do believe the United States Navy. And if the Navy is telling us that they got that commie sub, then I will take their word for it. The National Security Committee under my chairmanship has worked closely with the Navy to take our revenge for Norfolk, and I would ask all Americans to say a prayer of thanks for this rare good news."

The baying and barking started up again, and he let them run. It was good to let a dog pack stretch its legs.

When he felt they'd run enough, he jerked at the leash.

"Mister Winchell."

The *New York Daily Mirror* columnist nodded in acknowledgment. The pack fell quiet.

"Some people are saying, Senator, that you should be the new Vice President. Do you have any comment on that?"

McCarthy heard a few gasps at that, but otherwise they stayed remarkably quiet. Indeed, a great stillness came over them as they waited on the reply.

"It is not for me to make that choice, Mister Winchell," Joe replied. "That is the responsibility of the President, the Congress and the Senate. But..." he paused, just as Roy Cohn had taught him. "If I were called upon to serve..."

7

Moscow.

THE FLUORESCENT TUBES hummed like wasps, casting their cold white light on the stone floors of the Lubyanka. Flanked by his personal guards, Lavrentiy Beria descended into the bowels of his old kingdom, noting with some satisfaction how the harsh new-style lighting stripped away every shadow, every place where conspiracy might breed. He had ordered the installation himself, and the electrical engineers had worked through the night, stringing the glass tubes alongside the old fixtures set into the weeping walls.

The smell down here was a living thing. Fear-sweat had seeped into the walls over decades, and beneath that, the sweet-sick perfume of vomit and blood. But through this familiarity wound all the new things, too: the clean bite of ozone where electricity dreamed in copper veins, the sharp whisper of magnetic tape spinning its secrets, and the dry heat of the computing machines sighing through their cooling fans where screams had once been the only music. Through an open doorway, he glimpsed a technician coaxing life from a televisual eye that blinked its grainy judgment down on a cell three stories beneath the earth.

Progress, Beria thought, though today the word tasted as bitter as yesterday's cheese blinis.

He fingered the buff-coloured folder in his hand, feeling the thickness of so many newspaper clippings inside. The *Times of London*. The *Washington Post*. A gaudy spread from the picture magazine, *LIFE*, with the wretched Kolhammer's face splashed across the cover under the headline: "THE ADMIRAL STRIKES BACK." His jaw clenched involuntarily.

So many of his best plans, undone. The yanki pindos were supposed to be mourning their fallen president, not celebrating his replacement.

Two guards and the Watch Captain snapped to attention as he approached the interrogation suite. Unlike much of the Lubyanka, this section had been completely rebuilt to his specifications. Gone were the medieval stone chambers with blood drains in the floor. In their place now, clean white tiles, stainless steel fixtures, and a long window of one-way glass. The interrogation room itself looked like a medical lab, which in a way it was. In this suite, they could dig deep inside a man's head for whatever he had hidden there. Along one wall, the traditional tools remained on display—the rubber truncheons, the thumb screws and such like—but First Comrade Beria knew from long experience that the mind broke long before the body failed, especially when the subject knew his family was just three floors up.

"Has he been prepared?" Beria asked Watch Captain Volkov, who stood at attention by the door.

"As you ordered, First Comrade. No food for thirty-six hours. No sleep for forty-eight. His wife and daughters are in the family wing."

"The daughters. How old? Seven and nine, yes?"

"Yes, First Comrade."

Beria nodded. This, at least, was perfect. Old enough to understand, young enough to cry without guile. He handed his coat to Volkov but kept the folder. "Temperature?"

"Fourteen degrees, First Comrade."

Also perfect. Cold enough to be miserable in the thin prisoner's smock, but not cold enough to provide the mercy of numbness. Beria considered himself quite the scientist about these matters. Stalin had been a brute, of course, but brutishness was inefficient. Science got to the heart of things.

When he entered the interrogation room, Admiral Grigory Zhuravlev was trying to cling to some thin semblance of military bearing and dignity despite the chains, the cold, his hunger, and exhaustion—oh, and the fear, of course. One must not forget the fear. That was the most important thing, and Beria wondered if this proud admiral knew that yet?

This man, who had been afforded the privilege of commanding the Soviet Union's sole aircraft carrier battlegroup, sat shivering on a metal stool, his wrists shackled to a ring in the steel table. His face, once round with the privileges of rank, had hollowed out in the week since his rescue from the North Atlantic. His eyes, though, still held a spark of defiance.

Hmm. This would not do.

His guards took up station behind him as Beria settled into the comfortable armchair across from the admiral, taking his time arranging the folder on the small table between them. He produced his silver cigarette case, a gift from Franklin Roosevelt himself, back in the Tehran days, and lit a French cigarette, blowing smoke thoughtfully toward the ceiling where it swirled in the fluorescent glare.

"Admiral Zhuravlev," he began, his voice conversational. "Hero of the Soviet Union. Victor of the Battle of Sakhalin. Commander of my newest, most advanced carrier battlegroup." He paused, tapping ash into a crystal ashtray that caught the harsh light like frozen tears. He was quietly hoping Zhuravlev might say something stupid about that battlegroup being the people's fleet, not Lavrentiy Beria's. Still, despite his ravaged appearance, not all of the man's wits had abandoned him.

Beria continued, "Tell me, Grigory, how does a man such as you allow a single Amerikos, just a corrupt politician, really, playing at being a warrior, how does such a man, as you, allow his entire command to be destroyed by this degenerate clown?"

Zhuravlev's jaw worked, but he said nothing.

Probably wise. They both knew there was nothing for him to say that might help, not even a little bit.

Beria opened the folder slowly, noting how Zhuravlev's eyes tracked the movement. The first clipping he withdrew was from the *Times of London*: "PRESIDENT'S HEROIC FLIGHT DECIMATES SOVIET FLEET." The second, from *Le Monde*: "KOLHAMMER'S TRIUMPH IN THE ATLANTIC." But it was the *LIFE* magazine spread that he laid out with particular care, smoothing the glossy pages that showed an artist's dramatic rendering of the attack, the F-35 diving like an avenging angel, the poor ship Stalingrad erupting in blue white fire.

It wasn't entirely accurate, Beria knew. Kolhammer's accursed plane had never got that close.

"Our enemies have made quite the hero of your opponent," Beria observed, stubbing out his cigarette. "Look, look, Grigory. They're calling it the most daring pilot action since our countryman Pokryshkin shot down an entire Japanese squadron in the Great Patriotic War."

A muscle jumped in Zhuravlev's cheek. Good. That was a start.

Beria leaned forward like an eager child with a picture book. "Oh, but look at this one, Grigory!" He traced his finger along the *LIFE* magazine's garish illustrations with theatrical delight, his voice taking on an almost sing-song quality. "See how they've painted your poor *Stalingrad*? Such stark beauty in the explosion, don't you think?"

He turned the single page with exaggerated care, as if handling a precious storybook. "And here—oh, this is my favourite—they show Kolhammer's plane diving on you like the sky chariot of some Roman god of war. The Americans do love this rubbish, do they not?" His finger lingered on the image, and he made a soft "whoosh" sound, like a child playing with toy aeroplanes. "Down, down it comes, bringing death to the godless commies. That is what they call us, yes?"

He looked up at Zhuravlev with mock innocence, his eyes bright with feigned wonder. "Isn't it marvellous how they have made a delight from our shame? Such talented storytellers, their propagandists."

He sat back and folded one leg over the other. Lighting a new cigarette.

"Seventy million Americans have seen these pictures. Children now play at being Philip Kolhammer, diving their toy planes into our ships. Hollywood is planning a film, I'm told. Mister Gary Cooper has been mentioned for the lead, though I do not think he looks much like the new president, no?"

"The aircraft was invisible," Zhuravlev said, his voice barely above a whisper. "Our radars couldn't—"

Beria clicked his tongue and wagged a finger, silencing the admiral.

"The poor worker blames his tools."

Zhuravlev's chains rattled as he shifted. "But our defensive systems never saw it until—"

"Until it was too late. Yes, I've read your report." Beria stared at him, letting the silence stretch. Somewhere in the building, a door slammed. The sound echoed through the ventilation system like a gunshot. The man's Adam's apple bobbed as he swallowed.

Beria stood and began to pace, his footsteps clicking on the tiles. "I am a practical man, Grigory. A scientific man, I like to think. I want to understand how this happened. Not to punish you, but to ensure it never happens again."

He returned to the armchair, leaning forward over the back of it. "So I ask you again. How did one American pilot—for that is what he was, not the president, not some hero, just one pilot, and somewhat out of practice, I would have thought—how did he destroy the most advanced battle group in the Soviet Navy?"

After a long interval, Zhuravlev spoke, the words seeming to physically pain him. "Their fighter was at least three or four generations ahead of anything we have. The robot rocket he deployed, we had no defence. Thousands of kilometres per hour, it flew."

"So you're saying our Soviet science is inferior to American capitalism?"

"No, Comrade Secretary, I—"

"Because that's what it sounds like you are saying. It sounds like you're making excuses for cowardice and incompetence by blaming our scientists and engineers."

Zhuravlev's face had gone pale. "That's not what I meant—"

"Let me tell you what I think happened," Beria said, sitting back down and opening the folder again. This time, he pulled out a clipping from Pravda. The headline read: TRAITORS AND SABOTEURS.

"I think someone in your battlegroup, perhaps multiple some-ones elsewhere in the Navy, betrayed us to the Americans. I think they knew exactly where you'd be, exactly when you'd be there. And I think Kolhammer's 'miraculous' attack was only possible because of treason."

"That's not true! My men were loyal—"

"Your men are dead," Beria snapped.

He stood again, walked to the one-way glass, and tapped on it twice. A moment later, the door opened and Guard Captain Volkov entered, carrying a small tape recorder, another uptime innovation he rather liked. Some nights, when the burdens of being the First Comrade felt like a crushing weight upon him, he would play tapes of his favourite interrogations in his private quarters.

"Play the recording," Beria ordered.

Volkov pressed a button, and a young girl's voice filled the room, high and frightened: "Papa? Papa, where are you? The men say you're a traitor. Papa, I'm scared—"

"That is enough," Beria said, and Volkov stopped the tape. Zhuravlev had gone rigid, his face a mask of anguish.

"Your daughter Katya," Beria said conversationally. "She is a bright girl. She understands what happened. Why can you not see the truth, Admiral?"

"Please," Zhuravlev whispered. "They have nothing to do with—"

Beria waved his tutting finger again.

"Tut-tut-tut. Everything is connected. Every success, every failure. Every loyalty, every betrayal." He pulled out another Western clip-ping, this one from the *New York Times*, showing Kolhammer being greeted as a hero on his return to America. "Look at him. Look at what you've made possible. All because you couldn't stop one man in one plane. What would little Katya say?"

Zhuravlev was weeping now, silently, the tears cutting tracks through the grime on his face.

"Of course, Grigory, if you could name the traitors in the Navy, and perhaps the Army, who betrayed us..."

It was important, that little word. 'Us.'

It drew a protective circle around the two of them, made of Zhuravlev and Beria, a small team who might unite against the greater threat. The threat of traitors and saboteurs who would undo everything.

Any moment now, Grigory Zhuravlev would understand what he must do.

But before he could, a knock at the door interrupted them. Beria kept the annoyance from his expression as Volkov answered the knock, whispered a conversation, and then approached Beria urgently.

"First Comrade, Comrade Serov insists on speaking with you immediately. He says it's about the Ukraine."

Beria grunted. He could not help it.

Serov, his new NKVD chief, was a competent butcher who'd personally eliminated all the Politburo members Beria had known to be plotting against him. If he was interrupting this interrogation, it was serious. There might be more plots. Especially if there were Ukrainians involved.

Beria looked back at Zhuravlev. Perhaps he might confess to his knowledge of this Ukrainian business?

"We'll continue this conversation, Admiral. In the meantime, think carefully about what you want your daughters to remember about their father. Hero or traitor, it's entirely your choice."

He followed Volkov into the corridor where Serov waited, his usually composed face tight with concern. The man was holding his own folder, and Beria could see radio transcripts poking out.

"What is it?" Beria demanded.

"First Comrade, Ukrainian fascist elements have raided the missile base at Pervomaysk. They've executed all the political officers and tried to turn the missiles on Moscow."

Beria felt his stomach clench. Pervomaysk housed forty-six R-16 intercontinental ballistic missiles. "How?"

"Americans, First Comrade. Special forces and CIA, too, we believe. The guards reported hearing English commands during the assault."

Of course. Kolhammer again. Beria's chest tightened at the merest thought of the name as if a giant fist had closed around him. His free hand found the wall, fingers pressing against the cold stone as a wave of nausea rolled through him. The American pindo's shadow fell across everything like a curse, and Beria could taste bile at the back of his throat—sharp and acidic, mixing with the lingering flavour of French tobacco.

He swallowed hard, forcing his breathing to steady.

"Secure the traitor," Beria ordered Volkov, gesturing back over his shoulder at Zhuravlev. "Keep him alive. We may need him later."

He turned to Serov. "Get me the Stavka. I want to turn around the 3rd Shock Army. I want those khokhol bastards in Kiev back under our boot within twenty-four hours. Arrest every Ukrainian division commander. We cannot show weakness."

"Yes, First Comrade," Serov barked.

8

Washington.

KOLHAMMER STOOD at the windows of the Oval Office, gazing out over the flower beds and thinking about his wife. Every day, Phillip Kolhammer forced himself to remember Marie. It had been more than fifteen years since he had last seen her, last touched her, since he had lain beside her in bed in their modest Santa Monica home. And so, he made himself think of her each day—even when it would have been so easy, particularly now, to let the remembrance slip by for one day, which might become two or even three in a week like this, a month like this. Before long, he would not have forgotten his wife; she would always be there with him, but she would no longer be what she had been. Kolhammer was determined, however, that he would see out his days devoted to Marie.

Outside, a gardener was at work, digging up the old rose bushes to replace them with agapanthus—Marie's favourite—that had surrounded their house back home. The morning heat was already building, promising another scorching D.C. summer day. Even at this early hour, the humidity pressed against the armour-glass windows like a living thing, and he could see the first wavering heat haze beginning to shimmer off the South Lawn's immaculate grass.

A knock at the door interrupted his thoughts. He glared at the dozen or so newspapers crowded on his desk, then quickly smoothed away the scowl as the butler entered, escorted by a Secret Service agent. "Mr President, your breakfast," he announced.

"Thanks, Willie," Kolhammer said. "Just wheel it over. I'll eat it while I work." He wasn't supposed to be eating in the Oval Office; a whole wing of the White House was reserved for domestic routine. But then again, he was the goddamn President of the United States of America. If he wanted to have his steak and eggs at his desk, he would have his steak and eggs. He brushed off his irritation. After all, it wasn't Willie's fault that Joe McCarthy was a gigantic, sucking asshole. Lia had said he was up to something, and now they knew what.

Willie responded with a slight bow before he and the Secret Service withdrew from the room.

Kolhammer dabbed away a few beads of sweat from his forehead. The workout had elevated his core temp. Although it was already 80 degrees outside—heading for a stinker of a day in Washington—the office was chilled with air con so crisp that steam rose from his scrambled eggs and rump steak. The climate control system was a Davidson Industries upgrade, installed along with a bunch of new comms gear. Grunting, he sat down to eat, determined not to allow McCarthy to steal this small pleasure from him. Just half an hour ago in the gym, while bench pressing and getting after his barbell rows, he'd pushed aside any thoughts of the bastard. If he was going to enjoy his protein and caffeine, he couldn't let him get in the way now.

Kolhammer attacked the medium-rare steak as he scanned the headlines. He knew he shouldn't—really, he should focus on eating and think about anything else—but the news invaded every corner of his mind. Every paper, from the *New York Times* to Hearst's shittiest tabloid (which he read just as rigorously and grimly as he performed his leg day routines every Wednesday), carried reports of the sinking of the Russian submarine. "God damn it," he muttered, chewing on a piece of rump and washing it down with a mouthful of black coffee before scooping up all of the neatly arranged newspapers, shuffling them into a thick pile, and dropping them onto the floor next to him with a thud.

A few deep breaths and some determination carried him back to the last time he'd had breakfast with Marie, the day before they shipped out for Indonesia. He couldn't be sure whether he was recalling that morning accurately or merely calling up memories of memories, carefully tended and preserved yet inevitably shifting with each recollection. But it helped him to think of her and the conversation they'd shared. He couldn't remember every word, of course, or even much of what they'd discussed, but he did recall how they never discussed work at the table. That was one of the reasons he loved her. That final morning, she would have taken him through her plans for the day, chatting about the shopping, the gardening, some friends she might catch up with, and the reading class she ran as a volunteer at the local school. Far more engaging than the day ahead of him, which he'd spent pulling together the first elements of the Multinational Force.

After a few minutes, he realised his scrambled eggs were gone, his steak nearly finished, and the coffee had cooled. So had he. He was almost ready to pick up those newspapers and quickly scan the first couple of paragraphs of each story when another knock sounded at the door. Looking up, he saw a Secret Service agent admitting his Chief of Staff. Lia Pao looked terrible. Still wearing the same clothes from the makeshift TV studio the previous night, her eyes were smudged with puffy, dark half-moons, and her bloodshot gaze testified to an all-nighter.

"You look like shit," he said. "Did you even go home last night?"

"Home's where my head hits the pillow on the couch," she replied, nodding toward the coffee pot on the sideboard. "You gonna drink all that yourself?"

"Knock yourself out."

"You got any creatine?" she asked.

"Not up here, no. I can have Willie bring some in if you need it."

"Maybe later." Lia poured herself a long cup of joe, adding two heaped teaspoons of sugar and a dash of oat milk. Kolhammer preferred his coffee black, but he kept a supply of alternative milk substitutes on hand since Lia couldn't take dairy. Walter Winchell had been obsessed with that discovery, penning three columns in one fortnight about Lia Pao's un-American, anti-milk proclivities, as if almond milk were somehow a communist plot.

Carrying the pot over, Lia topped up his coffee and noted the pile of newspapers on the floor. "Solid choice," she said. "D'you read any of those, or should I have somebody take them out to the crapper right now?"

"I'm sure you've read them," Kolhammer said. "Why don't you tell me what our favourite senator's been up to overnight? I can already see he's claiming credit for sinking the *Alexei Shastney*."

He nodded down at the papers, which all carried front-page stories about the Navy's sinking of the Russian sub. Lia pulled up a chair in front of the Resolute Desk, took a long pull on her coffee, inhaled the rising steam, and then carefully placed the mug on a desk jotter.

"He called a presser last night," she continued, "Print only, no electronics, and, of course, it was mostly Hearst guys. He spoke to them about fifteen minutes before their deadline. They didn't have time to double-check anything."

"Not that they would have anyway," Kolhammer said.

"Yeah, I know," she nodded. "So he sold them his version of the hunt for Red October."

Kolhammer gave her a pointed look.

"Okay, fine, the fucking Alexei Shitboat or whatever," she said, throwing up her hands. "He spun the whole fucking charade with CBS, the Aussie PM and Templesmith into a fairytale with him slaying the Russian dragon at the end."

Kolhammer looked down at his plate. A couple of pieces of rump steak remained, but his appetite had deserted him. "Well, we were going to tell everybody the full story today," he murmured. "I guess that frees up an hour or so for me to do some real work. And nobody's gonna believe McCarthy swam out there with a knife between his teeth and shanked them himself."

Lia returned his look, with a few extra cranks on the handle. "I know you think this stuff isn't important."

"Oh, I know it's important," he admitted. "But I just don't think it's as important as my real job. And that's kicking Lavrentiy Beria's ass all the way back to Moscow and, hopefully, into one of his Lubyanka dungeons where the next mad fucking butcher can put a bullet in the back of his head. And the merry-go-round can start all over again."

Her expression softened, if only slightly. "Don't hold out much hope for a liberal renewal in Russian politics going forward, boss?"

He snorted. "That fuckin' fairytale was already falling apart by the time we left," he added, his tone nervous for a moment. "We had one Russian on the whole Multinational Force, and he was an accident. An observer with Lonesome's unit. Some UN bullshit. I didn't even find out until after we got here."

"Ivanov," she said. "I met him once. He's okay. Half-Crimean, I think. Really fucking hated Putin and Stalin."

"Yeah, I know, just ignore me, Lia," he said. "I was thinking about home. I don't care to ponder how it turned out after we ended up here."

She shrugged. "That future might not exist anymore." Then, noticing his troubled look, she added softly, "Sorry, I forget about Marie sometimes."

Kolhammer shook his head. "I try not to forget, but don't worry about it. Tell me about McCarthy. I don't suppose he overreached? Left himself exposed, so we could give him a small tactical nudge and send him over the edge into well-deserved perdition? That'd be a nice way to start the day."

"It would," Lia agreed, "but no such luck. I'm afraid Roy Cohn's fingerprints were all over the presser."

She leaned back in her chair, and Kolhammer noticed how exhaustion had carved deeper lines around her eyes. Outside, the gardener's electric hedge trimmer buzzed to life, the mundane sound threatening to go from irritating to enraging if he didn't get his temper under control.

"If you read the comments McCarthy made, he didn't give away anything we could nail his ass for. And who'd be doing that anyway?" Lia continued, her voice picking up some heat. "He's got Hearst in his pocket, or they've got him in theirs; it hardly matters, they're all the way into this weird fucking parasitic/symbiotic relationship by now anyway."

Kolhammer pushed the remaining steak around his plate, his

appetite completely gone. The air conditioning cycled on again with a soft hum, fighting against the rising heat outside.

Lia continued, "So, none of those headlines you decided not to read this morning actually brush up against the truth, which is that this asshole came *this* close to blowing the OPSEC on a top-secret naval operation." She gestured toward the scattered newspapers on the floor, then angrily threw her hands up. "And of course the useless fucking legacy press, the fucking *New York Times* and—"

Kolhammer waved away whatever she was about to say.

"Decided to both-sides it all the way down, did they? This is my surprised face."

He wore an utterly stone-faced expression.

"Yeah, well, that's not the worst," Lia said.

"Really?"

If missing an opportunity for a day of good press wasn't the worst of it in Lia Pao's judgment, Kolhammer wasn't sure if he wanted to hear what qualified. "What else did he do?" Kolhammer asked.

"He shanked Martha Griffiths in the exercise yard."

"He what?" Kolhammer asked incredulously.

"Right at the end of the presser, when everyone was straining at the leash, desperate to phone in their stories because the deadline was closing out, he said the National Security Committee was opening an investigation into Griffiths because of suspected un-American activities."

"Oh, for fuck's sake, not again," Kolhammer muttered. The air conditioning hummed louder for a moment, as if the building itself were sighing in exasperation.

"Yes, again. Three times is a charm," Lia confirmed.

He opened the top drawer of his desk, searching for the antacid pills he kept there. His breakfast had decided it wasn't happy. Two of his previous VP nominees had gone the same way, sandbagged by McCarthy and Hearst before he could present the nomination to a joint sitting. The tablets rattled in the bottle like dice in a cup as he stared at the scattered remnants of breakfast, the weight of the day already pressing in.

Through the windows, the gardener had moved on to trimming hedges, the mundane rhythm of maintenance continuing even as the world teetered on the edge of destruction. Marie would have approved. She'd always believed that living in the ordinary moments kept you sane when everything else went to hell.

"Lia," he said finally, "what do you think McCarthy wants out of all this? I mean, what's his endgame?"

Her expression shifted, becoming sharper, more focused. "Oh, I know exactly what he wants." She stood up and came around the desk, bending down to rifle through the newspapers on the floor. "Here we go," she said, pulling out the *New York Daily Mirror*. She flipped it open and stabbed at the page with two fingers. "Walter Winchell, today's column."

Kolhammer leaned forward to read. The headline made his stomach clench: "AMERICA NEEDS A PATRIOT: Why Joe McCarthy Should Be Kolhammer's Deputy."

Below it, Winchell's prose breathlessly sang the senator's praises as the only man tough enough to stand beside the new president against the Red Menace.

"Son of a bitch," Kolhammer muttered.

"That's unfair to the blameless bitches of the world," Lia said, straightening up. "But, yeah, this is his game. Or Hearst's. Or Getty's. Whoever is backing him."

"He wants to be VP? Seriously?"

"No, boss. He wants to be President."

Kolhammer popped another couple of antacid tablets. He closed his eyes and rubbed them slowly, trying to fend off the headache that was coming in hard.

"Get him in, Lia. No. Better yet, get the Natsec Committee in. Let's at least try to make this look legit."

"You can't be thinking of giving in to this fascist asshole, boss?"

"I'm not. But ignoring him isn't gonna make the problem go away."

"The problem isn't just him. It's the big money shitheads behind him. A bunch of oil men and newspaper barons. Bunch of fucking vampire squids trying to keep their feeding tubes stuck down everybody's throats."

Kolhammer grunted. Maybe it was even half a snort of laughter, but there wasn't much humour in it.

"Yeah, I know. I get it. It's like they're so frightened of some faraway future without them, they can't see the fucking tsunami about to flatten us all next week. Just get the National Security Committee in. Today, if possible, the senior members at least, and we'll pull McCarthy aside at the end. You got anything we can use against him?"

Lia smiled.

"With guys like that, there's always something."

9

Los Angeles.

SLIM JIM LAUGHED his ass off as the bombs fell. It was pretty funny watching Moose Molloy try to dodge them, especially with a Hollywood lovely perched on each of his massive shoulders. The girls screamed and squealed as Moose heaved left and right, sending tidal waves sloshing up and down the rooftop pool, knocking everyone off their inflatable loungers, and even upending the floating cocktail bar. But it was no goddamned good. Slim Jim nailed him with all three water bombs.

"No fair, no fair!" Moose cried out.

"Nah, I nailed you fair and square, Moose-man," Slim Jim laughed, holding the drone controls aloft like a trophy. "You gotta pay up, big fella."

Moose couldn't argue with the logic of that. With a giant heave of his shoulders, he sent both of the lovelies tumbling into the water with twin shrieks of delight. He waded to the edge of the pool where a tray of shots waited for him and downed them - one, two, three. One for each water bomb that'd struck him. House rules.

The crowd cheered, and the DJ dropped the needle on a new track.

But as Slim Jim watched the riot unfolding around him, he had to admit it wasn't quite as awesome as some of the parties he'd hosted here before the war. When was that? What, five or six weeks ago or something? There were only half as many people here as last time, and not everyone had been called up or volunteered. It was like peeps just didn't want to party anymore, like they thought there was something wrong with it.

Slim Jim tossed the controller aside, knocking over the tray of margaritas he'd been meaning to drink.

Goddamnit.

If some commie buzzkill really was gonna send them all to the salt mines soon, the only logical thing to do was to get your party on while you could. He was pretty fucking sure Siberian salt mines didn't run to rooftop pools and floating tequila bars.

He watched the three humming little drones navigate their way back to the loading table, where a couple of tech guys from one of his companies—he had no idea which—began reloading them with more water balloons. The drones were fucking slick, about the size of dinner plates, and brightly painted in Davidson Enterprises' corporate blue with silver trim. They hummed like angry wasps and could deliver a decent payload with fair accuracy on a target as big as Moose.

But the moment had gone sour.

He looked around the rooftop party again. The laughter sounded thin and even a little forced against the vastness of the California sky. The splashing in the pool seemed frantic, not fun. High above, the contrails of jet fighters stitched silver threads across the deep blue, a constant reminder of the world beyond this rooftop bubble.

"Jimbo!"

The voice was harsh, female, and familiar enough to make his nuts try to crawl up inside his body.

"Oh, hey," he said, turning and shading his eyes against the sun. Maria O'Brien stood there, dressed in a black suit as usual, holding some sort of flexi-pad as usual, and looking pissed off with him, as per fucking usual.

"Can I speak to you away from the orgy for a moment?" she said.

"Sure, whatever."

He pushed himself up out of his sun lounge. He swayed a little on his feet; he'd lost a couple of games of water-bomber to Moose earlier and had paid up with tequila slammers. "It's not much of an orgy, anyway, man. Just a pool party."

"We have stuff we need to discuss, Jimbo. Now."

Maria reached into her jacket and pulled out a small blue pill, holding it out to him like it was a communion wafer or something.

"Oh, man, really? I just got my drink on, Maz."

"And now you're going to get your drink off," she said. "This is important."

He sighed, took the pill and dry-swallowed it, making a face. He had no fucking idea how the thing worked, but he knew what would happen. Within a few seconds, a warm flush rolled up his body from his toes to the top of his skull. For a moment, he could have sworn he'd pissed himself, but he knew that wasn't so; it was just a weird effect on the nerves of whatever the hell was in that little blue miracle. Five nine-nine, retail, minimum pack of six. One of the most reliable cash cows in the whole of Davidson Enterprises. It didn't sober him up completely, but it swept the legs out from under his buzz, and suddenly he was able to concentrate on what was happening instead of just enjoying it. Or trying to.

"What's that?" he said, nodding at the envelope Maria was holding. He hadn't even noticed it before, and now he had a sinking feeling about it, the kind you got when the doctor called and said he needed to see you immediately.

"Another subpoena," she said, and the sinking feeling dropped through the bottom of his stomach and kept on going, heading for his ass.

"Fucking McCarthy again? Seriously? Come on, man."

"Yeah, and I think he's serious this time, Jimbo. He's talking about sending federal marshals to bring you in if you don't agree to testify."

"Can't we make this go away?" Davidson said, hearing a whine creep into his voice and hating the sound of it. "Don't we have some guys on that committee? Couldn't you give Kolhammer a call? We did save the world a couple of weeks ago. Remember that, when our sneaky satellites took out Stalin's fucking space stations or whatever the hell they were. Don't we get any credit for that?"

"The President is busy," Maria said flatly. "And the anti-satellite weapon system we built inside our supposedly civilian satellite network is exactly why the National Security Committee wants us to testify."

"Well, I didn't build the fucking thing," he complained, his voice taking on even more of a wheedling tone. He waved a hand towards the two tech guys still loading the drones. "That was my tech guys. Well, maybe not those specific guys, but some other guys. I got a lot of fucking guys, Maria. Send them."

Maria's frown softened a little, which was about as close to sympathy as you ever got from her. "I know, Jimbo, but they don't want your guys. They want you. And it's not just McCarthy with a weed up his butt."

"Yeah, I know, I know," Davidson sighed, running a hand through his hair. It was much thicker than it had been, thanks to the treatments he'd been getting, and running his hands through it was normally one of life's pleasures. But the new growth felt weird and greasy today, and it just reminded him of how badly it had been thinning before the treatments. "It's fucking Getty, man. I know it is. And Hearst. And those fucking railway goons. Why do they hate me so much, Maz? I'm just trying to make a buck here. An honest buck for a change. And have a good time. And—"

She smiled at that and cut him off. "Because you stole the future from them, Jimbo. Junior Hearst knows you are building out your satellite internet that will destroy his newspapers and magazines. Getty hates you for the magloop and the EVs, and you'd have Ford and GM on your ass too, if you hadn't licensed the battery tech to them. This is just the old world trying to hold off the new. Nothing more. They might be the industries of the past, they totally will be soon enough, but right now they still have plenty of money and power." She held up the subpoena again. "And this is them trying to hold on to it."

"But I don't want to testify," he complained. "I hate it. It's fucking triggering, man. Reminds me of how I ended up on that fucking chain gang in Georgia. That's what it feels like every fucking time,

Maria. Like I'm back in front of Judge Gamble, waiting to find out how many hundreds of years I'm gonna spend breaking rocks. Can't I just plead the Fifth or something?"

She laughed, and the sound was nothing like the horselaughs and raucous shit coming from the pool party. It was light and almost musical. "There's nothing to plead the Fifth to. You haven't committed any actual crimes, Jimbo. You've just pressed up against some international law, and that isn't even a real law. It's just a bunch of gentlemen's agreements." She leaned in to share a secret. "And there are no gentlemen."

Slim Jim nodded and breathed out. Starting to calm down. He looked out over the city again. In the years since the war ended, LA had turned into something that woulda looked like a science fiction movie to the poor bastard who'd walked off of that bunko charge and into the Navy back in '42. A lot of those towers, sleek and impossibly tall, were his. They didn't just dominate the skyline like steel and glass mountains. They were the fucking skyline. Down below, ribbons of freeway glowed with traffic, and beside them ran the silent, vacuum-sealed tubes of his mass transit system. He'd built this future, or at least paid for it to be built, or took a tax break for it. Maria was across the details.

But some people hated him for it.

It just didn't seem fair, so many people with so much aggravation for Slim Jim Davidson, who only wanted to make an honest dollar and a chilli margarita.

"You know, Maz. One thing I remember from the chain gang," he said quietly, his voice taking on that Georgia drawl that still came out when he did some hard thinking on serious shit. "When a guy gets himself cornered in the exercise yard, or the showers, that's when he's in the most danger, but he's at his most dangerous too. And you tell me if I'm wrong, but Getty and Hearst and those rail-road fucks... they're acting like they're cornered in a fuckin' shower block."

His gaze drifted back to the pool. Moose had one of the drone controls now and was showing the wannabe starlets how to fly the little gizmos. They were swooping and diving on everyone in the pool, dropping water bombs to roaring laughter and squeals of delight. The drones moved like hummingbirds, all quick darts and sudden stops, their rotors whining in the warm afternoon air.

He noticed Maria wasn't listening to him anymore. She was staring at Moose, and there was something in her expression he couldn't quite read.

It wasn't surprising, he supposed. Moose was a big guy, a hard-muscled lunk of a man. All rocky lantern-jaw and boulder-shoulders and a full head of hair with it. None of that DNA treatment Slim Jim had flown to London for. Had to admit, if you were a dame, Moose probably wasn't hard to look at. He stared at Maria staring at Molloy, and he didn't think she was seeing anybody at the moment. He knew she'd had that fling with the Tarzan actor a while back, but that hadn't gone anywhere. She was married to her work, she always told him. *And I appreciate that, babe*, Slim Jim would say, *but your work ain't gonna go upside your head if you have a little piece on the side.*

"Maria?" he said. "You still with me?"

She blinked and looked back at him, then glanced at the drones buzzing over the pool like giant mechanical dragonflies. "They're the new ones, aren't they? The ones coming out at Christmas."

He shrugged. The blue pill had really cleaned up his buzz now. He felt sharp and focused in a way that wasn't entirely pleasant. "Yeah. I wanted to put them out for the summer, but we only got the production line set up two months ago, and the marketing guys said we should go large for the holiday season, so we're waiting. Building inventory. I think we were planning to take a loss on the first batch, maybe even give them away with a satellite box subscription. I don't know, Maria. They're great fun to play with, but you know me. I don't spend a lot of time in the books, so you'd know better what the hell we're actually doing with them."

She nodded slowly, and he could practically see the gears turning in her head. "Yes," she said. "I would know. We've got at least 600,000 sitting in the warehouse at Encino, and the production line is currently running at 50k per month."

She stopped talking then, and he saw her go to that place she sometimes went, like she'd stepped into an office inside her head and closed the door behind her. When Maria O'Brien got that look, he knew there was no point trying to talk to her.

Instead, he watched Moose splash one of the drones directly into the pool to the great uproar and delight of the partypeeps. The little machine went down like a shot duck, its rotors sputtering and dying as it hit the water. Everyone cheered.

"You know what," Maria said suddenly, fanning herself with the subpoena in the hot afternoon air. "Let me see if I can take care of this McCarthy situation. You've got better things to do than worry about some drunkass try-hard from Wisconsin."

"I do?" He paused, thinking about it. "Yeah. Yeah, I do," he said, more certain now. "Of course I fucking do. You take care of that, Maria. That sounds real good to me."

He turned back towards the party, already wondering how many margaritas it would take to get over the effects of the blue pill. It would be an interesting experiment to run, he thought. He didn't get the chance. Maria took him by the elbow, her fingers digging in hard enough to leave marks.

"Ouch," he said. "What the hell?"

"No. You're done with the party today, Jimbo. Moose can entertain your guests. You and I are going to take the chopper out to Encino."

EXTRACT

'The Transitions: An Oral History of the Future by Studs Terkel'.
The New Yorker, March 13, 1954, Vol. 29, No. 5, pp. 51–56.

Eddie Gaines, bandleader and arranger.
(Interview conducted in November 1953, at his apartment in Las Vegas. Gold records lean against jazz biographies on improvised shelves. Gaines is forty-one. He talks rapidly, moving from topic to topic like he's improvising a jazz solo.)

It was a helluva time. A helluva place. You had concrete drying in the desert, gangsters wearing cowboy boots, and every second lounge act claiming they'd invented jazz. The town didn't sleep, but man, it dreamed. And we were part of that. We had our dreams, too.

What people forget about that place, it's not just putting black and white folks in the same room. Any fool with a liquor license and a death wish can try that. It was making them want to stay together. Making them listen to each other, maybe forget for a couple hours what they'd been told to think their whole lives.

I had this duo come in, country boys, scared stiff. One of them called himself Rex Rivers. Wasn't his real name. That was Dieter something. (laughs) Dieter Rivers, can you dig it? Anyway, their manager tells them if they go onstage with us, they'd never see radio again. I dunno how much radio they'd had, but they came anyway. Stood there like deer in the headlights the first night, but they played. That's what I think is cool. Not the stars or headliners, man. The ones who had to choose, every single night, whether to be part of it.

The tech helped. We had the best gear out of L.A. All the Davidson rigs, compression stacks. Even Skywire patches. Our sound system could lift a whisper to the back wall without touching the front row. When Frank or Dean sang, the girl at table six felt like they were whispering in her ear. That kind of gear, it levels the field. Makes the music about the music, not who's allowed to make it.

We had this janitor, quiet kid, polite, kept the place clean as a whistle. But he'd hang around the engineers at night, asking questions, fiddling with the dials when it didn't matter. Brown, I think his name was. Light on his feet. Real good ear. One night he fixed a blown crossover mid-set, and our trumpet section never even noticed. You tell me it's a bad thing that kid learned how to do that, I'll call you a liar.

B.B. King dropped in just to listen to the system. He'd stand in the wings with a kid guitarist, teaching him how to play the rests. Said the music lived in the silence. "The song ain't the notes," he says. "It's the air you leave between them." That kid's playing sessions in Chicago now, last I heard.

And the crowd... man. You'd see beat kids and hippies sitting next to ad men from back East. Some bug-eyed Kansas couple on vacay, right next to a biker outta Fillmore. Half the Air Force was in the audience some nights. Frankie, the pit boss, he comes up between sets, whispers to me about some lawyer from the coast. Talking about live broadcasts, beaming jazz into Alabama. Wild, right?

Of course, it didn't last. The official line was "safety breaches," but what really happened was the Mob wasn't copacetic. I don't care, I'll tell it to you straight. Those guys hated the future, 'cause they could see how they all ratted each other out and ended up in the slammer.

But man, the nights when it worked? That was enough for me. You could feel it. The room choosing what it wanted to be. The whole country, too.

10

_____

Los Angeles.

HE DID LOVE THE CHOPPER. It was probably his favourite toy. The rotors thumped overhead as Slim Jim pressed his face closer to the side window, watching the sprawl of LA roll beneath them like a living map. For sure, having a private jet had been awesome when the Russians started rolling on Paris, but he took the jet everywhere. It was just a flying bus with martinis, and he was used to spending a lot of time in it. You could get used to anything, they reckoned, but Slim Jim knew that just wasn't so. You never got used to breaking rocks in the Georgia heat, and although he'd tried hard, he never quite got to zero fucks about the looks they gave him when he rolled into one of those fancy-schmancy joints in New York where guys like Getty and Hearst preferred to hang out.

The helicopter shuddered slightly as they caught a thermal updraft, and Janet made a small correction at the controls. "Little bumpy today," she said apologetically.

"All good, I don't mind," Slim Jim grinned, settling back into his custom seat. The staff in those fancy joints were always cool. He figured they recognised a Joe like them, a guy who'd done some shitty jobs to make ends meet, but a guy who got lucky. They were always good to him, especially since he tipped like a motherfucker, and not just the waiters or the barkeep either. When Slim Jim Davidson went to one of those snooty fucking restaurants or clubs for some bullshit business meet-up, he made sure everyone earning minimum wage there knew they were good for a payday, because Slim Jim Davidson was a guy who looked after guys like him.

The city was thinning out below them now, suburban developments giving way to the brown hills of the San Fernando Valley. He could see the geometric patterns of orange groves in the distance, neat rows of trees. Everything in its place, everything serving a purpose. Like being a decent guy with the hired help.

For once, it wasn't Maria's idea, but she approved, which had surprised him a little. Ms O'Brien disapproved of most of his ideas on general principles, but with that one, she was on the Jimbo train. "Yeah, spread it around," she'd said. "Adds to the legend. You do these guys a favour, Jimbo, and one day, I guarantee you, some lowly waiter or a doorman or a garbage collector will be in a position to do you an atomic solid."

So he always tipped big. He always thanked the staff.

And when he flew in his helicopter, he liked to sit up front with the pilots. They'd even installed a special seat for him so he could watch them at work. Right now, Bob was checking his instruments while Janet handled the stick, both of them professional as hell, but relaxed enough to chat.

"How's the fuel looking?" he asked, because he liked to understand how things worked.

"Plenty for the round trip, sir," Bob replied. "We'll be there in about fifteen minutes."

He was like a kid again every time they took off. The world fell away beneath them, LA shrinking to a toy town, the new freeways sparkling like steel rivers. He'd press his face to the glass, grinning at the way the rotors thudded overhead, the whole machine humming with power. The pilots, Bob and Janet today, would point out the landmarks—there's the Hollywood sign, there's Venice Beach, there's the tar pits—and he'd nod, pretending he was on a secret mission or something. There was just something about the chopper that was cooler than any plane.

"Encino coming up," Janet announced, and Slim Jim could see the change in the landscape ahead. They'd bought up a ton of ground out here, even before the end of the war. Land banking, Maria called it. Just picking up the asset and putting it on the shelf for later use. They did a lot of that, actually, with land, people, companies. Elvis. He'd picked up Elvis that way, and man, that'd paid off.

The helicopter's shadow raced across a golf course, dark and swift like some fat bird of prey. A few golfers looked up and waved, probably wondering who was important enough to be flying around in a private chopper on a Tuesday afternoon. Probably saying, 'Slim Jim!'

Those Beatles kids, too. He'd put them in his pocket even if he wasn't so sure if they'd turn out as good as Elvis. It wasn't a done deal that whatever magic they'd had the first time around would loop back through time and work again under different circumstances. Really fucking different circumstances, he thought. But what the hell, he owned their entire catalogue. What did it matter if they never wrote another *Twist and Shout* or *Sgt. Pepper's*? Those were his favourites. They'd written them the first time around, and he owned them, and they'd done good out of the deal. Their families were super wealthy now, and four Liverpool kids who'd grown up poor in the rubble of the war now had good lives, completely transformed by Slim Jim's buying up their intellectual property. Paying top dollar for it, too, because O'Brien said he had to. Maybe that meant they weren't going to turn out to be the artists they were the first time, but so what?

Slim Jim had no time for that crap, anyway, for the shit people went on with about artists starving in their garrets. He'd done some hungry fucking days himself when he was younger, and he'd bet a shiny dollar for every one of them days that mostly what your starving artist did in his fucking garret was go hungry. He didn't make a shit ton of art.

The chopper banked over to the left, giving him a better view of his factory, a big, shining hive full of all sorts of stuff, dazzling under the California sun, all glass and steel, crawling with people and machines. Thousands of solar panels, drinking up the free power.

Fuck, he loved that idea. Partly because he remembered shivering in a fucking one-room apartment with no power, one miserable winter in Chicago. Partly because it tickled him silly to think of the Gettys and those Texas assholes like Hunt and Richardson eating their fucking livers every time somebody didn't have to pay them a buck.

"There she is," Bob said with obvious pride. He'd been flying Slim Jim around long enough to take personal satisfaction in the boss's big wins, and the gigafactory down there was one of the biggest.

A minute or so later, they touched down on the helipad to the south of the main facility. He knew to wait a few moments for the rotors to stop spinning. He could have hopped out and bent over, of course, like Maria did, but to be honest, it kind of freaked him out, the way those things whirled around up there like rotating guillotines. So he sat and waited until the pilot told him it was safe.

He clapped both of them on the shoulder. "Thanks, guys. Y'all go get yourselves a coffee or something." Then he exited through the rear of the cabin, stepping out of the helicopter's plush, leather-lined interior—soft seats, polished wood, a little fridge stocked with cold brewskis—onto the tarmac, where Maria O'Brien was already waiting, briefcase clutched protectively to her even as the rotors slowed to a complete stop.

There was a greeting party to meet them, of course. There was always a greeting party everywhere he went. And it was a matter of some pride to Slim Jim that people always looked happy to see him. His people, anyway. He imagined that if he flew into one of John Paul Getty's oil refineries, he might get some stink-eye, what with all the solar panels he was building out here and down in Texas. But *his* guys always looked like kids the day the school commissioner turned up to give them a holiday for some visiting senator or something.

That had only happened once, when he'd been a little 'un in his old backwoods public school, a slumping shack with a patchy playing field full of gopher holes and no running water in the crappers. That time the school commissioner turned up with some Senator and told them they didn't have to come to school the next day; that was his only good memory of school days.

He heard lots of "Welcome, sir," and "Mister Davidson," and

"Thank you for coming out, sir," but Slim Jim held up his hand and said, "Come on, y'all know the rules." To which all the older, senior guys shuffled from side to side and looked a bit embarrassed.

"Yes, Jimbo," they said, while his younger employees all snickered and grinned.

"So, we're good to go?" Maria asked.

And Weedon, the senior guy, nodded. "We can tour the facilities on the way, if you would—"

"No, we wouldn't," Maria cut him off. "We get the weekly reports, Byron. You're doing a great job out here."

"Bonuses for everyone!" Slim Jim said, throwing up his hands. There was a small cheer and some laughter at that. But Byron Weedon didn't look happy. "Yeah, yeah, like she said, you're doing a hell of a job, Byron," he went on. "But Maria says she's got this idea, and I wouldn't mind seeing it myself, straight up, if that's cool."

"Well, of course, everything that you want is... cool, sir," Weedon replied.

"Outstanding," Slim Jim said. "Let's get after it."

The small crowd parted to reveal a couple of golf buggies waiting for them. Slim Jim, Maria, Weedon, and some other guy piled in, the electric buggies humming as they set off. Slim Jim waved to the greeting party as they departed like some kid at a state fair, stealing a bumper car, grinning as they rolled away.

They drove through the facility, past gleaming buildings and busy workers, the future exploding into being all around him. He didn't always understand everything that went on out here, but he was smart enough to know his people were building the future, and he'd be fucked if he was gonna let some asshole like Joe McCarthy or Lavatory Beria take that away.

The trip took them from the main facility, through what had once been raw countryside; now corporate land, a strange blend of old ranchland and orange groves giving way to weirdly curvy concrete bunkers and glass-box laboratories. It took them a while to reach the testing facility, nestled in a small valley with lots of trees all around. Slim Jim looked up and sure enough, he spotted the two really big drones that were constantly circling around the site, keeping an eye on it. They were massive, and not that high up, but he couldn't hear them. What he could hear was the gnat-like buzz of the much smaller drones they were building and testing out here, the same model he'd been playing with at the pool party yesterday.

He hopped out of the golf buggy, feeling the sun starting to burn his fair skin as soon as he was out from underneath the shade canopy. Maria handed him a wide-brimmed straw hat and a tube of sun cream, and before he could object, she said, "Just put it on, Jimbo. Fifteen minutes in this sun and you'll be a walking melanoma."

He rolled his eyes, but put the hat on and slathered sunscreen over his exposed skin, even the back of his neck, though the hat probably covered it. She'd shown him some pictures of what skin cancer looked like when it got hold of you, and it wasn't pretty. Even the memory made him feel all dizzy and green.

That's what they told him had done for him the first time around, his computer guys were pretty sure. That was the story of Slim Jim Davidson in the universe where Maria and the K-Hammer, and all those future guys, didn't turn up like a goddamn personal miracle, just for him. Where and when they'd come from, he'd been in and out of jail all over the South. Spent a lot of time on work gangs out in the sun, and in the end, it'd done for him. James Earl Davidson died in a prison infirmary in Little Rock, Arkansas, in 1963, skin cancer, they said.

There were no prison infirmary records in FleetNet, of course. They told him Arkansas didn't even computertize that stuff until the late 1990s, and those files never made it into the wedge of the internet that came through with Kolhammer's people. But there were breadcrumbs. A mugshot from the Pulaski County Sheriff's archive, mirrored on an old genealogy forum. A digitised death certificate stub from a Department of Corrections report that had been scraped into a forgotten VA health-data cache. And weirdest of all, a single post on something called a 'blog' from 1998, written by an old lag who remembered a white guy called Davidson dying in the infirmary next to him with 'his whole neck gone to rot from the sun.'

Close enough for government work.

So he wore the big hat, and he slathered on the sunscreen. He did as he was told. They walked from the little car lot, which had a lot more golf buggies than cars in it, towards the building where the trials were being run. The building was all made of wood and stone, and glass. It was pleasing to look at, like a holiday home a millionaire might spend his summers at down by some lake in New England. It said something about the people he had working for him, he supposed, that they put so much effort into making this weird little science shack look like that. He wasn't exactly sure what it said, but he supposed it was good, and he was glad they hadn't cheaped out on the air conditioning after walking just a minute from the car lot in the dazzling California sun.

"Through here, Mr Davidson," Weedon said, and Slim Jim didn't bother correcting him, telling him to call him Jimbo or anything. Weedon wasn't like those whizkids he had working for him back at the big factory. He recognised the type of guy Weedon was: a fucking country club Republican. He woulda been running a shoe store chain or a glue factory or something back in the original history, and woulda been running it really well too, which was why he'd been hired to do this job. Maria said he was an operations genius, but Slim Jim knew him for who he truly was: just a natural boss. The kind of asshole who'd kept guys like him down all his life. So while he was glad that Weedon was doing a good job running his factory, making him money, he didn't feel like he had to be friends with him. Not the same way he felt he had to be friends with everyone else. That was weird when you thought about it, but it was just something he'd always felt.

It was why he'd chummed up with Moose on the *Astoria*, because if you were friends with Moose Molloy, you weren't gonna have to take any shit from anybody. It was satisfying to him now when he pondered on it, which he did as he closed his eyes and cooled off in the AC, it was satisfying to him that he'd been able to pay Moose back for all that. The big fella had a good job with Davidson Enterprises, the best kind, really: one that paid a heap of money with all the benefits, but didn't expect much of a guy, mostly that he was on hand to hang out with Slim Jim whenever he was in town.

"Jimbo," Maria said, breaking through his reverie.

"Oh, sorry, man. Sorry, Weedon," he said. "It's the heat. How do you guys even handle it out here?"

Weedon was staring at him, looking perplexed. "Well, the facility is air conditioned, sir."

"Yeah, I know, but still, it's a long drive, and it bakes the old noggin, doesn't it?"

"Yes, it does," Weedon agreed. "If you would care to join us at the viewing deck?"

"Sure, sure. Can I get a fizzy water?"

"Yes, sir," somebody said, and hurried away to fetch him a drink.

"Maria, are you okay? Do you need a fizzy water? How about you, Weedon?"

"I'm hydrated," Maria said.

"I'm fine," Weedon agreed.

"Okay, cool. Just the heat, you know. Brings back bad memories."

"Of course," Weedon said awkwardly as he led them to the small viewing area.

The space was corporate but comfortable, with big glass windows looking out over the testing area. Slim Jim could see half a dozen technicians out there, all of them dressed for the heat and the sun. He knew they were scientists and technicians and stuff, but none of them wore lab coats. They were all in shorts and surf shirts, and they wore floppy hats and sunglasses. There were a couple of trestle tables, and it looked like maybe twenty or thirty of the drones he recognised from the pool were laid out on the trestle table. There were another ten to twelve drones, he couldn't tell the exact number, buzzing around in the sky.

A siren sounded, and the science guys quickly packed up whatever they were doing, bringing the last drones in to land.

Another siren sounded, and a two-minute countdown started on a screen in front of them. After thirty seconds, the testing area was clear. Nothing and nobody moved out there.

"How many have you got in this test flight, Byron?" Maria asked.

"Just three, ma'am," he answered.

"We're gonna need more than three."

"I understand, Ms O'Brien."

Slim Jim kept his grin to himself. He remembered Maria rinsing Weedon for calling her Miss, the first time they'd come out here.

"But building the swarm turned out to be much harder than

reconfiguring the load bay for the weapons package. We'll start with three, but I hope to demo a complete fight today, with EM interference, before you leave."

"Okay," she said. She sounded mollified.

Slim Jim wasn't sure why, or what any of that meant. He was just looking forward to the fireworks.

The countdown continued, the room going quiet at the end.

"Three... two... one..."

Slim Jim looked but couldn't see anything.

"What am I looking for?" he said.

Weedon pointed to the horizon.

"A thousand metres down range, sir," he said, before quickly adding. "Sorry... Jimbo. Or you can just follow the monitor."

He pointed at a bank of screens in front of them.

Slim Jim nodded, seeing three of the little drones he'd been playing with at the pool party. They swept across the landscape like angry hornets, moving faster than he'd expected. On the monitors, he could see them clearly; sleek, dark shapes racing low over the scrubland, their cameras giving crystal-clear views of the terrain below. To his naked eye, they were just dots against the brown hills, but the screens showed everything: the way they moved in perfect formation, the subtle adjustments they made to stay on course.

"Target acquisition," someone announced quietly.

On the main monitor, a crosshair locked onto what looked like a pile of old cars and scrap metal, maybe half a mile away. Slim Jim squinted through the window but couldn't make out much except heat shimmer and distant brush.

"Releasing ordnance," the same voice said.

He watched the screen as three small objects dropped from the drones, wobbling at first but quickly stabilising as they fell. They looked no more threatening than the water balloons he'd dropped on Moose and those girls in his pool.

The explosions bloomed all at once, three brilliant flashes in one that turned the target area into a fountain of dirt, smoke, and flying debris. Even on the monitor, the violence was shocking in its suddenness and precision. Where there had been a pile of junk, there was now a crater surrounded by scattered metal fragments.

Slim Jim jerked back in his chair, his body reacting before his brain caught up. The flinch was pure instinct, and maybe some muscle memory from the *Astoria*.

Then the sound hit them - a sharp triple crack that rattled the windows, followed by a rolling thunder that seemed to go on forever.

"Jesus Christ," he breathed, his heart still hammering. "That was…"

"Effective," Maria said calmly, but he caught the slight smile at the corner of her mouth.

11

The Med.

THE THING HARRY appreciated about nuclear submarines was all the hot water. You'd never go short of a nice cup of tea or a long, hot shower. He stood under the showerhead, massaging his scalp, trying not to think too much about the last time he'd been on a sub. That'd been HMAS *Havoc*, off Timor, just before everything kicked off. He'd been with Viv and the boys, preparing to go ashore, when he passed out and woke up in the wrong bloody century. It'd been a while since Harry had thought about that. Not so long, though, since he'd thought about Viv.

Squeezing his eyes shut, he pushed the memory away. Nothing to be done for it. Viv was dead, and the cunt who'd killed him, Alexei Skarov, was gone. Probably in Marseille. That's where Harry was headed, too. But he wasn't chasing Skarov; he had another mission there. It was frustrating for sure. But the best way to deal with frustration was to let it go. As the Stoics used to say, suffering comes not from circumstances but from how we respond to them, which was fine as far as it went, he supposed, but not all that useful when you walked into an ambush by some filthy Russian blagger, which his old sergeant major had.

Let it go.

Harry rolled his shoulders and tried to let the hot water wash away his anger.

They would settle with Skarov, one way or another. While he might be otherwise engaged in Marseille, Charlotte and Ivanov were free agents, and they were still working commissions to find the NKVD man.

Reluctantly, Harry turned off the hot water and stepped out of the narrow shower cubicle. He grabbed his towel, which was surprisingly thick and soft, not the threadbare rag you'd expect on a military vessel. He dried off quickly before changing into the thin disposable paper jumpsuit hanging just outside on a hook.

From the bathroom, he made his way to the galley. Charlotte and Ivanov were already there, both in their paper onesies. The Russian was shovelling giant spoonfuls of rice and spicy pork mince into his mouth, washing it down with black tea. Charlotte had finished her breakfast and was sipping coffee. Both looked up and nodded as Harry slid into the booth beside her; there wasn't much space on Ivanov's side.

A wardsman appeared, placed a plate of bacon and scrambled eggs alongside two thick slices of buttered toast, and asked whether he wanted tea or coffee.

"Coffee, thanks," Harry said.

"You are an Englishman. You should drink tea," Ivanov said, not looking up from his plate, lest some errant grain of rice or morsel of fried meat escape his spoon.

"You drank all the tea on the boat," Harry said, nodding toward the steaming mug in front of his Russian friend.

The galley was small, with seating for six, unless one of them was Ivanov, in which case it was more like three or four, depending on how cozy you felt like getting with an enormous Russian psychopath in a thin paper Snuggie. Still, like most of the crew spaces on HMS *Achilles*, the Royal Navy's newest AUKUS boat, it felt surprisingly roomy. Then again, maybe not that surprising, Harry conceded. They'd cribbed everything from Jane Willet's boat and used the Combat Intelligence from HMAS *Havoc* to push the design and build as far and fast as humanly possible. *Achilles* was augmented tech from bow to screw, probably one of the most advanced war machines on the planet, along with her sisters.

Nuclear subs had already been the most complex machines ever built back upwhen he'd last enjoyed a long, hot shower on the *Havoc*. Before everything went sideways. A decade later, and seventy years earlier, if you could get your head around that—and Harry found it was best not to bother trying—they still held the title, even with the whole world turned upside down by time-shattered madness.

"Ready for a swim?" Harry asked, spearing a strip of bacon into his mouth.

"A little vacay on the French Riviera? Who wouldn't be?" said Charlotte.

"Marseille is not the Riviera," Ivanov grunted, chasing the last of his meal around the plate. "It is major Soviet fleet base. Before that, it was hive of scum and villainy."

"Reference acknowledged," Charlotte said, raising her mug to him.

"Well, it's the generous supply of scum and villainy that makes it so attractive," Harry pointed out.

"Are you confident your villainous friend will be there for us?" Charlotte leaned back in the booth, one foot propped on the bench like she was lounging in a café, or maybe an opium den.

"Ronsard? Yeah. He'll be there," Harry said. "I worked with him in the war. He's solid. Reliable."

"He has been long in Marseille?" Ivanov asked.

"I don't know. Wasn't in the briefing packet. But I trust him."

"What about the local villains?" Charlotte said.

Harry shrugged. "That's the thing about villains, isn't it? You can't trust 'em. That's why we need Ronsard."

"Trust does not matter," Ivanov said. "The only thing that matters is what a man wants. And what do these men want? Communists gone. Hard to run mafia business under communist regime. If you're not in the regime, you're not in the business."

Harry chewed on that, chasing it with another piece of bacon. "Fair point," he said.

"You think he'll give us a line on Skarov?" Charlotte asked.

Harry noticed she didn't mention Professor Bremmer, the whole reason they'd been chasing Skarov across Sardinia. Finding Bremmer, whether to extract him or deny him to the Soviets, was technically the secondary objective of his Marseille mission. But looking at his teammates across the table, Harry knew their real focus was on the NKVD man who'd taken him.

At 0245, an ensign escorted them down to the deployment bay tucked into the torpedo room. It was a cramped, no-frills space carved into the submarine's belly, a shadowed chamber dedicated to prepping special forces operators for insertion. There was no separate changing area.

Charlotte didn't blink. Years of working with Viv had stripped away any shyness. She peeled off her disposable paper coveralls without hesitation and began gearing up alongside the others. They each slipped into the sleek black wetsuits they'd wear inside the deployment capsules.

Their gear was laid out next to the pods for final checks. Harry ran through his kit quickly. There wasn't much. His disguise was simple: scuffed blue overalls in the livery of a Marseille stevedoring company, plus two changes of civilian clothes, local cut, mid-1950s waterfront chic. His field loadout was equally lean: a digital radio with quantum encryption, original uptime kit, still in perfect working order. From the looks of it, the unit had been drawn from a reserve cache, likely untouched since before the Transition.

He also carried a knife, a pistol, and six mags of 9 mm. That was it. Nothing like the full kit he'd prepped aboard *Havoc*, back when they still thought deployment was happening in 2021.

Charlotte and Ivanov finished just as fast. Their loadouts matched his, with a few personal additions and freelancer perks. They zipped each other up, and then the crew moved in to lock them into their pods.

The pods looked somewhat like torpedoes, but they weren't especially sleek. These one-man submersibles were purpose-built for offshore insertion, engineered for function, not comfort. Claustrophobic as hell. Each capsule required the occupant to wear an oxygen mask, breathing from a tank stashed inside the coffin-like interior.

Not everyone could handle that. Harry remembered a couple of hard-bitten 21st-century operators who'd flat-out refused to board far more modern, roomy versions.

The crew of HMS *Achilles* helped him slide into the cramped capsule and sealed the hatch behind him, plunging him into total darkness for a second.

Once sealed in, there was no HUD. No comforting readout counting down the minutes to splash. Nothing like the uptime kits he'd used before. Just a small red light LED which blinked on shortly after the hatch closed. The capsule was semi-autonomous. It would navigate to the insertion point, surface, and pop the hatch. Hopefully. Unless it hit a submerged rock shelf, or got tangled in a net, or triggered some Russian subsea monitoring system they didn't know existed.

Any of those outcomes meant he'd die alone in the dark.

All those possibilities jostled for space inside the capsule with him.

Harry had spent nearly all of his mental prep for this mission avoiding exactly that line of thought. In fact, he hadn't thought about the mission at all. He'd focused instead on getting out of his head, meditating himself away from the capsule, out of his body, into a space where panic couldn't find him.

He knew panic could strike. He'd seen it happen. Once, a chief petty officer he'd served with, twenty years in, 43 capsule drops to his name, had started screaming and pounding on the hatch less than a minute after lock-in. No one ever spoke of it again. Harry never asked. But everyone had a limit.

That bloke's was 43.

The memory passed through Harry in less than a second, and he let it go. He didn't fight it, because fighting it meant touching the idea that this might be his 43rd. That this might be the one. The one where he started screaming and pounding on the hatch.

Instead, he focused on his breathing. Slow, deliberate inhalations. Measured exhalations. He counted each breath silently, letting every outward flow carry away a little sliver of anxiety. He visualised a gentle wave washing through him—cool, calm, and slow—creating a buffer between his mind and the black steel shell encasing his body.

So when the launch came, it caught him off guard. A sudden hiss. Then motion, violent and fast, shoving him forward into the dark. He immediately regretted the scrambled eggs from half an hour ago.

The jolt of acceleration gave way to a hard slap of deceleration as the capsule cleared the flooded tube and punched into the water off southern France.

For a moment, Harry did wonder if this was his 43rd. The cursed one. But then the pod stabilised, slipping into a steady glide as the electric drive kicked in. The motor's hum was low and constant, and it grounded him. He returned to his breathwork.

He stayed in that headspace for thirty minutes.

Eventually, he sensed his orientation shift, his head rising, feet falling. One minute later, a chime sounded. A second followed two minutes after that. Thirty seconds later, the hatch popped.

Now cruising on the surface, no longer twenty meters under, Harry was at the mercy of the sea state. It was calm, thankfully. But even so, it felt a hell of a lot livelier than the silent deep.

Now came the tricky part, getting out of the capsule. After a couple of minutes motoring toward the shoreline, Harry felt the pod scrape a sandy incline. He heard the soft lap of wavelets against the hull, and further off, the crash of surf. Every movement was a slow, deliberate shuffle in the cramped space, a graceless exit from a steel coffin that hadn't left much room to breathe, let alone move.

He hit the big green button, triggering the capsule's exfil routine. It would crawl back into deeper water, then sink, hopefully to be recovered later. Preferably not by the Russians.

Wading through the gentle swell, Harry scanned the dark water for any sign of Charlotte or Ivanov. The sea was warm, and he was already sweating inside the wetsuit. The swell was modest, barely a foot high, but the buoyancy tugged at his legs, lifting him off the pebbled bottom. A larger wave rolled in and broke behind him, dumping him into the shallows, nearly taking him under.

His kit was sealed and waterproof. Saltwater damage wasn't the issue. Losing a bag in the dark, though, having it caught in the current and dragged off into the night, that was a problem. Especially if it ended up in Soviet hands.

It had been a while, but the Special Boat Squadron course he'd completed had drilled one lesson into him: don't fight the ocean. When the next wave slammed into him, he let it carry him forward, tightening his grip on the gear bag and letting the surge do the work.

Eventually, he got his feet under him in waist-deep water. Another wave pushed past, and he turned to scan the horizon.

There, two more capsules broke the surface, a hundred meters offshore.

Despite the nerves that had clawed at him during insertion, despite climbing into something that felt like a giant soda can cobbled together from bleeding-edge tech and Cold War leftovers, Harry allowed himself a breath of relief.

Achilles had delivered.

The next waves pushed him further inshore. The beach break began to crash around his knees, the water sucking at his legs as it pulled back in a constant, hissing rhythm. He paused, scanning their landing point, a secluded cove tucked into the rugged wilderness south of Marseille. Faint starlight etched the shape of the coastline - rocky outcrops, lichen-cloaked cliffs, whispering scrub reaching down to the tide.

No sign of Ronsard. Not that Harry had expected the Frenchman to be waiting with aperitifs.

He peeled off his wetsuit and dug a Tesalate towel from his kit, drying himself quickly. The sweat was no concern. The locals in the '40s had, by his recollection, a much more liberal relationship with personal hygiene than anyone in the 2020s. After an hour sealed in neoprene, he figured he'd just regressed to the mean.

Changing in the dark wasn't easy, but he managed to pull on a pair of sturdy dark coveralls, dock worker's gear, period-appropriate. As he dressed, the surf finally relinquished its grip on Ivanov and Charlotte.

Under different circumstances, a proper gentleman might have offered Miss François a hand with her kit. Charlotte would've told him to go fuck himself.

Harry looked up into the hills surrounding the cove, searching the shadows for any sign of Ronsard. Nothing yet. He turned back toward the water and froze at the sound of footsteps crunching over wet pebbles. Charlotte and Ivanov.

They didn't speak. Just began stripping off their wetsuits.

Charlotte changed into a sharp 1950s getup: form-fitting skirt, pressed blouse, low heels dangling from one hand by their straps. Ivanov pulled on a dark, stiff-looking suit in shiny Russian synthetics, the kind of thing a mid-tier apparatchik or NKVD officer might wear while terrorising the local proles.

He gathered the wetsuits into a black plastic bag, then disappeared into the brush to find a discreet burial site.

Charlotte's voice came low in the dark. "There he is."

Harry followed her gesture. A lone figure stepped out from the forest edge, emerging from the deep shadows like a conjuring. His pulse skipped. He forced himself to stay calm. If this were a Russian ambush, it wouldn't be one man. It would be a whole platoon, searchlights, machine guns, and lots of shouting.

But the silhouette kept coming. No sudden movement. No backup.

Harry's hand hovered near his weapon when the starlight caught a glint of metal. A gun?

Then the shadow holstered it, and a familiar voice broke the silence.

"Harry, my friend. It has been too long."

12

Cairo. Five weeks ago.

FOR A LONG TIME, he could not be himself. That poor bastard had died many years ago. Many lifetimes ago, it felt like. The man he used to be had vanished so completely it no longer seemed a loss to anyone but him. He'd worn many names, been many things since they'd disappeared him in the burning wreckage of that aeroplane in Hawaii, and the men who'd orchestrated his vanishing had told him he could never return to the world, not as himself. He hadn't minded, not back then. But that was a long time ago.

In his mind, in his soul, which was surely condemned, he knew who and what he was. His name was Dan Black, and he was a killer.

A bare minute after adding the names of more dead men to the long indictment of what he had become, Dan walked away from the chaos at the Cairo Hilton and disappeared back into the city's old quarter. He didn't care about the, of course. But he did care about what he'd become.

He entered the old town through a small, densely-packed food market, where the air was thick with the scent of cardamom and roasting goat meat. Here, it did not matter that he stank with sour sweat, because the funk of unwashed humanity surrounded him. Laundry hung between the wooden balconies overhead, creating a flapping canopy above the narrow alleys. In some passages, he could touch both walls at once as he twisted and turned through the ancient maze. Life carried on much as it had for thousands of years, with merchants hawking their wares, children laughing and playing. He disappeared into the clatter of tin trays, a shopkeeper bellowing out the price of lemons and a hundred conversations drifting like incense through the crooked sandstone corridors in the late afternoon heat.

For thirty minutes, Dan threaded the alleys and courtyards, doubling back through the maze like a man expecting his own shadow to betray him. He counted blind turns, marked doorways, and scanned every window. A routine, yes, but not a perfunctory one. He paused at corners, glanced in shopfront reflections, always looking for the small details that betrayed a stalker, shadows that darted where others lingered, footsteps that hesitated when his broke stride. But there was nothing, no signal that he'd drawn undue notice.

If the Russians had tagged him on a satellite, he'd never know. But at least on foot, in the old way, he was certain. He'd shaken them.

For now.

He found the street he was looking for, a crooked stretch of sunbaked earth lined with low mud-brick buildings, each nearly indistinguishable from the next. He paused only once to confirm the faded number painted on a wooden shingle. The heavy wooden door groaned open into a dusty, silent stairwell that smelled of Nile river clay and forgotten millennia. He climbed fast, two steps at a time, as though the stairs might vanish behind him. The apartment at the top was simple to the point of sorrow: some mattresses on the floor, stained and sunken; a few crates posing as tables or chairs. It was clear that three or four men were living there, but he was the only one present for the moment.

He looked down at his watch, its face scratched and sun-faded. The others were still out, hunting for Bremmer. They'd be back soon enough—thirty minutes, give or take. He would've called them back if it had been safe, but it wasn't. It never was. That was one of the first things they taught him. No electronics. The only message you could trust was a final whisper into the ear of a dying man.

He undressed without ceremony and stepped into the makeshift shower, a modest corner space with a tin bucket strung from the ceiling and plumbed, more or less, to a rooftop tank. A tug on the chain released a reluctant stream of lukewarm water that traced its way across the curve of his shoulders. It was tempting to linger under the water, thinking about her. Of course, she was here. He'd known that much, and it would have been impossible to miss anyway. Julia remained a minor celebrity even now. And of course, her engagement to Harry only reinforced that celebrity. He scrubbed his face with both hands, but the thought of her clung to him, heavier than the dust he'd come in with.

He grabbed the cheap, coarse bar of local soap and began to scrub hard. He worked the soap into a lather, dragging it across his skin and rubbing the bar through his hair, still thick and dark, with only a few strands of grey. The suds ran down his face, stinging his eyes. He spent the last few moments of the shower bent over, flushing them with what little water was left.

As he stepped out and reached for the towel, the sound of the door opening froze him mid-motion. His hand was already drifting toward the shoulder holster slung from the towel rack when a voice called out:

"It's Carter."

Dan reached for the towel instead of his gun. He patted his hair and face dry, blinking to clear his vision, then wrapped the towel around his waist. He caught a glimpse of himself in the old mirror. It was streaked with dust, untouched by steam, and wholly unforgiving. He saw a man in middle age, tall, thick and powerful through the upper body, but badly scarred in places, with the signs of age gathering on him. He pulled on a clean t-shirt and left the bathroom.

Carter stood by a tea chest they were using as a table, unscrewing the cap from a bottle drawn from the shrink-wrapped 24-pack in the corner, their hedge against the undrinkable local water. He tipped up the bottle without ceremony, as if trying to rinse out a bad taste.

"You hear about the Hilton?" he asked.

"I was there," Dan said. "That was me."

Carter didn't seem surprised. "What happened?"

"Russians," Dan said. "If you don't mind, I'll wait until the others get here so I don't have to tell the story four times over."

Carter shrugged. "Suit yourself."

Dan disappeared into the small room they shared as a barracks and dressed in a fresh pair of cargo pants and a loose linen shirt. When he emerged, buttoning his shirt, the other two members of his team had arrived. Blair Soneski, all sinew and restless energy, paced with the agitation of an impatient man waiting for permission to act. John Merrill, stockier, slower, the team's medic, sat with the watchful stillness of someone long accustomed to waiting out trauma.

"You right, boss?" Merrill asked. He'd stitched up a lot of the scars that ran like train tracks over Dan's body, and he was a half-decent amateur headshrinker as well.

"Yeah, I'm good, Johnny," Dan said.

That's when he should have told them about Julia. They were going to find out.

But the words refused to be spoken. He parted his lips and felt the shape of her name form, but nothing emerged because to say her name aloud would unleash everything he'd spent years containing. And he'd done such a careful job of it, too: high walls erected, iron doors bolted, the past sorted into locked, labelled drawers he no longer dared open. And all of it—every last defence—felt as thin as rice paper. Just one word. *Julia*. That's all it would take to tear it all down.

"You guys go first," he said. "Did you get anything?"

"I'm still working on a clerk at the Ministry of the Interior," Carter began. "For a few more bucks, he'll get us a look at the landing cards for all the German nationals arriving in the last month. But nothing yet."

Soneski shrugged. "I was tailing one of Bremmer's old college pals. Still not sure what he's doing here, but he wouldn't be the only Nazi in Cairo. Hoping they'll meet up at some point."

"I paid a visit to the Anglo-American Hospital," Merrill said. "Made a donation, talked to a few of the nurses. They had nothing about any German kids coming in recently. So, I dunno, that rumour about his kids being sick, it's probably nothing."

Dan pulled a bottle from the block and twisted off the cap. He drank half in a single motion, the water loud in his throat. His hand trembled slightly, and a few drops escaped, running down his chin.

He wiped them away without comment. But Merrill would have noticed.

"Boss," the medic said, his voice soft.

Dan held up a hand. "It's okay. I just… had a day, is all."

"You want to tell us about it?" Merrill asked.

"Not really," Dan said with a shake of the head.

Carter, never one for delicate ambiguity, cut to the point. "It was her, wasn't it? That bitch was at the Hilton."

Dan said nothing. Not even a flicker of expression. But the room contracted slightly, as if drawing breath. He didn't rebuke Carter. It wouldn't have been fair. He'd said worse over the years. They all knew the history.

For a moment, though, he didn't know what to say. He'd worked with these men for three years now. They were his friends, perhaps the closest thing he had to family. But they were not her. Seeing Julia again, even for a brief moment, sent a jolt through him. Like pulling back the edge of an old wound and finding it as fresh as ever.

"Yeah, man," he said, his voice low. "She was there. The Russians went for her." The others said nothing, waiting for him to go on.

Still unsure of what to say because he truly didn't know what to think about any of it yet, Dan recapped his day for them.

"I picked up the Russians leaving that safe house they've got over by the City of the Dead," Dan began, his voice firmer now that he was on ground he knew and trusted. "They were sloppy, easy to follow. They did the rounds, then led me to the hotel." He paused. "I saw her coming out of the main building. She was heading for this garden party, some peace conference thing, and as soon as Ivan saw her, they tried to grab her."

"How'd that work out for them?" Soneski asked.

"Yeah, not so well," Dan said. "She crippled one of them straight away, then stabbed him in the throat. But there were three of them, one of her, and anyway, they're dead now."

Carter set down his water bottle with deliberate care.

"Because she killed them?" Merrill asked, "Or because you did?"

"It was a joint effort."

"Did she make you?" Soneski asked.

Dan shook his head.

"No. I'm pretty sure of that, at least. She had other things on her mind. She got swarmed by hotel security. Last I saw, they were taking her back up to the hotel. She wasn't looking for me; she wasn't even looking back at the Russians. She didn't make me. I don't think she even saw me."

"And what about the Ivans?" Soneski asked.

Dan shrugged. "They're not gonna be telling anyone anything."

"If she's here, then Harry's here," Carter said. "The Brits must've had a pretty good lock on Bremmer if they sent Windsor."

Dan nodded.

"Yeah, if Harry told Bremmer to jump off a cliff, he'd do it. Harry saved him and his family once before. He'd probably..." Dan trailed off.

Dan stared at the water bottle, his thumb worrying at the label where it started peeling. The silence stretched out, filled only by a donkey braying somewhere in the maze of alleys below and the rhythmic thump of a rug being beaten.

"You're okay, boss," Merrill said.

Dan shook himself out of his fugue. "Yeah, I'm good. So we need to find Windsor. Shouldn't be too hard. He'll be all over the social page of the *Cairo Times*."

"You haven't heard, then?" Carter said. "About the Hilton?"

Dan shook his head in confusion. "I just told you about the Hilton."

Carter shifted his weight from one foot to the other. Soneski stopped pacing and looked back at Dan, waiting. Merrill sat perfectly still. The silence grew into the sort of quiet that made a room feel smaller.

"No," Carter said at last. "Not your old girlfriend. Harry was there. Same time as you. There was a big shootout in the main bar. Half the hotel's been locked down."

Merrill sketched a grin. "Half the fucking spies in Egypt are going to have to find a new place to sleep."

Dan ran a hand through his still-damp hair. He knew for sure now. He'd messed up. He'd gone after the Russians to save Julia. But if he'd stayed on target, even after intervening to save her, he could've grabbed Bremmer himself. The rocket scientist was the whole reason they were all stuck in this shithole. The room seemed to shrink around him. He closed his eyes.

"Jesus, fellas. I'm sorry. I could've got him."

"Or you could've just walked into a bullet, boss," Merrill said. "Sounds like there was plenty to spare today."

"So what next?" Carter said. He was never much for hugging it out. "This fucking city feels like it's about to explode. Bremmer could be the spark that does it."

Dan shook his head. "No, it won't be Bremmer," he said. "Cairo's been ready to blow for years. One of the reasons Farouk is still king is that he's pretty good at stamping out sparks. This won't do it, but we're going to need better intelligence if we're going to grab up this guy."

"You gonna talk with Siregar then?" Carter asked.

"Yeah, reckon so. " Dan said reluctantly. "If the big boys are shooting up Hilton hotels over this guy, we're gonna need to...you know... to..."

He trailed off.

"We're going to need bigger guns," Soneski finished for him.

He was right.

They'd come light into Cairo, hoping to find Bremmer fast, put a bag on him, and deliver him up to Siregar without any messy bullshit. But nobody else was playing by those rules.

"Maybe," Dan said, still not quite ready to surrender the plan.

"Definitely," Soneski replied, without a flicker of doubt.

Dan crossed to the window and pushed aside the tattered curtain. Cairo unfolded in every direction, flat rooftops cluttered with water tanks and satellite dishes, laundry lines flapping between buildings as the muezzin's call to prayer drifted across the narrow alleys.

"Yeah, okay," Dan sighed. "I'll talk to him about tooling up. Shouldn't be a problem, but we need to be smarter about this. I'll get us some heavier kit, but we need better information, too."

He let the curtain fall back into place. He didn't want them to think he was looking for her.

13

Los Angeles.

THEY HAD six uniformed guards in the foyer of this place. When Cherry had been a punk patrolman in the Honolulu PD, they'd sent him off to a two-man station on the outskirts of East Kapolei. The goddamn foyer of Davidson's Tower had three times the number of cops as his first posting.

Of course, they weren't real cops, and at least he didn't have to check in at the desk like a mope. He didn't keep an office here; that wouldn't be *seemly*, according to O'Brien. But he did have come-n-go privileges.

"Good evening, Mr Cherry," the girl at the front desk said. She was a hottie, of course. It seemed to Cherry that Davidson only ever hired absolute smokestacks. Though if you got him after two or three shots, he'd tell you that from what he'd observed over the years, Maria O'Brien employed Davidson, and not the other way around. It seemed obvious to Cherry that the woman wore the pants in that relationship, even if it was a purely business setup. Same way, she wore pants every time he'd met her. Hell of a thing when you thought about all the shit these people had changed.

But he wasn't one to complain. His good fortune was part of the change. Cherry didn't care to think about how things might have gone for him if he hadn't got this... thing... with Davidson. The uptimers had saved him twice; he was man enough to admit it. Once on that beach in Hawaii, and again five years later when he washed up in LA.

Not that you'd call what he had here a job, exactly. His name wasn't listed on any employee payroll anywhere in the tower; there were no pay slips with his name on them. He kept an account at the track, and every two weeks, on the knocker, a couple of grand would drop onto the balance, whether he came calling on Davidson Tower or not. Whether he did anything for them. Or not. Two grand on the knocker every couple of weeks. A man would be a fool to turn that down, especially when the money got better when they *did* have something for him to do, like now.

"What are you fuckin' lookin' at?" one of the rent-a-cops snarled.

Cherry stopped and unfurled a slow smile for him.

The guy bristled, working up some backchat, but Lou Wanamaker, the shift supervisor, an old hack out of the 27th Precinct, gave him some supervision with the back of his leathery old hand.

"Just do your job, Neilson", he said, nodding at Cherry, who returned the nod and got moving again.

The mouthy rent-a-cop went back to whatever porno mag he had on the desk, and Cherry snorted quietly to himself. They must be paying old Lou some good coin for him to wear a clown costume like that. Unlike Cherry, who was forced out by the toe-cutters, the guy had retired on a good pension. Cherry lost his retirement and and nearly ended up in the jug. That's why he had no trouble with the changes Davidson and his crew had made in LA, because those changes had worked out pretty good for former detective Lou 'Buster' Cherry.

He rolled into the elevator and waited for the doors to close.

No attendant. Not even a button to push. The elevator was smart enough to just take him where he was going. Helluva lot smarter than Nielsen back there.

He rode up in the silent, gleaming box of brushed steel and blue glass. Soft music hummed from unseen speakers, and a wall of those weird three-dimensional movie screens glowed with abstract art, shifting cityscapes, and market data. A gentle, barely audible chime announced their arrival, and the doors slid open.

He no longer expected to find O'Brien waiting for him up here. He never expected even to meet Davidson. But the chickadee on the other side was a new one. A hot one, too, this being Davidson's personal floor. And his personality flaw, Buster thought. The woman waiting for him, seventy-two stories above the sprawling grid of Los Angeles, was a vision from a pin-up calendar, all curves and coiffed blonde hair, but that suit she wore was cut razor sharp, and her eyes, framed by sleek, wire glasses, held a knowing glint.

He knew that fucking glint.

He'd seen it on plenty of women the last ten years. First, they got ideas, then they got the glint.

Buster kept these thoughts to himself. That was one of the other things he'd learned: to keep his opinions to himself, at least around these characters. That's how he kept the big numbers dropping into his account at the track. Getting the job done and keeping his mouth shut.

He followed the young lady along the corridor, a long tunnel of polished concrete and dark wood, punctuated here and there by stark lighting fixtures. It felt less like a business office and more like an art gallery, or maybe a Japanese temple with all the deliberate emptiness, a helluva contrast to the streets seventy-plus floors below.

He almost chuckled. The Japs had done some terrible things in the Pacific. They'd done some of those things to him, sticking a bunch of bayonets in his ass back on Honolulu. Killing those poor kids, Rosanna and Wally. So, fuck them for that.

And yet, here was Davidson fitting out his playroom like he's best buds with Tojo.

It was hard to understand, was all. But, Cherry supposed, as bad as the Japs had been, they'd got it back with compound interest. They'd lost their goddamn country out of it, or at least half. The commies had taken the north of Japan, and the southern half was still full of white men with guns. Although he supposed the Japs would be happy to have them there now, with the commies trying to take over the whole show.

They arrived at the main entrance, which the hottie opened by placing her thumb on a small glass plate. He assumed it was reading her thumbprint, but you could never be sure with these guys. Mighta been taking a picture of her immortal soul for all he knew. The heavy wooden doors clicked open, and he had the distinct sense of passing through the gates of some castle in medieval Japan about five hundred years ago, which was weird, because when he got through to the other side, it was like he was five hundred years in the future. He resisted the urge to shake his head. He'd been in this office three times, and every time was a trip to fucking Disneyland.

The office was less an office and more your private sky-palace. Seventy-odd stories above the sprawling grid of Los Angeles, the entire outer wall was a massive glass wall offering a dizzying, panoramic view. That was no exaggeration, neither. Buster got dizzy if he looked at it too long. Wasn't natural to live up here like this. Drones orbited the building, red and green lights blinking in the perpetual nighttime haze. Further out, military jets carved figure-eight loops over the city. But it was the apartment that truly stole the breath away. The space was fucking vast, with soaring triple-height ceilings and a floor of polished black granite that reflected the city lights like a pool of wine. Sculptural furniture seemed to float on the huge expanse. A living wall of vines and ferns climbed one entire inner surface, misted by unseen nozzles, and a burbling, shimmering waterfall cascaded down another, disappearing into a rock pool. The air was cool, faintly scented with something alpine. It was a space designed to overwhelm, to make a man like Buster Cherry feel both insignificant and privileged to be there.

And sitting in the middle of it all, in his old bathrobe and socks with his feet up on the couch, was the big man himself, James Earl Davidson, watching a replay of a football match on a TV screen that was about half the size of your average football field. He perched a bowl of corn chips on his lap and drank a beer.

"Hey, Buster," he said, "you want a brew?"

"No brew for Buster," Maria O'Brien said. "He's on the clock."

"Just being sociable," Slim Jim said. He pointed the magic stick at the giant television screen, and onscreen, the action froze: a replay of a college football game, the USC Trojans, locked in a brutal tackle with the Bruins. Buster fucking hated the Trojans. Too flashy, too arrogant, too many of their players in the news for all the wrong reasons. Fucking crooks, every last one of them, in his book.

But so fucking what. He'd ended up working for the world's wealthiest criminal, hadn't he? That's what James Earl Davidson was, a two-bit bunko man who'd grifted his way into this joint. But Cherry wasn't here to judge. He was here for a job. And who the hell was he to judge anyway? The reason he'd needed the work was because they took his pension away from him, because he'd been moonlighting for hoodlums with much less money and much shittier connections than Davidson there in his fucking socks and jimmyjams.

"You called? I came," he said to Maria O'Brien. She nodded, fetching a large envelope from a desk on the other side of the room. It was such a big room that it took her a minute to walk over there and back.

"You know who won this game, right?" Buster said to Davidson while they waited.

"Yeah," Davidson shrugged. "But you know how it is. There's no games on anywhere at the moment."

"You had money on this?" Buster asked.

Davidson snorted, then huffed out a brief laugh. "Yeah, I had a grand on the spread. Did my dough cold."

"So what're you watching it for now?"

"Tryin to learn from my mistakes."

Cherry snorted. "Amen to that, brother."

O'Brien returned. The envelope she handed him was thick and heavy. It had real heft, but it wasn't like phone book weight or anything.

He didn't bother to open it in front of her. "What's the job?" he asked.

"Joe McCarthy," Davidson smiled from the couch, sucking at his beer, looking like he was enjoying watching for Buster's reaction almost as much as he'd been enjoying re-watching the football game. Buster gave him nothing; after all, McCarthy wasn't the biggest name they'd fed him.

"It's gonna cost you," he said.

"It always costs something," O'Brien pointed out. "We'll make the deposit into your betting account as normal, $10,000 a week for the next four weeks. Sound about right?"

"For the retainer?" Buster said. "Yeah, that sounds about right."

"Usual arrangement for expenses in the file," she said. "There's a new Amex for you. Rack up your legitimate travel and investigatory spend on that. There's five grand in cash in there for anything you have to cover that we can't tell the IRS about."

He laughed. "Lady, if I thought you were telling the IRS about any of this, I wouldn't be doing the job for you."

Davidson laughed at that, too, but O'Brien did not. "That's why we like working with you, Buster," she said. "You are the soul of discretion. You're flying to DC tonight, and no red-eye bullshit. You're taking our jet. There's a car waiting downstairs for you."

"What about my cat?" he asked.

"The usual arrangements for the cat," Maria O'Brien replied.

"Okay," he said. "But just tell that Mexican witch not to tidy my apartment this time. I like it the way it is. And the cat does too."

"I'll let her know," O'Brien said.

"So, what's the brief?" Buster asked, holding up the packet. He knew they wouldn't have committed anything to paper; the envelope would contain information but no instructions. It was safer that way.

"It's just a look-see this time," she said. "We don't need you to do anything. We just need you to have a look at this guy and figure out where he's going to fall apart if you press in hard."

"But you're going to want me to press in hard at some point, right?" Buster asked, "Because that's usually how these things go. There's a logic to it."

"For the moment, you're just having a look."

"What about cover?" he asked. "What sort of cover do I got?"

"All the money in the world, man," Davidson replied before O'Brien could say anything. "That cover enough for you?"

"I'm not talking about legal or medical expenses," Buster said, holding the envelope up. "This is political. This guy's got enemies— I'm looking at two of them. I can think of another one who lives on Pennsylvania Avenue."

O'Brien said nothing, and Davidson kept his mouth shut for once, too.

"But a guy like this has friends too," Buster said. "Or if they're not friends, they're at least people who share mutual interests. They're the people I need cover from."

O'Brien nodded. "You'll have it," she said.

"When do you want the information?" Buster asked.

She looked at him. "Why are you still standing here?"

"Right," he said, and he left.

EXTRACT

'Studs Terkel Talks About The Transitions: An Oral History of the Future'
   The New Yorker | March 13, 1954 | Vol. 29, No. 5 | pp. 51–66

Margaret "Maggie" O'Sullivan, copy editor, Playboy magazine.
(Interview conducted July 1953 in a coffee shop near the magazine's offices. She speaks with the clipped precision of someone who has spent years squeezing long stories into cramped column inches.)

The penthouse meeting?

You have to picture it: top floor, Michigan Avenue, the glass wall looking out over the river. The ice bucket sweating on the liquor cart. Everybody smoking like the world was running out of air. The Features boys in their shirt sleeves and loosened ties, making a show of their progressive chatter while the secretaries topped up their martini glasses. Hef in the doorway, backlit like a saint in a Renaissance painting, never saying a word.

And then she came in. This freelancer. Betty Friedan. Pitched us an op-ed on housewives and retail. She carried a folder under her arm like it was full of dynamite. Said she had the research. Charts, data. They were calling it the "second shift" fifty, sixty years from now. She spread her photostats out on the coffee table. Numbers stacked like shoe boxes. Women working eight hours behind a typewriter, or standing all day on the floor at Marshall Field's, then going home to another eight of unpaid labor. Cooking, cleaning, children. No overtime. No paycheck for the second gig.

The boys all leaned forward, blinking like they were staring at a misprint on the cover.

Features says, "We run a magazine, not a manifesto."

Another one leans back, puffing his Chesterfield like he owns the skyline. "Our readers want legs, bourbon, and a good laugh, not some lecture about dirty dishes."

There were chuckles around the lounge room. I kept my mouth shut until I couldn't anymore.

I heard myself answer, very calmly, "We run manifestos all the time, for the promotion of a fantastic lifestyle. If you've got a dick."

That shut them up. For a second, anyway. You could hear the ice settle in the glasses.

The smoke just hung there, thick as gauze. Nobody wanted to cough first.

Features tried again: "Come on, Maggie. Next, you'll want us to put the cover girl in a boilersuit."

I didn't blink. "You put a red-check apron on Miss August last year."

"And she sold her ass off."

They started laughing, yucking it up, but Hef finally spoke up. Two words. "Pitch approved." Then he turned on his heel and vanished back into his office, like a director calling "cut."

What do the kids say? Game over.

Betty gathers up her papers. She was calmer than I was, but she's reading the room. She can see the boys aren't happy. Before she left, she gave me a business card. "If they try to kill this piece in committee," she said, "call my friend Maria."

I still have the phone number. I haven't had to call it yet. I sorta wonder what would happen if I did.

Anyway, we ran it as an op-ed and the letters came in. Said it was shrill, said it was dull, called it communist propaganda. Sometimes in the same letter. But a lot of women said, "Finally!"

Hef just looked at the subscription numbers.

They went up.

14

Germany.

THE THOUGHT CROSSED Geert's mind for perhaps half a second. Surrender.

He dismissed it immediately. The stories were too consistent and too detailed. The Orcs weren't taking prisoners. They'd accept the surrender of any equipment, so they could strip it down for use or study. But they'd line up the crews, and the lucky ones would get a bullet.

The unlucky ones were still screaming when the tank tracks rolled over them.

"Gun One, Gun Three. Report ammunition status," he transmitted, scanning the wooded ridge where they'd taken shelter. The pine trees offered good concealment but limited fields of fire. Below them, perhaps four hundred meters of gently sloping pastureland stretched down to a narrow stream, then rose again toward a series of low hills where the Soviet forces were massing.

"Gun Three, Gun One. Four rounds HE, two Willie-Pete." Klaas de Boer's voice shook with the strain they all felt. Through gaps in the treeline, Geert could see Klaas's position fifty meters to his left, his gun's long barrel barely concealed behind a stand of young oak.

"Supply Two, report."

"Three, Supply Two." The medic's voice, tight with worry. "The Lieutenant's stable but unconscious. We've got small arms ammunition and some rations, but no artillery rounds."

Marvelous. Against what his binoculars told him was at least twenty Soviet vehicles spread across the valley floor.

Geert adjusted his commander's periscope and studied the grim shape of his impending death. The northern force—eight T-72s with BMPs and BTRs in support—had deployed along the stream line. They were advancing by bounds, using a few scattered farm buildings for cover as they closed the distance. The southern force massed at least twelve tanks with what looked like a full motor-rifle company in support.

Both formations were converging on him like the jaws of a trap.

The terrain told the story. The Reds controlled the high ground to the east and south. The valley floor offered no cover for a retreat. To the west, more open farmland stretched for kilometres before reaching the next defensive position, if any such positions still existed.

They had a few minutes before the northern force reached effective range. Less than five or six minutes before both Soviet formations could coordinate a final assault.

Geert frowned as he peered through his binoculars.

The tanks were moving too fast, he thought. Racing to close the trap before their prey could escape. The BMPs and BTRs were falling behind, struggling to match the pace across the broken ground. The infantry that should have been advancing with the tanks was losing contact with their armoured spearhead.

The Russian commanders wanted this finished quickly, and they were getting ahead of their infantry, leaving their flanks exposed.

"All elements, listen carefully," Geert transmitted. "We're not engaging the tanks. Repeat, do not engage the main battle tanks. We're going after the soft targets, the infantry in those troop carriers. We strip away their support, then displace immediately."

"Understood, Gun Three." Klaas sounded relieved.

"Gun One, you take the northern BMP formation advancing along the stream. I'll target the southern infantry concentration near that burning farm. We fire everything we have, then we run."

"Roger, Gun Three."

Everything they had wasn't much, but then neither was the armour on a Soviet troop carrier.

Through his periscope, Geert could see the target now. Soviet motor-rifle troops advancing in extended formation across the pastureland, perhaps eighty men spread across two hundred meters of open ground. Behind them, three BMPs provided fire support, their 30 mm cannon raking a treeline where they must have suspected NATO forces might be hiding.

"Target infantry, bearing 145, range 800 meters," Geert called to his crew.

"Identified," Ter Velde replied from the gunner's position.

"HE, time fuse."

"Up!" Aukema confirmed, sliding the shell into the breech.

An airburst would be devastating against troops in the open. The shell would detonate perhaps twenty meters above the ground, showering the entire area with deadly fragments.

"Fire!"

Bernadette lurched as the 155 mm round left the tube. Through his periscope, Geert watched the shell's flight path, counting seconds. The explosion bloomed above the advancing Soviet infantry like a malevolent flower, white-hot fragments sleeting down.

Men dropped. Others scattered, seeking cover that didn't exist. The neat tactical formation fell into chaos.

"Gun One, engaging!" Klaas's voice crackled over the radio.

The wooded ridge erupted in coordinated fire as both Dutch guns engaged the Soviet support elements. Geert grinned as one BMP shuddered to a stop, smoke pouring from its fighting compartment. Another was reversing frantically, its crew abandoning the advance.

"Reload, HE!" Geert ordered, and Aukema was already ramming another shell into the breech, targeting the Soviet infantry trying to reorganise behind the stream.

The second shell was even more effective than the first. The airburst caught a platoon in the open, crossing the stream. Bodies dropped into the water, and the survivors broke completely, running for whatever cover they could find.

"Willie-Pete, next target!" Geert called, shifting his aim to a group of BMPs that had stopped to provide covering fire. White phosphorus wouldn't penetrate their armour, but it would force the crews to button up, maybe even panic them into abandoning their vehicles.

The third shell struck directly between two BMPs, and suddenly the valley floor was obscured by billowing white smoke. Through the chemical haze, Geert could see the infantry retreating, their advance completely disrupted.

But it wasn't enough. The T-72s were still coming. In two or three minutes, the tanks would be close enough to engage with main gun fire, and no amount of artillery could stop them.

He laughed.

No amount was exactly how much ammo he had left.

"All elements, displace now!" he transmitted. "Supply Two, you should be moving!"

"Already gone, Gun Three!"

"Driver, get us out of here!"

Bloemsma threw Bernadette into reverse, backing through the trees toward a logging trail that led west. Behind them, Geert could see Gun One moving fast, Klaas's vehicle weaving between the thickest pine trunks as tank rounds began servicing their abandoned firing positions.

They crashed through the treeline into a potato field, and immediately, Geert knew they were in trouble. Eight hundred meters of ploughed earth stretched ahead, the neat furrows creating a geometric pattern that would have been beautiful under other circumstances. Now it was simply a killing field. Flat, open ground with nowhere to hide, nowhere to take cover. The next woodline seemed impossibly distant.

Bernadette's tracks churned through the soft soil, throwing up clods of dark earth as Bloemsma pushed the engine to maximum power. Behind them, Geert could see Gun One following, Klaas's vehicle weaving slightly as it fought for traction in the churned mud.

"Come on, come on," Geert muttered, watching the treeline behind them through his periscope.

The first T-72 appeared at the edge of the woods, its low silhouette unmistakable against the pine trees. Then another. Then three more, spreading out as they prepared to engage targets in the open.

They were perhaps four hundred meters into the field when the tanks began their advance, rolling down into the potato furrows with the confidence of wolves loping after a wounded lamb. Playing with it. Perhaps they even meant to loop around and fully encircle him. The lead T-72 was maybe a hundred meters into the field, close enough that Geert could see the commander's head and shoulders in the cupola, when the tank simply vanished in a ball of fire and smoke.

Then another. And another.

"What the fuck—" Ter Velde started, but his words were lost in the roar of more explosions.

Through his periscope, Geert could see thin trails of smoke reaching out from the western woodline. Missiles. Wire-guided anti-tank rockets, striking the Soviet formation with devastating precision.

"Somebody's got Milans!" he called over the radio, hardly believing it.

The T-72s tried to locate and suppress the missile positions, but their supporting troops were scattered across the valley floor, still dealing with white phosphorus and the aftermath of the airburst attacks.

Without infantry to spot for them, without dismounted troops to clear the missile teams, the Soviet tanks were helplessly exposed. One by one, they died. The lead commander spotted the first missile team too late. Through his periscope, Geert watched the Soviet tanker's head swivel frantically in his cupola, searching the western treeline. The man had seen the smoke trail, the thin white line stretching across four hundred meters of open ground, just before the wire-guided Milan struck the T-72 just below the turret ring.

The explosion wasn't Hollywood dramatic. Nothing like one of those movies from the future. No towering fireball, no secondary detonations. Just a sharp crack and a puff of smoke, followed by the sudden stillness of a sixty-ton machine that had simply stopped being a problem.

The second T-72 tried to reverse, backing frantically through the potato furrows as its commander realised the trap they'd driven into. Another smoke trail reached out from the woodline. This missile struck from above, punching through the rear deck plate, and this time there was a fireball—the engine compartment erupting in filthy orange flame as diesel fuel ignited.

Tank number three pivoted toward the suspected missile position and fired, the 125 mm main gun sending a high-explosive round crashing into the treeline. Trees splintered. Earth erupted. But the Milan team had already displaced, moving thirty meters down the woodline to a new firing position.

Geert imagined he could see the thin line of the guidance wire catching the afternoon sunlight as a third missile streaked across the killing ground, but his rational mind told him that was impossible. The T-72 commander saw the missile coming, too. Geert watched the man's desperate attempt to traverse his turret, to bring the coaxial machine gun to bear on the missile team. Too late. The shaped-charge warhead punched through the turret's side armour, and suddenly two figures were climbing out of the commander's hatch, moving with the mad desperation of men who knew their vehicle was about to cook off.

They made it perhaps twenty meters before the ammunition storage exploded. The turret lifted completely off the chassis, spinning like a coin tossed by a giant, before crashing back to earth fifty meters away.

The fourth T-72 commander was either very good or very lucky. He was using the burning wrecks of his comrades as cover, advancing by short bounds from one smoking hull to the next. He almost made it to effective range before a fourth Milan team found him.

The missile struck home, and it seemed the tank might survive. Then smoke began pouring from the driver's vision blocks, and the giant vehicle ground to a halt, its crew already climbing out through their hatches.

"Unknown allied artillery, this is Stalker Six." The voice on the radio, calling on the Brigade fires freq, was crisp, British, and utterly calm despite the carnage unfolding around them. "Rally on my position for extraction. Grid reference follows."

Geert didn't question the miracle. He simply followed orders.

Ten minutes later, Bernadette crashed through a hedgerow into a small clearing where perhaps thirty infantrymen had established a hasty defensive position. British paratroopers and German panzer grenadiers, mixed together by circumstance and defeat, but still fighting.

A British major approached Geert as he climbed down from his commander's hatch. The man's uniform was torn and muddy, but his bearing remained parade-ground perfect.

"You're the senior officer for this artillery unit?" the major asked.

"NCO. Opperwachtmeester Veenstra, sir. B Battery, 3rd Artillery. For what it's worth."

"Major Blackwood, 2nd Para. And it's worth the drink we owe you, Opper. Outstanding work back there, carving away their ground support like that. You absolutely pantsed those tank crews for us."

Geert blinked, and it felt as though he had a handful of sand in his eyes. He didn't quite know what to say, and didn't have to, as the low, throaty, unmistakable growl of turbofan engines grew to a world-ending roar.

"Ah," Major Blackwood said with evident satisfaction. "The Americans. Late as always, but right on time."

The A-10 Warthogs came in low and fast, their distinctive twin engines and straight wings making the tank killers instantly recognisable.

"All ground elements, this is Hogsbreath Four-Oh," a drawling American voice announced over the radio. "We have Reds in the open. Beginning gun runs now. Keep your heads down."

The first Warthog rolled into its attack, the pilot lining up on the surviving Soviet tanks from the southern force and opening up with the GAU-8 Avenger cannon in its nose. The sound was grotesque, huge, and industrial. A mechanical roar that seemed to tear the air itself apart. BRRRRRRRRT. Seven barrels rotating at enormous speed, firing depleted uranium rounds at nearly four thousand rounds a minute.

The retreating T-72s didn't stand a chance, DU penetrators punching through their armour like wet paper, turning fighting vehicles into funeral pyres.

"Jesus Christ," someone whispered behind Geert. Through the

smoke and chaos, he could just make out men running. The survivors of his artillery barrage, now fleeing the destruction of their heavy armoured units.

The second Warthog banked sharply into its attack run, its straight wings slicing the sky like razors as it dipped into the smoke-streaked valley. Geert watched, mesmerised, as the beast screamed in just above treetop height, so low he could see the pilot's helmet glint in the sunlight. The twin turbofans howled with a banshee's fury as the GAU-8 Avenger opened up again—BRRRRRRRRT—a mechanical war cry that sent ripples through the earth itself. The cannon's thunder didn't just echo, it punched, shaking ribcages and shredding steel. The southern tank group never had a chance. One T-72 was caught mid-pivot, its turret blossoming open like a steel flower as depleted uranium shells ripped through it, ammo cooking off in a gout of fire. Another tried to reverse into cover, but the A-10's strafing run stitched a row of molten craters across its hull, peeling it like a tin can. Hatches blew open. Men boiled out, some on fire. One crewman made it five steps before the second Warthog swooped in for a finishing burst, turning him into a red mist.

"All ground elements, this is Hogsbreath Four-Oh. The target area is clear. Have a nice day."

Major Blackwood clapped Geert on the shoulder. "Righty-o then, Sergeant. Time to collect your wounded and get moving. The Sovs will send more cannon meat our way, and we can't count on having the good luck of a footloose artillery unit passing by next time."

Geert looked around the clearing at the mixed group of British and Dutch soldiers. Paratroopers who'd been dropped behind enemy lines, infantrymen who'd escaped the encirclement, artillerymen who'd lost their guns.

"Sir," Geert said to Major Blackwood, "what are our orders?"

The British officer raised an eyebrow as though amused to be asked. In the distance, smoke still rose from the burning Soviet tanks. "Orders, sergeant? Let's start with buggering off, shall we? Everything else we'll figure out as we go."

15

Germany.

JOACHIM BOOSFELD STOOD in Panzer 59's commander's hatch, watching the intersection where Highway 46 crossed Route 229. He'd grown to hate that particular stretch of German tarmac with the passion other men reserved for unfaithful wives. From Brilon to Meschede, from Meschede to here in Arnsberg, his company had fought the communists along every inch of that accursed road. Forest to intersection, intersection to town, town to forest, an endless, bloody retreat along which it felt like he had left pieces of his command every few yards. Pieces of men, machines, himself.

Yesterday, he'd commanded fifteen main battle tanks. Today, five. Tomorrow he might go back up to twelve or fifteen. Or he might die before tomorrow came. The nearest replacement M-60 had arrived with the morning supply convoy and sat hull-down behind a stand of birch trees, its paint so fresh it seemed to glow against the muted greens of the German forest. It boasted factory-new road wheels, unblemished armour, and that distinctive smell of a fighting vehicle that had never seen combat; grease, leather and hydraulic fluid instead of cordite and fear.

The crew was another story entirely.

Sergeant Niehauser, the tank commander, had to be pushing fifty. His weathered face showed the lines from squinting through vision blocks during the long retreat from Moscow. He was a veteran of Kursk and Stalingrad, one of the few old comrades who'd survived both the Ostfront and the post-war denazification trials to emerge with clean papers and a Bundeswehr uniform. Boosfeld knew he could trust the man.

But Niehauser's loader was some schoolteacher from Düsseldorf, recalled from the reserves with two weeks' notice and a wife who'd screamed at him not to go. The gunner had been selling insurance in Cologne until the mobilisation orders arrived. The driver looked old enough to be Boosfeld's father.

Alte Hasen, the others called them. Old stagers. Men who'd learned to survive one war only to face the grim and very likely prospect of dying in another.

But they were tankers, and tank crews were what Boosfeld needed. He'd split his five remaining vehicles into two sections of two tanks each, with himself as the reserve, ready to plug holes, exploit opportunities, or simply die in whatever manner best served the day.

The ogre's grumble of artillery carried across the forest from Rumbeck, three kilometres southeast. German guns this time, judging by the direction and the distinctive crack of 155 mm shells. Between the explosions, Boosfeld could hear the irregular chatter of small arms fire, and his radio crackled with terse reports of an increasingly desperate situation.

"Lehr Six, this is Ranger Two-Seven. We are in close contact. Request immediate fire mission, grid 347829."

"Ranger Two-Seven, guns are unavailable. Break contact and withdraw to Phase Line Hotel."

"Lehr Six, we cannot break contact. We are decisively engaged. Request close air support."

Static. Then: *"Ranger Two-Seven, no assets available. You are on your own."*

On your own.

The unofficial motto of this war. Boosfeld had heard those words so often that they no longer surprised him. What did surprise him was that anyone still bothered asking for support. Better to save one's breath for a final cigarette, he thought.

The sun climbed higher, turning the forest into a verdant green hall of light and shadow. Boosfeld was grateful for the canopy; his tank's air conditioning had failed two days ago. Below him, his driver had fallen asleep with his head pillowed on the rim of his hatch. Hoffman was barely nineteen, young enough to sleep anywhere under any circumstances. Boosfeld envied him for that. But not for much else. Hoffman would most certainly die in this hot, stinking steel box. They all would. At least Boosfeld and the old rabbits had lived a life of sorts. Not much of a life, granted. They whored where other men loved and drank and smoked while other men devoted themselves to finer pursuits. But at least we got a few good times in, Boosfeld thought.

Not like poor fucking Hoffman there, eh.

The sound of an engine and tires on forest loam made him turn. A jeep threaded through the trees, following a trail that existed more in the driver's imagination than on the ground. Boosfeld recognised the vehicle before it stopped. Oberstleutnant Müller's personal transport, the small, waving forest of antennae marking it as a command vehicle.

Lieutenant Colonel Müller climbed out and approached Boosfeld's tank with the stiff, awkward movements of a man who was getting too old to run about in forests full of Russian orcs. He was a small, compact fellow with intelligent eyes and the kind of moustache that had been the fashion when the Kaiser sat the throne. Under his arm, he carried a map case that had seen better wars.

"Mind if I come up, Joachim?" he asked.

"Visitors from the rarefied heights of Regimental command are always welcome, sir. What delicacies have you brought for us today?"

Müller hauled himself up the front slope with a few grunts and a long grimace that took over his face entirely until he'd made it all the way up the steel slopes. Hoffman opened one eye, nodded, and immediately resumed his unconsciousness. Müller nodded down at the sleeping driver and spoke quietly.

"Priorities. Smart lad."

"How can I be of service, sir?" Boosfeld asked.

Müller settled on the turret roof and pulled out a silver cigarette case. Real silver, too, probably a family heirloom. He offered a smoke to Boosfeld, who accepted and lit it up with his Zippo. The tobacco was smooth but tasted incredibly rich after all the ersatz rubbish they'd been smoking for weeks. "Looks like you brought work as well as smokes," Boosefeld said, gesturing toward the sound of gunfire from Rumbeck.

Müller puffed out his cheeks like a hamster and blew a thin stream of smoke into the hot, still air. "Here's what we know. Your current opposition is the Second Hungarian Motor-Rifle Regiment, backed by the Czech Third Tank Battalion. The Russians are holding their units in reserve for now, at least in this sector. They feed their kulaks into the meat grinder during the day, then hit us with their Guard divisions after dark."

"Smart," Boosfeld admitted grudgingly. "If the Guards have night vision. Keeps us engaged around the clock, draws down our ammo reserves."

Through the trees, Boosfeld could see thicker smoke rising from Rumbeck. The artillery fire was walking closer, individual explosions distinguishable now rather than a general roar. Someone was adjusting fires, probably a Soviet forward observer with a good view of the German positions. They hadn't seen any signs of drone activity yet, for which Boosfeld would have said a prayer, if he were even a little bit inclined to believe in such nonsense.

It was a wonder to him that the Russians had not swarmed the battlefield with drones, but not entirely wondrous. Orbital bombardment systems did not come cheap, especially when you had to build them in secret. He assumed that's where most of the Red Army's R&D spend had gone. And look, who was he to argue with the result? It was the fucking Russians crawling all over Germany, forcing him to give up more and more of his soil every day, not the other way around.

"And what do you need from me, sir?" Boosfeld asked, though he suspected the answer would be the same as always: more than he could give.

Müller sighed. "Keep the road open as long as possible, Joachim. Cut them down in windrows when they come. Try not to get killed for no good reason." He paused to take another drag. "Oh, and about replacements, don't expect any more for a while."

Boosfeld nodded. Germany was running out of tank crews faster than she was running out of tanks. "We'll manage," he said, because that's what good commanders always say. Sometimes they even mean it.

"I know you will. You always do." Müller dropped his cigarette onto the armour plate and ground it under his boot. Boosfeld frowned. The man had wasted half the smoke.

"Can I give you the big picture? Off the record?"

"Please."

Müller pulled out a map from his case and unfolded a tactical overlay on top of it. Red arrows showed Soviet penetrations, blue lines marked NATO positions. There was too much red and not enough blue. "We're not going to stop them here," he said without preamble. "Not in Arnsberg, not anywhere along this line. Third Armoured is finished as an effective fighting force. So is First Dutch Corps."

The words hung in the air like smoke after an action.

Boosfeld studied the map, noting the gaps in the blue line and the thick red arrows driving west. "Then what's the point?" he asked quietly. "I assume it's not just to die facing fearful odds for the ashes of our fathers."

Müller snorted softly, finishing the quote for him.

"Nor the temples of our gods. No. It's for time," he said, and tapped the map with his finger. "We're buying time for the Americans to get their heavy divisions across the Atlantic. Time for the British to reinforce from BAOR reserves. Time for the French to have a second *café au lait* before making their way, ever so carefully, into the fight." His smile was as bitter as week-old coffee. "Every hour we hold off the beast costs Beria more casualties he cannot afford to take."

Boosfeld laughed out loud.

"Beria could fill the ocean to overflowing with the blood of all the casualties he can afford to take, *mein Oberstleutnant*. He's probably killed more men in his dungeons than he's sent to their deaths out here."

Boosfeld waved airily at Route 229.

"I know," Müller said, his voice thin and raspy. "We're trading German lives for American shipping schedules. But that's the war we're in, Hauptmann. It will be another war when they arrive."

Boosfeld absorbed this information with the professional detachment of a man who'd made peace with his own mortality years ago. "How long?"

"Two weeks. Maybe three if we're unlucky." Müller began folding his map. "Then the real war begins. Assuming any of us live to see it."

"I make no assumptions."

"Probably wise."

The conversation was interrupted by the distinctive sound of rotor blades; close, fast, and getting closer. Both men ducked instinctively as two dark arrowhead shapes roared overhead at treetop level. Boosfeld's hand moved automatically to his .50 calibre machine gun before his brain processed the familiar silhouette of the Cobra helicopters, flying nap-of-the-earth, their skids barely clearing the tree tops as they raced southeast toward Rumbeck. Their stub wings bristled with rockets and missiles, and their chin-mounted cannon swivelled like robot predators tracking scent.

"Jesus," Müller breathed.

The Cobras disappeared over a hill, then suddenly popped up like evil twin jack-in-the-boxes. Boosfeld watched through his binoculars as they executed a perfectly coordinated attack, sixteen Hellfire missiles streaking toward targets he couldn't see, followed by devastating bursts from their 20 mm cannons. The sound of distant explosions reached them like hammer blows from Thor's foundry.

Both choppers nosed over into what looked like suicidal dives, and for a heart-stopping moment, it seemed they would carve their rotors into the German countryside. But they levelled out mere meters above the deck and raced west along a different route, seeking concealment and distance from the inevitable counterfire.

"Impressive flying," Müller observed.

"The ones who can't fly are already dead," Boosfeld replied. "Natural selection."

Müller nodded, gathering his maps as he prepared to leave. "Any other questions?"

"Just one." Boosfeld met his commander's eyes. "You are closer to the throne than we mere jesters out here."

Müller paused, one leg already over the side of the tank. "Not much closer, Jochem. What do you ask?"

"The schwarzer," he said. "Jones. Your assessment of him."

"I do not know the man," Müller said stiffly.

"No, but you have watched his plans in play now for three weeks. I would have your assessment of the man asking me to fight for a shipping schedule."

The lieutenant colonel said nothing for a moment. And then, he shrugged.

"A month ago, I thought Beria would be in Paris by now. I thought we would all be dead." He shrugged again.

Boosfeld nodded.

"So did I."

Neither of them said anything for a while. Boosfeld was thinking about scavenging the cigarette butt Müller had ground out under his boot heel when the man spoke up again.

"He is a fighting general, I think. Even though he fights backwards for now."

"You think?"

Müller nodded.

"Yes. He arrived here with their Medal of Honour, you know. It is not the Knight's Cross," Muller nodded in acknowledgment of Boos-feld's decoration. "And he was only fighting Arabs, but the Americans do not just give them away. And he fought off a Russian airborne assault on Naples at the start of this. Probably saved the whole show down there."

"He fought them off? Or his men fought them off?"

"He did," Müller said. "Picked up a gun and led them into the fight. They say he shot his way up into a control tower full of Spet-snaz, with a company of cooks and bugle players."

"They say a lot of things," Boosfeld snorted, but he had read the reports too, in a torn, half-burned copy of *Die Welt* a week ago.

"Kolhammer trusts him."

"A good name that, for a fighting man," Boosfeld conceded. "I knew a Kolhammer from Baden-Württemberg."

"A fighting man?"

"While he lived, yes."

Müller sighed. "While we all live. Good luck, Joachim."

They nodded at each other, the caution against saluting in the field second nature by now.

Müller dropped to the ground and walked back to his jeep without looking back.

Boosfeld watched the command vehicle disappear into the forest, leaned out to retrieve the crushed cigarette, and tucked it into a pocket before returning his attention to the intersection. The artillery fire was growing more intense, and he could see smoke plumes rising from what had been a quiet farming village an hour ago.

His radio crackled with the voice he'd been expecting: "All Lehr elements this net, be advised friendlies bounding toward your position. Stop Line Hotel untenable. Prepare for passage of lines."

The defence of Rumbeck had collapsed. Surviving German units were retreating toward his position with the Red forces in pursuit.

"You hear that, Verrenkamph?" he asked his gunner over the intercom.

"Yes, sir. I can see friendlies coming this way. LAVs and M-60s in tactical withdrawal."

"Any sign of the orcs?"

"Not yet, sir. But they won't be far behind."

Through his binoculars, Boosfeld watched the retreat unfold with professional detachment. German armoured vehicles bounded backward in tactical sequence, one unit providing overwatch while another displaced, then roles reversed in well-drilled choreography. It was a textbook retrograde action, the kind of thing he'd had his company practise endlessly at Grafenwöhr before the war began.

The difference was that this time, men were dying, not practising.

A distant flash and a deep roar marked the death of a German tank. Boosfeld spotted the muzzle flash that had killed it, a T-72 behind a farm building, at a range of approximately 1600 meters. An easy shot for an experienced crew.

"Tank," he called to his gunner. "Bearing 110, range 1600."

"Identified," Verrenkamph replied. The turret traversed smoothly as the gunner laid his sights on target.

"SABOT, load."

His loader, Tomas, slammed a depleted uranium penetrator into the breech. "Up!"

"Lasing." The laser rangefinder confirmed the distance. "On target."

More German vehicles raced past his position, some trailing smoke, others carrying wounded on their rear decks. The retreat threatened to become a rout, but it was still organised for now. These men would live to fight another day.

Unlike the crew of that T-72.

"Fire."

The 120 mm gun boomed, and across the battlefield, the Soviet tank disappeared in a spectacular fireball that painted the afternoon sky orange and black. Its turret separated from the hull in a lazy arc, spinning end over end before crashing into a wheat field, where it bounced like a discarded toy.

No other targets appeared for a moment, but he knew more Soviet armour would follow, and his five tanks couldn't hold this position indefinitely.

They could, however, buy time. Precious minutes that might somehow matter in the larger scheme.

Captain Joachim Boosfeld and what remained of the 2nd Company would hold Highway 46 until they could hold it no longer. Then, if they lived, they would fall back to the next intersection, the next patch of forest, and the next killing ground.

Until there were no more roads to defend.

Until the Americans arrived.

Or perhaps just until their luck ran out.

The radio crackled again. More units reporting contact. More calls for support that wouldn't come. More men dying for time.

He lit Müller's cigarette and waited for the next wave.

16

Marseilles.

"It is not like the last war, *non?*" Ronsard said, as the small cargo van crested a hill and Marseille unfolded before them, lights twinkling in the darkest hour before dawn.

"No blackout," Harry observed.

The Frenchman nodded. "With guided missiles, I suppose it is not necessary."

Harry shrugged. "There are only so many guided missiles in the world," he said, "and I think we've fired off quite a lot of them already. Don't they get air raids here out of Naples and Gibraltar?"

He looked at the fires on the horizon, about twenty miles north of the road they were driving on. As he watched, a new bloom of orange light erupted from one of the distant blazes, momentarily illuminating the industrial landscape on the far side of the city.

"That was not an air raid," Ronsard explained. "That is our friends in *le Resistance*. They blew up an ammunition dump all the way over there so that we might make our way into the Old Port unbothered by too many roadblocks and inspections. At least, such is the plan."

"And I do love it when a plan comes together," Harry said. "So here's hoping."

Ronsard drove on, Harry in the passenger seat next to him, Ivanov and Charlotte out of sight in the cargo compartment behind them, but ready to emerge, guns hot, if necessary. Ronsard had provided them with much heavier weapons than they had brought, including a couple of shoulder-launched anti-tank rockets, which had impressed both operators.

The road wound through the Massif des Calanques south of Marseilles, a wasteland of jagged limestone outcrops and ghostly brush. By night, the hills were little more than hulking silhouettes beneath a faintly luminous sky, their slopes cut with narrow, twisting lanes barely wide enough for the van. Occasionally, the headlights caught glimpses of wild thyme and low cypresses clinging to the rocky soil, while the chill, salt-laced wind carried hints of the sea far below. The route was completely unlit, the silence broken only by the crunch of gravel beneath their tires.

Harry had only been to Marseille once, back up in the 21st, and that for less than twenty-four hours. He thought he recalled flying in over these hills and remembered them as rugged enough to claim to be at least modestly mountainous.

The city before him seemed smaller, perhaps two-thirds the size of the Marseille he knew, even though he would admit to not knowing it very well. It was remarkable, however, just how much of the port and its hinterland was lit up. It was just after 4 a.m. local time, with the first hint of dawn lighting the horizon to the east, yet the city was blazing with light, as though illuminated for a carnival.

To the north, the new port sprawled in a vast landscape of concrete quays and prefab warehouses. Towering cranes loomed over the waterfront, while clusters of searchlights swept the sky. On the dark mirror of the water, the hulking silhouettes of Russian warships still lay at anchor—ghostly, half-sunken giants, their hulls marred by fire and entangled in rusted mooring lines, shrouded in an eerie mist rising from the sea.

"It is the Russian way," Ronsard explained as Harry admired the handiwork of the RAF and the US Air Force. They'd smashed Stalin's Mediterranean Fleet within hours of the Soviet orbital strikes. Then he corrected himself. It had been Comrade Beria's fleet by then. Not Stalin's.

"They light the streets up, but enforce the curfew, "Ronsard continued. "They want to see anybody who is moving around after dark."

"And how do we negotiate our way through that?" Harry asked.

"I have papers," Ronsard explained, tapping a bundle of documents in the console beside him. We are drivers for a company that supplies the Old Port with hand wipes and toilet paper, all Russian-made. It's very dull. But good cover, which I have been using since I arrived here six months ago. It has not failed me yet."

"That's good to hear," Harry said, "but I'm sure six months ago you weren't tooling around after curfew with a lorry full of foreign spies and rocket launchers."

"*Non*," Ronsard admitted with a rueful grin, "but we must all adapt to the times, Harry. How have you been, my friend? You must tell me. Have you adapted?"

Harry shrugged. "One tries, Marcel," he said, "I'm engaged to be married now."

"*Magnifique!*" Ronsard's eyes flashed with delight as he let out a sharp, triumphant laugh, his gloved hand thumping Harry's chest with unexpected force. The corners of his mouth curled into a wide, lopsided grin, and he drummed his fingers on the steering wheel.

"This is your friend, the American woman writer, right? I have seen you in the news magazines and once on the television, too. You were at a movie festival, I believe."

"Probably," Harry nodded. "Jules gets around to a lot of those things. She's still working, although she freelances now. She doesn't need to, but she enjoys it."

He tried not to think about his fiancée and the last time he'd seen her. She was being loaded onto an emergency evacuation flight out of Cairo with a lot of tubes punched through her ribcage for all the IV lines running into her. He hadn't been able to speak to her since then, but he'd received an update on her condition upon joining the *Achilles*. Julia was at a private clinic, according to MI6, and doing much better than expected.

Harry had never heard of the clinic, but Dr. Yasmeen Collins, an uptimer from Karen Halabi's old ship, the *Trident*, ran it. He was grateful that Julia was in the care of somebody who understood proper modern medicine. If she'd ended up in a regular hospital, the bloody temps might've given her a spoonful of cod liver oil and a bag of leeches.

Harry hoped she'd be moving around soon, just a little to help her recovery, but not so much or so easily that she might feel it necessary to pick up her old job as an embed with the US military. Beside him, Ronsard was enthusing about married life, which was odd since Harry understood him to be divorced, but perhaps he was just being very French about it all. He steered the van through a series of switchbacks, during which Harry lost sight of the city. A few minutes later, they emerged from the hills and the scrubby forest that covered the lowest slopes, crossing quickly into Marseille's outer suburbs. Although they weren't suburbs, he thought, not as he understood them.

The city had not sprawled the way so many cities uptime had. It had grown, yes, he'd seen the evidence of the New Port from high up in the hills, but the growth seemed constrained by a planned intensity. It made sense, he thought. The Soviets did nothing without a plan, and they'd taken the city and most of southern France at the war's end. They'd had the better part of a decade to bugger everything up around here.

He didn't know what the newer arrondissements looked like, but he could picture them; vast, ugly tracts of ferroconcrete horror boxes stacked atop one another in endless, miserable repetition. Apartment blocks with windows like dead eyes, pitted and grey beneath the glare of security floods. In captured cities like this, the Sovs seemed to savour erasing everything at human scale, burying it all beneath tectonic slabs of concrete and rebar. There'd be none of the chaos and glory of the old inner city they were headed towards.

"Tell me about these characters we're meeting," Harry said.

"Criminals," Ronsard replied flatly.

"Mafia?"

"They call themselves *le Milieu*," Ronsard explained. "Effectively, they are the Marseille Mafia, yes."

Harry frowned. "I thought the Corsicans ran all the underworld rackets in Marseille." He wasn't sure why he thought that. Possibly, he'd seen it in a movie sixty or seventy years from now.

Ronsard nodded. "Originally, in your time, yes, that was true. The Corsicans imported heroin from Indochina. They brought it through Marseille and sent it to America from the same docks."

"Ah," Harry said, realising he had indeed seen it in a movie. "The French Connection."

"Oui," Ronsard said, nodding vigorously. "An excellent film, yes. When I first watched it, I thought it would be about France, but obviously not. Still a great film, however. Much better than so much of the rubbish you brought here with you." He was smiling as he said it, and Harry shrugged.

"Can't argue with that. Sorry, mate. So these blokes are local hoodlums, then?"

"Oui. Yes," Ronsard agreed. "It is complicated to run a port without finding a few rats underfoot. And the rat, he is a resilient creature, Harry. So it is with the Milieu. The communists tried to suppress them, but they had no more success than the Nazis ten years ago."

Harry recalled what Ivanov had said on the sub about not being part of the business if you weren't in the regime.

"So what are they looking for to get our help?" he asked. "Because I can't imagine the Hammer is going to sign an executive order allowing them to run heroin into New York, even if it was the CIA who greenlit that originally."

"Yes, but... we adapt, as you say," Ronsard said.

The van plunged deeper into the city, the broader avenues of the outer districts giving way to narrower, older streets. This was the First Arrondissement, the heart of the old port, a place that felt both ancient and neglected. Grimy tenement buildings crowded together, their ground floors often boarded up or repurposed into makeshift workshops. The air grew heavy with the scent of diesel fumes, stale fish, and something indefinably industrial. Soviet propaganda posters, faded and torn, peeled away from crumbling walls, depicting stern-faced workers and heroic soldiers. Occasional figures, hunched against the pre-dawn chill, hurried along the pavements, their faces obscured by shadow.

"These are not the Corsicans, remember, Harry," Ronsard continued. "I am sure they would love to smuggle all the heroin into North America, but they will be content for now with simply getting the communist jackboot off their necks. Many of their members have ended up in mass graves, and many of the Russians have followed them into the darkness as a matter of revenge. I cannot speak for their plans five or ten years from now, but I can speak for what they intend to do in the next month: kill as many Russians as possible, blow up their train lines, sink their ships, cut throats and burn warehouses."

"Sounds marvellous," said Harry. "I can't wait to meet them."

"And they are very enthused to meet you, Your Highness," Ronsard smirked. Harry rolled his eyes but did not ask the Frenchman to refrain from calling him that. He was here because Number 10 had ordered him to Marseille. He'd been going anyway, because that was where MI6 judged Skarov and Bremmer to have gone after Sardinia. But securing the German rocket scientist and settling up with Lavrentiy Beria's hatchet man had become a secondary goal.

The Milieu, as Ronsard had called them, wanted assurances that if they went to war with the Russians infesting their city, they would be properly supported by the Allies. Harry had been judged a sufficiently significant interlocutor, and they would accept any deal he offered. It was a matter of no small irony to him that the reason he'd been dispatched into the heart of southern Soviet Europe was the same reason Ronsard had been teasing him about his place in the line of succession. He did not have one. Having cut through the Gordian knot of any succession issues arising from his travelling back here from the future, Harry was entirely expendable. That didn't make him insignificant, however. He was, in that sense, something of a unicorn. MI6 could deploy him, as he had been in Egypt, because of the perceived eminence of his role, and he could be abandoned or denied just as easily because of his insignificance in truth. He didn't care to dwell on it too much. It wasn't the sort of thing that made a chap feel good about his place in the world.

The landscape outside the van window shifted, the residential blocks giving way to the grimmer, more functional architecture of industry. Warehouses, their corrugated iron sides streaked with rust, loomed on either side of the road, interspersed with low-slung factories whose chimneys stood out against the pre-dawn sky. The traffic, though still sparse, was heavier here, a few lorries rumbling past, their hooded headlights cutting through the gloom. Foot traffic, however, remained thin, save for the occasional dock worker, trudging towards the distant glow of the port. Harry felt a familiar sense of purpose settle over him; they were nearing their objective.

His heart skipped a beat when he saw a security checkpoint ahead, but Ronsard assured him it would not be a problem. "We are not going that far anyway," he said, turning left deeper into the warehouse district before reaching the roadblock.

The walls closed in on them, quite literally. Harry expected to hear the scrape of old stucco against the van, so confined was the winding alleyway through which Ronsard took them. Harry quickly lost his bearings. The passage was tight, and even tighter passageways and cut-throughs branched off it at irregular intervals.

Ronsard waved a hand at the windshield. "The Nazis, they often swept through this area, gathering up everybody and displacing them," he said. "The whole of the Old Port was declared a nest of terrorists, which allowed them to handle it in a rougher than usual fashion."

"Rougher than usual for a Nazi? That must have been quite something," Harry said.

Ronsard answered with a very Gallic shrug. "You remember what they were like, Harry. Barbarians with clipboards." Harry grunted. He understood what Ronsard meant.

The van continued its winding journey, deeper into the labyrinth of the Old Port. The air grew cooler, damp with the proximity of the sea, and the sounds of the city faded, replaced by the clang of metal on metal and the mournful cry of gulls. The alleyways became even more convoluted, a bewildering tangle of brick and stone, occasionally opening onto small, deserted courtyards filled with stacked crates and rusting machinery. Finally, after what felt like an eternity of twists and turns, Ronsard brought the van to a halt outside a large, nondescript shed, its corrugated iron walls scarred with graffiti.

"Nice work, Marcel," Harry said. "Safely home."

The Frenchman scoffed. "My friend, nothing is safe about what we must do next."

17

London.

TODAY, Julia Duffy gripped the iron bar. She lifted her weight, her whole body, a little to adjust her position so the bar was directly above her eyes. She wrapped her fingers around the knurled steel, breathed in, tensed her entire body, and pushed up. The barbell lifted out of the metal cradle, and she held it over her chest.

"Five reps, please, Ms Duffy," the therapist said.

Julia lowered and raised the barbell five times. It was frustrating. She knew she could lift much heavier loads than this, but they wouldn't let her try. They didn't even have the proper plates on the end. She was lifting a naked barbell, not even a proper Olympic standard 25-kilogram barbell. They'd made her start with the 15-kilo 'lady bar'. Still, she admitted to herself as the bar clanked back into place, two weeks ago she wouldn't have imagined she could make this much progress.

"Alright, we'll take a three-minute rest," the physio said, "and then push out the second set. How did that feel?"

"Like I'm wasting my time," she said. "Seriously, dude, you can put some plates on the end of it."

The physiotherapist smiled. "I could, I could. But that would be more than my job's worth, Ms Duffy. We have your rehab program, and we're going to stick to it. If you think you could walk out of here today and start jumping out of aeroplanes, running around, doing whatever you used to do, you'll need to take it up with Doctor Collins."

"Three minutes, though, seriously. There's no weight on the bar. I don't need that much of a rest period."

"Three minutes is what it says on my clipboard, so three minutes is how long we'll wait," the physio said primly.

She knew it was pointless to argue. He'd said the magic phrase: more than my job's worth. You couldn't get an Englishman to do anything once he'd said those words. So she was going to do a 5x5 rep with a naked lady bar, even though she was pretty sure she could get a one-rep max of forty or even fifty kilos out. Nothing like her actual 1RM of a hundred and forty kegs, but that was before a couple of Lavrentiy Beria's weird little meatpuppets stuck a bunch of sharpened steel into her, back in Cairo.

That was, what, four or five weeks ago?

Her recovery was fucking amazeballs as the kids didn't say any more and probably never would. Those kids would never be born now.

Yazmeen Collins had saturated her in a bunch of uptime and augmented technologies. But Julia suspected the Doc was right when she told her the peptide therapy made all the difference. Peptides, short chains of amino acids, had been a radical innovation in medical science back upwhen, but they were just coming out of clinical trials when Julia, Yazmeen and ten thousand other time travellers got sucked into Manning Pope's wormhole.

The journal articles promised a revolution in healing – a revolution that had been rudely interrupted for Julia and the Multinational Force when they dropped ass-backwards into the middle of the Pacific War in the 1940s. She'd begun the peptide therapy three weeks ago and hadn't even noticed because Collins had her doing so much recovery work. Some of it involved active physio, like today, and a lot more had her sitting in machines, being bathed in various sonic and radiation treatments. The injections delivering the peptides to her badly damaged tissue had been a handful a day amidst the thirty-plus shots she'd had to endure. Broad-spectrum antibiotics to ward off infection from her multiple stab wounds, potent painkillers to manage the constant throb, and various anti-inflammatories and nutrient supplements to aid her body's monumental task of repair.

"Alright, second set," the physio said. "Eyes under the bar, try and bend the barbell like it's made of rubber just before you pick it up, pushing down through the heels, clenching the whole body like a fist."

She dropped her hands from the bar and said, "This is not my first time in a gym, buddy. Like, did you even lift weights before we came here?"

The physio looked at her, confused. "Oh, you mean uptimers," he said. "I thought you were talking about the hospital. Because when you came into the hospital, you looked like a bag of sausages somebody had dropped on the ground in a dog pound. So that was confusing to me. Bar, please."

"Sorry," she said, realising that she was behaving badly. "It's just frustrating, you know," she said as she settled under the bar again. "I can feel myself getting better every day. I know my recovery is miles ahead of the schedule on your clipboard. And I just want to get the hell out of here."

He smiled, not unkindly, and said, "It's understandable. But you also understand that there is a method to this. The scientific method. We can't just kick you out the door because you say you're feeling better. You suffered severe trauma, which a normal person undergoing normal treatment might not recover from. And you need to accept that. You are..."

He trailed off.

She looked at him. "Are you about to tell me I'm getting old?"

He smiled. "I would not dare."

"Solid choice," she said. "You should put some heavy plates on this bar now, cos I gotta lot of feelings and they're all going into this lift."

"Please don't throw the barbell through the ceiling," the physio said.

The session lasted for another hour, and if Julia was honest, she would admit there were moments she found very difficult. Her core strength and mobility were still badly compromised, and occasionally she would suffer sharp abdominal pains for no reason whatsoever. Well, besides the whole murderous stabbing thing. At one point, a nurse was taking her blood pressure and heart rate, and it felt as though she was being knifed again. The pain was fierce enough that both the physio and the nurse noticed. But because she wasn't in the middle of a movement sequence, they were less concerned that she'd just done some damage to herself.

"It's not unusual," the nurse explained, "and it's not phantom pain either. Don't let the doctors tell you that, love. The pain is real. You suffered some very significant wounds. The body holds on to its damage, the mind too," the nurse said.

Julia didn't reply to that; she just nodded. She was sweating by the end of the session, and a little shaky, and she took herself back to her room to have a shower. She felt better after that, clean and even a bit hungry, which was a good sign because she hadn't had much appetite since waking up in the hospital. She was about to call the nurse and ask if she could get a cup of coffee – unlikely – and a sandwich – more likely – when she saw the book of matches in the bag on her bedside table. She frowned and fetched it out. For a moment, the strangeness of the object was baffling. It was as though she didn't recognise what she was holding, although she knew it was a book of matches. Then her memories came together.

It was from a club in Cairo. She and Harry had gone there for a drink with Viv. Her heart gave a violent lurch, and she broke out in a light sheen of sweat. Her hands were trembling as she examined the matchbook. There was nothing written on it. All of the matches were intact. There was no message here. She dropped to the bed, shaking, her appetite forgotten.

But, Dan, she thought. *I saw Dan in Cairo. I dreamed I'd seen him.*

She'd thought it was a dream, but looking back now, it felt like a memory. It had shape and weight. It had... possibilities.

Julia shook her head. This was insane. Dan Black had been dead for a decade. She was misremembering at best, and possibly hallucinating. Her hunger came roaring back. She would get that goddamned sandwich, she thought, and a cup of coffee too, no matter what the fuck they said. She could sneak down into the staff canteen and make it herself if she had to. She was about to call the nurse when one appeared at the door of her room with Agent Plunkett.

"Oh," she said, still flustered by the matchbook and light-headed from the session with the physiotherapist, which had been longer and harder than she would've admitted when she was bitching up a storm at the start of the session.

"Five minutes," the nurse said, "she's due for her afternoon rest."

Julia's eye-roll earned an indulgent smile from Plunkett as he stepped inside, one hand already reaching for the visitor's chair. "You're looking much better than the last time I saw you," he said. "Vertical, for one thing. But you've got some colour in the face."

"Is he okay?" Julia asked. "Is Harry okay?"

"He's fine, Ms Duffy."

"Julia, please. Come on, what can you tell me? Nothing, I'll bet."

"I can tell you he's fine. He's still working. We've had contact recently, and he sent you his best wishes, which, of course, is not protocol, but M thought it reasonable for someone to pass on his message."

She looked at him. "He thought it reasonable for someone to come and check on me to make sure I wasn't about to wander out the gate and start babbling, or even worse, writing about what happened in Cairo."

"Something like that," Plunkett said.

"Is he still in Cairo?" she asked.

He shrugged and showed her his empty hands.

"Okay, sure, whatever. Even if you told me, I wouldn't believe you because you'd probably be planting misinformation and hoping I would spread it somewhere."

"Heaven forbid," the MI6 agent said, with a confident smirk that made Julia want to throw something heavy at his head. If she had the energy, which she did not.

"Well, it's good to know he's okay. For now," she admitted.

"And what about you, Julia?" Agent Plunkett asked. "Are you okay? Your recovery does seem to be coming along."

She thought about showing him the matchbook, but was paralysed by the tangle of thoughts and feelings knotted around it. It could be nothing, of course. She could well have brought the thing from Cairo back with her, and some clerk or attendant had found it, tucked it away somewhere, and later fetched it out for her. A kind gesture, a memento mori, whatever.

Or, perhaps, she'd been visited by a ghost.

She wasn't going to tell David Plunkett that, of course. She had no desire to be shunted off to a psychiatric ward. So, she said nothing about it.

"It's going better than I would've thought. I lifted some weights today. Not very heavy weights, but I lifted them. I picked them up, I put them down, I moved them around."

"Well, that's marvellous," he said. "It sounds like remarkable progress, given the state you were in when last I visited. If we should get the opportunity to talk to Harry, I'm sure you would have a message to pass on."

"Will it embarrass you and make you go all weird and English if I ask you to tell him I love him?"

"Not at all," Plunkett said. "Anything else?"

"Yeah," Julia said, leaning forward and lowering her voice. "Could you find me a sandwich and a cup of coffee?"

EXTRACT

'The Transitions: An Oral History of the Future, by Studs Terkel.'
    The New Yorker, March 13, 1954, Vol. 29, No. 5, pp. 51–56.

Mae Donovan, chorus captain, *Moulin Rouge*
    (Interviewed November 1953 in her apartment off the Strip. The Moulin Rouge closed three months ago. She's packing, heading to New York, she says, shooting for Broadway.)

The pills? That was my idea. Well, mine and the union's.

See, most people talk about the birth control thing as morality. It's not. For us, it's about math. You miss your cycle, you miss work. Miss work, you lose your spot in the line. The bills come in. You can't pay them. Simple math.

Before the pills, a girl could be perfect on stage every night for three years, and then biology takes her out. Casino didn't care about biology. They cared about reliable bodies in reliable costumes hitting reliable marks.

So we made it reliable.

She pulls a small blue disc from a jewelry box, turns it like a prayer wheel.

Every night after last curtain, same time, same routine. "Roll call," I'd say. "Anita—set. Doreen—set." Down the line. We took them together because time gets slippery in Vegas. Drunk neighbors, late shows, missed alarms—any of that could throw you off schedule. But after curtain? That's a clock that never lies.

The casino doctor hated it. He'd show up wanting to do "compliance checks" in the hallway, just him and whichever girl he decided needed reviewing. The bosses, you see, once they got the idea they could save themselves the trouble of a girl getting knocked up, they were all over that shit. They wanted us on the pill, and they wanted to know we were taking our medicine. I put a stop to that fast. Union rule. No medicine in the halls. Any discussions happen with witnesses.

She laughs, but there's an edge to it.

The thing is, we weren't just taking pills. We were keeping books. My clipboard, my ledger. If any suit tried to cut a girl for "risk of pregnancy," the union could point to my records and say, "She's on schedule." It was protection we owned, not permission we begged for.

This new girl—Ruthie—I remember her asking, "What happens if I'd rather take mine at home?" A fair question. "Call the house phone by ten and say 'set,'" I told her. "This is a habit, not a sacrament."

But most nights, we wanted the company. Not because we needed help swallowing a pill, but because the world was getting strange and this felt like pushing back together.

She closes the jewellery box, sits back.

The Transition brought a lot of complications. But those pills? They brought us something simple.

Schedules we could keep.

18

Cairo. Five weeks ago.

THEY MET at a Japanese teahouse in a new shopping mall on the edge of the diplomatic quarter. Mirrored escalators glided past storefronts showcasing Parisian fashion and Swiss watches. The air, chilled to a morgue-like frigidity, hummed with the sound of the air-conditioning and the faint, tinny pulse of electronic music that shouldn't have existed for another five or six decades. It was all a bit much for Dan's taste. Outside on the concourse, Korean pop music blared from hidden speakers while a group of Saudi teenagers clustered around a shop window displaying the latest sneakers and music players.

Dan arrived early and spent an hour shopping, gathering a small bag of gifts: silk stockings from a Parisian boutique, a bottle of Chanel perfume, and a delicate silver bracelet. The sort of trifles a wealthy man might buy for his wife or, more likely, his mistress. It allowed him to scope out the location before Siregar arrived.

The mall was eternity, shattered into mirror shards and remade with air-conditioning. He'd been there when the centuries had crashed into each other. He remembered steel folding into flesh when the *Leyte Gulf* emerged inside *Astoria*. This wasn't that, of course. But it wasn't something entirely different either. This was a weird and otherworldly echo. Egyptian men in spotless galabiyyas shuffled past him, one of them tapping at a thick tablet that shimmered with scrolling Arabic. They moved under a light sculpture from Osaka, its shifting LEDs spelling out poetry in a language no one here spoke, while Dan waited for a takeaway coffee from a place called KaldiHaus. The biggest chain in the Arab world, it looked exactly like one of those uptime Starbucks places, except as dreamed of by a Libyan goatherd. They promised authentic Viennese roasts, but served everything with condensed milk from a tin.

Dan took his black.

Five minutes before the agreed time, he took a booth in the teahouse, ordering a pot of green tea and a plate of dumplings. The booth had a clear view of the main entrance and the staff exit at the rear. The bench was covered in genuine leather, buttery soft and aged to a rich patina that spoke of craftsmen who revered their trade, and an interior designer who didn't understand that you simply didn't find such seating in a real Japanese tea room. Everything had been imported at huge expense: the hand-carved wooden frame, the silk cushions with subtle geometric patterns, even the small ceramic dishes that held wasabi and pickled ginger. Still, the tea service was legit and came in a small ceramic pot with a bamboo handle, and delicate cups thin enough to feel as though they were in harm's way between his thick fingers.

Dan poured his second cup as Siregar slid into the booth opposite him.

"Mr. Dan," he said.

"Thanks for coming," Dan said.

"I didn't imagine I had much of a choice, given your message."

Dan shrugged and speared a dumpling with his chopsticks. He dunked it into a small bowl of soy sauce and chilli paste before popping it into his mouth. He chewed and swallowed before replying.

"Thanks anyway."

His eyes swept over the teahouse. Bamboo mats, low tables, and shoji screens that diffused the mall's bright white light into a soft glow. He scanned the other patrons without smiling. He'd stopped smiling at strangers years ago, after a job in Tbilisi where his dopey

American friendliness had nearly blown his cover. Here, he saw no apparent danger, only a pair of diplomats' wives trading gossip over matcha, a German businessman trying to impress a local official, and a young couple lost in their own world. All harmless enough, and it wasn't a pointless exercise. You could never let your guard down. But he knew Siregar's security people would have watched the joint for the past few hours. They'd be safe here. Safe enough to talk, anyway.

"Do you have good news on my shipment?" The other man asked.

Dan let the silence stretch for a beat before answering. Years of working in places where eager responses got you marked as desperate had taught him the value of measured pauses. He watched Siregar's face, reading the hidden text of micro-expressions.

"I was hoping we might've filled your order this afternoon," Dan said at last. "I came close to picking up the stuff you needed, but we ran into some pretty aggressive competition."

Siregar was a spy who styled himself as an importer of fine things —spices, electronics, the occasional crate of anything that could be bought low and sold high. He moved goods and favours along the ancient routes, and in so doing, enjoyed a level of freedom and agency few diplomats could match. Taking a contemplative sip of tea, he nodded once. "So I've heard. The city appears to be having one of its episodes."

"Cairo is always having an episode," Dan said with a faint smile. "But, yeah. Things got out of hand."

"You are still confident of securing the shipment for us, though?"

"As confident as I can be. We've been through this before, buddy, haven't we? High-value merchandise attracts a lot of competition, some of it pretty insistent. That's why I needed to talk to you as soon as possible."

Siregar eased back in his chair, and Dan watched his reflection ripple faintly in the table's glossy black finish, watching the fingers of his left hand fret unconsciously at the small scar on his right. A familiar tic. Dan had noticed it six years earlier, not long after taking his first contract with the Moertopo regime.

When Siregar lifted his teacup, Dan noticed the slight tremor in his hand, barely perceptible, but there. Stress, fatigue, or something else?

He was a man built of quiet compromises, his suit well-made but a season out of date, his face a patient mask that had carried him through any number of shifting allegiances in a poor but massive nation still finding its feet.

"I hope you are not attempting to renegotiate the terms of our contract, Mr. Dan," Siregar said.

Dan gave him a flat look. "When have I ever done that?"

He had the decency to look abashed. "You have not, of course. My apologies. I am used to dealing with others in your profession who do not share your sense of honour."

"In this line of work," Dan said, "I would rather fail with honour than succeed without it."

Siregar poured himself another cup of tea, his gaze fixed on the spirals of steam as if reading auguries. "You still refuse to acknowledge our profession, my friend? It is surely not just a line of work, as if we'd simply chosen careers in shipping or insurance."

Dan snorted. "You literally own a shipping company." But then he set down his teacup with deliberate care. He looked around the room again. The diplomats' wives were gone, the young couple folded ever closer and deeper into their world. "What would you call it?"

"Come now, Mr. Dan. We are professionals, are we not? We apply our skills to complex tasks, navigate difficult clients, and—more often than not—we deliver. If that doesn't qualify as a profession, I wonder what does."

Siregar said it lightly, almost as a jest. But there was a flicker in his eye that implied it was important to him that Dan agree.

Dan offered a thin, well-mannered smile. "Doctors have a profession. Lawyers, too, on good days. Maybe even soldiers. Or at least officers..." Dan gestured vaguely at the teahouse around them, or perhaps to the fallen world beyond. "A profession confers respectability. It implies wider acceptance. What we do, my friend," he paused, pushing a dumpling around the plate. "Is neither respectable nor accepted."

"And yet without people like us, the respectable world is lost," Siregar said softly. "We are a necessity, Mr. Dan.

Dan ate the dumpling, chewed thoughtfully. "Do they teach

Machiavelli in Jakarta? The promise given was a necessity of the past—"

"The word broken is a necessity of the present," Siregar grinned. "But I learned that at Eton. Not at home. In the republic, other lessons were necessary."

"And that's what we are, Siri. A necessity, I guess. But a service industry, really. We're just plumbers. Somebody's got to deal with the shit, and nobody wants to shake hands with the guy who fixes their toilet."

Siregar laughed at that as though delighted. "So you are an honourable plumber?"

"I try, man." Dan refilled both their cups. "Honour is what keeps you from becoming the shit instead of just dealing with it."

Siregar nodded, seemingly satisfied. "You have an interesting philosophy, Mr. Dan. So what is it you need, if not more money?"

"Equipment," Dan said.

"Ah," Siregar said.

"Heavy equipment," Dan added.

"I understand." The other man nodded. "I assume you have a list?"

"I do." Dan reached into his jacket, took out a piece of paper already folded twice, and passed it across. Siregar disappeared it like a conjurer.

"I shall review your requirements, Mr. Dan, but as long as they are not too outlandish, we should be able to re-equip you without delay."

"Thanks," Dan said. "I'll need it by tonight. Two of my Russian competitors are no longer bidding on the merchandise."

"Why not?"

Dan allowed a faint smile. Around them, the soft clunk of porcelain on wood continued like several ticking clocks. At the next table, a new arrival—a man in shirtsleeves, sweating profusely—murmured urgently into a satellite phone, the strain in his voice betraying the effort of managing chaos from exile.

"They're not doing much of anything after today."

"Ah, I see. You had developed them as sources?" Siregar frowned.

Sunlight slanted through the mall's glass ceiling, softened to a golden amber that made everything feel hushed and momentary, as if time had paused to listen.

Dan shook his head. "No, more like following a lead. I think it was a pretty good lead, too, but it died."

"At the Hilton?" Seregar asked.

"That's right," Dan said.

"And what sort of lead specifically were you following?"

"I'm looking for another Russian," Dan said. "A man called Skarov."

Siregar's teacup stopped halfway to his lips. His eyes darted reflexively toward the other patrons, the sweating man with the satellite phone, the young couple, as if the very name might have summoned the devil.

"Mr. Dan," he said quietly, setting his cup down with unusual care. His voice dropped to barely above a whisper. "That is not a name one utters without consequence."

"You know him then?"

Siregar's hand went back to the small scar on his right hand. "Who can truly know such a man?" The Indonesian glanced around the teahouse again, then back at Dan. "Are you certain this is the path you wish to take?"

"Yeah. I'm afraid so," Dan said.

Siregar was quiet for a long moment, his fingers drumming silently on the table's glossy surface. When he spoke again, his voice carried a weight Dan hadn't heard before.

"Then God help us both. I will do what I can. By tonight."

19

Washington DC.

HE TOOK a long drag on the cigarette, pulling it all the way down to the stub end so he could feel the heat of the burning tobacco on his lips. He crushed the butt in an ashtray already full of ash. A thin stream of smoke escaped him, momentarily obscuring the papers on the cheap plywood desk.

People are so fucking stupid, Cherry thought. They got no idea what's good for them and what's bad. They get all worked up over bullshit that means nothing. Meanwhile, they ignore the tiger that's ready to chew their ass to loose meat and bloody rags.

Leaning back from the desk, he picked up another cigarette, one of a dozen or so he'd pre-rolled so that fixing a smoke wouldn't interrupt his train of thought. Lighting it, he took a deep drag and squinted at the papers on the desktop through half-lidded eyes. "There's the fucking tiger," he muttered.

The uptimers called it "movement data and contact matrix", a lot of ten-dollar words to disguise the reality they described. He was looking at a fucking beast that was gonna devour the world. Unless the commies got there first, of course. Spitting out a stray scrap of tobacco, he doubted the commies would get away with their shit. Not looking at what they were up against.

The 'data and matrix' for Joseph McCarthy, a fucking United States Senator, for Chrissakes, it was something else. The packet they'd given Cherry got deep down into the weeds of every damn thing this asshole had done for the past six months, all of it doubtless compiled by some busy little smartass sitting at his thinking machine, probably squinting at the screen through coke-bottle glasses.

Taking another drag from his cigarette, Cherry reached for the brown bag across the other side of the desk, then paused. He'd have some professional drinking to do later on. Might be best to give himself a margin. Picking up his pencil, he leaned over the desk and his notepad. That was how it used to be done, and, he wagered, still was in most places; a detective poring over the evidence, filling a notebook with small, neat script of the sort they'd whipped into him on the job back in Honolulu. There was no pansy police academy back then, of course; if you were any good, you'd start out walking a beat, swinging a billy club. If you didn't get too much blood on your hands, too much blame for what the job made you do, you might eventually step off the beat and out of the uniform into a cheap suit. That's when the real police work began.

He laughed, a single short bark, and thought, here it was, the real police work, and he wasn't even a cop anymore. He wasn't sure what he was. A fixer, he guessed. A solver of problems. He had plenty of evidence to work with; he'd give them that.

The floorboards groaned in the hallway outside his door, followed by the wet slap of bare feet on linoleum. Some drunk heading to the can, probably. Cherry didn't look up from the papers, but his hand moved instinctively toward the .38 in the holster under his coat on the chair back. A place like this, you never knew. The footsteps passed by, and he heard the bathroom door slam shut with a bang.

Grunting softly, he turned back to the job.

The packet they'd passed him on McCarthy was thick. It had real heft when he'd taken it from O'Brien, and the promise of real possibilities when he'd first read it on the plane flying east.

That flight had been his first time on one of them private jets, his first time in an aeroplane of any sort, to be honest. It reminded him of the slow boat back from Hawaii in '42, a journey of months zigzagging across the Pacific to avoid the Japanese subs that probably weren't even there, and him in a cot most of the time full of holes from the bayonets those Japs had stuck into him on the beach, full of tubes pumping magical mystery stuff into his body, fixing him up, making him better.

Cherry didn't realise he'd lost himself in the memory. That happened sometimes. Not as much these days as it used to, but sometimes still. The past just sorta cold-cocked him, and he could never be sure where he'd end up. Right now, sitting at a desk with one short leg, in a shit motel, smoking, not drinking, and having to ponder some things, he wasn't even on that hospital ship anymore. His thoughts had started off there with all the other evacuees slowly chugging east for LA. But now, Buster Cherry was on that Australian submarine, the one from the future, the one that'd picked him up off the beach. Not the submarine, of course, but four guys off of it, wearing that weird grey-black camouflage they had, coveralls wrapped in black pads and thick armour.

They'd found him curled around his strongbox on the beach. His retirement fund, as he'd explained to Rosanna Natoli; twenty-three hundred bucks and a couple of notebooks, worth a lot more than two grand.

A siren wailed somewhere out on the street, getting closer, then fading away. The sound dragged him back to the present for a second, back to the stale air of the motel room, and the crackling of the radio next door. But the undertow of memory was strong, and it pulled him under again, back to those books, the ones that would keep him safe when he left the job. Or the ones that'd kill him, perhaps; that was always a chance too. But Cherry had bet they'd keep him safe. And in a way, he supposed that it did, not the notebooks but the other things in that strongbox. Rosanna had thrown her magical gadgets in there - the screen she carried everywhere that seemed to have all the books and newspapers in the world on it, and a pair of glasses that were too small for him to put on his big, fat head. The specs were like having one of those screens wrapped around your face, she told him. You could buy them now if you had a coupla thousand dollars and no common sense. But the ones in the catalogues and the computer stores these days were bigger and heavier than the ones in his strongbox, and he'd bet Rosanna's were a damn sight more powerful.

That's what those guys had come looking for. Not him, for sure. They'd come for all of her gadgets and stuff, the screens, the glasses, and whatever else Rosanna Natoli had put in there. Because you could find that stuff using the other stuff that they had. It was like all the gadgets and doodahs knew where all the other gadgets were at, and the uptimers were hell bent on making sure the one place they never ended up was in Tokyo or Berlin.

He had to laugh at that. All the money they'd spent rebuilding Tokyo or Berlin, because they were everyone's buds now. It wasn't much of a laugh, granted, but he still coughed it out, and the cough turned into a hacking spasm that threatened to rip up his lungs. Even that didn't stop him laughing; it made it worse.

Those weird-looking super-soldiers from the Buck Rogers future had ghosted up onto the beach where the Japs had already caught and killed Rosanna and Wally. The Japs must have thought they'd finished the job when they stuck their bayonets through him.

But you didn't pull a blade on Buster Cherry without paying a price for it, and he'd settled with those slant-eyed fucks, settled with them for killing Rosanna and that Wally kid, too. He was okay, that kid. Cherry didn't need a laser gun or flying robot either; he finished them with his service-issue .38. When the Australians finally came up on the beach, they found Detective Lou Cherry full of holes, bleeding out, still clutching his empty gun, surrounded by dead Japs, the two kids they thought he died protecting, and that box full of gadgets, and that's why they took him.

They didn't tell him that, of course. Later, on the submarine, they said they realised he was alive when they tried to get the lock-box away from him and he groaned. So then they had to take him back to the sub. But Cherry didn't believe a word of that. They had a choice; they could have left him there. He woulda left him there. But they were soft, or sentimental, or something. They thought he'd been trying to protect those two kids, but also Natoli's stuff, her flexi screen and the computer glasses and stuff. That probably bought him enough credit to get him onto that submarine into their med-bay, which was full of all sorts of magical machines that saved his life. He'd admit that, at least. He was a hard man; he didn't have to brag about it. But getting stuck with four long blades usually means curtains unless you fall ass-backwards into a miracle. Which he did; first on that beach, then five years later in LA when he ran afoul of a crooked cop named Johnson.

Another laugh, a small one, because Buster Cherry was quite the crooked cop himself.

That's how he'd ended up with $2,300 and a couple of notebooks full of secrets in that lockbox on the island. LAPD gave him a job when he'd halfway recovered, the department being shorthanded on account of the war, and in Los Angeles, Cherry picked up exactly where he'd left off in Honolulu. What he didn't pick up was a permission slip from Johnson to work his grift on Johnson's turf. Johnson was paying up to Horral, the chief back then, and so the departmental toe-cutters came for him and his pension. That was the second miracle.

He got up and walked to the window, pulling back the moth-eaten curtain with two fingers. The street below was dark, busted streetlights casting weak yellow pools on cracked asphalt, a few late-night stragglers weaving between parked cars. A woman in a too-short skirt worked the corner under the flickering neon sign of a fried chicken joint.

Even this was better than where he'd ended up in LA.

He was only two days off the job, sitting in a dive bar on Bleeker, when some guy fronted him, bought him another drink as payment for his time, gave him a business card and told him if he dried out and called the number on the card, there'd be work for him at the other end of the line. Cherry took the drink, naturally, pocketed the card, and it wasn't until a couple of days later, finally coming to in a Bunker Hill flophouse, that he found the card again, creased and grubby, with no memory of how he'd come by it. He called the number out of desperation; he was about to get the bum's rush for getting behind on his rent, and now here he was in Washington, D.C. Mostly cleaned up but back on the job.

He shook his head, shivering a little, when he realised how far down the rabbit hole he'd gone. He was back in the motel. The stinging burn of the forgotten cigarette in his fingers had brought him back to the world of real things. And as soon as he was back, the mouldy smell of this flea pit fixed him in the present. He could afford better than this, of course. He was on expenses from Davidson. He could've booked a presidential suite in the Hilton, and O'Brien wouldn't have questioned it; she'd have just paid the bill. That's how it was between them: he got the job done, and she picked up his tab.

But because he was on the job now, and that job was Senator Joseph Raymond McCarthy, he'd chosen to lie low in this Marshall Heights dive, ass deep in Spadetown east of the Anacostia River. Better here than to try to move openly west of the line, among the wealthy whites. It wasn't the senator he was worried about; that sweaty sack of shit was so cross-eyed with his own ignorance he couldn't see past the end of his pudgy little nose. But the people around him, and more important, the people behind him, they were serious fucking people. And if Cherry spent twenty-four hours snooping around their pet senator, someone would notice. He didn't know what they'd do about it; he doubted they'd go so far as to put a bullet into him, but there were plenty of ways of finishing a man that didn't involve pulling a trigger on him. So he'd fetched up out here with all of the black and white trash. It'd do for a stakeout.

He'd make his way in when he had something, when it was necessary, and standing over his notes, looking at what he'd written over the last couple of hours, Buster Cherry figured he might just have something.

He stubbed out the fag end of his last cigarette, stood up, pulled on his coat, and checked himself in the small, fly-spotted mirror. His eyes were red, he had a heavy five o'clock shadow, and his shirt was sweat-stained from going without a change. He grunted and shook his head. That wouldn't do. It wouldn't have done when he was working Homicide. Wouldn't even have done when he was on Vice. And it wouldn't do now, not for this part of the job.

He shucked the jacket off again, whipped off his tie, and grabbed a thin, threadbare towel and his shaving kit. He didn't even have a bathroom in this dump; he had to share the facilities at the end of the hall like some sort of con. But it was worth it to know he wasn't under surveillance.

The Belvedere was the kind of flea trap that sprang up all over D.C.'s outer reaches after the war, a grim, three-storey brick box wedged between a boarded-up grocery and a storefront church. Peeling green paint flaked from the lobby ceiling like dandruff; a single bulb buzzed over a counter scarred by cigarette burns. The clientele drifted in on greyhound fumes, busted tradesmen chasing day labour on the Beltway project. Army kids who'd missed their train, hookers working on hourly rates with the house, one card shark too broke to spring for the Statler. They paid by the night, sometimes by the hour, and left nothing behind.

Cherry knew them all. He'd been dealing with mopes like this his whole fucking life. He recognised the sour stench of defeat coming off of them. He knew that flat, dead look in their eyes because until they pulled him off that beach in Hawaii and fixed him up with their magical machines from the future, until Maria O'Brien had reached out and given him a second chance, he'd looked into those same eyes in the mirror every morning.

He'd gone dark out here, and he was sure nobody from the world of light and power had made him. Not yet.

But he couldn't take the stink of this place with him when he crossed over.

So he threw the towel over his shoulder and headed to the bathroom at the end of the hallway.

THE BAR WAS Cherry's sort of place. Hell, every bar was Cherry's sort of place. But this evening, he had a very particular set of requirements, and this joint met all of them. It was smoky, it was crowded, it was loud.

He grabbed himself a beer, a light beer, because he was working and he didn't know how long he was gonna have to sit here. Might turn out he had to neck six or seven drinks over the course of the night. Certainly not an ask for a man of his ample frame and long drinking history. But he wasn't an idiot. Running surveillance on people you hadn't studied in a town you didn't know, going up against a big money operation – it was all dangerous. He took his pint of pretend beer and grabbed a packet of Winchesters, glad this bar wasn't one of those joints that'd banned smoking outright.

A waitress squeezed past his table, balancing a tray of cocktails above the crowd. She was young, maybe twenty-two, and if he wasn't a paying customer, he'd have been invisible to her. He'd got to an age where he was an invisible man to most young people. Training and experience made him invisible to everyone else.

He lit up a fresh one. Cherry didn't need some pussy-ass Surgeon General telling him smoking was bad for him. He could feel it every time he hawked up a loogie of black phlegm or coughed his guts out over the side of the bed in the morning. Coughed 'em up loud enough to scare the fuckin' cat away.

But it wasn't the goddamn Surgeon General's business how Cherry lived his life, or how quickly he was motoring towards the end of it. The shit that'd happened to him, he wasn't just on borrowed time. Every day he had in the world felt like it was stolen. And there were days he couldn't help feeling the payback was gonna be heavy.

The jukebox switched tracks, going from something that sounded like 1940s swing, though Cherry knew it was actually from about sixty years in the future because he liked that fucking song, to some jazz piece that could have been from anywhere, anytime. Something about a new world and a new dawn. A few couples near the small dance floor started moving to the new beat, their movements looser, more aggressive than what their parents would have recognised as dancing.

He sat himself at a corner table, just vacated by a couple who were obviously work colleagues and even more obviously about to go and bump uglies together. The way their hands were crawling all over each other like pink spiders, they wouldn't be coming back. He didn't care that the table hadn't been cleaned, which was good because nobody came to sweep away the bar nuts or police up the martini glasses. Six of them, if you could believe it. Three with bright pink lipstick around the rim. So that broad had been holding her own, matched her boss or her colleague or whatever the fuck he was, drink for drink. What a world. Cherry had dropped himself into the chair where the guy had been sitting, and he looked to anybody who cared to look, like a working man glad to get off his dogs at the end of a long day.

From this vantage point, Buster Cherry took in the room. It was the kind of place that had ideas about how much better it was than his normal run of gin joint, but the scent of stale tobacco and cheap perfume clung just as hard to the velvet banquettes at the end of the night. The music occasionally skipped forward a decade or seven, and a holographic bartender shimmered in the mirror behind the main counter, mixing the same drink over and over again, while a flesh-and-blood barkeep, a man with a face like a prospector's beard, wiped down the counter between orders.

A man in an expensive suit stumbled past Cherry's table, drink in hand, laughing too loud at something his companion had said. The laughter had that forced edge that came after the fourth or fifth cocktail when everything needed to be hilarious because the alternative was admitting everything was shit.

Seven decades of drinking developments, Cherry mused, all crashing in on top of one another, yet somehow, it worked. He liked it.

The main thing he appreciated, however, was the sight line from this corner along the bar to the table at the other end, where he could see Roy Cohn leaning over a martini to give some poor bastard the full vulture treatment. Cohn looked like he was tearing strips of meat off the guy's carcass while he sat there. The other man was a mystery, but he looked like a pol to Cherry. His suit was well cut, and it needed to be. He was a big bowl of pudding, and his tailor had done a job of work concealing it all. His thinning hair was slicked back, but his eyes, even from this distance, held a desperate quality. Cohn, on the other hand, had the lazy confidence of a predator with an easy kill. Cherry could tell he was lacing into the other man, who sat there and took it like a chump.

Cherry studied the setup with professional interest. Cohn was the hard target - sharp and connected. O'Brien had warned him the guy had half the Justice Department on speed dial. But the fat palooka?

He was soft. Sweating through his expensive suit, taking whatever Cohn was dishing up to him without fighting back. He was exactly what Cherry had come here looking for. The movement data put Roy Cohn in the bar most nights of the week. The contact matrix would have that loser's name in it somewhere.

Cohn was a wolf. But the other man was a fat, soft sheep.

Cherry drank two beers and ate a packet of pretzels while he observed them over the top of the newspaper he was pretending to read. The crowd ebbed and flowed around him, government workers blowing off steam after another day of managing the war, business shills working their contacts over expensive drinks, even the occasional military uniform adding a splash of colour to the sea of dark pinstripes.

He drank enough beer that it caught up with him, not making him lightheaded or anything, but forcing him to take a walk to the latrine. Cherry waited until Cohn ordered another drink, then he draped his coat over the back of his seat, being careful to take everything of value out of the pockets first. This wasn't the sort of bar where sneak thieves and pickpockets worked the room, but there was no point asking to get ripped off.

A few minutes later, he was back, and for a wonder, they'd cleaned up the mess. The dead martinis were gone. His paper was neatly folded. His beer was still there. The ashtray had been emptied, but nobody had taken his place. Yeah, he was starting to like this bar even more.

He resumed his seat and his observation of Joseph McCarthy's maximum fixer. From Cherry's observation, Cohn was a man very much aware of his dark legend, and seemingly happy to lean into it. There were guys – McCarthy was one of them – who'd been discomforted by the arrival of the uptimers because they brought with them all sorts of tales of villainy and disgrace from the future. But Cohn was not one of those guys. Cherry didn't think much would ever discomfort him.

The waitress came by again, this time carrying empty glasses back to the bar. She moved through the crowd, never quite letting the reaching hands make contact, always a step ahead of the fat fingers.

Cherry would pay McCarthy the compliment of acknowledging

he'd done okay recovering from the knock to his reputation. He'd also done well, Cherry thought, as he lit a new cigarette off the end of the previous one, recovering from his reported death in the South Pacific.

Cherry had his theories about that; who'd done it, and who bene-fited. The newspaper said they'd just taken the story off a wire service. The wire service had no record of running with it in the first place. After the Transition, there'd been at least a dozen reports gone out on the wires about guys who would have been something in the 50s and 60s who weren't going to be anything now because they walked into a bullet they'd somehow dodged the first time around. Sometimes the stories were real. Sometimes, a reporter just got the names mixed up.

A burst of laughter from a nearby table drew his attention briefly. Three young men in off-the-rack suits, congressional staffers by the look of them, were sharing some joke that probably wasn't half as funny as they thought it was. One of them kept glancing toward Cohn's table, then looking away quickly. Cherry sighed inwardly. He might have to move soon.

He scanned the crowd around Cohn and his mark. There was some space at the bar up there. He went back to his paper, glancing up every few paragraphs to make sure Cohn was still there.

McCarthy had insisted it was his enemies trying to mess with him, planting that story of his demise in the press. But that was bull-shit. Joe McCarthy, in 1943 and 1944, didn't have any sort of enemies that were special to him. He shared the same enemies as everyone else. In his case, a million or so Japs who were trying to kill him - and everyone else in the Pacific theatre.

When McCarthy ran for office, he blamed socialists and fellow travellers for the story. Said it resolved him that he had a job to do, protecting America from them. He'd even hinted, when Eisenhower chose Kolhammer to run with him, that the soon-to-be vice president might've had something to do with it. That was a two-day sensation in the Washington press. But again, Cherry thought it was all bullshit. He had some personal experience of the mischief those guys got up to—because they'd paid him to do plenty of it.

He'd once helped Slim Jim in a knife fight with Ford and GM, who wanted the city government to build freeways all over LA. Davidson, meanwhile, wanted permits for some of the same ground for his electric subways.

Cherry made sure a few key land deeds went missing. He also arranged for the crash reports on Ford's prototype self-driving electric bus - the one they claimed would turn freeways into mass transit - to drop onto the front page of the *LA Times*. At least one of those reports was bullshit, but what'd they say about a lie? It could be halfway round the fucking world before the truth got out of bed and put its pants on.

So yeah, he was plenty familiar with how dirty the uptimers could play the game. They could be subtle. They could be brutal. But what they didn't do was fuck around and waste time. And planting a story like that about a nobody like McCarthy, in some podunk newspaper, that was a waste of time for them.

The bar's atmosphere grew thicker as more people crowded in for the mid-evening rush. Smoke hung in blue layers near the ceiling, and the conversation volume rose to compensate for the growing noise. Cherry had to lean forward slightly to keep Cohn's table in clear view through the shifting crowd. A woman in a tight red dress brushed past his table, her perfume cutting through the tobacco smoke for just a moment before being swallowed up again by the bar's ambient smell of alcohol and sweat.

He caught sight of Cohn again and sat back.

If they'd wanted to cut the legs out from under McCarthy before he got moving, they'd have sent someone like Cherry to do it. And he wouldn't have started with a sophomore prank like that. No, the whole thing reeked of people who thought they were smart because they'd never had anyone tell them just how fucking dumb they were.

A sudden surge of patrons heading for the exit thickened the crowd, and Cherry lost sight of Cohn again. He considered giving up his table, relocating, but then the crowd parted, and Cohn stood up, but the other man remained seated at the table.

Roy Cohn put on his hat, draped a suit coat over his arm, and, carrying a briefcase, he walked away. The fat guy sat there looking like a man who'd just been fed a shit sandwich and told it tasted like fried chicken. And not only that, he'd been told he's gotta go out and sell those shitty fried chicken sandwiches to his family and friends. Cherry folded up his newspaper, butted out his cigarette, and stood up. The chair scraped against the floor as he pushed it back, the sound lost in the bar's ambient roar.

Time to close whatever this deal was gonna turn out to be.

20

North Atlantic.

THE VEHICLE DECK occupied the lowest reaches of the ship, vast and echoing like some grim iron cathedral. Above, the ship's veins and arteries—pipes, conduits, bundles of wire—ran between towering steel beams that disappeared into shadow, far beyond the reach of the floodlights. Rows of armoured vehicles stood chained to the deck, hulking and mute. The chilled atmosphere was heavy with the bitter edge of gun oil and the dry metallic sting of air passed too many times through ducts and filters. And through it all, the sea announced itself. With every roll of the hull, tools clinked and whispered. With each climb atop some monstrous wall of water and plunge into the valley beyond, the hull rang like a giant tuneless bell. It was the voice of the deep, the cold, endless reminder of the world beneath them.

Bravo Company had endured seven days aboard the *Kandahar*. Seven long, slow grey days that might have been weeks. The sea was indifferent, rolling under them in endless swells, and the convoy stretched so far that ships dissolved into the haze over the planet's curve. Jack neither knew nor cared where they were bound. Better not to count the days, better not to imagine the end. He no longer troubled himself with thoughts of where they might make land, nor how many days remained in this ironbound purgatory.

All that stood between them and the depths was another day's grace, another lucky pass beyond the prowling reach of the Russian hunters beneath the waves. Evenings were the worst. The smoking lamp extinguished, the hatches sealed. No cigarette to quiet the nerves, no sky to gaze upon and pretend there was somewhere else to be. Below decks, the air grew dense with human funk, two thousand men confined to steel and routine, each one transmitting his unease to the next like a quiet contagion.

It was the absence of a cigarette that gnawed at him most. The rationale, of course, was sound. Jack, a man not wholly ignorant of a transport ship's inner workings, knew well enough the hazards of enclosed compartments, flammable residues, and air systems that might turn a careless ember into mass immolation. He accepted all that. Still, the craving lived in the bones, winding tight into the nerves, making his hands itch and his thoughts wander. Understanding the rules did nothing to ease their tyranny.

Of an evening, then, Jack saw to it that his fireteam gathered on the vehicle deck for training, less for their benefit than his own. It passed the time, and more importantly, it kept the mind from turning inwards where shadows pooled. Routine was for now the only defence against the encroaching pressure of the deep, the thought of all that black water pushing in from every direction. And training kept the men sharp. It maintained discipline, and beneath that, for Jack, it held a fragile line against the slow pull of despair, a way to hold back the dark with the simple rhythm of orders given and obeyed.

That night's session was devoted to the SINCGARS manpack, another of the future's gifts. No larger than a haversack and no heavier than his toolbox in the garage at home, yet it summoned voices across impossible distances and guarded frequencies as a sentry guards a palace gate. A mariner of Nelson's age would have called it sorcery. The *Kandahar*, too, was a miracle. One of the original ships of the Transition. The aircraft carrier that wasn't. Slab-sided, towering, utterly unlike the rust-streaked transports he'd known in the last war. And yet it groaned in familiar ways, carried the same smells, and its occupants suffered the same indignities, their coffee sloshing everywhere in the high Atlantic swells that forced a man to sit down when taking a piss. The ship was beautiful in the way giant dams are beautiful, he conceded: powerful, indifferent and terrifying. But the little radio appealed to him. It was a soldier's tool. The ship would carry them across the ocean to the war. The radio might save him when he got there.

Jack regarded it with wary curiosity. This wasn't just a tool but a glimpse into a world he should never have known. The thing was absurdly compact. Jack stared at the interface, its bewildering array of pushbuttons, the electrical readouts, and all the cryptic markings that spoke of functions not merely unknown in 1942, but quite unimagined. It looked less like military equipment than something lifted from a Buck Rogers movie.

Jack had assigned Private Waylon Brown to the role of instructor, a bold move in some eyes. Brown was a radioman, but he was also a sharecropper's boy, and there were plenty of fellows in the 37th who'd swear black and blue, but mostly black, that he'd never be any more than that. But Brown belonged to Jack's platoon, and Jack had made it his business these last weeks to learn everything he could about his men. You never knew what might come in useful.

Brown had told him of playing around on a sound engineer's board at the *Moulin Rouge* in Vegas. He was just a janitor there, but they let him into the booth out of hours, and the sound guys had been training him up on the equipment. Brown had revealed a technical fluency, explaining the mystery of comms gear that caught most everyone except Jack by surprise. You never knew who or what might come in useful.

"Alrighty, gentlemen," Brown said, his Southern lilt lending unexpected charm to the technical instruction. "Who remembers what the Z-FH switch actually does?"

His squadmates squinted at the control panel. "I dunno," Corporal Leroy Parmenter confessed. He was the only one of them man enough to fess up.

"Remember," Brown said, "that Z always means some kind of zero. What do y'all think FH means?"

Jack waited until it became apparent that nobody knew. "Frequency hop," he said.

"Roger that, Sergeant." Brown's smile was even wider than that first time he'd favoured Jack with it, in the back of a deuce-and-a-half headed to Ravenna arsenal. "You fellas all know what OFF means, but what else does that switch do?"

Parmenter brightened slightly, remembering last night's session. "It clears the stuff stored on the radio after five seconds, right?"

"Yeah, that's why you always switch the radio to STBY, or standby." Brown pointed to the antenna connection with the precision of someone who'd learned through experience rather than classroom instruction. "And how do y'all fuck up the antenna?"

Jack appreciated Brown's way of dealing directly with practicalities. In his experience, equipment failure on the battlefield seldom traced back to faulty kit. It usually began in the hands of the man using the gear. Same rule at the factory, too. "By carrying the radio by the antenna," Jack said. "Or if the long antenna comes in contact with a wire or something."

"You best believe it, Sergeant."

The class suddenly broke off as the sound reached them, a giant resonant boom. It was not the constant hammering of engines, nor the slap of a heavy sea against the plating. It was deeper, rounder somehow, and far more ominous. Jack felt it in his chest, a blunt force transmitted straight through water and rivet. The deck fell silent, and heads turned in unison, the drill forgotten instantly as something older than training took hold. Jack felt the quickening of his pulse, the bracing surge of adrenaline, every nerve awake and singing, every breath labouring as time stretched with the strange elasticity that often comes with mortal danger.

"Brown, might be time to stow that radio," he said as the ship changed course, heaving over to port. The entire vehicle deck groaned in protest, twenty-ton LAVs testing their chains as the deck tilted beneath them.

"Yes, Sergeant," the kid responded, jumping up and weaving across the deck to secure the SINCGARS in its designated storage compartment on the LAV's exterior rack.

The tannoy spoke with that familiar metallic authority, cutting through the noise of the compartment. A short burst of static, and then, "Captain speaking. All hands to action stations. I repeat, all hands to action stations. Embarked troops to standby positions."

Action stations. The call confirmed what Jack had feared since the boom first rolled through the hull. The convoy was under attack, and now their lives depended on sailors they didn't know, fighting with weapons as new to them as Brown's mysterious radio.

Getting into a standby position was one of several emergency protocols drilled into them during their first days aboard. Now, seated shoulder to shoulder along the bulkheads of the vehicle deck, they formed a neat row, each man's placement permitting swift movement to the upper stations should the order to abandon ship be given. A familiar unease settled in Jack's belly, no less potent for being so well known. Though the chilled air in the compartment was cool, sweat gathered under his arms, and his thoughts grew restless. Then came the craving for nicotine. Battle, he recalled now, did not just breed new discomforts but summoned back all the old ones.

First Sergeant Bennett and a Chief Petty Officer moved calmly through the ranks, checking each man's life vest. The bright yellow flotation devices were compulsory for all embarked troops, part of the uniform of the day, but there was always someone who thought the rules didn't apply to them. Jack slipped his off whenever he took a shit, the only private moment he had on board. He loathed the fucking thing. It was cumbersome, it chafed his neck and made sleep a trial, but more than that, it was a perpetual reminder of the vast and hungry sea beneath them.

He watched Parmenter with increasing concern as they sat on the deck and braced against the bulkhead and the ship's increasing violent, shifting passage. The man's complexion had gone the colour of old cheese, and his fingers worked the vest's glow-in-the-dark inflation handle with a nervous energy that hinted at a mind nearing the edge. A single bead of sweat traced a slow path down his cheek.

"Don't even think about pulling that fucking thing," Jack said quietly. "Remember the drill, the vest doesn't get a blow job until you're up on deck."

Parmenter jerked his hand away from the inflation tab, as if suddenly aware of what he was doing, and folded both hands into his lap. There, they twisted together with the same nervous energy, redirected but unresolved. Jack let his eyes move along the line. Each man in his team responded to the moment in his own fashion. Brown had closed his eyes and appeared to be speaking under his breath. His lips moved with a slow, deliberate rhythm suggesting prayer. Jack was not a believer anymore, but he didn't fault the kid. When the soul is strained past bearing, you go with whatever works for you. Hell, if it worked for him, he'd be on his fucking knees, not his ass, right now.

To steady himself, Jack fixed his gaze on the wheel of the LAV just ahead. Twelve large bolts held the hub in place, flanked by a scatter of smaller fasteners. When he reached the end, he began again. The numbers built a rampart against insurgent chaos, anchoring his thoughts to something he could control. He counted them one by one, examining each with care, then began again at the start, letting the process of counting and observing fill the roaring void in his head. To the counting he added breathing; long, deliberate breaths drawn in through the nose, then released in a slow, measured stream through the mouth. The rhythm he soon matched to the rise and fall of the ship, another exercise to keep body and mind in working order. A measured cadence to tamp down the panic, and keep oxygen flowing to the parts of the brain where reason still held. He'd learned all these things the hard way, but he *had* learned them.

Another boom sounded through the ship's hull, closer than the first. Jack lost track of his bolt count but immediately resumed from the beginning. Parmenter flinched visibly, while Brown's murmuring stopped briefly before resuming at slightly higher volume.

One of the men from Second Platoon, which had been revisiting first aid drills on the far side of the deck, suddenly broke into a sprint. His eyes were wide, his breath ragged, and he was heading for the stairs at a dead run.

"LET ME THE HELL OUT OF HERE! LET ME OUT!"

A sailor in his path reacted quickly, tripping him mid-stride and driving him to the deck. The runaway struggled to get up, but more hands arrived to subdue him and to drag him away. The scene passed quickly but left a noticeable stillness in its wake. Everyone had thought about running. He'd just been the first to try.

Jack resumed counting bolts on the LAV wheel.

A crewman jogged through the compartment, and someone called out, "Hey, what's going on?"

The man's response was brief. "Fucking commies, asshole, what d'you think?"

Before anyone could ask follow-up questions, he disappeared down to the lower decks.

Brown's murmur grew in volume until the words took shape: the Lord's Prayer, spoken in an unsteady rhythm that testified less to piety than need. The blast that interrupted him struck with such force that even the huge and heavily laden *Kandahar* pitched over in response. Jack banged his head against a steel plate. Nobody needed to ask what had happened. A vessel had been lost nearby.

Discipline faltered. Cries rose from the ranks, a chorus of fear twisted with fury at their confinement below the waterline. The NCOs responded instantly, Jack among them, roaring.

"SHUT THE FUCK UP! AND SIT THE FUCK DOWN!"

The language was coarse, the tone brutal, but authority had to speak louder than fear. You didn't reason with panic. You crushed it. And, Jack would admit to himself, roaring like a demon was something of a comfort to him, too. Way more so than counting fucking wheel lugs.

Someone retched. A single heave, wet and guttural, then another, and another, as the chain reaction took hold. It wasn't weakness. It was the body's rebellion against fear. The stench spread fast. Sour bile with the noxious tang of half-digested rations, sweat-soaked fatigues and the ever-present fuel vapours. In the steel confines of the compartment, every foul note was concentrated tenfold, pressing hard upon the spirit.

Brown began to rise, the movement abrupt and ungoverned, suggesting flight. Jack reached out and clamped a hand around his arm, forcing him back down, holding his gaze and digging his thumb into a nerve bundle until the younger man's eyes lowered in submission.

"The Lord is your fuckin' shepherd, Private. Act like it."

Brown resisted for a breath, then broke eye contact and sagged into place, cowed but still trembling.

Then his voice came, cracked and low. "The Lord is my shepherd, Sergeant."

Jack didn't ease off. "Again, like you believe it."

"The Lord is my shepherd," Brown repeated, his voice steadier, though his hands still trembled in his lap. The words carried something more this time, like belief or at least the memory of it.

Close enough, Jack thought.

"Look at me, Private," he said. "All of you. Eyes on me. What does the SC position on the Mode switch mean? Not you, Brown. Private Taylor? Martinez?"

Taylor blinked, mouth working silently before a dry stammer emerged. "W-what?" He wasn't hearing. Not really. Jack repeated the question, same tone, same cadence, nothing changed. Repetition was the point. Routine was the life vest.

When he got no answer, he turned to Leroy.

"Corporal Parmenter, take a moment and think it through. What does the SC position mean?"

The words worked their way through the fog. Parmenter blinked once, then again, and something clicked. "Uh... single channel, Sarge."

It wasn't crisp or confident, but Brown stopped praying and huffed a little laugh.

"That's right, corporal. Does anyone remember what the Z-FH switch does?"

"Frequency hopping and some shit about zero," Martinez replied.

"Zero shit detected, Martinez," Jack said as the *Kandahar* heaved over and the engine whine grew even louder. He thought he could hear choppers lifting off, although they were a long way down from the flight deck. "Private Brown. You were saying before we were so rudely fucking interrupted?"

"Who knows how to set the Function Control if you're being jammed?" Brown asked.

The training resumed, almost with a gasp of relief, like breath returning after a long-held choke. One by one, soldiers up and down the bay engaged, responding to questions and posing their own. They asked questions about radios, procedures, maintenance drills, anything that required coherent thought. Fear hadn't left the room, but it had been given less space.

More explosions followed, distant and indistinct, punctuating their resumed training with reminders of the engagement still raging beyond sight. But none carried the weight of the earlier detonation that had rolled through the ship like a judgment.

The ship's loudspeaker activated after what seemed like hours but was probably less than thirty minutes.

"Attention all personnel. This is the First Officer. Secure from general quarters."

Movement resumed with a collective groan, and the men unfolded themselves like rusted joints, rising slowly and with some difficulty, stiff from prolonged stillness. Jack felt the sting of circulation returning, sharp pins and needles in his thighs and buttocks where they'd pressed against the cold steel.

Beside him, Brown let out a nervous laugh. "That sho' was something, huh, Sergeant?"

"It was, Private. Good job. I'll make sure Captain Pearce hears about it."

Brown froze, eyes wide, uncertain whether he was being mocked or recognised. Then disbelief faded, and something flickered in its place, something obviously unfamiliar to the kid. Jack had seen it plenty of times before, though. The whipped dog who gets a pat from a stranger. Jack reached instinctively for his cigarettes, caught himself, and let the hand drop. Regulations still held, no matter how much his nerves screamed for nicotine.

"Don't get cocky, Private," he muttered. "The Army's idea of a reward for a good job is more shit work. And we got plenty of ocean left and plenty of work ahead."

21

Washington DC.

CHERRY LEANED AGAINST THE BAR, just a few short paces from the man Roy Cohn had been talking to. It hadn't looked like a happy meeting. The guy's expression was that of a man who'd recently endured a severe proctological examination—without lube or fresh gloves. For a long time, he simply stared at the tabletop, losing himself in a small puddle of beer.

Buster wondered about that. That puddle was big enough to suggest the man's hands had been shaking when he tried to take a drink. A heavy stillness had settled over him now, of a kind that comes over a body dropped in a back alley, never to get up again.

Around them, the bar was alive with a heaving late-night crowd: the clink of glasses, the low roar of conversation as everyone tried to talk over each other, the occasional burst of laughter. Waiters weaved between tables, balancing trays of cocktails and finger food. Buster played his part, just another face in the all-white crowd as he surveyed his mark.

He didn't know who this guy was yet, but he knew what he was; a solid lead. Cohn hadn't just been interested in him; the little ratfuck had been *invested*. Buster had spent the better part of an hour watching Cohn slowly tear strips of flesh from the poor bastard. It was like he was eating the guy alive, but slowly. Must have been good eatin', too. The complimentary peanuts still sat untouched on the table, in the beer puddle.

As Buster watched, the man seemed to return to himself, blinking and shaking his head as if waking in a room he didn't recognise. He stood awkwardly, grabbed his briefcase on the second attempt, his hands still trembling, and abandoned the table for a stumbling rush to the exit.

Buster smiled. He hadn't seen Cohn pick up the tab, and this guy had just done a runner. Not on purpose, he'd wager. He clearly had other things on his mind. Sure enough, a barkeep frowned at the departing man as he headed for the door.

Buster moved quickly, striding along the bar. "Hey," he said to the barkeep, jerking at thumb at the runner. "I need to fix the tab for my boss and Mr Cohn."

The bartender's features relaxed. He'd be used to staffers cleaning up after their delinquent bosses. "Of course," he said, ringing up the till.

Buster slid a five across the bar. "Keep that for yourself, pal."

"Thank you, sir."

He tried his luck.

"And if I could get a receipt made out to our office, that'd be good, too. Expenses, you know."

"Of course." The bartender rang up the sale and clipped the receipt to a handwritten invoice made out to the good offices of the honourable Dippy Schultz, Ohio 7. He even wrote "constituent meeting" on the receipt.

"Mighty white of you, pal. Thanks," Buster said, amused at the thought of O'Brien signing off on this one. He paid with Slim Jim's shiny black Amex, folded the receipt into his pocket, and hurried out of the bar after his 'boss'.

He needn't have rushed. Dippy Schultz stood on the pavement outside, looking up and down K Street as though he was lost. But Buster knew that he wasn't lost; he was trying to make a decision.

He fetched out his packet of Winchesters and joined a couple of smokers by the bus stop. Across the street, four cabs waited at a rank. Three drivers smoked on the pavement; one sat in his car, reading the paper. Smoking indoors hadn't been banned in Washington yet, but it was coming in a month, according to the papers. Maybe these guys were getting in practice for their exile, or maybe they just liked the fresh air so they could taste the smoke. When Buster wanted to slow down and enjoy a cigarette, that's what he did, found himself some clean air so he could appreciate all the poison he was pulling down past his teeth.

On his third drag of the Winchester, he watched Schultz make a decision.

Dippy's choice sent him heading off along K Street, striding purposefully now that he'd settled on a course of action.

Buster fell in behind, keeping a careful distance. It was late mid-evening in Washington, hot, but the city was busy because of the war. People worked around the clock, so the streets were crowded and well-lit, the air thick with the hum of traffic and bright with the glow of neon in this part of town. Buster moved through the throng, just another bar hopper, tailing Schultz as he cut through the city.

At Wentworth, Schultz took a left, leaving the main drag for a quieter side street. The noise faded, replaced by the hush of a residential enclave, big old oaks and elms arching over the road, their branches forming a dark tunnel of deep green. Here, Buster had to be more careful. Fewer people and fewer places to hide, but the trees offered some cover. He hung back, letting Schultz get ahead, watching as he turned left, then right, then left again.

The fat man was almost jogging now. Buster, who fancied he could hear Schultz wheezing from fifty yards back, put on a short burst of speed, reaching the corner just in time to see his quarry pull up in front of a three-storey brownstone. Schultz paused, and Buster faded behind the trunk of an old elm, certain the guy was about to check for a tail.

He waited a few seconds, then peered out again. Dippy Schultz was walking towards him.

Damn.

Buster started to pull back, remembering the difficulty of following a man from in front, even a man who wasn't trained to look for it, when Schultz turned on a dime and walked back to the brownstone. He took three steps, stopped, turned, stopped and turned again, then finally fetched up outside the same address.

Buster grinned like a shark coming up on a school of sardines.

He was sure now. Dippy Schultz was up to no good. He wasn't visiting a friend or a colleague; he was probably cranking up the courage to knock on the door of a cat house. And in this street, it would be a pretty swanky cat house too, the sort of place where you were expected to make conversation with the whores before putting it to them for fifty bucks an hour.

Schultz bounced on the balls of his feet, nervous energy radiating off him in waves. Buster had a bet with himself about how long it would take Schultz to build up the courage to go in, but he lost the bet. Schultz suddenly pushed through the gate and motored up the front path. The brass knocker hit the door with a rapid series of bangs loud enough to make Buster jump where he hid.

The door opened, spilling a warm wedge of soft, golden light onto the street. The light seemed to have a narcotic effect on Schultz, almost levitating him off the ground and pulling him inside. The door closed behind him.

Buster relaxed, lit another cigarette, and checked his watch: 10:07 pm.

He waited twenty minutes, long enough for even the classiest whorehouse to move a guy on to the business end of the transaction. He stubbed out his cigarette, flicked it into the gutter, and strolled down the street.

He walked up the pathway and knocked at the door. Gentle compared to Dippy's excited hammering. When it opened, he got a helluva surprise, so much so that it took him a second to realise he was surprised.

The woman who answered was tall and handsome. Some women get described that way because their features are striking, and they carry a certain authority. It's less about prettiness, more about presence. Buster had known some strikingly handsome women. O'Brien was one of them. But she was all woman, too. Plenty of va-va in her vavoom, he'd bet.

In this case, though, once his surprise settled, Buster realised this dame was handsome because she was a fuckin' dude. The voice was soft and lilting, and coulda passed for the real thing in a loud enough cocktail bar if you were a couple of drinks into the wind. Her silver-blonde hair was elegantly coiffed, and the make-up mighta been done by Marilyn Monroe's favourite fag, it was so deftly applied. But that big, chunky Adam's apple bobbing up and down in 'her' throat gave it away.

Dippy Schultz was a friend of fuckin' Dorothy.

"Please do come in," the 'madam' said.

"Thanks," Cherry nodded, still a bit off kilter as he followed her inside.

The reception lounge was nothing like he'd expected. This fairy castle was nothing like the top-shelf bordellos he'd tried to shake down for protection money back in LA, back before Clemmence Horral's toecutters came for him. It looked more like a high-end cocktail bar than the place he'd just left. Three "women" lounged on velvet chairs, hostesses, not just transvestites, and Buster had to admit, for a bunch of dolls with dicks, they made good-looking women.

The madam introduced him to each by name. Varna, Desiree and Leneen.

"Ladies, charmed, I'm sure," Buster said. "But ah, I think I got the wrong address."

"Are you sure you're sure?" Desiree asked, unwrapping a slow smile for him.

"Yeah, I know what I was looking for," he said. To himself, he thought, and I found it. But aloud, he went on, "But this ain't it. Sorry, ladies. No offence. Somebody gave me a bum steer. I'll show myself out."

He retreated the way he'd come and was met at the front door by the madam.

"I'm sorry, sir, was something not to your liking?"

He smiled, winningly, he hoped. "I was looking for something a little more... conventional. I don't suppose you'd know where I could find that?"

She nodded, as though she suddenly understood. "Ah, yes. You have come to the wrong address." She fetched a business card from behind the desk and pressed it into his hand. Her nails were long, her hands surprisingly soft, and for a second, Buster wondered if, had he been a different man... Nah. No point even asking. There's what was and what wasn't, and this wasn't for him.

"Our sister establishment, so to speak," the handsome woman said.

"Thanks, darlin'," he said, "No hard feelings."

"No hard anything," she smirked, and he left.

He spent an hour and a half waiting under the tree at the end of the street. Two men came past in that time, both heading for the cat house. Another turned around when he saw Buster smoking under the tree. He recognised the first two when they came out an hour or so later. But a third customer who exited was new to him. None of them was the representative from Ohio 7.

Schultz emerged shortly before midnight, looking a hell of a lot more relaxed than he had going in. He stepped carefully onto the street, checking—badly—that he hadn't been followed, and started walking towards Buster. Not with a spring in his step—someone had fucked all the spring out of him—but with none of the anxious energy Buster had seen outside the cocktail bar. It was no trouble following him now. Dippy Schultz was in his happy place, or maybe just walking home from it, but wherever he was, he wasn't thinking the kind of dark thoughts that would have him looking over his shoulder.

Buster followed him back to town, keeping his distance. Schultz returned to the Mayflower Hotel, and Buster closed the gap, entering just a few steps behind.

Schultz stopped at the front desk and picked up a couple of messages. Buster walked on past, heading for the elevators. He waited until Schultz was almost on him, then pressed the button to go up. He yawned, letting his shoulders slump, just a guy who'd worked late, looking forward to hitting the sack. He stepped into the elevator in front of Schultz, walked to the back of the car, and "remembered" he'd forgotten to punch in his floor number after Schultz hit the button for the fourth floor.

"Excuse me," Buster said, stepping around him and pressing five. He retreated to his corner, saying nothing else and looking at his shoes. That was the thing about elevators: They were great for tailing mopes because everyone was awkward about sharing the space, and nobody wanted to look at anyone else.

The car stopped with a chime. The door slid open, and Schultz stepped out, heading right. Buster pressed the button to keep the doors open and waited. One, two, three. He heard a key in a door, then stepped out. Schultz's room was two doors down the hallway to the right. He unlocked the door, turned the handle, and Buster charged.

Ten years ago, he couldn't have done it. A Mexican pimp in a zoot suit had put a .38 slug into his thigh. Buster had paid him off with a headshot, but the damage was done. His leg healed up enough to go back to work, but he was crippled by shooting pains all down his side if he had to run for more than a few yards. After signing on with Davidson, though, and getting some treatment from the company doctors, he was good these days for a hundred-yard dash.

He fairly sprinted the short distance down the hallway, sandbagging Schultz and forcing him through the door, knocking the man flat on his face inside the room. Buster closed the door behind him and slid the useless little chain across.

"Hey, Dippy," Buster smiled. "Dorothy says hello."

22

Washington, DC.

KOLHAMMER DIDN'T GET out of the Situation Room until mid-afternoon. The morning had been an executive hellscape, the usual cascade of unsolvable problems delivered to the one man who couldn't pass them on. The room itself, deep in the bowels of the White House, was a sterile theatre of crisis, its walls lined with screens displaying satellite feeds, encrypted communications, and battlefield maps flickering with the symbols of friendly and enemy forces. The air hummed with electronics and tension. Generals, admirals, spooks and cabinet secretaries sat around the main table, their faces blotchy with fatigue and lit by the cold glow of monitors and LEDs. Kolhammer had eaten a couple of sandwiches on the go, barely tasting the bread and meat as he absorbed data and issued commands that would determine whether thousands of soldiers lived or died.

At three o'clock, his chief of staff, Lia Pao, appeared at his elbow like a guardian angel with a clipboard. The senators from the National Security Committee were waiting upstairs.

"Do you need me along for this, Mr President?" Admiral Tisevich asked, his gaze not leaving the main screen where a crisis they had been wrestling with since dawn was still unfolding. Red markers blinked ominously along the German front, gathering around the town of Arnsberg.

"No, Paul," Kolhammer said, pushing back from the conference table. "I want you to stay here. Keep running this." He gestured toward the wall of screens. "I've got some politics to do."

"Understood," the Chairman replied, already turning back to the displays where the real war was being fought.

Kolhammer and Pao walked the corridors from the subterranean world of the Situation Room back upstairs toward the Oval Office. The transition was always jarring, like breaching the surface from deep water into blazing sunlight. They moved from the windowless, functional spaces of the national security machine, up stairwells and along hallways humming with a different kind of energy. The air grew warmer, less sterile. Aides scurried past with binders, White House Press Corps journalists milled around their designated feeding areas, and the faint, muffled sounds of the outside world began to seep in through the building's bones. It was a journey, and Kolhammer felt himself changing with it, sloughing off the features of a tired man who'd been making life-and-death decisions since before dawn.

The senators were waiting for them in the anteroom: Saltonstall, Jackson, Symington, and Joe McCarthy, looking like a cartoon hyena who'd just finished picking chicken pieces out from between his back teeth. He lounged in one of the antique chairs as if he owned the place, sweating a little in his heavy coat despite the air conditioning.

"Mr President."

"Mr President."

They all spoke, one after another, rising to their feet with varying degrees of deference.

"Gentlemen. Senators," Kolhammer replied with a nod. "If you'd follow me."

They trailed him into the Oval Office, McCarthy making a great show of inspecting the furniture as he entered, his eyes lingering on the presidential seal woven into the carpet, the flags flanking the

Resolute Desk. The AC hummed quietly, fighting against the afternoon heat that pressed against the bulletproof windows.

"Hell of a slick job convincing the Ruskies you were here last night, Mr President," McCarthy said with a shiteating grin that could have emptied a sewage farm.

"Even slicker job convincing the press you were too, Joe," Kolhammer remarked dryly.

That took the edge off McCarthy's grin and caused a few of the other senators to chuckle to themselves. Senator Saltonstall coughed to cover what might have been a laugh.

Kolhammer didn't retreat behind his desk. Instead, he turned the chair Lia Pao had been sitting in that morning and faced the four men directly. The late afternoon light poured through the windows, casting long shadows across the office and highlighting the dark shadows under McCarthy's eyes.

"I called you all here today because I appreciate the work you've been doing for the country," Kolhammer began, bullshitting them as smoothly as any careerist politician. "And I thought it would help your work to bring you up to date with the European situation."

"What about the situation in the Pacific, Mr President?" McCarthy asked, cutting in like a dull blade. "Plenty of commies running wild out there."

"There are, Senator," Kolhammer conceded, settling back in his chair. "But mostly they're running around in tight little circles on the Korean Peninsula and the northern tip of Japan. The Marines, the South Koreans, and the Free Japanese Forces are holding them back. Our allies are helping us keep the Russians bottled up inside Vladivostok and the first island chain. So, Asia, the Pacific, is not the priority at the moment."

McCarthy leaned forward on the couch, his eyes gleaming. "Then why waste time with the Australians and the British? That's what you were talking about with them last night, right? Not many kangaroos in Germany."

"Senator, you know I can't disclose the details of those discussions to you," Kolhammer said calmly. He noted to himself that as good as McCarthy's sources were, the senator didn't seem to be aware of the specific request he'd made: for the two Royal navies to redeploy their nuclear-powered submarines from the Pacific to the Atlantic. Small mercies, then.

Before the exchange could grow heated, Symington, the ranking Democrat on the NSC, interjected. "Mr President, we were wondering if you could give us any further and better particulars on the sinking of the *Alexei Shastny* last night. We've seen the press reports, of course, and we have a briefing from the Navy scheduled this evening, but you might have more up-to-date information."

Kolhammer shrugged, allowing himself a thin smile. "Thanks, Stuart," he said. "They're dead. That's my best information. We found those fuckers and we sent them to the bottom."

He did not mention the ruse he'd personally deployed in drawing out the Russian sub. They all knew what he had done, faking the brief media event with Menzies and Templesmith. Despite McCarthy's best efforts, even the morning papers had reported it as the former war-fighting admiral returning to his roots, using misdirection and deception to lure an enemy into fatal error.

"It's good that the Navy boys got them," McCarthy said, his voice taking on the cadence of a stump speech, "but the commies ain't short of submarines, last I checked, Mr President. Plenty of them out there, and your Reforger convoys are sitting ducks for 'em." He paused for effect, his gaze sweeping the other senators before returning to Kolhammer. "Frankly, I don't know why you're endangering so many ships and so many American boys when you coulda ended this war weeks ago. I'll put aside the impeachable negligence of allowing the communists to get the drop on us with their orbital rockets. We shoulda nuked those bastards back to the Stone Age on day one."

The air conditioning cycled on with a whisper, the only sound in the sudden silence. Kolhammer felt his jaw muscles tighten, but kept his expression neutral. More than wanting a reaction, an enemy needed it. Forbearance was a choice to deprive them of their needs.

McCarthy struggled to lean forward again, pressing what he probably thought of as his advantage. "They are still a decade behind us in atomic warheads and missile systems. We coulda wiped them out before they set a foot in Germany. Now they got half a dozen goddamned armies swarming all over the continent, and that opportunity is gone, because they are balls deep into Germany and southern France, and we can't take a clean shot anymore."

Kolhammer said nothing for a long moment, letting the weight of McCarthy's words settle in the room like smoke. He knew what this asshole was trying to do; goad him into losing it, into saying something that could be used against him later. Through the windows, he could see more gardeners at work on the South Lawn, tiny figures maintaining order in this quiet corner of the world.

He didn't bother pointing out that he hadn't been president when Stalin, Beria, or whoever it was, had launched the pre-emptive orbital strike. The Intelligence agencies were still trying to figure out when Stalin had died, even if it was a lay-down certainty that Lavrentiy Beria had given him a final, fatal shove.

There was nothing to be gained from pointing out that, as Eisenhower's Vice President, he'd been occupying the office so famously described as not being worth "a bucket of warm piss." Everyone in this room knew that for all the former president's reluctance to embrace what he called the military-industrial complex, Kolhammer, as his Vice President, had been pushing hard to build out that complex, to leapfrog it as far into the future as he could. He'd argued it would give them an advantage over the Soviets, which would mean the same outcome in this timeline as it had in his: economic stagnation and eventual collapse for Moscow and its client states.

Of course, Moscow had borrowed from the example of Beijing in the late 20th and early 21st centuries, loosening the chains on its economy even as it tightened the party's stranglehold over the state and society. However, as interesting a philosophical and political economy discussion as that would have made, he didn't imagine Joe McCarthy was equipped for such thinking.

Kolhammer watched the senator across from him, noting how the man's inner ugliness seemed to ooze from the pores of his skin, a physical manifestation of the poison he peddled. The afternoon light caught the greasy sheen of perspiration on McCarthy's forehead. The man was working himself up, getting high on his supply of febrile craziness. Kolhammer let him finish, then let the uncomfortable silence spin out, watching as the others shifted awkwardly away from

McCarthy. Senator Jackson examined his fingernails. Symington cleared his throat softly.

Lia Pao stood silently on the other side of the room, watching, remembering everything.

Finally, he spoke.

"Well, thanks for your thoughts, Joe," he said, his voice carrying the flat tone of command authority. "I wasn't aware that a former tail gunner could be blessed with such grand strategic insight. But it's good to see the Air Force doing its best." He paused, letting the dig sink in. "However... you can probably put your dick away and tie your pants up, because as long as I'm president, we won't be firing off hundreds of nuclear warheads in a fit of fucking madness."

He let his words sink in, watching McCarthy's face flush red with anger or embarrassment. The other senators suddenly found the carpet fascinating.

"The Russians chose to put their best efforts into their orbital system, and it almost paid off for them. But 'almost' doesn't win many prizes on the battlefield. They took their shot, and we absorbed the hit. They expected to be in Paris by now and London by next week, but they're still stuck in the ass-end of Germany." Kolhammer stood, moving to the windows, his hands clasped behind his back. "The forces they had in southern Europe are making headway into France, but they simply don't have the mass they built up along the border with West Germany. That's where the true threat lies. And that's where we have to hold until all the elements of Reforger hit the ground."

He turned back to face the senators, the light behind him casting his face into partial shadow. "We can't hold them with atomic weapons, because we'll kill just as many Germans and Dutch and Brits as we will Russians. And we'd have to use so many of them that Comrade Beria would inevitably counter-attack with his tactical nukes, leading—I guarantee you—to us trading cities with them at an accelerating rate until everyone on this goddamn planet is dead."

"So you're saying you won't defend America with every weapon we have," McCarthy said, his voice tight with barely controlled rage. "Good to know, Mr President. Good to know. "

Kolhammer focused on his breathing and on keeping his temper in check. Through the windows, a helicopter passed overhead.

"That's not what I said, Senator," he pointed out, returning to his chair. "I'm simply making the case that there is a time and a place for everything, and we are not in the place where I would consider using nukes. That doesn't mean we won't get there, and God help us all if we do. But we are not there yet. We have other moves to make."

The silence that followed was broken only by the soft hum of the air conditioning and the distant sound of D.C. traffic beyond the White House grounds. He hoped that each man in the room understood that they were discussing not just strategy but the possible end of human civilisation as they knew it, potentially the end of all life on Earth. But he couldn't be sure.

"Joe," he said, looking at McCarthy, who seemed surprised to be addressed by his first name.

"Yes, Mister President."

"You served in the Solomons and Bougainville, didn't you?"

McCarthy nodded.

"A gunner observer, yeah. Twelve combat missions."

Kolhammer nodded. He knew those twelve missions were about as safe as could be in a war zone. The Americans had air superiority in both theatres when McCarthy flew. But it wouldn't help to point that out, so he kept it to himself.

"You ever get out into the boonies in the Solomons after a big firefight? You were an intelligence officer, so I assume you must have."

McCarthy drew himself up a little, nodding.

"That was part of my job, yeah."

"Hell of a thing, isn't it?" Kolhammer said, "What you see after a battle."

McCarthy nodded. The other men looked on silently.

"I want you to think about the worst shit you saw in the South Pacific. I'm guessing it would've been on the Solomons. I want you to remember what a square mile of ground looks like when it's been fought over by tens of thousands of men. The scorched earth. The corpses. Now you imagine that a thousand times worse. Stretching on for as far as the eye can see. Death and horror piled up like some biblical nightmare, but not in some jungle nobody cares about at the ass end of the world. You look out the window and imagine that here. Because that's what's coming when we start throwing nukes around. You think about that senator. If I have to push that button, I will, but I'll do it knowing what it means."

McCarthy said nothing.

But he looked bitterly resentful.

Kolhammer let the moment stand long enough to become uncomfortable before letting go of a breath he'd deliberately held onto.

"On a closely related topic," he said, "Continuity of operations. What the hell is it I hear about this committee spinning up some bullshit witchhunt against Martha Griffiths?"

23

Washington, DC.

JOE MCCARTHY HATED this couch almost as much as he hated
socialism, but not quite as much as he hated Philip Kolhammer. The
damned thing was a trap, is what it was. You sank into the cushioned
crevice so deep you had no choice but to look up at the bastard like
some naughty schoolboy called to the principal's office. And Joe
knew, he just _knew_, that Kolhammer had chosen this particular piece
of furniture for that exact reason. The sneaky son of a bitch probably
had it custom-made by some communist furniture collective in
California.

The late afternoon light slanted through the bulletproof
windows, casting long shadows across the presidential seal woven
into the carpet. Outside, Joe could see the heat haze shimmering off
the South Lawn despite the arctic air conditioning that made the
office feel like a meat locker.

Meanwhile, Kolhammer perched himself across the mahogany
coffee table on a simple wooden chair, sitting on it like he was some
sort of regular guy, a man of the people. But Joe wasn't fooled by that
horsehockey, not for one goddamn second. The bastard did that

because it gave him an extra coupla inches of height over anyone trapped in the socialist crevice couch. You couldn't stop a smart fella from noticing tactical disadvantages like that.

And who the hell was Kolhammer anyway to be lecturing him about the dangers of nuclear war? This worthless bum looked like he hadn't slept in weeks, dark circles under his eyes, five o'clock shadow coming in early. Joe McCarthy had been to war, as Kolhammer had so unctuously pointed out, and Joe knew the dangers plenty well, thank you very much. He also knew the dangers of losing a war, which was what was happening here because this fellow traveller refused to do what was necessary when it woulda made a difference.

And now? Now the son of a bitch had the unmitigated gall to question him about Martha Griffiths! What did those people always call it? All that diversity, and equal silly stuff they went on with. Just another name for socialism, if you asked Joe McCarthy. Which not enough people did, more's the pity.

Joe shifted uncomfortably, deep in the crevice, trying to find a position that didn't make his back ache. His goddamn bladder was giving him trouble again, too—had been all morning—and that burning sensation at the tip of his man-fellow was coming on something fierce. Probably gonna need to see a doctor about that, but what was a fella supposed to do? Walk into some clinic and get judged by some quack who'd probably got his goddamn medical textbooks mail-ordered from Moscow?

He quickly glanced over to check on his so-called colleagues, who looked about as comfortable as three cats in a dog kennel. Scoop Jackson and Symington were sunk deep into their sections of the couch, trapped just as effectively as he was. Neither of them had wanted to open the investigation into Griffiths, but hell, they never wanted to open investigations into anybody. It was just a damned lucky thing they were more frightened of bad press from Mr. Hearst than they were of what this so-called president might think or say about them.

"I don't know why you'd be asking about that," McCarthy said, digging an elbow into the arm of the couch to lever himself up. He'd be damned if he was going to sit at the feet of Kolhammer and be lectured about the separation of powers like some pogue out of boot camp. "Because that would be entirely inappropriate, Mr. President."

He gained his feet with considerable effort and stalked around the office until he found a position he thought suitable for the lesson he was about to deliver; a few feet away from Kolhammer, safely out of arm's reach, where he could look down on him.

Unfortunately, the sneaky devil negated that advantage by simply standing up and looming over McCarthy again, now with his arms folded. Jesus Christ, the bastard was tall. Built like a brick outhouse, too.

"Really, Joe?" Kolhammer said. "You're going to give us a civics lecture?"

The condescension in his voice made Joe's teeth clench. And you couldn't blame a fella for getting his dander up when some Navy puke talked to him like that. Not even the real navy, neither, but some weird mutation of it decades hence, full of negroes and beatnik lesbians.

"No. I'm going to ask you why you think it's appropriate to interfere with the legitimate business of a Senate committee, Mr. President. Because unless I woke up in Moscow this morning, which wouldn't surprise me one damn bit, the way things have been going, you are not the supreme leader here. And questions like that, I'd suggest, are designed to interfere with the dignity and functioning of a co-equal branch of—"

"Knock it off, you fucking blowhard," Kolhammer said.

Joe stepped back like he'd been slapped across the face, and he felt that familiar tightness in his chest that always came when somebody caught him off guard. He nervously glanced at the other senators, who seemed almost as shocked as he was. Hell, even the little Chinese woman Kolhammer kept on a leash in the office like some yappy chihuahua looked shocked, as though she had no idea that was coming.

She started away from the wall where she'd been standing, raising one hand as if to interject, but Kolhammer didn't give her an opportunity.

"I don't know what game you think you're playing, Joe," he said. He was a big man, and the afternoon light from the windows backlit him, throwing his face into shadow. "But I do know what Hearst and Getty are playing at. They're trying to roll back history. They've seen what's coming, they don't like it, and they've picked you as their chump."

"What the hell are you talking about?" McCarthy shot back, though he knew exactly what Kolhammer was talking about. Hell, the only reason Joe was in this office, the only reason he'd made it into the Senate in the first place, was with the backing of Mr. Getty, the Hearst family, and, of course, some early help from the late and sainted J. Edgar Hoover. God rest his soul.

"I've put three nominations to the Senate," Kolhammer continued, and Joe could see that vein starting to pulse in his thick neck. The man's face was flushing red despite the air conditioning, and his hands were slowly clenching into fists at his sides. "Not formally, but quietly sounding them out so that we could avoid any unpleasantness."

He began to pace, moving around the coffee table like a caged animal, and Joe could hear the soft whisper of his shoes on the presidential carpet.

"And on each occasion, my approach has been thrown back in my face. A process which should have been a courtesy followed by the formality of a vote has been gummed up in the works because it didn't suit the interests of a couple of billionaires."

Kolhammer stopped pacing and turned to face Joe directly, his eyes boring into him like a drill press.

"I had been wondering why, until I opened the paper and saw your fine friend Mr. Winchell this morning, trailing your coat past my office, suggesting you'd make a much more agreeable choice for Vice President than any of the three highly qualified candidates I quietly requested, and—"

"How dare you, sir," McCarthy shot back, his voice cracking a little. The burning in his pecker was getting worse, and he had to fight the urge to reach down and adjust himself.

"No, how dare *you*, sir," Kolhammer jabbed back, and his voice dropped to something that sounded almost like a growl. He took a step closer to Joe, close enough that Joe could smell his aftershave— something expensive and foreign, probably, mixed with the faint scent of coffee and stress sweat. Joe was awful familiar with stress sweat.

"Understand this, Joe. You are always welcome in my office as a member of the United States Senate and as the chairman of the Senate National Security Committee. We are not just men here. We are officeholders, and I recognise the responsibility that you hold."

Joe could feel the heat radiating off Kolhammer's body, and being this close to him made Joe's mouth go dry.

"I suggest you take a long, hard look at yourself and try to come to the same place. You are here to serve your country, not to serve the interests of a couple of rich assholes who are freaking out because they looked at the future and didn't see themselves in it."

Kolhammer's voice was getting louder now. Joe could see the others pressing themselves deeper into the couch, as if they could somehow disappear into the cushions.

"Martha Griffiths would make a fine vice president," Kolhammer continued, his voice dropping back to that menacing growl. "And should anything happen to me, she would make an able and admirable president of these United States. You tell me why she wouldn't, before your pal Winchell goes pissing it all over the *New York Daily Mirror*."

Joe was aghast. He'd never been spoken to by anybody like this, not even when he was in the Corps. Sure, everybody got chewed on here and there by somebody in the Corps, that was just the way of it. He got chewed on plenty. Pretty much every day, it seemed. But this felt personal. This fellow seemed to have taken a real dislike to him, and Joe could only imagine it was because of the lies they had told about him back upwhen.

Who did this bastard think he was, talking to a United States Senator like that? Like Joe was some sort of errand boy. Sure, maybe Mr. Getty and Mr. Hearst had been generous with their support over the years. But that was just how politics worked. You couldn't blame a fella for knowing which side his bread was buttered on.

"This committee," he said, waving a hand in the direction of Saltonstall, Jackson and Symington, "this committee has received serious allegations about the Griffiths woman, and—"

"No, you haven't," Kolhammer cut in, and Joe blinked like an owl.

The president took another step forward, close enough now that Joe had to crane his neck to maintain eye contact. "There are no serious allegations to be made about Martha Griffiths. There's just a lot of lies and horse shit to be smeared around."

Kolhammer's voice had gone quiet now, which somehow made it even more menacing than when he'd been shouting. The office felt smaller, the air thicker, like the atmospheric pressure had dropped before a storm.

"And I suggest you knock it the fuck off and get on with your job, which is to do everything possible to win this fight against the Red Army, not to drag your fat, drunken ass a few inches closer to the Oval Office bourbon closet."

The words hit Joe like a physical blow. Fat? Drunk? Well, maybe he'd put on a few pounds over the years, and sure, maybe he liked his brewskis and the occasional shot to take the edge off. Who didn't? But you couldn't blame a fella for that, not with the stress of the job and all the vicious lies people spread about him. A fella needed a little something to help him get through the day.

His old persuader chose that moment to remind him of its existence, and the possible poor choice he'd made with that strumpet down in Biloxie last week. He shifted from foot to foot, trying to relieve the burning without making it obvious.

"Mr. President, please," the Chinese woman spoke up.

"Not now, Lia," Kolhammer said, not taking his eyes off Joe. "Don't interrupt me when I'm telling the truth. It's a hard enough thing to do in this job on the best of days, and we are a long fucking way from our best days at the moment."

He turned to Symington, sitting on the far right side of the couch. "I want to hear from you right now about whether you think this investigation you're proposing to open into Martha Griffiths is a legitimate use of your committee's time and resources. It's just us in this room. There are no reporters. We can check behind the curtains if you want, but I'm pretty sure Walter Winchell didn't sneak in here behind you. I just want God's honest truth from you. What the hell is going on with these nominations?"

All three looked intensely uncomfortable. They were sweating almost as bad as Joe was, and that was saying something.

"Mr. President, I'm sorry," Leverett Saltonstall, the junior Republican senator, started.

"You will be sorry," McCarthy barked at him, "if you don't shut the hell up and do as you're told."

Joe felt the sweat running down his back now, soaking into his shirt. His suit felt like it weighed a hundred pounds, and that burning sensation in his man-fellow was getting worse by the minute. He shifted uncomfortably from foot to foot, trying to find some relief.

"Come now, Joe," said Scoop Jackson, who looked like he'd rather be anywhere else in the world. "We're all on the same side here. We should be able to talk this through."

"There's nothing to talk through," McCarthy shouted, and he could hear his voice getting shrill. He hated it when that happened. Made him sound like some hysterical woman. "We have our job to do. And that job does not in any way encompass inviting a fellow traveller of Josef Stalin into the White House."

"Stalin's dead," Kolhammer said flatly.

"You know what I mean," McCarthy shot back, though the words came out sounding weaker than he'd intended.

The argument spiralled out of control with dizzying speed. Joe knew his fury to be righteous, because Kolhammer and his people, the place they came from, that was an abomination, but deep down, he knew the bastard was right about one thing. The investigation into Griffiths was horseshit. Cooked up by Winchell on orders from Junior Hearst. But what was a fella supposed to do? Say no to the fellas who put him in office? Tell them to go to hell when they'd been so generous with their support?

You couldn't blame a man for looking out for his interests, but you should blame him for not looking out for his friends.

"Gentlemen, gentlemen, please." It was the Chinese woman, slipping between them with her hands raised like she was trying to break up a bar fight. Joe was so shocked he almost woulda slapped her, but he managed to gain control of his legitimately outraged feelings. Also, she was probably a master of karate-fu or one of those diabolical oriental boxing styles. It simply wouldn't do to find himself slapped by a she-devil who looked like she'd fallen off a Confucian charm bracelet. Even Winchell might not be able to resist that story.

"There's more than enough fighting in Europe and the Pacific," she said in a schoolmarmish way that made Joe feel even more agitated. "I don't think we need to start a third front in here."

For a second, Joe wasn't entirely sure Kolhammer was going to listen to her. The man was a big, bald fireplug of barely contained fury, and his temper seemed to suck all the oxygen out of the air. There was a vein in his thick neck, pulsing under pressure, and his hands, still clenched into fists at his sides, looked like slabs of granite. The mad devil looked like he might take a swing at somebody.

And then, just like that, the fever broke. Kolhammer shook himself like an old dog coming out of a lake. The tension went out of his shoulders, and he took a step back, giving everyone room to breathe again.

"You're right. Sorry, Lia." He turned to the other Committee guys and nodded. "Gentlemen, my apologies. I can't stand bad manners, and I have shown appalling manners myself today. My apologies."

The senators murmured their apologies in turn, struggling up out of the crevice couch like a bunch of baby turtles trying to right themselves. They shook Kolhammer's hand with the nervous enthusiasm of men who'd just avoided a beating from their bookie's collector.

Then Kolhammer turned back to Joe McCarthy.

Joe squared his shoulders and raised his chin, as if inviting the president to take a pop at him. He did flinch a little as Kolhammer moved—couldn't help himself—but the sneaky bastard was simply putting his hand out to shake.

Joe looked at the proffered hand for a moment, then reluctantly took it. Kolhammer's grip was firm but not crushing. It made Joe feel small somehow, which only made him angrier again. The president's hand was warm and dry, while Joe's was moist with nervous sweat.

"We can agree to disagree on almost everything, Joe, including this," Kolhammer said, his voice back to that calm, reasonable tone that Joe found so goddamn infuriating. He held the handshake just a moment longer than necessary. "But you need to understand me. I do not have time to play politics. I am not going to have this fight with you."

Kolhammer released his hand and stepped back, but his eyes never left Joe's face.

"I am going to put Ms. Griffiths up for nomination, and the Senate and the House will vote. You can vote against her if you want. You can campaign against her if you want. But understand me—I will not play your game."

The president moved closer again, close enough that Joe fancied he could see his reflection in the president's eyes. "If you campaign against her, I will call out what you're doing and why you're doing it. Maybe it shifts a few votes one way or another, but the facts on the ground will be that Martha Griffiths becomes our next VP. If you wish to spend your very limited political capital opposing that, be my guest. For now, it's still a free country."

The pause that followed stretched for a small eternity. Joe could hear the distant sound of traffic from Pennsylvania Avenue, and even his own heart hammering against his ribs.

"But be assured, Senator, when I'm finished dealing with Lavrentiy Beria, I will turn around and curb-stomp you to jelly, if it's the last goddamn thing I do."

Joe felt his bladder clench, and for a terrible moment, he thought he might piss himself right there in the Oval Office. The burning sensation in his pecker flared up something fierce, and he had to bite back a gasp of pain.

He managed to keep his voice steady, but just barely. "You shouldn't threaten me, Mr. President."

Kolhammer smiled, but there was no warmth in it. "I don't make threats, Senator."

As they filed out of the office, Joe's legs felt shaky beneath him. The cool air in the hallway hit him like a splash of cold water. The burning in his johnson was getting worse, a steady throb that made every step uncomfortable.

Goddamn, but he needed a drink.

And maybe after that, he'd give Walter a call. See what the man thought about this conversation. See what kind of story might come out of it.

You couldn't blame a fella for wanting to set the record straight.

EXTRACT

"The Transitions: An Oral History of the Future, by Studs Terkel."
The New Yorker, March 13, 1954, Vol. 29, No. 5, pp. 51–56.

Frankie Maguire, importer and wholesaler
(Interview conducted October 1952 in a rented warehouse on the south side of Chicago. The walls are stacked shoulder-high with cardboard cartons, each labeled in block letters: PET ROCK. A single folding chair has been placed in the middle of the concrete floor. Maguire is sweating through his shirt. Every time he gestures, his cigar sheds ash onto the concrete like burning confetti.)

You've got to have a bit of the old entrepreneurial, right? That's what I tell people. Some folks, they call it grift. But I call it grit. This is business. The business of the future. You take what's gonna be hot tomorrow, you make it hot today. That's the secret.

Yeah, these boxes? Pet rocks. Don't laugh. They're gonna be huge. A big, big hit, I swear. Like millions. It happened, or would have, in the middle of the '70s. So I figure, why wait? I get a truckload out of

Joliet, clean packaging, nice copy: "Feed it nothing, love it forever." That's catchy, right? That's modern convenience right there.

He waves the cigar toward the cartons, almost like they might sell themselves if he gestures hard enough.

Problem is, I dunno, people here don't get it yet. They think I'm making fun or something. No, no. It's serious. Look at James David-son. He saw the angles. He knew the smart play. I'm just picking up the torch he laid down, is all.

I did hula hoops before this. Plastic tubing out of Cicero. Sold a heap in St. Louis, and the kids loved 'em. But, I dunno, it didn't take off like it should have. Too soon, they said. Always too soon.

He pats his shirt pocket, then produces a little plastic cube with crooked colored stickers. The thing rattles like it's got a loose tooth.

Doesn't matter though, cos this one's gonna be the killer. It's a puzzle toy. The whole world goes crazy for it in the 1980s I think. Early '80s. Or maybe late '70s. Doesn't matter. They go crazy for it. You twist it around and make the colours line up. Red, green, yellow, blue. Try it. But be careful, you don't get hooked. That's my only prototype. Except, uh...

He turns it once, twice. A sticker peels halfway off. The cube sticks, won't rotate. He frowns, wipes his hand on his trousers.

Of course, manufacturing is tough. Tolerances. Plastics, you know. But once I figure that out, forget about it. Every kid in America's gonna want one. Every grown up too. It's therapy in a cube, Studs. You'll see.

He drops it back in his pocket, lights another cigar off the stub of the last one.

That's the old entrepreneurial, you see? You keep throwing tomorrow at people. Rocks, hoops, cubes, whatever it takes. And one of these days, boom!

He leans back on the folding chair, smoke curling up to the rafters.

You'll see.

24

Cairo. Five weeks ago.

THE FIRST STAMMERING burst of gunfire reached them not long after sundown. They had been smoking in the semi-dark, sipping coffee from enamel mugs, and in Dan's case, beginning to think about food. But Merrill had rules, hard-learned ones. No eating just before an op. A gutshot stomach leaked acid and stew into the cavity. You didn't get hours. You got minutes

Carter stood by the window, unmoving, when the first, faraway stutter of gunfire reached them. He drew slowly on his cigarette, turned his head a few degrees—no more—like a man trying to pick out a tune from a distant radio. "Other side of the city," he said, not addressing anyone, not needing to.

Dan checked his watch with the faintest raise of an eyebrow. Siregar was late, though not without excuse. He'd sent word by way of a barefoot courier, a street urchin, no more than ten, with ribs like fence pickets beneath a threadbare shirt, and a serious look that didn't belong on a face so young. He announced, in the solemn tone of an errand boy far above his station, that Mr Siregar was delayed but would be upon them presently, despite the inconvenience occasioned by a city filling up with soldiers and sandbags. He put out his hand for consideration, and Merrill, working another cigarette between his fingers, like his nerves couldn't quite settle, stopped briefly to fetch a handful of crumpled banknotes from a shirt pocket. It was way too much money, of course, since they all knew Siregar had already settled the tab.

The boy did well at pretending he'd been shortchanged on the deal. Soneski dragged him to the door by the collar and tossed him out.

"You good, boss?" Merrill asked, voice low, like a man asking something bigger than the few words he was allowed.

"Those things will be the death of you, Johnny," Dan said, nodding at the cigarette.

Merrill smiled. "Probably not. If I kept smoking them for another twenty or thirty years, maybe. But I don't think that's likely, do you?"

Dan didn't answer. Soneski returned to pacing back and forth across the room, counting his steps with each circuit as though he expected the tally to change between one lap and the next. It never did.

"I meant, are you good about, you know... Duffy," Merrill said.

Dan shook his head, not admitting to anything, just denying he had a problem. "I knew she was here, Johnny," he said. "I knew there was a fair chance our paths would cross, too. I'm pretty sure Harry's working for the Brits. They both were in Rome at the same time as us."

"There's a lot of people in Rome this time of year," Merrill said. "It's very popular with newlyweds. You must have read the announcement."

"They're not married yet," Dan said.

Merrill nodded, acknowledging the technicality but refusing to let the wider point go. "No, they're not, boss. But that's what usually happens after you announce your engagement and spend a couple of weeks in Rome, taking in the sights, eating all the noodles," he said. "I'm just looking out for you, is all. There's a big hole inside you where she used to be. And you sure as hell can't fill it with us."

Dan huffed out a short laugh. "I wouldn't even try."

"And what about her?" Merrill asked. "Do you think she could fill the hole she made? If you took her back?"

"No," Dan said. "Not after what she did. I couldn't go back there. And she's engaged. To a prince, last time I checked."

Merrill exhaled slowly, watching the smoke drift toward the cracked ceiling. "You live back there, boss. When you're not on a job, that's where you hide. Maybe this—" he gestured vaguely at the room "—this is your vacation."

Dan didn't answer at first. He followed Merrill's gaze to Carter, still at the window, eyes on the skyline like he expected it to confess something.

"We all have our reasons, Johnny," Dan said.

Carter had worked for the Office of Strategic Services during the war and had a good war, as far as such things go. Maybe too good, because he'd never quite settled down when he got home.

Soneski, circling the room like a caged dog, hadn't even bothered with the pretence. He'd gone straight from the Marines into the freelance war biz, like a man who knew exactly what he was fit for.

And Merrill? Sitting opposite Dan, chain-smoking hand-rolled Turkish cigarettes, forbidding anyone so much as a spoonful of rice and goat meat. He told Dan he liked the freedom. And the pay. Said it beat working back home in a hospital or some tiny suburban practice. He made three times as much here, if you tallied all the hazard bumps and bonuses. But Dan knew better. Merrill gave most of it away. Just like he had before with the messenger boy. He wasn't a drinker. Had no love for the cards. And his heart didn't bleed for the sorrows of the world. The man simply had no use for the money once it was earned, and his necessities were met.

"Did Siregar offer you another job?" Merrill asked, seemingly out of nowhere, but again, Dan knew better.

"No," he said. "He's given up doing that. I told him, I don't mind working with Ali, but I don't want to work for him. Not like Siregar does. I prefer to pick and choose my jobs."

"You still got that nice little place in Bali, though? You thinking of retiring anytime soon? You can't do this forever, boss."

"And you can't keep smoking like that, Johnny. But yeah, I still got my place in Bali," Dan said. "I'm not thinking of retiring there, yet, no."

The conversation continued like this in fits and starts, attended only by the slow procession of Merrill's cigarettes. He was reaching for another when Carter, still silhouetted at the window, finally spoke.

"You know, it's getting pretty sporty out there."

Their street was quiet, but looking out across the old quarter towards the newer, more developed districts, gunfire rattled like hail on a tin roof. The sky lit in sudden, violent bursts too bright for gunshots. Grenades, maybe. Or even shoulder-fired rockets.

Dan was just about to rummage through his pack for the transistor radio—maybe see what the BBC was saying—when the bell rang.

It wasn't electric. Just a little iron thing, no bigger than a ping pong ball, rigged to a string that ran down a drainpipe to the street below. You pulled the string, and the bell answered upstairs, clear and light, like something you'd hear in a country kitchen or a one-room schoolhouse.

Dan started towards the door, but Soneski was already there, opening it with a pistol behind his back. He looked down over the tiny landing, down the stairwell, then turned back to them.

"It's Siregar," he said. "He's coming up."

The Indonesian arrived a moment later and entered without knocking, his suit crumpled from the day's exertions, and his expression more so. He paused just inside the doorway, the silence briefly his to hold.

"Mr. Dan. Gentlemen."

Merrill offered a crooked grin. "Hey, Siri."

Siregar tilted his head, the faintest trace of exhaustion flitting across his face. "Mr Merrill. If only I had a rupiah for every time I've heard that." He sounded as though he'd already spent and wasted the fortune.

"Are we good to go?" Dan asked.

Siregar gave a slight nod. "Transport is waiting, two streets over. At Port Said, everything has been arranged, equipment, passage, discretion."

Carter stepped away from the window, where the city was visibly coming apart. A plume of thick black smoke rose into the dusk a mile away. The building shuddered slightly as something heavy exploded nearby. Dust motes danced in the lamplight.

"Why the port?" he asked.

"Because that is where you will find our quarry," Siregar said. "Comrade Skarov and the engineer. My best information puts them on a merchant vessel, the MV Bulgakov, leaving Port Said in four hours."

Soneski stopped pacing. "Are you fucking kidding me?"

"I am not," Siregar assured him. "Events move quickly." He motioned toward the window, where the sound of automatic fire punctuated the slow percussion of something heavier. "The palace has put down two coup attempts since dusk. Maybe three. Nobody's certain."

Dan glanced out the window. Through the narrow aperture, the old city revealed itself, ancient and angular, its sunbaked mudbrick blocks stacked like forgotten parcels. And beyond, a rough beast stirred. Carter moved back to the window, drawn by a fresh burst of tracer fire that lit the skyline in brief, angry streaks.

"Has this got anything to do with our job?" Dan asked.

Siregar shook his head. "I do not believe so, Mr. Dan. My understanding is that Soviet advisors began redeploying across the neighbourhoods around their airfield, and certain factions took this as a signal to rise up against the crown. The Russians are denying everything, of course, but the British and Americans have begun to redeploy at the request of the King himself. It is confusing, sir, but I do not believe it has anything to do with our mission."

"It's gonna make it more complicated, though, isn't it?" Carter said.

Siregar nodded. "I am afraid so, sir. But this is not the only complication."

Dan rubbed his eyes, which were stinging from all the cigarette smoke in the room. Merrill started rolling another.

"Go on," Dan said.

"Don't mind if I do," Merrill grinned.

Dan ignored him. So did Siregar. "On the best of my information, the British had very lately seized the person of Professor Bremmer."

"Harry?" Dan asked.

Siregar shook his head, looking slightly confused or perhaps frustrated. "Perhaps," he said. "He was seen with a group of men who we know to have done work for MI6, but to the best of our knowledge, they were not working with His Highness on this matter."

"This matter being Bremmer," Dan said.

"Indeed, Mr. Dan."

"Popular guy," Merrill said, lighting his next cigarette. "For a Nazi."

"He is an engineer, Mr Johnny," Siregar said. "Not a Nazi. We knew of many factions, many interests who had set themselves upon acquiring the services of this man."

"Who didn't want to be acquired," Soneski said from the other side of the room. He had stopped pacing and was now preternaturally still, staring at Siregar, who shrugged. The smell of burning rubbish drifted through the window, mixing with Merrill's Turkish tobacco.

"Indeed, sir. But that is why my patron retained your services. You have proven effective and most efficient in these matters."

"Yeah, okay, we don't need the soft soap," Dan said. "So, Harry had the professor, and these other guys took him, or what?"

"His Royal Highness met Professor Bremmer at the Hilton. There was an incident almost immediately," Siregar said. "Possibly involving the Jews, perhaps the Russians, too. But not the incident with your Russians, Mr. Dan."

Dan shook his head. "They weren't my Russians, buddy, and they're nobody's anymore."

Siregar bowed slightly. "You make a fair point, sir. Nonetheless, I can confirm through a cousin of my cousin by marriage, Mr Al Nouri, who holds a most prestigious position with Mr Hilton, that His Royal Highness—"

"You can probably stop calling him that," Dan said. "He gave up the title years ago. Harry will do fine. We'll figure out who you're talking about."

Siregar bowed again. "That Mr... *Harry*..." It seemed to pain him to make the correction. "Mr Harry met the German, Bremmer, at the hotel. There was the unfortunate incident in the bar with the Jews and the Russians and possibly others—quite separate to your incident with the other Russians, Mr. Dan—and to the best of my knowledge, Mr Harry escorted Professor Bremmer from the hotel with the assistance of a member of this other British team."

"A second British team," Dan said, just to be certain.

"Indeed, sir." Siregar nodded, then nodded again, seeming more confident. "My information on this is good."

"How do you know?" Carter asked.

"Because we had been watching the other team for a week," Siregar said. "We understood them to be in pursuit of Professor Bremmer, too. Nothing in our observations led me to conclude that Harry had anything to do with this second team, until, by happenstance, his path crossed with one of them subsequent to the incident at the Hilton. At that point, it appears they agreed to work together, at least in the short term."

"So they took Bremmer," Dan said.

"And then handed him straight back to the Russians," Siregar said. He nodded once, then shook his head in disbelief. "This part, sir, this part escapes me."

Dan shared a look with Carter, who had worked with the Russians and against them, during and after the war.

"Skarov," Carter said. "Bremmer was the primary objective, but these other guys might've also had a catch-or-kill order for Skarov. Makes sense. That's a pretty juicy plum, if you can pluck it and squeeze it."

"Okay," Dan said, cutting to the chase. "So the Brits used Bremmer as bait to try and grab Skarov. Greedy and dumb. And now Skarov has Bremmer on the Bulgakov, and we are, what, competing with MI6 to grab him?"

Siregar shook his head. "Happily not, Mr. Dan."

"Why not?" Carter asked from across the room.

Siregar looked at him. "Because the MI6 team are all dead, sir. And Mr Harry and his fiancée, Miss Julia, have also been captured and are being held aboard the Russian ship."

Dan closed his eyes. He didn't need to be told the others were watching him; the silence pressing in was enough. When he opened them again, Siregar was still standing there, waiting.

"So, Mr. Dan, I have a van and a location for you. The only question, sir, is whether you can extract Professor Bremmer and deliver him to me."

Dan gave a nod, barely more than a tilt of the head. "Yeah. Fine. Let's get it done."

Outside, Cairo burned in patches across the horizon, orange light flickering against the low clouds.

25

Washington DC.

SCHULTZ LOOKED TERRIFIED. "No, no, no," he kept repeating, his triple chin quivering as he crabbed away on his back, butt-scooting across the carpet in a desperate attempt to put distance between himself and Cherry. The rolls of fat bunched and shifted beneath his ill-fitting suit, panic sweat soaking through the fabric. Schultz's face was blotched red, hair plastered to his forehead, eyes wide and glassy with fear.

"Careful, Dippy," Cherry said, flicking on the main room light. "You'll give yourself a hell of a rug burn doing that." The overhead bulb bathed the hotel room in unforgiving yellow light, throwing deep shadows into the corners and revealing the shabbiness of the Mayflower's mid-tier accommodations. Thin carpet, worn furniture, the lingering smell of old cigarettes and disinfectant. Cherry would bet good money that Schultz was spending his travel allowance on rent boys, rather than accommodation.

He took another step closer, his shoes whispering on the thread-bare carpet, getting up close enough to kick Schultz in the guts if he had to, to stop him from crying out for help. But the man's voice had that quavering softness that told Cherry he was so terrified he could barely breathe.

"What do you want?" Schultz stammered, his back now pressed against the foot of the narrow bed. The wooden frame creaked under pressure. "I've got money. You can have it."

"I don't need your money, Dippy," Cherry said, unbuttoning his coat slowly. He let it fall open just enough for Schultz to glimpse the shoulder holster underneath. "I just need some information."

"About what?" Schultz stammered, his eyes flicking between Cherry's face and the hint of gunmetal.

Cherry walked to the window, pulled the curtain aside with two fingers, and glanced down at the street four floors below. Late-night traffic was finally thinning out, just the occasional cab and a few drunks weaving home from the bars. The neon sign of an all-night diner across the street cast red and blue patterns on the hotel room wall, cycling endlessly through its promises of coffee and pie.

"About whatever Roy Cohn wanted."

Schultz's face, already flushed, went a deeper shade of red. The colour spread down his neck, disappearing beneath his rumpled collar. "I don't know who you're talking about," he lied.

Cherry laughed, a short bark which made the other man jump. "Everybody in this town knows who Roy Cohn is, Dippy. Joe McCarthy's fixer, for one thing. But more importantly, the guy you spent an hour sipping drinks with earlier tonight. Before you sipped enough to screw up the courage to visit your lady friends on Hobson Street."

He turned from the window, studying Schultz's face in the sickly yellow light. Sweat was beading on the man's forehead, threatening to drip into his eyes.

"Oh no, oh no," Schultz muttered, more to himself than to Cherry. His hands trembled as he pressed them against the carpet, trying to push himself further back against the bed frame.

"Oh yes, Dippy. I followed you there. I knocked on the door. I met the ladies—Desiree, Vana. I forget the name of the third one." Cherry moved closer, his shadow falling across Schultz's cringing form. The room's single table lamp flickered. "What I do remember is she coulda used a shave, and I'm not talking about her legs. You know what I mean, Dippy? You're fucked, pal. I know what Cohn has over you. And now I've got it too."

The air conditioning clanked, and somewhere down the hall, a door slammed. The hotel was alive with small sounds: footsteps overhead, muffled conversations through the thin walls, and the distant hum of the elevator machinery.

"Here's the deal." Cherry crouched down, bringing himself to eye level with the other man. This close, he could smell Schultz's animal fear sweat, sharp and acrid beneath his cologne. "You tell me what I need to know, and I walk out of here and forget I ever saw you tonight. I forget that I followed you a mile to that cathouse, and any memory I got of you waltzing out of there grinning like someone sucked a golf ball through your garden hose—all of it disappears. Just as soon as you tell me what I need to know. What was Roy Cohn talking about? What'd he want from you?"

"Nothing, nothing, I swear—"

"No, Dippy," Cherry cut him off, his voice dropping barely above a whisper. The quiet was always more menacing than if you shouted. "There's always an ask from guys like Cohn. I know, because I'm just like him. Only worse. So here's my ask. What did Roy Cohn want?"

Schultz's panic reached a breaking point. It could have gone either way, into defiance or collapse. Cherry watched the transformation with professional interest. He'd seen it plenty before, in the interrogation room, and back alleys. The moment when a man realises he's fucked and his mind finally stops racing in circles, looking for an escape that doesn't exist. The trembling stopped. Schultz's shoulders slumped, his eyes lost their frantic darting, and for a moment, he looked almost relieved, as if the crushing weight of his secret life had finally slid off his shoulders.

"Kolhammer," he said, the name coming out as barely more than an exhale.

"President Kolhammer?" Cherry asked, straightening up slightly.

Schultz nodded, his neck straining against his tight collar. "Cohn told me to vote for a House committee investigation."

Cherry frowned, processing this. Outside, a siren wailed in the distance, growing louder then fading as it passed the hotel.

"Kolhammer? What, you're thinking of impeaching the guy a

month into a war he's been warning us about for the last six or seven years? Are you fucking nuts?"

"No, no," Schultz almost shouted, causing Cherry to tense and hold up a warning hand.

"Keep your voice down, Dippy." Cherry glanced toward the door, listening for any sign that their conversation had drawn attention. The hallway remained quiet. "Tell me what Cohn wanted you to do to Kolhammer."

Schultz swallowed hard, his Adam's apple bobbing. "Griffiths," he said. "Martha Griffiths. Kolhammer wanted to nominate her to be his vice president. Cohn wanted us to stop Kolhammer from putting her name forward. He wanted the investigation."

"Into what?" Cherry asked, settling back on his heels.

"It doesn't matter," Schultz said, looking at Cherry as though he were an idiot. Some of his natural arrogance was returning now that the initial shock was wearing off. "Anything will do."

"But why Griffiths?" Cherry asked. "What's wrong with her? Apart from, you know, she's a broad—a woman. Unlike your little friends tonight."

Schultz laughed at Cherry's naivety, a bitter sound that seemed too large for the cramped room. "She's not Joe McCarthy. That's her fucking problem. McCarthy wants to be vice president."

Cherry shook his head slowly, genuinely puzzled. The overhead light buzzed, threatening to go out entirely. "I've shot dogs with more leadership potential than Joe McCarthy. What makes him think he can do that job?"

Schultz seemed to grow a little less frightened, even a touch more confident, as he realised Cherry wasn't about to beat him senseless. He shifted slightly, trying to find a more comfortable spot against the bed frame.

"You're not from around here, are you?" Schultz said, studying Cherry's face with new interest.

"Stick to answering the questions, Dippy," Cherry warned, standing up and leaning against the small desk by the window. The wood was scarred with cigarette burns and water rings from count-less glasses. "It'll go a lot easier for you than asking them. What's McCarthy's play?"

"It's not his play. It's not even Cohn's," Schultz said, some of his old political instincts reasserting themselves. "It's Hearst and Getty and all of them. They want their man in the Oval Office, and McCarthy's their man."

Cherry shook his head. Through the thin walls, he could hear someone's television, the late news, by the sound of it. "I don't get it. McCarthy wouldn't have a shot at this under normal circumstances. And we're a thousand fuckin' miles away from normal right now."

"I don't know what he's thinking," Schultz shot back, frustration creeping into his voice. "He doesn't talk to me. Don't you know anything? Do you have any idea who I am?"

Cherry snorted, pushing off from the desk. "You're a fat, sweaty fairy, butt-crawling across the floor to get away from me. To get away from the consequences of your perverted appetites."

Schultz's expression turned peevish, even nasty. Cherry tensed, ready to remind him who was in charge.

"Never McCarthy. Does that phrase mean anything to you?"

Cherry shook his head, genuinely ignorant.

"Do you even read the papers?" Schultz sneered.

Cherry stepped forward and casually stomped on the man's ankle. Not hard enough to snap it, but more than enough to remind Dippy Schultz that he was the snivelling fag in this exchange. Schultz howled with pain, and Cherry kicked him in the stomach, driving all the air out of him, and cutting off his cry of pain.

"I only read them for the ponies," he said, moving back toward the window as the other man doubled over and heaved up on the carpet. The neon light across the street painted half of Schultz's face red, the other half blue.

He lay on the floor, crying.

Cherry left him to his misery. Sometimes the best way to break a man was to say nothing – just let him sit with the stink of his own failure.

After a while, Schultz whined.

"Can I get up? Can I at least get up?"

"Sure," Cherry said, gesturing magnanimously.

Schultz climbed awkwardly to his feet, hauling his considerable weight up off the floor with a series of grunts and wheezes. The effort left him breathing hard, sweat staining his shirt in expanding circles. He eyed the bed but shuffled over to the little bar fridge in the corner. The compressor hummed loudly in the small space as he opened it, the fridge light reflecting off the small bottles inside. He pulled out a tiny bottle of bourbon, offered one to Cherry, who shook his head.

"Not interested. But if it's good for what ails you, Dippy, fill your boots."

Schultz twisted the cap off with trembling fingers, downed the bourbon in one go, then pulled out another bottle. The empty clinked as he set it on top of the fridge. He flopped into the armchair by the window, the cheap upholstery sighing under his weight, breathing hard.

"There are two dozen of us," Schultz explained once he'd settled himself and twisted open the second bottle. He seemed almost eager to talk now, and Cherry kept out of his way. You did when a perp started running their mouth. "Republicans like McCarthy, but nothing like McCarthy, if you know what I mean." He shook his head, searching for the words. "You know about him, right? What he would have been like if Kolhammer and the others hadn't turned up. He's a history lesson in what not to do, in who you *do not* want to be." Schultz's thoughts broke off, his head shaking more vigorously. The bourbon was hitting his empty stomach, loosening his tongue. "And people just... it was like some people just—"

Cherry studied how his face worked as he struggled with whatever he was trying to get out. "Some people, they just..."

He trailed away.

Cherry finished the thought for him.

"Some people took a good look at what he was and what he promised, and they said, yeah, we'll have some of that. Is that what you're trying to say, Dippy?"

He nodded, relief flooding his features. "That's exactly what I mean. He's just... he's a monster. And some people want that. But there are twenty-four Never McCarthy votes in the party. Every committee he stands for, every investigation he tries to get going, every piece of legislation he backs, we say no. We've always said no because we've always known what he is." He threw his hands up in a gesture of defeat. "And yet—"

"And yet," Cherry said, moving away from the window to perch on the edge of the desk again, "some people still want that."

He was leading the witness, he knew. But some of them needed it.

"Yes," Schultz said, sounding utterly exhausted. He took another pull from the little bottle.

"So Roy Cohn is trying to break up your little club. Is that it?" Cherry asked.

"That's close enough, yeah," Schultz answered, rolling the bottle between his palms. "He wanted to know where the soft votes were, who he might strip away."

Cherry watched him carefully, reading the tells. "Is that you, Dippy? Are you soft on McCarthy?"

Schultz looked physically sick at the suggestion. "I hate him," he said with surprising vehemence. "I hate him so much."

Cherry smiled grimly. "Because he knows who you are, doesn't he? Roy Cohn, too. They know who and what you are."

Schultz didn't answer, but he didn't have to. The silence stretched between them, filled only by more of the building's nighttime sounds; pipes settling, the distant elevator, that TV still playing softly through the walls.

"Who else is in your little club?" Cherry asked.

Schultz looked at him as though he were crazy. "You really don't read the newspapers, do you?"

"I told you," Cherry said, standing up and straightening his jacket. "The racing form. Sometimes the TV guide. That's all."

Schultz started reeling off names, counting them off on his fingers. Cherry didn't bother writing them down. He could get the names from any newspaper or just call up O'Brien. She probably had files on all of them.

"And Cohn," Cherry said when Schultz finished his recitation, "he's the spear carrier. McCarthy's point man, right?"

Schultz nodded, swaying slightly in his chair. "Yes. Normally, we don't talk. Normally, McCarthy won't talk to us. And I'd cross the street to avoid him."

"Normally?" Cherry said, picking up on the qualifier. "That sounds like something's changed recently."

Schultz gave him that half-pitying, half-contemptuous look again, emboldened by alcohol and the politician's natural arrogance. "The war," he said. "Eisenhower getting killed? Kolhammer moving into the Oval? Surely even you noticed that?"

Cherry thought about backhanding him for the attitude. Schultz was getting overconfident again, forgetting his station. Instead, Cherry just asked, "I mighta heard something about it. That's not what I was asking, but. It sounded to me like something changed in the way Cohn has been doing his job. Why don't you tell me what that is?"

Schultz closed his eyes and nodded, seeming to deflate again. "Right. Sorry. I understand now. He set up a meeting with us recently, a month or so back, just after the Russian attack."

"In Washington?" Cherry asked.

"No," Schultz said quickly, as if the very idea was ridiculous. "In Biloxi, Mississippi."

"Why there?" Cherry moved to the window again, checking the street below. A patrol car had pulled up to the curb, and Cherry watched as two cops got out and entered the diner across the street.

Schultz laughed, a sound with no humour in it. "That's the question that answers itself. Who the hell is going to look for anything in Biloxi? The three of us—the caucus leaders, the Never McCarthy caucus leaders—we were in Biloxi on business, legitimate business at the army base, and Cohn turned up with McCarthy. They wanted to meet."

"They wanted to meet about Martha Griffiths?" Cherry asked, turning back to the room.

Schultz shook his head, the motion making him wince slightly. "Her name wasn't out at that point. Kolhammer's people had approached the House and Senate leadership about Peggy Guggenheim. We shut that one down. She's a hippie freak."

Cherry stared at him.

"Glass houses, pal."

Schultz had the decency to look ashamed. Cherry wasn't being entirely truthful about his news-reading habits. But he tended to skim the political headlines, rather than dive in too deep. It wasn't like he voted or anything. He did remember seeing a few stories about the Guggenheim woman, none of them flattering. That Winchell asshole had given her a touch-up.

"They asked us to meet them in a hotel in Biloxi," Schultz continued. "And they asked for our support to put McCarthy's name to the White House for VP. We laughed in their faces." His voice grew harder. "That's when things got nasty with Cohn. That's when he came directly at me with..."

His voice trailed away.

"Yeah, I know what he came at you with," Cherry said. "I was there tonight, remember?"

The room fell quiet. Cherry moved to the bedside table where he'd spotted a pad of hotel stationery and a pencil. He picked them up and tossed them to the congressman.

"All right, Dipshit. This is how it's going to work." Cherry's voice took on a businesslike tone. "You write down everything you remember about your stay in Biloxi, particularly names, dates, and places you went. Especially the places you met up with Cohn and McCarthy. You do that for me, and we're square."

Schultz caught the pad clumsily, nearly dropping it. "What are you going to do?"

"You don't want to know."

"Are you going after McCarthy?" Schultz asked, suddenly animated. "Because if you're going after him, you need to go all the way. You need to get him."

Cherry studied the politician's face, the flush of alcohol and excitement, the desperate hope that someone might finally deal with his tormentor. "You need to start writing, Dippy. Names, dates, places. Just give me that, and I'm gone. You'll never hear from me again. And you don't need to lie awake at night thinking about what I know, cos all I wanna know is names, dates, and places."

Schultz started to write, his pen scratching across the hotel stationery in the quiet room. It took him ten minutes, his handwriting increasingly shaky as the bourbon worked through his system. He filled at least half a dozen pages with small, neat script, occasionally pausing to remember a detail or check a date. When finished, he tore the pages off the pad with exaggerated care and handed them to Cherry.

"Much obliged, Congressman," Cherry said, folding the papers without reading them and tucking them into his jacket pocket. He turned and started for the door, his hand already reaching for the knob. The hallway beyond was quiet.

Before he got there, he stopped and turned back to Schultz, who was slumped in his chair like a man who'd reached the end of everything.

"You know, Dippy," he said, buttoning his coat, "you're not doing yourself any favours living like this. You should think about moving out to California. San Francisco's full of fags like you, and nowadays, they don't go sneaking around in the dark."

Schultz just stared at him, his eyes unfocused and glassy. Cherry opened the door. The hallway was empty, lit by buzzing fluorescents. He stepped out and closed the door softly behind him, leaving Schultz alone with his bourbon and his choices.

26

Germany.

ALL ROADS MUST END SOMEWHERE, Joachim Boosfeld reflected as he surveyed the ruins of what had once been the 3rd Armoured Division. His personal road, and the accursed Highway 46 that had consumed his unit like some mechanical cancer, ended here in Hagen, amid the scattered remnants of eleven thousand men reduced to fewer than nine hundred.

The defeat was written in smoke and steel across the German countryside. Müller was dead. Torn apart by a Sturmovik's 30 mm cannon three days ago, his command jeep transformed into twisted metal and bloody fragments. The Division Commander was dead. The Chief of Staff was dead. Half the regimental commanders were dead or missing, probably in Soviet hands by now, if they were still breathing.

Boosfeld stood in the afternoon sun, his CVC helmet hanging from his belt for the first time in weeks, and marvelled at the simple pleasure of walking in the open without scanning the sky for attack aircraft. The front was fifteen kilometres east, close enough to hear the rumble of artillery, far enough away to allow what remained of his men to eat hot food and sleep without their boots on.

Three tanks. That's what remained of 2nd Company, 93rd Panzer Lehr Battalion. Three M-60s from an original fifteen, but not *the* original three, of course. Just like the mythical Ship of Theseus, 2 Company has been gradually replaced, piece by piece, until it was hard to tell if it still existed outside Boosfeld's memory. His few surviving crews were hollow-eyed wraiths. They were scattered across a field outside Hagen, their engines finally silent, their eyes finally closed in sleep, not death.

The relief by the British 1st Armoured had been less a military handover than an unholy rout dressed up in staff college politeness. "Passage of lines," the orders had called it. "Tactical withdrawal to prepared positions." Pretty words to disguise a piteous reality. The 3rd Armoured had broken under the hammer of Soviet steel, and what few remained had fled for their lives toward the imagined safety of the rear lines.

Boosfeld lit a cigarette with his old Zippo, a relic that had somehow survived two German defeats and looked more likely than he to outlast a third. The tobacco was harsh Turkish stuff, but it was real tobacco, and it was his to enjoy for the moment. He would take the small victories within the greater loss.

The sound of approaching vehicles made him turn. A jeep and a staff car picked their way through the scattered clumps of men and machines, both flying the pennants of senior officers. Boosfeld recognised the jeep's occupant before it stopped, and he climbed out. General Hoffmann, call sign "Volga Six," was a career panzer officer who'd earned his bones fighting T-34s in the Ukraine. The other passenger was unfamiliar: a British higher-up with intelligent eyes and the kind of performative moustache that suggested either supreme confidence or simple-minded naivety.

Carefully putting out his cigarette on his boot and saving the stub end, he came to attention as the two men approached. He judged the front close enough to make saluting inadvisable, but military courtesy demanded proper bearing. Besides, Hoffmann was the kind of general who'd earned respect the proper way, with track grease under his fingernails and the scars to prove he, too, had been wherever he sent his men.

"Gentlemen," Boosfeld said in English, the NATO lingua franca. "How may I help you?"

The British brigadier looked him up and down with the appraising gaze of a horse trader evaluating a nag which might be suitable only for the glue factory. His uniform was clean and pressed, his equipment precisely arranged.

"This is the chap?" the Brigadier asked Hoffmann, as if Boosfeld weren't standing three meters away.

"It is," Hoffmann replied. "Captain Boosfeld has extensive experience with ad hoc formations, and he's performed magnificently under impossible circumstances these past weeks."

Joachim Boosfeld didn't like the sound of this. When senior officers started using words like "magnificent" and "impossible," experience suggested someone was about to receive orders testing the previously established meaning of those words. The Brigadier, whose name tape read 'Stevens', nodded and fixed Boosfeld with pale blue eyes that held all the warmth of a January moon. "Good enough then. Let's cut to the chase, shall we? Captain Boosfeld, we need a chap who can look after an improvised armour-heavy battle group and deploy wherever the situation demands. Interested?"

As if I have a choice, he thought. Aloud, he said, "I have questions, sir."

"Best ask them then."

"Chain of command first. Who would I report to?"

Brigadier Stevens glanced at Hoffmann. "To General Hoffmann. We're pulling him back to corps staff, but he'll maintain immediate control of your area of operations."

That was acceptable. Hoffmann understood the power and perils of armour, the realities of tactical command, and, most importantly, that the world as viewed from headquarters bore little resemblance to conditions at the front.

"You mentioned improvised forces, sir. Improvised, how, if I might ask?"

"Six companies' worth of personnel from various nationalities and specialties. Bit of a lucky dip, I'm afraid. Survivors from broken units, replacement drafts, whatever we could scrape together." The Brigadier looked over the men asleep on the bedrolls in the field behind Boosfeld. "You'll retain your current men and equipment, of course, so you'll have a few familiar faces around you."

"I have three tanks, sir. A proper armoured formation requires forty-five."

"Yes, quite." The Brigadier nodded in sympathy. "However, needs must when the devil drives, eh? I can give you thirty tanks total, two companies. One German, one mixed Dutch and Belgian. Plus a 120 mm mortar section that's been orphaned, two companies of mechanised infantry, and two companies of light infantry with truck transport."

Boosfeld absorbed this information with growing apprehension. Mixed nationality units were difficult enough to command when they'd trained together. Throwing together survivors from different armies, different languages, different tactical doctrines, and expecting them to function as a coherent force within days... it was the kind of toy soldier fantasy that looked elegant on staff planning boards and proved disastrous in reality.

"Languages, sir? Will we be able to communicate?"

"English is NATO's command language," the Brigadier replied with the confidence of a man who'd never tried shouting fire commands in his second or third language at a Dutch tank crew under artillery bombardment.

Christ, Boosfeld thought. This one's never done it. Half his new command probably couldn't ask a whore for a handjob in passable English, much less coordinate complex tactical maneuvers. But he was a professional soldier, and professionals adapted to circumstances rather than complaining about them. He sighed, but not theatrically. He was just tired.

"Time frame and mission, sir?"

Hoffmann answered this time. "You leave immediately for Witten, where your new command is assembling. From there, proceed to the intersection of Highways 42 and 43 outside Gelsenkirchen. Establish defensive positions and hold until relieved."

"Expected duration?"

"Three days to establish your defence. After that..." Hoffmann shrugged. "You hold until you can't hold anymore. I'm sure you know what that's like, Captain."

Fuck, he thought. *Another crossroads, another delaying action, another butcher's bill to buy time for the Americans.*

"Yes, sir."

Hoffmann pulled a small envelope from his pocket and tapped out the epaulet sleeves of a major. He removed Boosfeld's three captain's pips with some ceremonial flair and pinned on the new rank; one pip with a wreath. Under different circumstances, promotion in the field might have been cause for celebration. Under these circumstances, it felt more like a death sentence with slightly better pay.

"Congratulations, Herr Major."

Hoffman stepped back, and Boosfeld came to attention, but exchanged no salutes.

"Thank you, sir. About those tanks..."

"M-60s," Stevens interrupted. "Mixed vintage but all operational. Your German company commander is Hauptmann Weber, a solid officer, knows his business. The Dutch-Belgian company is commanded by..." he consulted his notes, "...Major van der Berg. I know him well. He plays cricket! So language shouldn't be a problem there."

Fuck me, Boosfeld thought wearily.

"Questions?" Hoffmann asked.

"Logistics? Ammunition? Medical support?"

"All arranged. You'll find your support elements already in place at Witten. Your call sign," Hoffmann said as he prepared to leave, "is Kilo Six, Kampfgruppe Bravo. For Boosfeld," Hoffmann's smile held dark amusement. "Your reputation precedes you, Herr Major. Half the Wehrmacht survivors in this sector know someone who served under you in the last war. They're expecting miracles."

"I don't do miracles, sir. You will need a priest for that."

"We can get you one of those," Stevens said, brightening.

"Unless he can drive a tank, that won't be necessary. Sir."

WITHIN AN HOUR, what remained of the 3rd was rolling northwest toward Witten. The convoy was small enough to fit on a single stretch of highway; a dozen tanks, nine support vehicles, and a sorry collection of trucks carrying the men who'd survived the destruction of an entire armoured division. They moved with the weary resignation of veterans, maintaining proper intervals, scanning the sky for aircraft, ready to disperse at the first sign of enemy contact.

The countryside rolled past with deceptive beauty. Green summer fields, prosperous farms, small towns that might have been painted by Romantic landscape artists if one ignored the occasional burned-out tank or cluster of fresh graves. Witten appeared ahead, a modest industrial town cleaved in two by the Ruhr River and surrounded by the sort of mixed residential and light manufacturing districts that were so common throughout the region. Under normal circumstances, it might have housed perhaps eighty thousand people. Now they were gone, and it was a military staging area, its streets clogged with muddy vehicles in the livery of five different armies.

Boosfeld spotted his new command well before he reached the designated assembly area. A great mass of steel clustered around a major intersection; tanks, armoured personnel carriers, trucks, and assorted military vehicles in no discernible order. Through his binoculars, he picked out unit markings from German, Dutch, Belgian, British, and a few American formations.

"Park us on the edge of that mess," he told his driver as they approached the intersection. "Let's see what delightful surprises await."

Panzer 59 ground to a halt, its diesel engine rumbling. Some of the allied personnel turned curiously, but most ignored him. Boosfeld surveyed his new command from the turret hatch and felt his heart sink.

It was much worse than he'd expected.

Thirty tanks, as promised, but scattered randomly across several bombed-out city blocks without regard for tactical positioning or mutual support. The personnel were clustered in national groups, eyeing each other with the suspicion of rival crime gangs forced to share territory by a police crackdown. Much of the equipment had been parked wherever the crews happened to stop, creating a nightmare that would take hours to sort out, and would kill them all if the Red Air Force broke through.

His tank had a loudspeaker system, and Boosfeld grabbed the microphone. He keyed it on, his amplified voice echoing off the ruins of the surrounding buildings.

"This is Major Joachim Boosfeld, commander of Kampfgruppe B. All company commanders report to me immediately!"

He saw several officers start forward, then hesitate. What now? Did these idiots not know whether they were his company commanders? A series of brief conferences followed, conducted in three languages, before seven men approached Panzer 59.

There were two Americans, the first a chubby captain with the soft look of a rear-echelon fellow suddenly thrust into line service. His uniform was clean, his equipment new, and his bearing that of a man who was rather hoping for orders to relieve him of whatever responsibility fate had thrust upon his sloping shoulders. His nameplate read "Wilson."

The British lieutenant was barely shaving.

The German tank commander looked familiar, Weber. He was a regular army lifer with the vacant yet intense stare of someone who'd seen too much in too short a time.

The two Dutchmen were older, with the bearing of reservists called back to service. Resentful, he would have said, if pressed.

The Belgian was a major—technically senior to everyone present except Boosfeld, but there was no spark in his eyes. He would do as ordered, but Boosfeld doubted he could rely on the man to take over if his own Panzer ate a shell or rolled over a mine.

The second American, a Ranger captain, stood slightly apart from the officers. His name tape read "Rodriguez," and his equipment was arranged with the precision of a man who'd learned that sloppiness killed people.

Boosfeld waited until they'd assembled, then swept them with his gaze. Each man received the full measure of his attention for as long as it took to capture theirs entirely.

"Gentlemen," he said in English, "welcome to Kampfgruppe B. In two hours, we move to our operational area near Gelsenkirchen. In three days, the Soviets will try to kill us all." He paused to let this sink in. "Before that happens, we're going to turn ourselves into a disciplined military unit again, instead of the armed mob I see before me."

The German tank commander looked bored. The British subaltern appeared determined. Rodriguez, the American captain, smiled. The Belgians and Dutch exchanged glances, suggesting they didn't believe a word.

"Questions?"

Captain Wilson raised his hand like a schoolboy asking permission to visit the toilet. "Sir, about my men—they're not exactly infantry. They're musicians. The 799th Army Band."

Musicians. Of course. Good. Excellent.

"That is unfortunate for them," Boosfeld said drily. "Because now I must insist they keep their instruments as clean as their rifles. When we are done at Gelsenkirchen, they can play a jaunty tune for us over all of the dead Russians we shall pile up. Captain Rodriguez, I assume you were touring with Captain Wilson's... orchestra? Tenor section, perhaps?"

Rodriguez smiled.

"No, sir. Heavy weapons and mortar section. We were just collocated when this whole thing started."

"Mortars I can use. Musicians..." Boosfeld shrugged. "I can use them, too. Any man who doesn't want to die running away, that man I can use."

The British lieutenant spoke up. He sounded nervous. "My lads are all odds and sods, sir. Signals, engineers, supply specialists, whoever happened to be in the replacement pool when the call came."

"Can they shoot?"

"Oh yes, sir. Some of them rather well, actually. We've been practising, sir."

The boy seemed quite earnest and could not be a complete idiot if he'd been training his men while they waited in the depot. Some officers he knew would have left them to it.

"Then they're infantry. Major van der Berg, status of your command?"

The senior Dutch officer replied in careful English. "Mixed tank company. Fifteen M-60s, various modifications. Crews are experienced, but equipment is... how do you say... improvised."

"As long as the guns work," Boosfeld said. "Major..." he looked at the Belgian, whose name tape was too faded to read.

"Dubois, sir. Mixed mechanised company. APCs and truck-mobile infantry. Also... improvised."

"I'm beginning to detect a pattern." Boosfeld's smile held no humour. "Hauptmann Weber, your status?"

"Fifteen M-60s, all operational. Mixed crews—some regular army, some reservists, some replacement draft. But they know their business."

"Good. Sergeant Rodriguez, mortar capability?"

"Four 120 mm tubes, sir. Plenty of ammo, and I have good crews. We can provide immediate fires out to six klicks."

Boosfeld nodded. "Excellent. Final question for all of you. Can your people fight?"

The answers came in various accents and levels of confidence, but they all amounted to the same thing: yes, they could fight. Whether they could fight together remained to be seen.

"Outstanding. Here's how we're going to do this..."

The sun was westering, and shadows lengthened across the field. Soon, they'd need to move toward their new positions, where they'd have three days to prepare for whatever the Reds chose to throw at them.

A ripple of motion caught Boosfeld's eye, just a flicker, but enough to draw attention. A lone figure moved toward them at a half-limping jog. Helmet in one hand, a submachine gun slung and bumping slightly at his side, his uniform streaked with soot and dried blood.

He stopped just outside the loose semicircle of gathered officers, mud caked up to his knees.

"Corporal Geert Veenstra," he said without waiting for an introduction, his voice raw and rasping, his English thick with the marshy drag of his Dutch accent.

"Apologies for the delay, Herr Major. We had contact south of the canal this morning—BMPs with dismounts. Two vehicles lost. One KIA, two walking wounded."

Boosfeld looked him over. The corporal's face was hollowed by exhaustion, and his eyes carried that flickering, distant stare of a man who'd been under fire for more days than he could count. A fresh rip across the sleeve of his battledress had congealed with blood, but he gave no sign of favouring the arm.

"And you're the senior man remaining? Corporal?"

Veenstra nodded once. "Yes, sir. My gun section's down to a couple of effectives."

Boosfeld glanced at van der Berg, who simply tilted his chin in acknowledgment. The corporal's presence, however grim, had evidently been expected.

"You're late," Boosfeld said, flatly.

"Yes, sir. We stayed to burn the last of the Russian ammo before pulling out."

For a moment, no one spoke.

Then Boosfeld gave him a curt nod. "Good work. You'll take your brief with the others."

Veenstra gave a hoarse "Yessir," eyes red-rimmed with exhaustion.

Boosfeld studied him for another few seconds. Torn kit, blood-spattered, and barely standing, but upright. He wasn't asking for anything. Nor offering excuses. He would do for Kampfgruppe Boosfeld.

"Right then, gentlemen," he said, his voice carrying across the intersection. "Let us begin."

27

Biloxi.

BILOXI, Mississippi, was one of those places they rolled up the sidewalk at sundown. Or they used to, Cherry thought. These days, with a hundred thousand army and air force guys—and girls, he conceded—hunkered down a few miles out at Keesler Field, it was always busy.

The main stem of Biloxi was a slow-motion riot. For the second time in ten years, Uncle Sugar's green river and the endless churn of young recruits had transformed the sleepy coastal town. Neon signs flickered above bars and juke joints, their doors yawning open to the humid night. Military police patrolled everywhere, their white helmets bobbing through the crowds. The air was thick with the mingled scents of spilled beer and fried shrimp, and the sharp tang of gasoline. Chrome-plated dupes of seventies muscle cars idled next to battered pickups with rusted fenders and cracked windshields. Black kids in sneakers and hoodies darted between GIs in pressed khaki. Cherry moved through the chaos, scoping ahead, occasionally stopping and lingering to check behind him.

It was just after eight on a bitchin' hot evening as Cherry made his way to the Beaumont Hotel. He had a room there, but he wasn't stay-ing. The room, in the name of Kefauver, held a change of clothes, a suitcase, a fifth of bourbon, and a half-eaten sandwich, exactly what you'd expect to find if you tossed the place while he was out. But he was always gonna be out. He couldn't stay at the Beaumont; they'd come for him there, which suited him fine. If they were scratching their heads and their asses, wondering why he wasn't in the hotel, they wouldn't be looking for him where he really was: a motel on the road out to Keesler Field.

He rechecked his watch. The night manager had been on for an hour and should have been far enough into his shift that things had settled down, maybe even got a little tedious. Cherry climbed the three steps and pushed through the revolving door into the blessed chill of the hotel's air conditioning. Outside, the steam-press humidity of the summer's night was hell. He knew some bad heat from his time in Honolulu, but Mississippi was something else—rank, oppressive, and inescapable, unless you had AC. Dressed in a suit, top shirt button undone and tie pulled loose, he felt like a corpse gone AWOL from the freezer down at the morgue.

Like Biloxi, the Beaumont had seen a flood of money come through during the war, but nothing for ten years. It was enjoying its second act. The marble floors were polished to a dull sheen. Heavy velvet drapes framed tall windows, their colours faded by decades of sun. The front desk was a long, scarred slab of wood, its edges worn smooth by generations of elbows. A chandelier hung overhead, its crystals catching the light and scattering it across the lobby in frac-tured rainbows. The air smelled faintly of lemon polish and old cigar smoke.

The night manager was alone at reception—a thin, tweedy-looking little twist with high cheekbones and a cocksucker's mous-tache. Cherry stepped up to the counter and got into character, sliding a business card across the scarred wooden bench top. "Good evening, sir," he said.

The manager picked up the card and read it with a flicker of inter-est: "Good evening. How can I help you, sir?"

"You had a guest in here, about a month ago," Cherry said. "Sen-ator McCarthy, down from Washington, visiting the base."

"Oh yes," the manager replied, picking up the business card again and reading it with more attention this time. The card introduced Cherry as Robert Kefauver from the office of the Sergeant-at-Arms, United States Senate. Cherry saw a whole bunch of what-the-hell across the other man's face: mostly surprise, interest, and anxiety.

"Is there a problem? We haven't heard anything from the Senator's office."

"No," Cherry said, taking the business card back and slipping it into the pocket where he kept about a dozen other cards from other men he'd met, all with useful jobs. "The senator might have left an address book here," he explained. "A little black book, you might call it, if you get my meaning." The night manager returned the sly grin. His was more furtive than Cherry's. "I might do, sir. But we haven't had anything handed in. If one of the maids had found it, you can be assured she would have turned it in."

"Thing is, Mr...?"

"Boudreaux," the night man replied.

"Mister Boudreaux. Thing is, I'd be assured by you telling me that, but I'd prefer the maid herself to tell me. I'd like to ask her that question face-to-face. If you understand."

Cherry let his eyes fill in the details. Robinson started nodding. Once he started, he couldn't stop. He rummaged under the desk, pulled out a clipboard, and flicked through half a dozen pages. "Yes, it was Millie on duty. She had the third floor that day. The thing is, Mr. Kefauver, she won't be in 'til Thursday."

"That's not gonna work for me," Cherry told him. "I'm out of here tomorrow morning. I had some things to chase up at the airfield and figured I'd come in here this evening and put a line under this. When I get back to DC, I want to tell the Senator's office we did everything we could. Frankly, Mister Boudreaux, I reckon if they look down the back of the cushions in his office couch, they'll find it there. But I'm in Biloxi today, flying out tomorrow, and you can save me another trip if you give me the maid's phone number and address."

He slid a ten-dollar note across the counter. Boudreaux palmed it like a first-class magician—it was there, and then it wasn't. They were alone at the reception desk. An Air Force guy, a colonel, it looked like, sat in an armchair on the other side of the foyer, reading a copy of

Time-Life magazine. Two large suitcases stood next to him. He wasn't paying them a lick of attention.

When Cherry looked back at the night manager, Boudreaux had scrawled out an address and pushed it across the countertop. Millie Mae Washington. 1 Charleston Street. No phone number. Cherry disappeared it into his pocket almost as deftly as Boudreaux had made the ten vanish.

"Thanks," he said. I'll check on this tonight. Can you send some fresh towels to my room? It's the heat, you know. I think I'm gonna have to take a cold shower before I head out again."

"Of course, sir," Boudreaux said. "I thought you were staying with us. I recognised you when you came in."

"Room 307," Cherry said.

"I'll have them sent up right away, Mr. Kefauver."

"Thanks again," Cherry said. He walked away from the counter, past the Air Force colonel, who looked up at him, idly curious. "Evening," Cherry nodded as he went by. He punched the button for the third floor at the single elevator and waited, resisting the natural urge to look back over his shoulder at the sneaky little fuck of a night manager.

The rather grand old elevator arrived with a clatter and a sigh, its brass doors opening to reveal an ornate iron concertina gate. Cherry pulled open the outer door, then the iron grille, stepped inside, and closed both behind him. He pressed the button for the third floor, then, as soon as the car began to move, stabbed the button for the second. The car jerked to a stop a few seconds later, and he hopped out, hurrying down the staircase that wrapped around the elevator shaft. He pressed himself against the wall and edged up to the corner, hoping to see the reception desk in the reflection of the big windows at the front of the hotel, but lady luck wasn't with him. He had to stick his head out around the corner. Sure enough, Boudreaux was on the phone, his back turned to the Air Force colonel, his shoulders hunched forward, and his hand cupped over the speaker. He didn't look like a man calling up housekeeping to order fresh towels to room 307.

The ghost of a grin flitted across Cherry's face. He walked back up to the first floor and took the fire escape out the back, down into the alleyway behind the hotel. The alley was deserted, the walls streaked with graffiti. Dumpsters lined up like drunken sentries, smelling of rot and fryer oil. Somewhere nearby, a cat yowled. The alley led out onto a side street that fed back onto the main stem, where the city's pulse was still strong—music, laughter, the blare of car horns.

Cherry rejoined the crowds, walking three blocks down to where he'd parked his rental car. No air con, sadly. He rolled the windows down and took out the note with Millie the maid's address on it.

He wasn't familiar with Biloxi, but it wasn't a big town. He drove to a gas station at the far end of the main stip, pulled in, bought some gum and a Coke, and asked the kid behind the counter for directions to Charleston Street.

"That's the Black District, mister," the kid said, surprised.

"Didn't ask for the colour code, kid," Cherry said, "Just the directions."

He got them and returned to the car, glad to have the icy-cold Coke. The sun had beat down like a hammer when he'd driven in this afternoon, but he thought Mississippi's nighttime heat was worse, a malignant, living thing – thick, wet, and suffocating. It pressed in from all sides, turning the air syrupy and demanding an effort for every breath. Sweat pooled at the small of his back and trickled down his ribs. The steering wheel was slick beneath his hands, and the seat stuck his pants to his ass. The only relief was the cold Coke, which he pressed against his neck for a brief, blessed chill.

He drove for ten minutes, windows down, watching the city change as he left downtown behind. The neon faded, replaced by streetlights casting long shadows over cracked sidewalks. Houses grew smaller and closer together, their paint peeling, and their yards overgrown. He passed shuttered storefronts, a church with a sagging roof, and a corner store with bars on the windows. The neighbourhood was respectable but tired and worn down.

Cherry pulled up at the corner of Charleston and Sumner streets. Millie Mae lived in a little shotgun shack. He could already imagine the floor plan: two bedrooms up front, hallway down the middle, lounge room to the left, another bedroom to the right, kitchen, outhouse, laundry, all the utilities at the back. The place was lit up. Three children played on the front porch where an old black man sat, reading a newspaper under the porch light, smoking a crooked-looking hand-rolled cigarette. No sign of Millie Mae.

Cherry turned off the engine and climbed out. The kids stopped playing. The old man looked up from his newspaper and stopped rocking. Cherry walked around the car and up to the front gate. He didn't push through. "Good evening, sir," he said. "My name's Stan Kefauver." He took out the business card. "I work for the Senate, and if it's no inconvenience, I'd like a few minutes of Miss Millie's time. She's not in any trouble, but she might know something about someone who is, a guest at the hotel."

The old man nodded. The children went back to playing, already bored with this small, unexpected intersection between the adult world and their own. The old man rocked forward and looked like he was about to struggle up out of the chair. "Please don't inconvenience yourself, sir," Cherry said. "I'm happy to walk up there and hand you the card. A good rocking chair can be hard to find, and that looks like one of the better examples I've ever seen. I'd hate to be responsible for interfering with your enjoyment of it."

The old man nodded, looking half-amused and half-relieved. "Best you come in then, son."

Cherry pushed through the gate. He expected it to squeal on its hinges, but it swung back smoothly, freshly oiled and recently repainted, he thought. The garden was small but tidy, with beds of marigolds and zinnias, a row of tomatoes staked along the fence, and the grass clipped short. The porch boards were swept clean, and the paint, though faded, was carefully maintained.

An old woman appeared at the rear of the shack, silhouetted in the hallway, and behind her, a much younger woman. Millie Mae, he assumed.

On another job, under other circumstances, Cherry would've barged into the house and started firing questions right into her face. But that wasn't the play here. He handed Stanley Kefauver's business card to the old man, who held it up under the porch light, around which a cloud of moths and mosquitoes swarmed. He nodded and handed it back.

"Millie Mae!" he called out. "Company for you."

"Thank you, sir," Cherry said.

The young woman emerged from behind her mother, maybe her grandmother; it was hard to tell. But Cherry bet on grandma. Millie Mae was good-looking, with high cheekbones and clear eyes, but there was obvious tension in her shoulders.

"Is there something wrong at work?" she asked.

"Not at all, Miss... Washington, is it?" Cherry said, glancing at the old man for confirmation.

"Millie Mae Washington," the old man confirmed.

"No problem at all, Miss Washington. Not for you. My name's Kefauver. I work for the Senate. You had a few senators staying at the Beaumont about a month ago."

"The Beaumont's had plenty of senators through," she said quickly. "It's the big base out at Keesler Field. They're always coming down here for that."

"Understood," Cherry said. "This was Senator Joseph McCarthy."

At the mention of McCarthy's name, the old woman, who'd been watching him intently but saying nothing, somehow managed to go from saying nothing to completely closing down. Cherry saw the steel shutters slam down behind her eyes, natural wariness turning instantly to cold reserve.

"Oh," said Millie Mae. "Yes."

She left it at that.

"He says he lost a notebook," Cherry said. "He thinks he left it behind in the room."

He let that hang there, too. If he'd been a hotel detective or a beat cop investigating a petty theft, he'd have had a lot more to say, and it would have arrived on a freight train full of threats and allegations. He didn't want her scared of him, though; he wanted her help.

"Well, I didn't see anything like that," she said.

"I'm not saying you did," Cherry smiled. He tried to make the smile as friendly and collegial as possible, rebuilding the frame around the story he'd used with Boudreaux. "Frankly, ma'am, the Senator is forgetful. This is not the first time he's left something behind and... well, you know."

The old man spoke up. "And tried to blame it on someone else, you mean, sir."

Cherry left his smile in place. "You might say that, sir, but the office of the Sergeant at Arms couldn't possibly comment." He let the grin grow wider, and as it grew, he felt the tension beginning to break up and float away.

"Miss Washington, would you mind if I asked you a couple of questions about what the Senator was doing when he was down here?" Cherry asked. "The more I know about his routine, the more likely I am to find his notebook."

Millie Mae hesitated, not knowing how to respond. The older woman said, "Would you like some iced tea, sir?"

"That would be very nice, ma'am. Thank you," he said. "I'm not from around these parts, and the heat, well, as the good Lord said, these things are sent to try us."

The old woman nodded and shuffled off to the rear of the house. Cherry wondered if they had a refrigerator or if she'd chip a few chunks off a block down in the root cellar. He had his answer a few moments later when he heard the clunk of a heavy fridge door opening and the crack and rattle of ice cubes being twisted out of a tray. All the mod cons, he thought. Good for them.

"Hey, mister," one of the kids tugged at his suit. "Do you have a gun?"

"Not on me, son," Cherry replied. "Why? You think you could beat me in a quick draw?" He mimed a cowboy pulling his six-shooter and squeezing off a couple of rounds. The kid squealed with laughter, and the other two joined him, swarming the visitor, who, it turned out, was much more interesting than the average adult.

"You kids get going now!" the old boy said. "You leave Mr. Kefauver be, less'n he pulls out his gun and shoots y'all for real with it. Go on. Git!" He leaned forward as if to get up from the rocker, and the kids scurried away, giggling.

"Well, don't just stand there," the old woman called out from the far end of the cottage. She held a jug full of ice cubes and dark liquid. "You can come in now, if you agree to ignore the mess. Three children underfoot, you know, worse than three literal demons."

Cherry nodded and stepped in through the front door. The house was immaculate. Basic, but clean and comfortable. He saw some furniture that looked like it might have been carved by hand, which gave him an idea that grandpa out front was rocking a chair of his own making. In the kitchen, he confirmed there was a General Electric fridge, an old model, but bigger than the one he had in his apartment back in LA. The table sat on steel legs, and the Formica top was faded and scratched, but spotless. Granny had already laid out three glasses with doilies under them, and she poured the iced tea.

He sat in the chair she indicated and waited for her to serve. She'd cut up an orange and a lemon and put the slices in the jug. Cherry sipped the drink out of good manners, then blinked in surprise. It was a hell of a lot nicer than the Coke he'd just had. Even though it meant he was going to have to take a piss behind a tree on the way back to town, he drew off half the glass in a couple of gulps. "Damn," he said, then hurried to apologise. "Sorry, ma'am, but that is a fine iced tea."

The old woman nodded, but he could see she was pleased. Sitting opposite him, Millie Mae looked nervous and kept her hands in her lap. Grandma poured one for herself and her husband, presumably, and excused herself to deliver his drink. Silence dropped like a heavy curtain between Cherry and the young woman. It quickly became uncomfortable.

"Don't y'all have some questions for me?" she said at last, sounding both scared and resentful.

"I had a couple of things I needed to ask, sure," he said, "but don't you want to wait until your grandma gets back?"

"She's talking to Pop now," Millie Mae said. "She's probably forgotten you're here. She forgets things these days. More things every day."

"Sorry to hear that," Cherry said.

Millie Mae looked at him. This time, she didn't drop her eyes. "With all due respect, sir," she said, "I doubt you care."

He nodded, acknowledging her point, but said, "Good manners never cost a man anything, Miss Millie."

"Not many men around here would agree," she pushed back.

"White men, you mean?"

She said nothing to that.

"I never saw any notebook," she said after a moment.

"That's because there was no notebook," Cherry said. "That's not what I'm here about."

Millie Mae's glass stopped halfway to her lips. Her shoulders went rigid, and her hand trembled slightly when she set the tea down. She pushed back from the table, the chair legs scraping against the linoleum.

"Then why are you here?"

"Not because Joe McCarthy sent me. I can tell you that much."

"You gonna need to tell me a hell of a lot more'n that, if'n you want my help, sir."

Her eyes flicked over his shoulders, down the hallway to where her grandparents chatted on the front porch. "Am I in trouble?" she asked.

He shook his head gently.

"It feels like I'm in trouble," she insisted.

"No, ma'am," he said. "You are not in trouble."

Her eyes narrowed. "You don't work for the Senate, do you?" she said. It wasn't a question.

"I do not."

"Who do you work for?"

"Miss Millie—" he started.

She cut him off.

"Please don't call me that."

"Okay. But, ma'am, it's best you don't know who I work for."

"Oh, this feels like trouble," she said.

"Not for you, ma'am. Regarding anyone who'd care, you spoke to Mr. Kefauver about Senator McCarthy's missing notebook. Mr. Boudreaux at the Beaumont, who gave me your address for ten dollars, will confirm that."

Something shifted in her face, not surprise, but a kind of weary recognition. She shook her head slowly. "Ten dollars," she repeated, her voice flat. She looked up at him, pushing her shoulders back. "And what is it that you want me to talk about that's worth a whole ten dollars?" she asked.

Millie Mae Washington was a smart woman, Cherry thought. Almost certainly didn't have her high school diploma, but that didn't make her dumb.

"You cleaned his room every day he was there?" he asked.

"Yes, sir," she said, "every day."

"Did he have anyone with him?" he asked.

"Mr. Cohn stayed in the hotel," she said. "He was on another floor, though."

"That's not what I meant. Did he have any visitors? Any guests staying overnight in the room?"

She looked at the iced tea sitting in front of her. The beads of perspiration had grown large enough to start trickling down the side. She said nothing, which was half an answer.

"The maids can always tell," Cherry said. "When someone's had company. Can't they?"

Millie nodded. "You can always tell," she said.

"So when I asked if McCarthy had anyone stay over, you didn't say no."

She shook her head. "It's a sin to lie, sir."

Cherry leaned back, letting that sit between them. He was not a good man by most measures, but he understood men and their nature. Women, too, for some things at least. He knew when to press and when to play out the line. He'd already hooked something important. He knew Joe McCarthy hadn't brought his wife to Biloxi, and he hadn't slept alone here. That was something to be getting on with. But he could sense Millie Mae knew more, and he didn't need to jerk the line. Sometimes, the best way was to say nothing, just let your subject fill the silence with what they needed to say.

"There's something else, ma'am," he said. "There's something you don't want to tell me, isn't there?"

"It is a sin, sir, to tell a lie."

"Yeah," he said, "it says so right up at the front of the Bible, as best I recall."

"Do you read your Bible, Mister Kefauver?"

He shook his head. "Sadly, no, Millie. Not for a long time."

"You should," she said.

"I cannot argue with the truth," Cherry agreed. "And I would not have you tell me lies, ma'am, but I'm afraid that telling a lie isn't just a sin of commission. You can offend the Lord with what you don't say. And there is something you're not telling me, Miss Washington, something I need to know. I don't want to presume on you in any way, but I'd suggest that whatever that thing is, it's weighing heavily on your conscience. So heavy that perhaps the Good Lord needs you to unburden yourself of it."

She opened her mouth and closed it, took a drink of the iced tea so quickly that some slopped over the side. She stood up with a little groan. She'd soaked the knitted doily, which the glass had been perspiring on. She hurried over to the kitchen sink and pulled a tea towel off a hook, coming back and cleaning up her mess. She didn't sit down again. Cherry stood up.

"Is there a name you can give me?" he said. "Just a name. That's all I need."

She opened her mouth and closed it. She turned away from him, clutching the tea towel, and turned back. "My friend," she said. "Willamina, my friend." She had screwed the tea towel into a tight binding around her hands, as though shackled by whatever she was trying to tell him. "Poor Willy," she said.

The night had gone quiet around them. Even the children on the porch had stopped their chatter. Cherry could hear his heartbeat, the tick of a clock somewhere in the house.

"Tell me," he said.

But before she could speak, the gunshot cut her off.

28

Biloxi

FOR ONCE IN HIS LIFE, Cherry wasn't lying, not entirely. He'd told the kid he didn't have a gun when what he meant was that he wasn't carrying his gun. It was out in the car. He'd left it there, not wanting to scare Millie Mae Washington when he turned up. He regretted not having it when he heard the pop of gunfire outside.

But then he heard the squeak of brakes and the grumble of tires on gravel, and he knew it wasn't gunfire. It was just a backfiring tailpipe from some shitty pickup or sedan. Cursing, he told Millie Mae to stay in the kitchen.

He stalked down the hallway, through the house, and back onto the porch. Sure enough, a flatbed truck had pulled up behind his rental sedan.

"Y'all get inside now," Grandpa Washington told the three kids. They started to protest. Cherry growled at them. "Do as your grandfather says. Now." They stared at him with big, wide eyes. The kid who'd approached him earlier gulped and led the others into the house.

The truck doors clunked open, and three men climbed out. The driver first: a thick-set, flat-topped, broken-nosed plug of a man with ham hocks for arms. On the passenger side, a six-foot-tall rattlesnake in human form uncoiled himself from the front seat and slithered down onto the footpath. He wore stovepipe jeans, a grey t-shirt that might have been white once, and a thick belt with an even thicker belt buckle. After him came the shortest of the three, small enough that Cherry might have picked him for a jockey, except for the pot belly hanging over his blue jeans.

They walked past the gate, up to Cherry's rental sedan, and lounged against it, watching.

"Do you know them?" Cherry asked quietly.

"That's Delroy Moody," the old man said, "the longhaired rattlesnake is Morgan Stover. Short fella is Darby Poole. He's the sheriff's nephew."

"Great," Cherry said. "Just great. You should go inside now, all of you."

Grandma Washington tried to pull Millie Mae back into the house and scolded her husband for still sitting in his rocker, but neither the young woman nor the old man seemed inclined to follow Cherry's advice or listen to her demands.

He stepped off the porch and walked a few steps down the path towards the three men. They roused themselves and pushed off his rental.

Cherry stopped just short of the gate. He gave them the professional courtesy of a brief once-over. At least they weren't carrying guns, not that he could see. But he wouldn't be surprised if one or more of them had a straight razor or a flick knife in a back pocket.

"Can I help you boys?" he asked.

Delroy Moody elected himself their spokesman. "You can tell us what you're doing here."

"What makes you think it's any of your business?" Cherry said.

"Because we're making it our business," Delroy growled.

Cherry nodded, appeared to think that over, and conclude that it was an entirely reasonable response. "Furniture," he said, which surprised them. Genuinely surprised them, he was happy to see. "I heard the old man made furniture. I want a rocking chair. For my old man. So I came out to see if he'd make me one."

"The fuck you did," Delroy said.

"The fuck would you know about it?" Cherry pushed back.

"You came out here to ask questions." Stover hissed at him.

"I did," Cherry said, "about a rocking chair."

"You shut the fuck up about the rocking chair, you dumb Yankee fuckpig," the fat jockey said.

Cherry huffed out a laugh. "You still fighting that war, pecker-head? You know your useless fucking grandaddy lost it, right? A long time ago. Or you were too stupid to notice?"

They'd crowded up around the gate, and he stepped back a little to give himself more room.

"You come out here and say that!" Derby Poole challenged him.

"Why? Are you hard of hearing as well as comically short? Fatso?"

That did it. Enraged beyond all hope of rational thought, Derby tried to scramble over the gate rather than just opening it and walking through. As he threw one leg over, Cherry stepped forward and grabbed a handful of hair in his meaty fist. He yanked hard, and the short man yelped, trying to pull back. But he was only standing on one leg, the other leg half over the gate, robbing him of all his balance and most of his strength. It was nothing for Cherry to step back again, pulling hard and slamming him face-first into the concrete path.

Delroy and Morgan tried to dog pile him, the bigger man having the presence of mind to undo the latch before trying to charge through. But the confined space worked in Cherry's favour. They had to funnel through in single file, slowing them and ruining any chance of coordinating their attack. Delroy came first, his broad shoulders jamming momentarily against Morgan, almost knocking sideways into the flower beds. Cherry stepped forward and drove his knee straight up into the big man's groin. He doubled over with a strangled grunt, blocking the narrow opening completely.

Morgan tried to jump over his writhing friend, but stumbled instead, arms windmilling as he fought for balance. Cherry grabbed a heavy terracotta planter beside the gatepost and swung it hard. The pot exploded against Morgan's skull in a shower of dirt and ceramic shards, dropping him like a sack of shit.

In less than five seconds, all three men lay broken and bleeding on the ground.

Cherry turned around. Millie Mae and her grandmother stood on the porch, their faces distorted with horror. Grandpa Washington stood by his rocking chair, a double-barrel shotgun now cradled in his arms, a satisfied grin playing on his lips.

"Sorry about the mess," Cherry said. He opened the gate and dragged Derby Poole and Morgan Stover back onto the grass verge. He picked them up like bags of feed, one after the other, and threw them into the back of the flatbed truck. They each landed with a dull thud and a groan.

He went back for Delroy, who was still doubled over from the boot to his nuts, but he was giving it the old college try, reaching for his back pocket with a shaking hand. He pulled out a flick knife and tried to lunge at Cherry, a woeful, clumsy attack that Cherry avoided easily. He grabbed Delroy's knife arm, extended it, and snapped it at the elbow. The sharp, wet crack echoed through the night, followed by two screams, Delroy and Millie Mae Washington's.

Cherry dragged Delroy Moody around to the driver's side of the truck. The flat-top crew cut offered no purchase, so Cherry grabbed a handful of ear, using his crushing grip to steer the man. He yanked open the driver's side door and bundled Delroy in. He was broken, a snivelling, snot-and-blood-covered mess. Cherry took a handful of his throat, closing his fingers around Delroy's windpipe. Then he put the flick-knife up to his neck.

He glanced toward the front of the shack. The two women were hurrying back inside. Grandpa Washington still stood with his shotgun, watching it all go down. The smile was gone.

Cherry squeezed another quarter inch on Delroy's windpipe and dug the knife into the skin under his ear. He slowly twisted the point. "Who sent you?" he said quietly.

Delroy struggled to get away from the sharp steel. Cherry dug his fingers deeper into his throat and twisted the blade again. "Who sent you?"

He blubbered up a name, coughed it up with a ball of snot as blood ran freely from the growing incision in the side of his neck. "Ha- Ham- Hamilton," he gasped.

"Never heard of him. Who's Hamilton?" Cherry squeezed and twisted again.

"Mr. Hamilton," Delroy babbled. "Edgar. Edgar Hamilton."

"Good boy," Cherry said. He took the knife away, thumb-pressed the button and pushed the blade back into the handle until it clicked shut. He slipped the knife into his back pocket but kept his grip on Delroy's windpipe.

"I'm gonna let you go now, Delroy," he said. "That's going to be the highlight of your day. You're going to be able to breathe free again. And that's gonna be so fucking sweet, you won't believe it." He closed off another quarter inch on the windpipe, then let go. As Delroy Moody gasped for air, Cherry chopped his hand back into his throat, took the grip again, and squeezed just as hard as before. "But if you come back at me, boy—if you come back at these people—next time I'm gonna keep squeezing. Do you understand me?"

Delroy blubbered out that he did. This time, Cherry let go of his throat for good.

"Are you a good driver, Delroy?" he asked. The other man was crying wretchedly now, his face a mask of snot, tears, and blood, his body trembling. He stared at Cherry, eyes wide and unfocused, the question seemingly too complex to process.

"I asked if you are a good driver, Delroy. I assume you must be, because this piece of shit truck of yours looks like it'd fly apart if you farted too hard. So, you gotta be a pretty good driver to keep this heap on the road. Am I right?"

He nodded, a pathetic, jerky motion. "I'm okay, I guess."

"Good," Cherry said. "Because you'll need to drive yourself and your friends to the hospital. And that won't be easy, because I broke your arm at the elbow. You'll never fully recover from it, and you sure as hell won't be getting any better in the next five minutes. So I suggest you get one of the fellas to work the stick while you steer and manage the clutch. That's why I asked if you were a good driver, because that'll be a hell of a challenge."

"Okay," Delroy blubbered.

"The other challenge for you, Delroy, is pride. Your pride will start whispering to you in the next day or so. It's gonna tell you a bunch of lies about what happened here, about how it coulda turned out different. If you listen to those lies, Delroy, you might be tempted to come back, to prove that what went wrong here for you was just an accident. But it was no accident, son. I meant to hurt you. And here we are, because you're a bunch of fucking redneck fools and you don't know what you're doing. But let me ask you, Delroy, do you think I know what I'm doing?"

Delroy, still blubbering, nodded vigorously. "Yes, sir. You know what you're doing."

"That's good, son. I'm glad to hear that. Because if you do come back here, if you so much as look sideways at Millie Mae, or her grandparents, or those children, I will fall on you like the angel of fucking death, my friend. I will take your lives. Do you believe me? Do you believe I am the sort of man who would take your life from you, Delroy?"

Delroy nodded frantically. Cherry nodded and patted him on the shoulder.

"That's good. I'm glad we got to have this chat. I feel like we understand each other now. Which of the retards do you think would be the most useful in helping you drive away from here and never come back?"

"Morgan," Delroy mumbled. "He's... he's..."

"The tall one, yeah, I know," Cherry said. "Morgan Stover. I know all your names, and in an hour or so, I'll know where you live."

Cherry walked back to the flatbed of the truck, dragged Stover off, and threw him bodily into the cabin next to Delroy.

"You drive careful now, Delroy. You understand? You wouldn't want your little friend to roll off the back."

He watched as Delroy attempted to start the truck. It took them two or three minutes to get going, and even then, they kangaroo-hopped away around the corner and into the night.

Cherry watched them go until the taillights had been swallowed up by the thin, scrubby forest between this neighbourhood and the edge of town. He returned to the front gate, frowned at the mess they'd made of the flower beds, and walked up to Grandpa Washington.

"I'm sorry about that," he said, and he surprised himself by meaning it.

"I'm not," Washington said. "Those boys are Klan."

"Yeah," Cherry said, looking off up the street where he fancied he could still hear the coughing of the truck engine. "Figured as much. I told them not to come back."

"And they probably won't," the old man said. "But..."

"But somebody else might," Cherry conceded. He looked at the shotgun. "A black man is not going to get away with pointing a shotgun at white men in Biloxi, Mr. Washington. Besides, that's a double-barreled duck gun. You can get off two rounds of buckshot, and then they'd swarm you."

Washington nodded. "Sounds about right," he said. "So, what would you suggest I do, Mr. Kefauver, seeing as how you brought this to my doorstep and dragged my granddaughter into it?"

"Seeing as how I did, yeah, I'd suggest you get the hell out of town, sir."

"Uh-huh," Washington said. "And go where? This is our home."

Cherry reached into his jacket and took out the envelope full of cash. He'd figured Millie Mae Washington would have to make herself scarce after he'd spoken to her. He hadn't imagined it would go this bad, this fast.

"You got two thousand dollars in here," he said. He pressed the envelope into the old man's hand, but Washington didn't move to take it, his grip firm on the shotgun. Cherry dropped the envelope onto the seat of the rocking chair. He reached into his back pocket, took out his wallet, and pulled out a business card. A real card this time, with an LA phone number on it.

"Take the money," he said, "and get out of town tomorrow. Call this number. Tell them what happened. Tell them Lou Cherry told you to call and said they would handle the problem. Can you do that, Mr. Washington?"

This time, he took the card. He reached down and picked up the envelope. "Damn you," he said. "Damn all of you white devils to hell."

"Will you do it, Mr. Washington? It's important. You need to get yourself gone from Biloxi, all of you. The people at the end of that phone number will help you."

"I can do it," he said.

"Good," Cherry said. "I'm going to swing by here tomorrow before I head out of town. I'd like to think you'd be on your way by then."

"What choice do we have?" Washington said.

"There's always a choice, sir," Cherry replied. "I'm just suggesting you make the right one."

EXTRACT

'Studs Terkel Talks About The Transitions: An Oral History of the Future'
The New Yorker | March 13, 1954 | Vol. 29, No. 5 | pp. 51–66

Clarence "Clay" Foster, filmmaker

(Interview conducted September 1953 on a rented soundstage outside Watts, Los Angeles. The paint on the walls is flaking, the air smells of dust and burned celluloid. Foster is thirty-two, wearing a porkpie hat and a jacket that looks one size too big. A Steenbeck editing table sits in the corner, reels stacked like poker chips. The hum of a borrowed projector fills the room.)

I'm twenty years early, brother. That's what I keep telling people. Twenty years minimum. But if you give me seventy years of movies to steal from, you best believe I can meet the future halfway.

Hollywood? Nah, Hollywood don't want me, not as a director. They'll take me as a porter, a driver, maybe an extra if they need a body in a crowd scene. But a camera? A dolly track? Forget it. So we got to do it ourselves.

Davidson Pictures wrote my first check. For *Low Rent*. No, the irony was not lost on me. Not a big one, but enough to buy short ends, rent lights, feed a crew. They didn't have a Hollywood lot then. So we shot in warehouses, jazz clubs after hours, a church basement where the pastor leans radical.

It was a straight rip of *Double Indemnity*. I mean straight. Same bones, same shadows, same cigarettes burning down in the dark. Good artists copy. Great artists steal. Right? We stole everything but the location. Set that in Central Avenue, the hood. And we shot fast. Two takes, three at most. You know our first night shoot? We didn't have a generator. We ran extension cords through three different yards and blew half the block's fuses.

Props? Half of them borrowed. We shot a love scene in a Buick the pastor's brother loaned us. Told him it was for "transport sequences." He never asked questions. The kiss steamed the windows so thick we were blind, and I was ready to call cut, until Donna Maree wipes at the fog like she's drowning in pleasure. To the camera it looked like she was raking at the world in ecstasy with those white gloves on.

He leans back, grinning like the Cheshire cat.

That's where the poster came from. *That* image that went all the way to the Supreme Court. Mr Davidson cut a bigger cheque for the lawyers than he ever did for the movie!

The thing is, my audience is hungry. You ever sit in a colored theater on a Friday night when *Low Rent* is playing? Or *Midnight Contract*. Or *The Switchman*? Folks see themselves big on the screen— not maids, not porters, not jokes—but as heroes, lovers, detectives. It's like a cool drink of water in the desert.

Hollywood still laughs at us. Calls it back-alley junk. But I know how to frame a shot. I know how to see the world with my third eye. And when whiteywood finally wakes up and sees our ticket sales, they'll know: the future wasn't theirs to stop.

29

Marseille.

WITH A BRISK MOTION, Ronsard pulled open the van's rear doors. Ivanov emerged first, adjusting the lapels of his suit. Good cloth, but hard miles and tailored to imply some rank and privilege. Charlotte followed, her appearance just as composed and deliberate: the flat shoes, the grey blouse, the heavy wool skirt were the choice of a young French woman with a job to do and no interest in drawing notice. One might take her for a junior clerk in the customs office, or a librarian for the city council.

"This it?" Charlotte said, looking at the warehouse, unimpressed.

"Almost," Ronsard said, "we have to go the last part on foot."

He tapped twice, paused, then rapped again on the narrow wooden door beside the yawning steel shutter. A code, Harry thought, unmistakably practised. The door cracked open at once. A man beckoned them inside with a quiet rush of French, waving them through with a glance into the alleyway. No names, no pleasantries. From a dim hallway, a second man appeared, accepted Ronsard's keys as though retrieving a valet ticket, slid behind the wheel of the van and drove off, tires whispering over the cobblestones.

The first lookout patted them down for weapons.

Ronsard was allowed a handgun. Harry and the others had to go to the meeting unarmed.

They trailed behind Ronsard through a winding circuit of narrow corridors that seemed to run between many warehouses, along alleys that stank faintly of diesel and old piss, doubling back more than once, as if the path were designed not just for discretion but to disorient. At intervals, the path opened briefly to glimpses of the night sky before the following passage swallowed them again. It was a rat's nest in every sense: a junction where the Resistance and the remnants of Marseille's criminal underclass shared uneasy ground.

After ten minutes, they emerged into a low-ceilinged storeroom reeking faintly of mildew and old oil. Wooden crates were stacked haphazardly to the rafters. Harry first saw pallets of butter sealed in wax-paper bricks, corned beef from Manchester and tins of meat labelled in Cyrillic. He noted sacks of flour stamped with a red star and plastic-wrapped blocks of cheese stencilled with the logo of USAID.

Then he saw *le Milieu*.

Twelve men. Harry counted them almost reflexively, his mind already sorting them by allegiance. To the left, in front of a wall of what looked very much like stolen Allied rations, stood Jacques Fournier—better known, and not without cause, as "The Ferret." Thin, sharp-featured, and constantly in motion, however constrained, Fournier radiated nervous apprehension, like a man perpetually listening for the sound of boots on the stairs. His narrow face and darting eyes completed the impression; rodent-like, yes, but also cunning. His nose and jaw came to sharp points, and when he moved, he made quick, nervous cuts through space, like he was always halfway to the nearest door.

Opposite stood Guy "The Phantom" Vidal, a name bestowed with some irony, as the man himself was about as inconspicuous as a bloodied butcher's apron at a tea party. Stout and flushed, with the heavy-lidded look of a man more accustomed to long lunches than dodging bullets, he exuded the weary self-importance of a well-fed shopkeeper playing at empire. He wore a serviceable grey suit, pressed to within an inch of its life, a burgundy tie knotted with an almost painful precision, and shoes buffed to a shine that only emphasised their rather cheap leather. Respectability for Vidal was more costume than nature, Harry thought.

Each man had a second at his shoulder, and behind them loomed the muscle—thickset, brooding, and clearly not there to talk.

Standing at Vidal's shoulder, his lieutenant cut a sharper, more austere figure, lean to the point of gauntness, with angular features and a gaze that flicked from face to face like a pickpocket's fingers. His suit, ill-fitting and frayed at the cuffs, did little to obscure the impression of someone more familiar with alleyways than accounting ledgers. Whatever past he'd dragged behind him, it hadn't included counting coins at some shop counter.

Opposite him, Fournier's second was broad-shouldered, impeccably groomed, and possessed of that effortless confidence you found only in cavalrymen and con artists.

Harry wondered how each lieutenant had come to tie his fate to the man beside him, what debts were owed, what loyalties bought or betrayed. But he was not in Marseille to satisfy his curiosity about its criminal ecology. He had come, against the odds and perhaps his better judgment, to broker unity among men unaccustomed to thinking in terms beyond their own gain. To make something whole, however briefly, out of men who made their living breaking pieces off the world.

"Gentlemen," he said, dipping his head in a respectful bow, carefully calibrated to fall precisely between each man so that neither might think the other had been favoured.

"Your Highness," Vidal clicked his heels together and executed a quite creditable formal bow.

"Monsieur," Fournier said pointedly, lifting his chin almost as if inviting Harry to pull out a duelling glove and give him a smack across the chops for his insolence.

"You, of course, are known to us," Vidal said evenly. Then, with a glance that lingered a beat too long on Charlotte, "But who, may I ask, is your charming companion?"

He stared at her as if she were the last bonbon in the box; rare, tempting, and not long for this world.

"My colleagues," Harry began. "Madame Charlotte François,

formerly of the United States Marine Corps, now, like yourselves, engaged in more entrepreneurial pursuits. And from my own time, Captain Pavel Ivanov. No friend of the Bolsheviks, I assure you."

That last name hit the room like a flicked switch. The muscle tensed. They knew. Ronsard had promised they would. Still, knowledge was one thing, proximity and confirmation another.

"How can we trust him? He's a Russian," the Ferret hissed in French.

Ivanov smiled mildly and replied in French. *"How could anyone trust you? You're a fucking ferret."*

Vidal's men chuckled and sniggered at that; Fournier's did not. "You expect us to believe he can be trusted?" Fournier said, this time in English.

"I've been fighting communists a lot longer than you have," Ivanov said.

"Really?" the Ferret sneered. "And how many Russians have you killed?"

Ivanov's smile was slow and deliberate, like a blade being drawn for show, "I've killed many more Russians than I have French vermin. But I'm willing to make a change."

Vidal's men were laughing openly now; Fournier's looked like they might be about to draw guns. Ronsard stepped in between Ivanov and Fournier, holding up both hands. "Gentlemen, please," he said, "we share the same enemy, at least for today. Prince Harry has come as the personal envoy of Her Majesty's government to assure you that if you make common cause with us, you will be supported to the full extent of our means."

"And what form might that support take?" Guy Vidal asked.

"Tell me what you need, tell me why you need it, and I will make it happen," Harry said. "Weapons, money, whatever."

"Freedom?" the Ferret repeated, voice curling around the word like smoke. "And when the Russians are gone? Whose boot finds our neck then?"

Harry raised both hands, palms open.

"Monsieur Fournier," he said softly, "I won't insult you with promises my government wouldn't honour, or with futures none of us will see if we don't survive the present emergency. What you're asking, I suspect, is whether the black market channels you once ran —say, the opium trade out of Indochina—will reopen."

He said it without accusation, but without apology either.

They hadn't expected him to be so blunt. That much was clear from the way both the Ferret and the Phantom paused, like men caught off guard by someone naming the thing they'd all agreed to tiptoe around. But Harry had learned something long ago, many decades from now—in desert tents and shattered mudbrick towns— that you didn't build trust by making easy promises. You built it, if at all, with the kind of truth that made everyone more than a little uncomfortable.

"So no," he concluded quietly, "I can't promise you a return to empire—the heroin routes, the docks, the quiet complicity of a shadow state. I can assure you that should we lose, you'll find your-selves not at the helm of Marseille, but in a gulag. Worked slowly to death most likely, executed quickly if your luck is in, and buried in either case without a name in the clay beyond the city you once ruled."

Both men paused, letting the weight of the argument find its place.

"He makes a fair point," said the Ferret with a reluctant nod.

"Indeed," said Vidal. "Sufficient unto the day are the evils thereof."

Harry smiled at Vidal, needing to show himself off as a man of letters.

"Naturally, I would welcome your answer now," Harry said with a polite nod. "But I understand these things require discussion." He paused, just long enough. "As you consider this, I hope you'll keep in mind that my government—and those aligned with it—are sincere in their offer of support. We understand that Le Milieu possesses certain... capabilities. Capabilities acquired over very long careers, and skills of a sort that make life a nightmare for your enemies."

He tried not to look at Ivanov or Charlotte, particularly Charlotte, whose smirk might be contagious.

"This is all very well," the Ferret said. "And we accept the serious-ness of your mission. Your presence here speaks to that. If the Russians were to take you, I imagine you'd fetch a high ransom?"

Harry barked out a short laugh. "This isn't Agincourt, my friend. No heralds, no terms. If I'm taken in Marseille, I'm not a bargaining chip. I would be just another prisoner behind the wire."

"Interesting," Fournier said. "But it strains belief."

Harry gestured lightly to himself. "Nonetheless, I stand before you. You wanted a gesture of good faith. I am that gesture."

"And what of your colleagues?" Vidal asked. "The Russian and an American, if I am not mistaken. What do they betoken?"

"We're here on personal business," Charlotte said. She teased open a pocket and paused, letting them see she was not reaching for a weapon. From within, she pulled out a picture of Alexei Skarov. "We are looking for this man," she said.

Neither Fournier nor Vidal betrayed the slightest recognition. To Harry, that was telling. If Skarov had operated here, their response would have been very different.

But then again, if he had worked this city, it was unlikely either man would be alive to respond at all. They'd be long buried, with the rest of their colleagues.

"Who is he?" Vidal asked. "Or perhaps I should say, what is he to you?"

"Comrade Skarov is a senior operator for Beria's NKVD," Harry said. "He's currently escorting a German scientist named Ernst Bremmer, by which I mean, he's taken him. They're en route to Moscow, assuming they're not there already."

He paused. "We've been chasing Bremmer since before the war began. But with hostilities underway, my superiors have judged him a lesser priority, which is how I find myself here, with you. You are my mission, specifically organising the resistance in Marseille, along with my colleague Captain Ronsard. My friends, however, have personal business with Skarov."

"Ah."

"I see."

"Then it is blood vengeance," said the Ferret, as if naming a favourite wine.

Ivanov let his smile emerge by degrees, "You see, we do understand each other," he said. "Harry is here for you. We are here for Skarov. And if he is not here, we shall move on. Or," and at this he turned to Charlotte, "I shall. It will be easier for me to track him to Moscow."

Charlotte raised an eyebrow at him and replied in perfect Russian, "You keep saying that, but I don't think those words mean what you think they mean."

Ivanov shrugged. The clan bosses simply looked confused.

"At any rate," Harry said, "if you agree to this arrangement, you will work with us, not for us, and we will support you with whatever resources we can bring for the duration of hostilities."

Fournier nodded, and Vidal looked satisfied.

"Let us talk then," the Ferret said.

"We will discuss it now," Vidal agreed, casting a sidelong glance at Fournier, whose answering nod was short but sufficient.

The tension, once as thick as paste, began to loosen. It was not a win, not yet, but it might be progress. Perhaps this would hold. Maybe he'd be on a plane back to England within the week. And to Julia.

"If you'll excuse us," Vidal said.

The men crossed the warehouse, their footsteps scraping and scuffing against the cracked concrete. Around them, crates and barrels loomed in the shadows and the air held the strong aromas of roasted coffee, tobacco, and onions.

The Frenchmen formed a tight circle, their conversation hushed but clearly animated.

"I think this will work," Ronsard said. "The arrangement, at least. As for your Russian spy," he glanced between Ivanov and Charlotte. "That's less certain. If Skarov made it to Marseille with a prize like that, he won't have lingered. Your German scientist is likely already sitting in a Lubyanka cell having his options explained to him."

"Then I will go to the Lubyanka," Ivanov said. "You have your war; I have mine."

Harry looked over at Charlotte, half-bracing for some promise of revenge. For Viv, for Cairo. But she didn't say a word.

Harry had just begun thinking about exfil. How long it would take to reach the submarine, how soon he might be home, when gunfire roared.

He had maybe a heartbeat to understand. No time for reason, just a rush of noise and heat and the taste of metal in his mouth.

His first thought was chaos. That Le Milieu had turned on itself.

The Ferret was already on the ground, half his head gone, his expression, what was left of it, frozen in surprise.

Gunfire raged. Vidal's men cutting down Fournier's. But not all of them. Two of the Ferret's own had turned, firing into their comrades.

Harry saw it for what it was: betrayal.

It was over almost before it began. Two seconds. Maybe less.

Ronsard went for his gun and took two rounds to the chest before he cleared the holster.

Harry, Charlotte, and Ivanov raised their hands.

Vidal strolled toward them, pistol in hand. Russian issue, Harry noted.

"My sincerest apologies, Your Highness," he said, almost as if he meant it.

Charlotte spoke softly, as though exhausted, "He's not even a real highness."

Vidal regarded her again, as though she were a particularly sweet treat he was soon to enjoy all on his own. "Indeed," he said, "if the English had been serious about these negotiations, they would have sent a serious interlocutor. Instead, they sent this playboy. This... refugee.

"And who did Comrade Beria send?" Harry asked.

"Oh, a very serious interlocutor, indeed," Vidal replied, turning aside.

From behind a row of cargo crates, a figure stepped into view. Tall, imposing, flanked by two men with dull-eyed expressions and gleaming automatic weapons.

Alexei Skarov.

30

Cairo. Five weeks ago.

THE DRIVE across Cairo ate up two and a half hours. More than they could afford. That left just ninety minutes to gear up and get aboard the Russian freighter before it sailed. Dan was pretty sure they could delay or even stop her departure if it came to it; taking out the pilot would do it, but they still needed to get on board before the *Bulgakov* slipped her moorings.

Dan rode up front with Siregar. The others were crammed into the rear of the van, quiet and alert, weapons resting across their laps. They were armed well enough for a street fight but not for the sort of war that seemed to be erupting outside. Cairo was convulsing; faction against faction, no one fully in control.

Carter had a small transistor radio pressed to his ear, tuned to the BBC's emergency broadcast. With every passing kilometre, the pattern grew clearer. What had seemed chaotic was not without purpose. The whole place was coming apart, and not just here. Maybe everywhere.

"Can you fucking believe this?" Soneski said, as the latest report of the communists' orbital strike on West Germany came in.

"The world is full of wonders, and some of them are terrible," Siregar said from behind the wheel.

It said everything about the mission that he was driving himself, not one of his underlings. Siregar did not look like a spy, which is what made him such a good one. Nor did he look like a commando, or what some idiots these days liked to call an 'operator'. He did not look like Dan, or Carter, or even Merrill. He was a short man, somewhat on the dumpy side, in a crumpled suit, the collar of his shirt sweat-stained, the tie pulled loose. But Dan had worked with him on and off for six years, and in a shadow world where most would sell you for parts, Siregar had never let him down.

Siregar belonged to that peculiar breed of fixer who flourished at the blurred margins of the intelligence world, a creature of utility and appetite. Even as the city came apart, block by block, Dan had the uneasy sense that Siregar understood it all via some map of the moral ruin that others couldn't see. Part confidante, part opportunist, he occupied the dim space between espionage and enterprise with a confidence that suggested both were, in the end, the same thing to those who understood how rules bent, how people broke, and what could be salvaged when they did.

Only once were they stopped for more than a few minutes, at a roadblock manned by a squad of royal guardsmen whose uniforms were crisp but whose loyalties were already fraying. Siregar sized them up quickly: still nominally loyal to the palace, but more reliably loyal to transactional virtue. He didn't argue. A bundle of American dollars changed hands, neatly extracted from a strongbox in the back of the van, and the sergeant, now warmly affable, cleared them through and offered the most reliable route to Port Said, along with a few unsolicited warnings about areas best avoided.

They took the American-built freeway at speed, slipping past units of U.S. mobile infantry who were too preoccupied establishing what looked like a defensive, or possibly containment, line to pay them much attention.

No one flagged them down. Nobody wanted the paperwork. On the shoulders and overpasses, American soldiers were rolling out barbed wire, stacking sandbags and looking in all directions at once.

They reached the port's edge under the cover of full night, pulling into a desolate warehouse district. The van stopped among rows of low-slung warehouses and cranes frozen in silhouette. Dan stepped out into the warm Mediterranean evening. The air outside was salt-tinged and heavy with the distant stutter of gunfire. Cairo wasn't just falling apart now. It was devouring itself.

"This way, my friends," Siregar said, waving them inside with a flick of his hand and a glance at the street behind.

Two of his men stood guard by the steel roller door. One held an old German Schmeisser, worn to the shine at the grips. The other cradled a newer Russian rifle, its matte-black finish glistening with oil.

Inside, the place bore all the contradictions of its owner: an import-export business on paper, something else entirely in practice. Sacks of coffee beans stacked high, crates of cinnamon and clove pressed in tight rows. It could have been a scene from any port in the world, until you reached the centre.

A folding table had been laid with the tools of another trade: body armour, firearms, ammunition, and night-vision rigs. The four carefully prepared kits showed off not just excellent logistics, but considered intention.

"Nice," Carter muttered as he surveyed the equipment.

Merrill went straight to his medical kit, checking it and nodding approvingly. "Looks good, boss," he said.

"Thank you," Dan said, shaking Sirega's hand. "We will get it done."

"Please see that you do, Mr. Dan," Siregar said. "Your equipment came from another operation. I was able to secure it only through intervention from the very highest level of the palace."

Dan tilted his head in confusion. "Farouk?"

"No, Mr. Dan," Siregar breathed, leaning forward to impart a great confidence. "President Moertopo himself."

Dan let that sit. Siregar was no braggart, and never had been, save for the polite fictions his trade required. He did not look pleased by the connection. If anything, he was deeply troubled, as though the attention of the palace in Jakarta came not as a favour, but a dire omen.

This bullshit, right here, was why Dan didn't move to Bali and retire to his house in the hills of Ubud. There would be no rest for him there. When the powerful can be bothered to remember your name, they rarely forget it. Once you'd been useful to someone like Moertopo—or Hoover and the Bulwark—you would not be allowed to rest. There would always be requests, encouragements, and eventually demands made of you.

"You will bring the engineer here," Siregar said evenly. "I will arrange his departure from the city. But first, you must pry him from that ship."

Dan spread his hands. "We'll make the attempt. But I don't offer assurances I can't honour. If Bremmer is aboard and alive, we'll do our best to secure him for you. If not, we'll keep after Skarov until we find him."

Siregar's eyes narrowed. "And His Royal Highness? What if Mr. Harry should take him?"

Dan allowed himself a thin smile. "Not much of a prince anymore, my friend. Not much of a highness, either. In this matter, Buckingham Palace is not our sponsor."

Dan caught Merrill's gaze. The exchange was almost imperceptible, a glance, gone before Siregar, preoccupied with his own burdens, could notice.

"One thing would help us," he said. "Tell me where the *Bulgakov* is headed."

"Securing the ship's papers is simple," Siregar observed. "What cannot be secured is certainty."

"I think I can guess," Dan said. "It's either Genoa or Marseille. Genoa's closer, but they'd have to slip past the U.S. fleet out of Naples. Marseille's a longer haul, but safer waters. Can you get us there, if it comes to that?"

The question caught Siregar off guard. "Of course I could. But you astonish me, Mr. Dan. Would you truly go into the very heart of Occupied Europe?"

"You asked me to do a job," Dan said. "If the job takes us to Marseille, then we go to Marseille. If you can arrange transport. But I'm gonna try hard to bring him back here to you in Cairo. Because I don't want to go to Marseille, Siri. And I'm pretty sure my boys won't either."

They both looked across at the team. The men were finishing their preparations, the rip of velcro straps and the solid click of magazines seating in their weapons cutting through the quiet. Carter raised his night-vision goggles to his eyes, the green glow painting his face in alien tones.

"It will be done," Siregar said. "But Allah willing, Mr. Dan, we will meet again this very night, and I will take charge of the professor."

"Allah willing," Dan said. "So you've got a guide for us?"

"Indeed, Mr. Dan." He snapped his fingers. From the far side of the warehouse, a young Egyptian approached at once. He had been unloading sacks of coffee from a pallet, but now came forward with almost boyish eagerness. Slender and restless, perhaps twenty at most, his gaze moved quickly from Dan to his men, then back to Siregar, eyes dark, wide, and bright with anticipation and unease.

"This is Muhammad," Siregar explained. "He works at the port and was helping load the *Bulgakov* earlier today. From him, we have the information about his royal highness Harry and Miss Duffy."

Siregar paused over Julia's name. He knew some of the history between Dan and her. Not all of it, but enough to understand why Dan had chosen this life.

Dan nodded at the young man. "Muhammad," he said. "You get us inside the port, and we'll do the rest."

"I will wait for you, sir. With the van."

"Good man."

THEY TRAVELLED in a different van this time, larger, more anonymous, a Port Authority vehicle in the standard grey, dulled by grime. The cabin was sealed from the cargo bay by a canvas curtain, and the four men sat in silence, each in his own quadrant. The journey was short, no more than ten minutes by the clock, though time has a habit of stretching and warping in such circumstances. No words passed between them. Each man retreated into his own thoughts.

Like a leaf caught in a current, Dan's mind drifted toward Julia. He believed Siregar. Had no reason not to. If the Indonesian claimed she was aboard the *Bulgakov*, that's likely where she'd be. With Harry.

That, too, he accepted. Julia wasn't the mission—Bremmer was—but Dan knew himself well enough that he couldn't walk away from that ship without her. Nor, he supposed, without Windsor. Harry had done nothing wrong by him. His life had simply intersected with Julia's after Dan's had veered away.

A smile nearly crept across his face. Not a happy one. It wasn't just Julia he'd walked away from. It was the whole damned world, the day he joined the Bulwark. It had all started with her, of course. The only way to bear the loss was to make it final. And so he'd vanished. She thought him dead, as did everyone who wasn't in on Hoover's project. There was even a gravestone in Arlington with his name on it. He'd never asked who lay in the box. But for years, he'd consoled himself with the notion that whoever the poor bastard was, he'd died in service of something.

Ten years on, and this was the payoff: his ass wedged in the back of a stolen Egyptian Port Authority van, en route to a firefight with Russian hoods over a German rocket scientist who, for reasons too tangled to recount, had already been kidnapped once and was to be grabbed up and regifted to a junta on the far side of the world. If Dan did his job right. He no longer troubled himself with untidy questions of conscience or complicity. Those distinctions—right, wrong, ways and means—had all blurred into something much less absolute. Morality was a matter of looking after his crew. Better to concentrate on that because the rest, he'd learned, would sort itself out, or it wouldn't, regardless of his contribution.

The van pulled up. Muhammad teased the curtain aside and whispered, "We're here."

Dan suppressed a sigh at the pantomime. No amount of hushed voices would mask the presence of four well-armed men spilling out of a stolen van. He caught the crunch of Muhammad's boots on gravel, a small reassurance that they were indeed in a deserted section of the old port. Then came the dull mechanical clunk of the rear doors as the kid threw them wide. Sodium lamplight, jaundiced and flickering, spilled in with the warm stink of rotting kelp and sea salt. Dan followed the others out, eyes already scanning for cover and angles.

This sector of Port Said hadn't been abandoned, but it was clearly marked for redevelopment. A new chain-link fence topped with razor wire ran around the area. Carter was already unshipping his bolt cutters to get through the gate, secured with a heavy chain and padlock.

"No, sir, please," said Muhammad. "Allow me." He produced a key from his back pocket and unlocked the padlock.

"Thanks, kid," Carter said. "Couldn't have done it without you."

Muhammad didn't get the joke. "That is why I am here, sir."

"And now it's time for you to go, Muhammad," Dan said. "Don't hang around waiting for us."

"But Mr. Dan," he protested, "the Honourable Siregar, he commands me to await your return."

"Well, the Honourable Siregar isn't here," Dan said, his voice even but firm. "It's quiet now, but this place will go to hell before the hour's out. Soldiers. Looters. Whatever. If they find you here, they'll want to know why." He looked Muhammad in the eye. "So you tell my friend Siregar that I told you to go. That I ordered it. You tell him I put a gun to your head and said that if you didn't, I'd shoot you myself."

Muhammad's eyes went wide.

Dan offered him a thin smile. "Don't worry, kid. I won't. You've done good work tonight. I'll make sure your boss hears that. But I want you gone now."

He looked ready to argue the point, until a distant burst of automatic fire snapped whatever courage he'd been gathering.

"Yes, sir. Mr. Dan. Thank you, sir," he said, repeating himself as he backed away.

He climbed into the van, started the engine, and drove off without looking back.

They eased through the gate, which protested with a long, mournful creak. But it was barely a whisper against the bigger storm. Gunfire chattered in all directions now, three, maybe more hot zones flaring up across the port. Off to the east, a curling trail of yellow tracers arced into the sky. No aircraft in sight. When two more lines of green and golden fire followed, Dan figured it for another local feud conducted at high velocity.

"Let's go," he said, and they slipped into the darkness.

They moved with care, weapons ready, through the husk of the old port, a 1930s relic awaiting a future that would likely never arrive. The buildings squatted low and heavy, their concrete walls streaked with oil and salt. Rusted cranes stood like weird modern sculptures, their long booms arrested mid-motion. Empty oil drums lay between enormous coils of steel cable and broken wooden pallets gone silver with age. The air was thick with the stench of diesel and just beneath it, the faint breath of the sea.

The team advanced without a word, each man watching his arc of the world. Carter took point, leading them around a heap of rusted winches. He raised his hand, signalling a halt at a collapsed shed.

From the shadows, two stray dogs bolted, vanishing into the dark.

They pushed on, threading through dead forklifts and piles of splintered crates. When Merrill caught his boot on a coiled cable loop, Dan instinctively reached out, catching him by the arm.

They regrouped in the shadow of a shipping container, the sea much closer now, breathing just out of sight. The container had been repurposed as an admin space, windows cut into one side, folding chairs scattered around a small step into the office, hundreds of cigarette butts ground into the concrete. It was deserted. The entire wharf area was deserted.

Carter and Soneski took up positions at each end of the container. Dan scanned the area before joining Merrill in cover.

Between the container and the edge of the wharf, Dan saw the remnants of a loading operation abandoned mid-task. A broken crate spilled machine parts on the cracked concrete. A battered handcart lay overturned, its wheels still. A pair of cargo nets hung from a crane, one half-filled with boxes, swaying gently in the night breeze. The wharf was littered with debris, discarded gloves, a broken lantern, and a clipboard with pages fluttering in the wind.

The *Bulgakov* rested at the dock. She was no modern container ship, but rather an old-fashioned cargo carrier, her hull streaked with rust, her decks cluttered with winches and booms. Cargo was still hauled aboard with small cranes, loaded in big nets and lowered into cavernous holds. The gangway was extended, but the operation had clearly been interrupted. A pallet of crates sat half-lifted, suspended above the deck. Ropes and chains lay tangled, as if dropped in haste.

The evidence of conflict was plain and immediate. Blood, dark and fresh, had collected in a pool beside the gangway, while the body of a man—face down, limbs thrown wide as if caught mid-fall—marked its source.

From aboard the ship came the sharp reports of gunfire, close and sustained. A sequence of sharp cracks sounded, followed by the glint and scatter of broken glass. Through the portholes, brief flickers of gunfire lit the interior like fireworks glimpsed through a storm.

Pressed against the container wall, they remained still, the metal cool against their backs.

"So what do you think, boss?" Merrill said.

"Quickest way is just to do it," Dan replied. "We don't have time or the equipment for an approach across the water. We've got to go up that gangway."

"It's a choke point."

"Yeah, and it won't be the last one," Dan said. "We'll go two by two, port and starboard, work our way from bow to stern. Hot zone ROE. Anybody who isn't Bremmer is hostile. Any threat gets taken down."

Merrill stared at him. "What about Duffy and Windsor?"

Dan looked at the asphalt beneath his boots. "If we can extract them or help them extract themselves, we will. They're friendly forces. But their interests don't align with ours."

"This is starting to get complicated, boss."

Dan smiled. "Life is complicated, Johnny. It always has been."

He pulled the team in at the corner where Carter had been watching the ship.

"No change," Carter said. "One dead guy at the base of the gangplank, nobody on deck. A lot of gunfire from inside. No sign of Skarov or Bremmer."

"OK," Dan said. He recapped everything he'd just discussed with Merrill. Taking a peek around the corner, he took a sight picture of the cargo ship. The gunfire, though muffled by steel, continued He caught the brief stutter of light, muzzle flashes within the dark geometry of the superstructure.

"We don't know who's shooting at the Russians on board," he said. "Could be friendlies, could be hostiles. Anybody who threatens you, kill them. But if we do encounter friendlies and there's no blue on blue incidents, we team up. OK?"

"Acknowledged."

"Copy that."

"Sure."

Dan held out his fist. The other three men put their fists into the circle.

"Let's get it done," he said.

In concert, they abandoned their cover and made for the gangway, their movements economical. Every step was measured; every breath, deliberate. Floodlights spilled their pale glow across the concrete, stretching shadows like dark fingers.

Dan let the rest of the world fall away, cutting the static from his mind, tuning into the fine details instead. He focused on his footsteps crunching, the metallic hammer of gunfire, and the occasional eerie stillness between shots. The wharf was strewn with wreckage, and he picked his way through broken crates and spilled cargo. They advanced in an arrowhead formation, each man covering a 20-degree arc left and right, their fields of fire overlapping. At the base of the gangway, Dan signalled, and they moved up, weapons ready. He took the first step aboard, low and deliberate, his body crouched to reduce his profile. Sweeping the deck, he tracked for movement. His finger rested just outside the trigger guard, a three-round burst a breath away.

Siregar had done well by them.

Their gear was borrowed from multiple decades. Each man wore ceramic-plated body armour and carried an assault rifle patterned on the uptime M4, its silhouette familiar, if subtly off. Each rifle bristled with a flash suppressor and a boxy laser module — infrared for the night, red dot for the quick kill. Thirty rounds of subsonic, armour-piercing per magazine — no tracers, no warning. Night vision gear waited on their helmets, ready for deployment as soon as they moved beyond the sodium light glow of the wharf. None of it was quite twenty-first-century spec. The designs were modern enough, but the materials—composites, alloys, circuitry—still lagged. The edge was there, though. More than enough to do the job.

He saw two bodies on the deck. One looked a little like Muhammad. A local dock worker, perhaps. The other was a Russian sailor, judging by his dirty grey coveralls.

They split up, port and starboard, heading for the superstructure. Dan led Merrill, and Carter took Soneski. The gunfire below decks was constant but not overwhelming, sounding like a small unit engagement, or maybe a couple of them.

Dan listened, parsing the chaos. Most of the weapons were Russian AK variants, their distinctive industrial chatter echoing through the steel plates. But once or twice, he heard the muted cough of something more advanced, similar to the rigs they carried. Occasionally, the crunching metallic explosion of a hand grenade reverberated through the decks, the shockwave felt in his boots. He took it all in, ghosting forward.

Dan positioned himself on one side of the first hatch they came to, Merrill on the other. Both pressed into the steel, breathing tight. The uproar inside was immediate and overwhelming. Shouts in Russian and a harsher cadence, perhaps Bulgarian. He heard no English, which suggested that any friendlies were disciplined enough to operate in silence or scattered far from this entryway.

He met Merrill's gaze and raised three fingers, then two, then one. Merrill nodded.

Together, they stepped across the threshold and into the noise and heat of the MV *Bulgakov*, the din swelling around them.

Their first encounter was with two Russian sailors, noisy, ill-equipped, poorly trained. Dan cut them down with short, controlled bursts. The second was much the same, another pair of sailors, panicked and firing wildly. They fell quickly.

The third encounter was different. Two goons in suits, their clothes torn and bloodied from the firefight. They had the build and bearing of military men. They fought with discipline and skill, using cover and communicating in clipped Russian. The firefight was intense, bullets ricocheting off steel bulkheads, and the shouting all in Russian. Simultaneously, another battle raged on the ship's far side, audible but unseen.

The ship's lighting was already poor. Flickering and uncertain. Then Merrill located a junction box and, with a quick snip of his wire cutters, extinguished it completely.

Darkness fell like a curtain. Dan dropped his NVGs into place. The world lit up in monochrome green, the edge of things now slightly fuzzed. The Russians shouted in confusion, their voices sharp with fear and frustration. Dan and Merrill moved on them like phantoms, sweeping forward and cutting them down.

Dan was breathing hard, heart hammering loudly in his ears. The tunnel vision of close-quarters combat was compounded by the narrow view through the goggles, but it was a trade he was willing to make. The advantage was his. He raised his hand, gave the signal. They moved out again, clearing the companionway room by room, fast and hard. Boots hit doors, muzzles swept corners, voices called out. Clear! Then, move!

At the third room, Merrill's voice crackled over the comm net.

"Boss, you better come see this."

Dan hurried into the cabin beside Merrill and froze.

Three bodies lay inside. A woman, and two children, perhaps nine or ten years old.

He blinked once, hard, and for a moment Dan simply stared.

It didn't add up. The boy's features were oddly peaceful, as if caught in sleep. The girl had died differently. Her face told the story. Blood was everywhere—so much of it—and in their tiny hands, not toys or makeshift blades, but real weapons.

In death, the girl still held two curved knives with the shape and purpose of talons, forged for slashing, not stabbing. Her fingers remained curled tightly around their black handles.

The boy had wielded a trench knife, brass knuckles fitted with spikes and a fixed blade, a grim artifact from the Great War. Dan stared.

Children, armed like shock troops. Berserkers. The cognitive recoil was immediate and sharp. He had no mental file to place this in, no protocol or language.

"Boss, focus."

Merrill's voice cut through the fog.

Dan turned to see him kneeling beside the woman, working fast, hands pressed to the worst of it, but there were too many wounds, too much blood flowing out too fast. He moved closer, trembling, dreading what he already knew.

It was Julia. It was a shock, but not altogether a surprise. Had the two children done this to her?

Had she done for them in turn?

To see her again—so shortly after the hotel, so broken—was startling. Julia, up close, bloodied and barely breathing. He had loved her. And had left her. She'd been carrying his child and ended that pregnancy without talking to him. Dan felt whole worlds collapse inside him. A quiet implosion of horror, betrayal, and memory. He kept his face blank because he had to. But inside, the annihilation was total. Two more children lay dead by her hand, but were they children or creatures torn from dark myth and nightmare?

"Boss, boss, I got this. You just get out of here," Merrill said.

"What?" Dan said.

Merrill grabbed him by the face, dug his thumb into the hypoglossal nerve under Dan's chin, and squeezed. The jolt of pain brought him back to reality, to the world of murdered and murderous infants, to his former lover bleeding out on the floor of a Russian vessel.

Gunfire echoed through the hull. Carter and Soneski were in it.

"I've got her. You're no use here. Go."

Dan hesitated, one last glance.

Then he nodded and moved. He could move or drown. Everything else could wait.

Dan stepped out, leaving Julia behind. He didn't look back.

The first Russian he saw went down in a three-round burst.

He was changing mags when the second came at him, a heavyset brute, fast despite his size.

The fight was ugly. Dan ducked under a swing that would've broken his jaw and drove his boot into the man's knee. The joint gave with a sickening pop. He caught him by the collar and smashed his skull against the bulkhead. Then he used a knife. There was no grace to it, just what had to be done.

Reloading, Dan pressed on towards Carter and Soneski. He found them at a corner, the intersection of the main starboard companionway and a passage cutting across the ship. He didn't join them, instead moving forward on the port side, twenty yards up at another juncture. He stepped over two dead Russians into the next companionway that cut across the ship.

Four Russians appeared in his firing arc. One looked up, raised his weapon, and Dan cut them all down with a long burst of automatic fire. Another Russian came around the corner. Dan shot him in the head. More gunfire out on the deck, tracers zipping past, then silence, broken only by the ringing in his ears.

Dan pressed his throat mic. "Sector clear," he said.

"Confirmed," came Carter's reply through the headset.

"I'm coming out," Dan said.

He emerged onto the ship's outer deck, the steel walkway vibrating beneath his boots. The whole port was chaos. Gunfire crackled in bursts. Tracers streaked like falling stars. Fires burned deep in the warehouses, sending up dense black columns. The air was thick with hot ash and smoke. On the ground, possibly dead, possibly unconscious, lay His Royal Highness, Prince Harry.

31

Moscow.

AT BERIA'S instruction the long room had been turned into a kind of cold tomb. Windows locked tight, chandeliers extinguished, the only light a hard white glare from the fluorescents strung along the cornice. It washed across the men at the table, flattening their features until they looked like death masks. The polished surface before them shone the colour of dried blood. No tea. No pens. Even the stenographer was gone. Nothing left in the room but silence, and the knowledge that no court, no witness would ever recall what was about to be said.

"Comrades," Beria said as he took the chair at the head of the table and placed his hands flat, the better to still the small tremor that had been in his fingers all day. "Shall we begin?"

They assembled as if summoned to a final reckoning: the ministers with eyes as flat and lifeless as coins; the marshals, shoulders squared in heavy coats that smelled of wool and machine oil; Molotov, neat in his black tie, the undertaker of foreign policy; Kaganovich drawn tight as a spring; Sokolovsky pale and rigid, his map-case clamped to his side. Even Serov, whose presence alone could turn any chamber into a prison cell. The door closed softly behind them.

"I would have the operational picture," Beria said softly.

Sokolovsky delivered his report to the centre of the table, as though the lacquered wood itself might judge him. Western Front continues to press on the Kassel–Paderborn axis. Third Shock Army executed the pivot order—with delay. His voice faltered. Ninth and Sixth Guards Tank held position, awaiting confirmation. The gap at Hofgeismar widened. Overnight, two German armored divisions and a British corps slipped through, across the Weser. Bridges destroyed behind them. A droplet gathered at his temple, incongruous in the chilled room. Beria felt bile rise in his throat and pressed it back. His chest cinched tight, then loosened at the order of his will.

"The pivot order, comrade," Beria said. "Repeat it."

Sokolovsky's voice was careful. "Third Shock Army to reorient east by southeast, secure the Ukrainian hinterland to the Dnipro line, priority on rail nodes Poltava–Kremenchuk–Dnipro. Secondary priority: stabilisation of rear-area political situation."

"In the army's vocabulary," Beria said, "that is a simple order, yes?"

"Yes."

"Then why was it misunderstood?"

No one answered. The fluorescents hummed.

"It was not misunderstood," said Marshal Grechko finally, his voice a rumble. "It was... disbelieved. A field commander holding encirclement will assume he prosecutes the advantage. He would not imagine that such..." He stopped himself. "That a reorientation of this magnitude is required when the enemy is in the bag."

"You do not imagine," Beria said. He shaped a smile so small it might have been a twitch. "You obey. Fascists in Ukraine burn our grain fields. The rails are cut. The political situation is not a situation; it is a storm. Do you propose we march on Paris with a knife pressed at our spine?"

"No," Grechko said, and his jaw worked.

Beria could hear Stalin's dry chuckle where it lived now, in the bone behind his ear. Timing. He placed one finger on the table and tapped twice.

"Serov," he said.

The security chief did not turn his head. "Yes, Lavrentiy Pavlovich."

"In the Third Shock Army, who signed for the delay?"

Serov's words came neat as typed lines. "Colonel-General Rogov asked Front for confirmation. He also tried Stavka's signal office, to be certain the order was", he allowed himself the faintest inflection, "authentic." The word gave off a strange warmth. Beria let it settle in him, tasting it.

Authentic.

He imagined the colonel-general's hand hovering over a tele-phone like a hungry peasant over the soup pot.

"And Front?" Beria asked.

"Front did not reply within the hour. When they did, they did not contradict the order. By then, the corridor was open. The enemy had begun to move."

Kaganovich cleared his throat. "The Ukrainian matter—" he began.

"It is not a matter," Beria said without raising his voice. "It is a rebellion. And it is to be put down."

Silence again. It was beautiful, in its way. The cold gave shape to their breath; the drapes and carpet devouring what little sound they made. Beria felt the tremor in his thumb and slid his hand below the table, steadying himself with the knowledge of the pistol in the drawer. He recalled the evening the Guard had been relieved of their arms at Stalin's dacha, an image that sent a wave of vertigo through him. He let it rise, then fall away. One does not struggle with tides; one waits for them to recede.

"There is no advantage," he said conversationally, "in naming stupidity. Stupidity is not a man. It cannot be shot. It is a draft in the walls. And we fix drafts. Do we not, Serov?"

"Yes, First Comrade."

"Marshal Grechko will transmit a summons to Colonel-General Rogov. He will report to Moscow within twenty-four hours. If the press of duty delays him, you will drag him here, personally, Comrade General."

Grechko did not so much nod as he *inclined*.

"We proceed," Beria said. He lifted his eyes to the room. "The escape at the Weser is a nuisance. The trap will be reset, and it will close. Meanwhile, Ukraine must be secured; militarily first, then politically. To that end, Third Shock *will* complete the pivot. Two rifle corps to the Dnipro bridgeheads. One tank army will not be wasted chasing partisans through beet fields; it will sit on the rails. Every train that moves will move under guns."

Sokolovsky said, "Yes."

"We will affirm our control of the air," Beria went on, pleasantly. "But I do not want our fighter jets hunting goats. I want every runway we do not control, every radio mast, every relay station between Kiev and Kharkov made into a fire. But not a forest fire. A stove. You simply add wood as it burns. We will yet need the stove."

"Understood."

"Molotov," Beria said, allowing the name to hang like a question.

The foreign minister folded his hands. "Yes."

"You will instruct our friends in Warsaw and Prague. Their news-papers will find Ukrainian fascists under their floorboards. In Budapest, they will discover Russian saints being martyred by Ameri-cans. In Berlin, they will discover both on alternating days. They will publish lists. Lists are always useful."

Molotov looked almost content. "Of course."

"Kaganovich," Beria said. "Find me printing presses. Old ones. Loud ones. Ship them to Kiev under the control of the political officers."

Kaganovich nodded once.

"We will cut this ulcer out," Grechko said, seizing the moment. "Give me another two armies—"

"You have enough armies," Beria said, and the words came out as a caress. "We will cut, yes. But we will also stitch. The people must be able to walk when the surgery is done."

He paid out the silence slowly, the way a fisherman lets his line uncoil into dark water. And when he felt the weight of it was enough, he pulled it home again.

"There remains," he observed, "the matter of the American plan."

What followed was not an ordinary hush but the stillness of

sailors watching the horizon darken, a fearful quiet born of storms approaching over an empty sea.

Beria let the silence stretch until it became unbearable. Then he said what none of them had dared voice, even in their private thoughts.

"The Vozdh was premature."

The words fell like stones into a deep lake. Around the table, men froze. Some mid-breath. In forty years, no one had spoken such words aloud in an official meeting. Not about Stalin. Not ever.

"Five years," Beria continued, his voice steady as a surgeon's blade. "We needed five more years. The orbital platforms required full deployment. Our submarine fleet needed completion. Most critically, the Americans needed time to grow... comfortable. Soft. Distracted by their prosperity and their new toys."

Molotov's face had gone the colour of ash. Even Serov looked shaken.

"Instead," Beria said, "he struck while they were still alert. Before they had grown soft. The elimination of Eisenhower," he continued, almost idly, "it was an elegant operation on paper and most gratifying to see their magazines fill with pictures of the corpse of their warlord president, to watch the veils of their widows flapping in the wind."

He arranged his mouth into something like sympathy. "But elegance is a luxury for men of a quiet era. We are not such men."

Molotov said, "You propose further operations there."

"I propose an argument," Beria said. "Between Americans. With our encouragement."

He leaned back, making a show of ease he did not possess. The cold had crept into his bones, settling at his ankles. "The Americans are not a singular people. They are valleys despising mountains. They are tribes and clans, bound more by feudal grievance than by fraternal ties. A South chastened, resentful of the North's dominion. Labourers fearful of their employers, employers fearful of the unions. The Negro, daring to raise his head and punished for it. They are the corrupt press baron who loves a scandal the way a drunk loves a bottle. They are warlords who think they saved the world, and fascists who think they own it. This can all be turned to our advantage, even now."

Kaganovich's eyes flicked up; there was a small, private amusement in them that Beria despised. "And how will we turn their eyes away from their dead warlord?" he asked softly. "Sing to them through the snow?"

The fluorescents hummed and ticked overhead as Beria pushed back from the table, the tremor gone from his hands now. This was familiar ground. This was where Lavrentiy Pavlovich Beria excelled.

"We will turn them," he said, and his voice carried a new warmth, like a professor before eager students. "Because they wish to be turned. Look at their bourgeois newspapers, comrades. Even their so-called serious press questions everything about the promised future."

"There is much to question, First Comrade," Serov said, and the thin smile cut his face in two.

"Indeed," Beria nodded. "This false future they promise, it cannot be. A world without the Soviet Republic? Ridiculous. Chinese state fascism dressed as socialism. Obscene!"

Molotov adjusted his spectacles. "But the theoretical basis for the Emergence—"

"Academician Markov has explained it perfectly," Beria interrupted, warming to his theme. "The dialectic tells us that the Emergence happened *because* this future was impossible. The contradictions of capitalism should have collapsed their system decades before the Emergence. The proletariat should have risen. The worldwide revolution should have swept away the bourgeoisie by 1980, perhaps 1990 at the latest."

He leaned forward, energised. "Instead, what do we see in their 2021? History twisted into unnatural forms and held in impossible tension. The workers distracted, pacified. The revolution... postponed indefinitely. Capitalism rotting, but refusing to die."

Kaganovich grunted. "An abomination of the laws of dialectical materialism."

"Precisely!" Beria slapped the table. "Late-stage capitalism, they call it. The reign of super oligarchs. The rise of corporate feudalism. The collapse of their so-called democratic institutions." His voice grew stronger with each phrase. "They have shown us the terminal phase of their cannibal capitalist experiment - a system that should have been overthrown by the workers, instead devouring itself like a cannibal chewing on his own innards. It is hideous and wrong. And the work of Academician Markov proves that spacetime itself rejected it, tearing apart the very fabric of reality."

"History had to correct itself," Molotov murmured.

"We all agree on this," Beria smiled. "The Politburo and the board of Standard Oil."

They laughed at that, and he let the sound loosen the room, just a little.

"So when we whisper to the American farmer that the future will destroy him, we speak the truth. When we tell the factory worker that automation will cast him down into poverty and wretchedness, we quote their own economists. When we warn the foolish churchgoer that their future promises only godless greed and moral decay. We will be their prophets."

"But surely they will not listen to us, First Comrade," Molotov said quietly.

"Surely not, comrade. But they will listen to their own kind, their own voices. And these voices speak already. We will simply help to amplify them."

Kaganovich smiled—actually smiled—for the first time that evening.

Grechko grunted approval. Serov's dead eyes showed something like hunger.

"The oil barons already fund campaigns against this so-called clean energy. The displaced factory workers already rage against robots and computers. The Southern slavers nurse their grievances from their lost war. Let them contemplate the next war. Let us help them believe they will win this time."

The room had warmed. Men who had entered like pallbearers now sat like hounds scenting blood.

"When we are finished," Beria concluded, settling back into his chair with satisfaction, "the Americans will be too busy fighting each other to bother with us."

The room went still after he spoke, the quiet stretching long and taut. Men shifted in their chairs, but no one dared break it. Beria savoured the hush like a hunter listening to the forest go silent, certain his quarry was close. He let the silence do its work, reading the faces as he had been trained to read reports: for omission, for hesitation, for the telltale trace of doubt. What he saw pleased him. He leaned forward again.

"Comrades," Beria said, noting with surprise the uneven catch in his breath, which he recognised—at last—as excitement. "Our purpose is plain, our hours too dear to waste. You will proceed exactly as directed. Should anyone wish to question the necessity, he must do so promptly, so that I may dispense with him just as promptly."

No one did.

He stood, and the others stood with him, chairs shifting in unison. At the threshold of the room, he faltered, not for theatre, but because nausea struck, sudden and sharp, like a flashbulb behind the eyes. He forced it down. The fluorescents hummed their assent. And behind him, at the thick stone walls of the Kremlin, he could almost feel the next winter breathing against the window, wanting in.

32

Washington DC.

LIA PAO's long day began at 04:30. "Omigod-thirty," she used to call it when she worked in the field for USAID. But that was a long time ago in a century far, far away.

Though not that far away, really. She remembered the Admiral telling her once that Einstein had said that home was closer than the space between his thumb and forefinger as he held them up and squeezed them together. "This close, but a universe away." Sometimes, Lia felt that way about her old life, too.

Her day began a second time at 4:40 am, when the snooze button betrayed her and the alarm started blaring again. She cursed softly, threw her feet out of bed, and squeezed tight every muscle in her tiny body as she stood up. The apartment was still dark, but she could tell dawn wasn't far away; the sun came up early at this time of year, and she didn't have the blinds shut completely in her bedroom. The first hint of the grey pre-dawn had crept in through the slats.

Her tea maker, one of the new Sony models, was already up and hard at work, and she poured herself a mug of jasmine tea while nuking a couple of eggs in the microwave. It pinged as she took her second sip, and she slid the two perfectly poached eggs out onto a slice of wholemeal toast.

Well, okay, fine, they weren't perfectly poached. She would've had to fuck around heating up water, getting it to just the right tempera-ture, tying the cracked eggs up in some cling wrap, and... seriously, who had time for that bullshit? Lia speared her fork into the first yolk, which burst and spilled over the toast. She ate without thinking about it while she flicked through the daily brief on her flexipad, cursing when she saw the link to Walter Winchell's column that she'd been warned about the previous night.

"Rat bastard motherfucker," she muttered under her breath as she skimmed the opening paragraphs.

Flash! The Nat'l Security boys are knife-sharpening for Kolhammer's VP pick Martha Mitchell... Sources whisper the Committee's plotting behind closed doors... Late-night phone calls... Senator McCarthy particularly hot to trot, citing 'national interest' (You go, Joe!)... The President girds for battle while the city holds its breath... Will Mitchell survive the gauntlet? What could she possibly have to hide? Your correspondent predicts fireworks ahead... Remember, you read it here first!

Lia grimaced as she realised her jasmine tea had gone cold while she read the whole thing and fell down a rabbit hole of all the fractal possibilities it suggested. "This fucking guy," she growled, cursing McCarthy, not Winchell. Just why the hell he thought sandbagging her boss was going to get his ugly ass into the vice president's chair, she didn't know. Satan would be selling Eskimo Pies on the seventh level of hell, before Kolhammer picked that guy for any job other than tweezering dried-up dog turds out of the Oval Office rugs.

She tossed the rest of her tea into the sink, poured another cup, and took the flexipad with her as she returned to her room to prep for the day.

"HAL, read me the rest," she said, tossing the pad onto her bed and plucking her workout gear from the basket in the corner. The AI started reading items from her daily brief in its clipped, cheerful voice as she pulled on her sneakers, a new pair of Air Jimbos.

"The Australian Prime Minister is scheduled to meet with Congressional—"

"Skip that," Lia instructed.

"Next item: The Secretary of Agriculture—"

"Skip."

"Next: The ranking members of the Joint Intelligence Committee will meet with the President in the Oval Office at..."

She skipped that one too; she'd set the meeting up herself and knew exactly who was coming and why. She finished getting dressed and grabbed a clean gym towel from the closet.

Her apartment block was a new build, and boasted a fitness studio that was empty when she got there just after five. She was grateful for that, if unsurprised, as few of the other residents seemed to use the facility, at least not this early in the day. Lia was the only uptimer living here. The other residents tended to be younger. Half of them worked for the administration, and so they did lean more future-forward in their choices, but unlike her, they hadn't lived through a forty-year obesity epidemic, so they weren't as obsessed about counting macros and getting their reps in.

People still looked at you funny if you went jogging in this town, as a civilian, at least. No one looked twice at Marines in PT gear humping it around the Mall. But if Lia pulled on her runners, it was a righteous certainty she'd get a lot of weird looks and the occasional evil eye as she logged her miles. Part of her knew some of that was about her being a 5'2" Hmong lesbian, but it was also because the temps mostly still thought exercise was weird.

She wasn't long on the treadmill, a NordicTrack salvaged from the *Kandahar*, that she'd talked the owner's association into adding to the gym. Despite its age and the annoying line of failed pixels running across the screen, it was still better than any of the commercially available options. She did 20 minutes of high-intensity intervals, returned to her apartment, showered, and changed for the office.

Lia met her driver in the foyer and tried to be pleasant. She still wasn't used to this arrangement. The Secret Service had insisted on it after Eisenhower, and she was quietly resentful of the alone time it had stolen from her. The short walk from her condo to the White House was the only time, most days, she got to spend with her thoughts.

Her driver, a Marine private she hadn't seen before, snapped to attention as she exited the elevator. "Miss Pao, if you would follow me, ma'am," he said, giving her a brusque nod rather than a salute.

"Sure," Lia said, refusing his offer to carry her day bag. The same way she refused to correct him when he called her Miss instead of Ms. One day, some young woman somewhere would set him straight on that if he was lucky.

When they left, it was still early, but the sun was starting to come up. Her ride was an open-top Jeep, which she thought probably undid a whole bunch of security protocols, but she was fine with it because she got some wind on her face and the first rays of dawn on her skin. Her aggressively short cut meant she wasn't worried about getting her hair mussed up.

As they arrived at the White House, passing through the first checkpoint, she eyeballed the sharpshooters on the roof and some army guys with shoulder-launched anti-aircraft missiles. There was a whole anti-aircraft missile battery nearby, in Lafayette Park, and Combat Air Patrol over the city at all times. Inside the White House, where the national security machine ran 24/7, the night crew was finishing up, handing off to the day shift. Lia took a quick handover briefing from the Deputy White House Chief of Staff, LaBrea Davis, who didn't tell her any more than the brief she'd had earlier from HAL. With the handover complete, Lia Pao headed to her office, next door to Kolhammer's.

The gardeners on the South Lawn were already out in the heat, the hedge trimmers and leaf blowers going hard. The boss's door was cracked when she came by. He was finishing breakfast, or at least glaring at the remains like they'd betrayed him.

"Get him in, Lia. No. Better yet, get the Natsec Committee in. Let's at least try to make this look legit."

"You can't be thinking of giving in to this fascist asshole, boss?"

"I'm not. But ignoring him isn't gonna make the problem go away."

The calendar would have had them in the Oval by mid-morning, because calendars are optimists. The Situation Room had other ideas. They went down, and the day narrowed to screens and voices and long, tight silences while Europe bled out inch by inch. It was the part of the job she loved and hated in the same breath: the puzzle and the price tag. The boss's voice was all gravel and caffeine; the intel kids looked like they'd slept under their desks; the lines on the map were never where you wanted them.

Every now and then, she felt the building above them, imagined a distant thump of footsteps, the unkillable bureaucracy doing laps around the track while the war machine ran on underneath. It tickled a memory of the future out of her while they waited for the secure link to General Jones in Paris. Some line Stephen King wrote in one of his short stories, she thought, something about the great black engine of the universe rumbling on in the basement of the world. Or something. Weirdly, he wasn't a big deal here. People just weren't into horror stories.

She pushed the thought away.

The McCarthy meeting slid itself to "later" without anyone having to say so. She told three different reporters from the White House Press Office the same story three different ways and fed each of them a big fat nothingburger.

When she finally dragged the boss out of the bunker, he was all serrated edges and deep, impacted fury. She walked him out and up past the new data cables taped to the floor, feeling him change temperature as they climbed. The senior committee men were waiting in the anteroom, three sitting politely while McCarthy smirked like an alligator in a necktie.

She took the wall in the Oval and tried to measure all the moving parts at once. Lia expected light sparring. She hadn't expected the moment the Admiral jumped the guardrails. It was a pressure drop, the kind you feel in your eardrums when the plane falls into an air pocket, and then a hard burn. She felt the room shrink. She felt her stomach clench. She opened her mouth once and shut it again. Sticking to the wall rather than coming off it as her instincts demanded.

The Admiral was right, though, and the other senators found their courage right on cue; it's amazing how often it gets lost under the couch cushions until somebody else picks it up. For one brief shining moment, she indulged herself, catching McCarthy's eye and giving him the kind of smile you measured by the millimetre, to see how far you could get away with it. He didn't return it.

After that shitshow, she fanned the boss like a prizefighter between rounds: water, a fresh daily brief, they were up to three now, two calls to Churchill and De Gaulle. Aides popped like bubbles in their wake. The nonsense came next, because it always does. A troop of Girl Guides in the East Room with cookie boxes and merit badges, smiling like they'd practised in a mirror all summer. The admiral bent his big shoulders, took his photo with them, and said something fatherly that would make a hundred thousand grandmothers cry when they saw it on the six o'clock news tonight. Lia Pao would make damn sure of that. On the way out, one of the girls asked him whether he'd ever been scared, and Lia watched him tell the truth of it, and she had to step out of the Oval for a moment for her own little cry.

Back to her office then: budgets and grudges. A committee chair wanted a pound of flesh; Lia countered with paper-cut politeness. HAL kept sliding things into her peripheral vision: Europe, the Pacific, convoy counts, the irritating math of time zones. She ticked what she could, shoved off what she had to, and saved a little oxygen for later.

What mattered—what she'd decided would matter today—was the ceremony. She pulled it together with the kind of threats and favours you could only pull off from this place. The pilots who'd flown across the Atlantic with the Admiral that night—the night that broke a Russian fleet and Lavrentiy Beria's fucking teeth—came in their dress uniforms. One of them refused his cane for the photos. A widow's hands shook, and the ribbon shook with them, while Lia watched the boss pin medals on them and keep his face steady. He shook their hands and met their eyes as if he were filing them away, one more thing to carry.

She made sure the one female pilot didn't get shunted off to the margins of the hero shots by the Hearst photographers.

She skipped the reception because some calls can only be made in private. She found the boss a quiet five minutes and waited by the door while he spoke to another newly-made widow. She fixed the edges of the official condolence letter, got his signature, and sent it where it needed to go.

By the time the West Wing lights took on that late glow and the press pool thinned to die-hards, she left by the Northwest Gate with exactly enough energy to be civil to the security guys and not much more. Outside, in the humidity, the city moved differently at that hour: taxis prowling, soldiers laughing too loudly, sirens far away.

The place she went to on the way home didn't have a name on the door. There was a bell in a small brass plate. Inside the pianist was finding all the spaces between three good chords. The dress code was mixed. Coveralls and WAC jackets and shirtsleeves, haircuts sharp enough to cut steel. Nobody looked twice if you sat alone and ordered a soda water with a lime wedge. You don't have to explain yourself to The Switchboard. It understood connections.

A welder with freckles and a laugh like a dropped toolbox offered to split a plate of fries with her. "Carbs after six. Sorry. I'm not that adventurous," Lia said, and they both smiled like they were in on a joke neither of them had time to tell. She had a burger, double beef for the protein, and mineral water, because she hadn't taken a real drink in eight years.

Home again, and her apartment still held onto the morning's shape. HAL dimmed the lights and she toed off her *Air Jimbos*. She showered and changed into her PJs. The flexipad blipped as she pulled the covers up, and there it was - Winchell's column for the morning, three hours before the presses ran, provided by one of her ghosts. In Lia's head, his bullshit came on like a meatgrinder possessed by a gossip demon, its needle-sharp fangs carving shrill little trenches straight through her frontal lobe. The sentences preened. The metaphors screamed to be seen from space. Some-where in the middle, italics twisted into the shape of a word he hadn't used until now but had obviously been dying to.

Impeachment.

She swore, set the pad down on the nightstand, and watched the ceiling for a while, listening to the air conditioning hum.

"HAL," she said finally, "start me a new project list."

"Title?"

She thought of the Girl Guides and the Situation Room and McCarthy's eyes, of medals and mothers and that welder at The Switchboard.

"Storm watch," she said.

33

Biloxi.

CHERRY WAS UP EARLY, woken not by his alarm clock—set for 4:30, with a backup call booked with the motel desk for 4:35—but by the racket outside his door. He trusted the little Japanese clock he travelled with more than the hotel desk, noting that while it was a cheap, rinky-dink piece of crap, you could rely on it. This morning, however, he didn't need either, as a couple of asshole long-haulers got into it right outside his door, their fight loud enough to drag him from sleep.

He woke sober, which was significant because there had been plenty of years when that didn't happen. He could hear the unmistakable sounds of a fight. Cherry reached for his gun out of habit, then paused, realising he didn't have to. He put the gun aside, pulled on his pants and a shirt, and stormed outside.

Two morons were punching on, surrounded by four or five other idiots, laughing and cheering them on. Cherry shouted, "Hey! Shut the hell up!" They ignored him. He tried again, louder: "Knock it off, you assholes, decent people are trying to sleep!" A couple of the truckers looked over at him, but not for long, seeing a guy standing there barefoot, his shirt not tucked in. One of them smiled, and they went back to cheering on the fight.

Cherry thought about getting his gun, knowing he wouldn't need to shoot them, just pop off a couple of times. A few shots in the air would do it. But there was no guarantee with long-haulers that they wouldn't be carrying either. The mob was active along this part of the coast, and they would steal anything—cigarette shipments, beef coming up from Texas bound for the northeast markets. It wouldn't be unusual for a trucker to carry a piece or stash a sawn-off shotgun in the cabin.

The two men were slowing down, having reached that stage of the fight where each realised he wasn't as tough as he thought, and his opponent wasn't as weak. They both had beer guts and jowls, and their faces were blotchy under the sodium light. The onlookers continued to laugh and cheer them on.

Cherry stalked back into his motel room, cursing the instinct and the experience that made him choose this place away from Beaumont. In town, all he woulda had to deal with was some guy trying to get into his room at two or three in the morning to put a few slugs into him, or maybe tool him up with a baseball bat while he slept. The gun was out, but the little wooden stool in the corner of the motel room would do just fine. He reached down and picked it up by the bottom of one of its four legs, so that it was a kind of awkward, heavy club.

He stalked out of the room, saying nothing this time, as he shouldered past one of the onlookers. Cherry barked again, "Hey!" and raised the stool over one shoulder as though to smash it down on their heads. The first man took a shot at him; Cherry ducked the wild roundhouse, swung the stool at the man's head, but dropped the arc at the last moment, swinging it into the side of his knee and hacking his legs out from under him. It was a surprisingly well-built, sturdy little stool and it didn't shatter at all. The trucker collapsed as his knee folded under him.

Cherry allowed the momentum of the swing to carry through. On the backswing, he swept the other man's fist aside, took a two-handed grip on the stool and punched him in the face with it. It wasn't enough to knock him out, but it was enough to shock him out of the adrenaline-fuelled haze that had kept him fighting.

Cherry spun quickly to confront the man he knew was coming up behind him. He held the stool like a shield now, with the feet pointing outward, ready to jab into the guy's face. "You looking for a taste, pal? Because I got plenty to spare." They'd gone quiet now. The fighters were no longer interested in fighting, and the onlookers had lost their appetite for the spectacle. With his feet bare, his shirt untucked, two men bloodied and hacked down in front of him with a cheap piece of furniture, Cherry wasn't the comic figure they'd assumed when he emerged from his motel room to complain about the noise. He knew what they were seeing: a genuine crazy man.

A few doors opened up and down the line of motel rooms, and other guests put their heads out. They'd probably been lying in bed cursing the truckers, too, Cherry thought, but none of them had the nuts to do anything about it. He could see someone moving around in the office, maybe calling the cops, probably not, though. He assumed this sort of thing was a regular occurrence.

"I gotta go get ready for work," Cherry said. "I suggest you gentlemen do the same. The business of America is business, after all. Why don't we all get on with it?" Somebody mumbled something, but he ignored it. All the piss and vinegar had gone out of them. He held onto the stool, just in case, but he could walk back into his room with his back turned to them. Partly because he'd broken their spirits, mostly because he could see them reflected in the window, and if anybody had come at him again, it would be a matter of no great inconvenience to swing around and take his head off with the stool.

He'd grown pretty fond of the stool in their short time together. It was a pity he'd have to leave it behind. Inside, Cherry closed the door behind him, had a shower, cleaned himself up, and got dressed, all pretty quick, six or seven minutes at the most. As he knotted his tie and shrugged his suit coat on so that it sat properly across his shoulders—he'd always been a big-shouldered man and had to get his suits made special—he heard sirens outside.

He clipped his .38 into the shoulder holster and opened the door of his room. The truckers were gone. The only evidence they'd ever been there was a couple of blood spots on the tarmac. He looked out to the main road, wondering if he was going to have to bullshit a couple of local law enforcement yahoos about tooling up some rowdy neighbours. He'd already settled on posing as an FBI guy if he had to do that, carrying the business card of Special Agent Newhart for just such occasions. There was no Special Agent Newhart as far as Cherry knew. Unlike the random business cards he carried—collected from restaurants and hotel lobbies for quick cover stories—Special Agent Newhart's card was a bespoke affair, crafted for him by a guy he knew and trusted, from the track.

It was still dark, but the sky was beginning to lighten in the east; the sun would come up quickly. In twenty minutes, you could call it dawn and not risk a perjury charge. What was left of the dark began to strobe, but the flashing lights weren't the blue and red of a police cruiser. The night throbbed fire engine red. He shrugged. Just as he'd thought. The cops wouldn't make their way out of town for a penny-ante punch-up between a couple of long-haul truckers.

Cherry returned to the room, slapped on some aftershave, picked up his hat, and stepped out. He walked to his rental car and pulled out of the car park, heading south, going in the same direction as the fire truck.

Dawn was coming on quicker than he expected. The grey morning light was enough to navigate by, although he left his head-lamps on. In a place like Biloxi, you never knew when you'd encounter some drunken cracker weaving across the road, full of moonshine and an inflated sense of their driving ability. He drove through the scrubby, swampy backwoods. He rolled the window down and could smell the swamp gas, but he could hear the sirens, more than one, he thought now. And he frowned. He was going out of his way, driving in this direction, but he wanted to make sure the Washington family got on the Greyhound bus this morning. If they were smart, that's how they'd get out of town—they had no car of their own, and the nearest train station was 10 miles away at Gulfport. Cherry cranked the window all the way down and eased off the gas to cut back on the wind roar. Yeah, there was definitely more than one siren. He recognised fire trucks, the local police, and maybe an ambulance.

"Shit," he muttered to himself, a bad feeling creeping up from his gut, threatening to give him heartburn before he'd even pulled into the roadside diner where he'd been planning to grab a breakfast sandwich. For the first time in a long time, Cherry regretted not driving in a police cruiser; he would've flicked on his own flashing lights and siren by this point. Instead, he just stomped the gas. The Chrysler leapt forward and started chewing up tarmac as it raced towards Charleston Street. He was muttering and cursing the whole way, swearing and praying that what he feared to be true hadn't happened. But his prayers had always meant nothing.

He came around the corner to find two fire trucks, a police cruiser, and an ambulance parked higgledy-piggledy at the intersection of the two streets where the Washington residence had sat only last night. Now, only burned-out ruins remained.

The whole neighbourhood was out, almost entirely black people in their pyjamas and nightclothes, watching the scene. Emergency services were doing their thing, with fire trucks training hoses onto the smoking ruins. The ambulance officers weren't moving much at all; just smoking, looking at the scene. Cherry knew why. There was no one for them to take away. They'd finish their cigarettes soon enough and give up their parking space to the meat wagon from the local coroner.

34

Cairo. Five weeks ago.

THE HOSPITAL surprised Dan with its stillness. He had braced himself against the sense memories of chaotic wards and blood-slick floors, but this joint offered no such theatre. Its hardwood floors, waxed to a polish, squeaked beneath his boots. Chilled air purred discreetly through hidden vents. It all felt unnaturally pristine, and at odds with the chaos outside. Cairo was convulsing, streets thick with panic, embassies shuttered, rumours as thick in the air as the oily smoke over Port Said. But within these walls, one could almost imagine that war had not dropped from the sky. If there was any sign of the greater catastrophe, it lay only in the tightness behind the nurses' eyes, or occasional guard detail of soldiers standing at quiet ease, their rifles slung low.

He found her on the third floor, Room 314. With the air of a man late for his third consultation of the morning, Dan bustled through the hospital corridors, his dark suit offset by a modest tie and a white lab coat lifted from a hook in the doctors' common room on the ground floor. That was all it took. The trick wasn't looking important. It was looking important and tired. Nobody stopped him. They never did. He'd long ago learned that the right attitude opens more doors than any badge.

The floor was hushed. Through the glass partition of room 314, he could see her—pale against white sheets, tubes running from her arms and chest, machines tracking her vital signs with soft, persistent beeping.

He slipped inside and closed the door behind him.

The doctors, he gathered, had not yet made up their minds about her survival. That much, Dan could tell from the machinery around her and the dense, urgent script crowding the chart at her bedside. Multiple stab wounds. Severe hemorrhaging. Post-operative complications. She looked so small beneath the sheets, her skin drawn tight over the bones of her face as she lay there, unnaturally still.

The images rushed at him—small bodies on cold metal deck plates—but he shut the hatch on them, hard. Dan retreated to the shelter of another memory: the Moana Hotel, the night in Waikiki when the world hadn't yet turned on them. She'd worn a black silk dress that shimmered in the candlelight, laughed at some dumb thing he'd said, her head thrown back, unguarded, free. They were both still whole then.

The memory felt like the tip of a blade between his ribs, but he leaned into it anyway.

Julia's eyes fluttered open. Not fully conscious—the sedation was too heavy for that—but wide enough to focus on him with obvious effort.

"Dan?" Her voice was barely a whisper, thick with whatever they'd pumped into her.

He cursed quietly.

He should leave. This wasn't why he'd come. He'd wanted to see her alive, nothing more. To know that pulling her off that freighter hadn't been for nothing.

"You're gonna be okay," he heard himself say. The words came automatically, from some part of him that remembered how to talk to her.

Her eyelids fluttered open, heavy with pain or sedation, perhaps both.

"I'm sorry," she said softly. "I'm so sorry, Dan."

The words caught him like a cold gust through an open door, and he stepped back without meaning to. Outside, voices murmured down the corridor, the world carrying on in that maddening way it does. Dan retrieved a matchbook from his inner pocket, from a club in the old quarter where he'd waited for something that never materialised. He placed it gently into a drawstring cotton pouch on her bedside table, holding a few personal items. A lip balm. Some jewellery. Her wallet. He almost smiled at that. She'd always refused to carry a woman's purse.

"I'm sorry, Dan. I loved you."

He couldn't be sure if she'd spoken, or if the words belonged to his own unravelling mind. The room held only the beeping of machines and the soft murmur of approaching voices.

He didn't wait to find out.

Dan slipped away, back through the service corridor, past unattended carts and sleeping monitors, down the staff stairwell, still smelling faintly of disinfectant and floor wax. Outside, the sky was just beginning to pale. Heavy gunfire rumbled in the distance. An ambulance idled nearby. No one looked at him twice.

Tomorrow, he'd restart the search for Skarov and Bremmer. Siregar still wanted him. Moertopo was still paying. They didn't know where the Russian had gone, but he would bet it was to Marseille, in occupied France.

Fine. They'd follow him there if they had to. Siregar was already organising passage.

Dan Black didn't understand why that should make him feel better.

But it did.

World War 3.2 is over.

The Axis of Time will return in *World War 3.3*.

ALSO BY JOHN BIRMINGHAM

The *End of Days* series.
Zero Day Code.
Fail State.
American Kill Switch.

The Axis of Time.
Weapons of Choice
Designated Targets
Final Impact
Stalin's Hammer
World War 3.1
(World War 3.2 & 3.3 coming in 2024)

A Girl Time in Time.
A Girl in Time.
The Golden Minute.
The Clockwork Heart (coming in 2025)

The Cruel Stars series.
The Cruel Stars
The Shattered Skies

Also by John Birmingham

The Forever Dead (2026)

Dave vs the Monsters series
Emergence.
Resistance.
Ascendance.
A Soul Full of Guns.
A Protocol for Monsters.

CHEESEBURGERGOTHIC

Hi. It's me, JB. If you liked this book and you'd like more of the same, sometimes for free, please join me over at my blog/book club/dive bar on the internet.

At the moment, it's hosted on Substack, but it kind of moves around, and wherever it ends up, it's *always* called CheeseburgerGothic.

Just throw that into el Goog or whatever AI chatbot runs the world now, and I'm sure they'll hook you up. I give away free stories there at least once a month. And my faves—everyone who signs up at the Burger is my favourite—get steep discounts on new releases.

Everyone else? Well, my friends, don't be like them.

I look forward to seeing you there.

John Birmingham

PO Box 437

Bulimba, Queensland 4171

Australia

❀ Formatted with Vellum